"Prepare yourselves for greatness."
—JAMES DASHNER, #1 *New York Times* bestselling author of *THE MAZE RUNNER*

"Addictive as a puzzle, moving with breakneck speed, *Nemesis* had me guessing until the very end. Try to predict what *Nemesis* is. I dare you."
—VICTORIA AVEYARD, #1 *New York Times* bestselling author of *RED QUEEN*

"Reichs builds plots like the Swiss build watches. *Nemesis* is a fascinating, twisty page-turner that will keep surprising you until its final page. I loved it."
—RANSOM RIGGS, #1 *New York Times* bestselling author of *MISS PEREGRINE'S HOME FOR PECULIAR CHILDREN*

"My favorite thriller since *The Maze Runner*—dark, fast-paced, and intense."
—MELISSA DE LA CRUZ, #1 *New York Times* bestselling author of *THE ISLE OF THE LOST*

"Reichs keeps you at the edge of your seat without compromising depth and heart. Prepare to think about these characters long after you've closed the book."
—ALLY CONDIE, #1 *New York Times* bestselling author of *MATCHED*

"Born from the imagination of an apocalyptic mastermind, *Nemesis* is an addictive read filled with mystery, conspiracy, and terrifying possibilities. I can't wait for the sequel!"
—KAMI GARCIA, #1 *New York Times* bestselling author of *THE LOVELY RECKLESS*

"My favorite kind of thriller: smart and action-packed, with twists and turns galore. You won't be able to put this book down."
—RENÉE AHDIEH, #1 *New York Times* bestselling author of *THE WRATH & THE DAWN*

"*Nemesis* disarms every expectation and lures you down a dark, gripping road. You think you know what's coming . . . You don't."
—ALEXANDRA BRACKEN, #1 *New York Times* bestselling author of *THE DARKEST MINDS*

"An utterly thrilling read with a deviously clever twist I never saw coming!"
—CARRIE RYAN, *New York Times* bestselling author of *THE FOREST OF HANDS AND TEETH*

"So scary it's heart-stopping—and so good it's scary."
—MARGARET STOHL, #1 *New York Times* bestselling author of *BLACK WIDOW: FOREVER RED*

"A twisted web of conspiracy and apocalyptic mayhem that kept me reading all night."
—JAY KRISTOFF, *New York Times* bestselling co-author of *ILLUMINAE* and author of *NEVERNIGHT*

OTHER BOOKS YOU MAY ENJOY

The 5th Wave	Rick Yancey
The 39 Deaths of Adam Strand	Gregory Galloway
As Simple as Snow	Gregory Galloway
The Conspiracy of Us	Maggie Hall
The Edge of Nowhere	Elizabeth George
Genesis	Brendan Reichs
Matched	Ally Condie
Nearly Gone	Elle Cosimano
The One Memory of Flora Banks	Emily Barr
The Reader	Traci Chee
The Sacred Lies of Minnow Bly	Stephanie Oakes
The Virals series	Kathy Reichs and Brendan Reichs
The Young Elites	Marie Lu

NEMESIS

NEMESIS

BRENDAN
REICHS

speak

SPEAK
An imprint of Penguin Random House LLC
375 Hudson Street
New York, New York 10014

First published in the United States of America by G. P. Putnam's Sons,
an imprint of Penguin Random House LLC, 2017
Published by Speak, an imprint of Penguin Random House LLC, 2018

THE LIBRARY OF CONGRESS HAS CATALOGED THE G. P. PUTNAM'S SONS EDITION AS FOLLOWS:
Names: Reichs, Brendan, author.
Title: Nemesis / Brendan Reichs.
Description: New York, NY : G. P. Putnam's Sons, 2017.
Summary: As the Anvil, an enormous asteroid, threatens to end all life on Earth, sixteen-year-old Min begins to uncover a lifetime of lies, a sinister conspiracy involving all students in her sophomore class in Fire Lake, Idaho.
Identifiers: LCCN 2016021737 | ISBN 9780399544934 (hardcover)
Subjects: | CYAC: Asteroids—Collisions with Earth—Fiction. | Survival—Fiction. | Conspiracies—Fiction. | Science fiction.
Classification: LCC PZ7.R264467 Nem 2017 | DDC [Fic]—dc23
LC record available at https://lccn.loc.gov/2016021737

Speak ISBN 9780399544941

Printed in the United States of America

1 3 5 7 9 10 8 6 4 2

Design by Marikka Tamura
Text set in Adobe Caslon Pro

For Emily, who believed

NEMESIS

THE SUN RISES. BUT NOT FOR ME.
I KNOW WHAT DAY IT IS.
WILL HE COME SOONER, OR LATER?
I DON'T KNOW, BUT IT DOESN'T MATTER.
HE'LL COME.
AND WHEN HE DOES, I'LL DIE.

PROLOGUE

SUNDAY, SEPTEMBER 17, 2017

I swore to myself I wouldn't die that day.

Up and down.

Come at me, you bastard. Sweaty-palmed as I gripped a battered Louisville Slugger, eyes glued to my bedroom door.

He was already inside the trailer—early this time, as the first slanting rays of sunshine began peeking over the mountains. While Mom was still away at work. I'd heard the front stoop creak, and instantly knew who had come.

That I was trapped.

Right here. In my own home.

Another unpleasant first.

I wasn't scared. Not of him. Of this. That's just not how it worked anymore.

But my anger simmered near the edge of control.

A floorboard groaned.

I took a calming breath. Narrowed my focus to audible noises beyond the door, a flimsy piece of sliding metal that couldn't stop a toddler. All that separated me from a monster who'd come to snatch my life away.

Silence stretched, then another muffled step. I tensed, prepping for battle.

There's no sneaking quietly across my crappy, not-so-mobile home, a fact I'd established many times during my sixteen years of life. I knew *exactly* where he was standing. How his weight was aligned. What the man was seeing as he peered across our shabby single-wide, eyes glued to the only other place I could be.

So why the delay?

I thought furiously, cycling through possibilities. Was he waiting me out? Could he possibly believe I didn't know he was there?

The first shot exploded through the door. High and left, but I panicked just the same.

A gun this time.

I dropped into a crouch, options rapidly dwindling.

The window.

I darted toward a grimy, dirt-streaked square of glass overlooking my single bed.

Too quick. I never sensed the trap.

The second bullet punched through the closet, slicing into my right shoulder and spinning me like a top. I gasped in pain. Fell against the bedside table.

The third shot tore into my chest.

My legs faltered. I tumbled to the floor, struggling to breathe, blood bubbling on my lips as I stared up at the drab fluorescent lights on the ceiling. Pain tinged everything red.

He'd been waiting for me to flee. I'd accommodated him. Checkmate.

I lose. So I die. Happy birthday to me.

The door slid open. I barely flinched.

A man entered, tall and thin, with coal-black hair cut short. High cheekbones. Narrow, elegant nose. He wore the same unadorned black suit as always. Silver sunglasses. Shiny black boots. His work clothes, I supposed.

Behind the opaque lenses, his face was utterly expressionless.

That always got to me. What kind of human could do such horrible things, yet show zero reflection of them in his features?

A psychopath. That's who.

The black-suited man stood over my punctured, broken body. Squaring his shoulders, he pulled the slide on his weapon, a gleaming black handgun that fit snugly into his palm. The barrel rose.

"Why?" I croaked, as my heartbeat lost its rhythm.

We'd been through this before.

Same question. Always the same question.

"I'm sorry," he said quietly, taking aim directly between my eyes.

Same reply. He always apologized.

I wasn't going to scream. I'd done it before, and refused to give him the satisfaction. I wasn't going to beg either. I'd learned that didn't get me anywhere.

But I wanted an answer.

"Why?" More gurgle than words. Liquid was filling my mouth, hot and wet. The hole in my chest burned like a sliver of the sun.

I knew a response wasn't coming. So, ever so slowly, marshaling my last remaining strength, I lifted my left arm. Hand shaking like a storm-tossed willow, I crooked my elbow, turned my palm inward, and carefully extended my middle finger, thrusting it at his blank, stone-carved face.

"Go to hell," I whispered, choking on my own blood.

"I'm already there."

A thunderous bang, followed immediately by another.

Agony. Then, nothing.

Hello, death. Long time no see.

Darkness enveloped me.

PART ONE

MIN

1

MONDAY, SEPTEMBER 18, 2017

My eyes slid open.

Blink.

Blink blink blink.

Birds zipped by overhead, squabbling as they rode the up-drafts. Inhaling deeply, I smelled huckleberry and red cedar, mixed with the indescribable sharpness of evergreen trees. Pine straw was jabbing me in the back.

A sour tang filled my mouth, like I'd been sucking on pocket change.

No pain. No lingering hurt. Or sadness. Or rage.

I felt nothing. Absolutely nothing. Just a tenderness to the scar on my left shoulder.

Exactly like last time. And the time before that. And the ones before those.

I was lying in the center of a forest clearing. *The* clearing, of course, tucked inside a stand of longleaf pines, on a jagged slope to the north of my tiny Idaho hometown. A glance at the sky told me it was early morning, but not the same day as before.

Though I knew it was pointless, I tried to remember how I'd gotten there. But I was grasping at smoke. There was nothing. No hazy impression. No magic flash. No blast of white light, or sensation of weightlessness, of flying, of rising through the clouds to my continually denied eternal rest.

That's not how it worked. I simply felt pain, died, and then woke up again.

Here. Always *here*. In this place.

"I'm *not* crazy. I am not."

I liked saying it out loud, as if challenging the universe to argue the point.

I bumped a fist against my forehead, then rose, pawing twigs and leaves from my short black hair. Unsnarled my necklace. No iPhone to check—I'd find it charging on my nightstand, right where I left it—so I smoothed my jeans and crumpled Boise State tee, the same clothes I'd been wearing during the attack.

No blood. No singed holes. No acrid stench of panic sweat. Not a misplaced thread to evidence the .45 caliber slugs that had ripped through my body. The faded garments looked and felt the same as always.

I shivered, and not from the temperature. Though it *was* chilly. My breath misted in the gusts swirling down the mountainside. Fall mornings at this altitude are no joke. It's a wonder I hadn't frozen to death while lying there exposed.

I snorted in a most unladylike fashion, then hugged myself close.

Yeah, it'd be a shame if I died, right?

I'm not immortal. At least I don't think so, anyway. I age normally, even though I have this curious habit of dying and coming back to life. I'm not like a ghost or vampire, either. Those guys are *un*-dead, or so I've been told.

No. I just . . . reset. Open my eyes. Get up. Start walking home.

If there's ever a zombie apocalypse, head for my town.

Tucked high in the Bitterroot Mountains, Fire Lake might not be *the* most isolated place in the United States, but it's close. Go any farther north and you're in Canada. There's only one way in or out of the valley—a slender, two-lane bridge spanning a three-hundred-foot drop into Gullet Chasm, some of the toughest river country in Idaho.

People make the trip, however, since the town is surrounded by national parkland. The lake itself is a tourist pull in summer months, balancing out winter ski-bum traffic and keeping the valley stocked with visitors nearly year-round. A few magazines have named Fire Lake the most beautiful vacation spot in America. I can't disagree.

Not that I cared that morning as I crept down the mountainside. I had one goal in mind: to slip back home without being noticed.

It took ten minutes to reach the first houses. There I paused to tighten my sneakers—had I been wearing them when shot?—before slinking into a park area north of town. I scurried along back roads, skirting the neighborhoods above the main village.

I had no intention of telling anyone what had happened. Not after my experiences as a child. I was cold, hungry, and demoralized. Desperate for a shower. An emergency sit-down with my psychiatrist would qualify as torture.

I already had a little blue pill. Mandatory counseling. There was nothing I enjoyed less than my sessions with Doctor Warm Smiles, the two of us fencing while pretending not to be. For fifty minutes every seven days, I fought to protect my secrets while he pried at them with all his shrewd kindness. Exhausting.

Dr. Lowell hadn't believed me when I was little. No one had, not even Mom. My horrifying memories were "the product of a troubled mind."

So forget it. I wasn't saying a word.

Reaching the business district, I hurried west, toward the rougher end of the valley. The typically vibrant neighborhood felt deserted. I passed small-but-charming hotels with no signs of guests. Most of the vacation houses had their shutters locked up tight. The streets had an almost ghost-town feel. Strange, even that early.

Then, with a wince, I remembered what day it was.

The Announcement is tonight, genius. Think that could be it?

September 18, 2017. The most anticipated press conference in history. That evening, just after sunset in the Rockies, Asteroid 152660-GR4 would clear Jupiter's gravitational field, allowing its path to be definitively calculated.

We find out if the Anvil will kill us all.

Fear gripped me. It was a measure of my own problems that I'd forgotten the one tormenting everyone else.

I crossed a footbridge, then turned right onto Quarry Road, heading back upslope. Almost home. I knew time was short—I was pretty sure it was Monday, which meant school, which meant I had to hurry. The road dropped behind the ridge, and I turned left onto a gravel driveway plunging out of sight.

Fire Lake may be romanticized for its beauty, but the brochures aren't discussing my neighborhood. I hurried through the gates of Rocky Ridge Trailer Park, a sloppy collection of run-down mobile homes wedged conveniently out of sight from the rest of the valley. My mother and I shared a depressing tan-and-peach unit slumped in the far corner.

A few heads turned as I slunk along the dusty rows—dodging clotheslines, stepping over Fred and Joe Wilson, who were passed out in the mud beside their fire pit, Fred's lawn chair overturned and resting on his face. Early risers were puttering about, watering plants or coaxing dogs to do their business. But no one spared more than a passing glance. It wasn't that kind of place.

The gazes I did meet carried an unspoken anxiety. People moved stiffly, almost robotically, frowning to themselves, as if even mundane tasks were nearly more than they could bear. I bristled at the tension.

Yes, humanity was in danger of extinction. I knew the awful truth. If the Anvil struck the planet—at any angle—almost nothing would survive. Doomsday might be at hand, and we'd find out in just a few hours. But I couldn't deal with both things at once. Not then. Not after what had happened in my bedroom.

Sorry, world. I've got my own problems.

My steps slowed as I drew close to home. I'd been gone nearly twenty-four hours this time. In all the deaths before, I'd never missed an entire night. My mother had grown used to my unexpected comings and goings—a pattern I'd cultivated to cover this very situation—but I was definitely pushing it this time.

She might not even be here.

Mom had been working the graveyard shift for three weeks, pouring coffee for the glory of minimum wage. It was possible I'd beaten her home, but there wasn't a car to tip me off. We didn't own or need one. I couldn't remember the last time we'd left the valley. Mom walked into town every day, same as me.

I studied the stoop for signs. A smudged handle. Wet footprints on our grubby welcome mat. But nothing outside the trailer caught my attention.

Then a shudder passed through me.

The black-suited man was here. He came right through to end my life.

Anything I detected could be *his* doing.

My pulse accelerated. It took me several moments to calm down. Then, disgusted with everything, I lurched forward and pulled the screen door wide.

She was home.

Keys on the counter. Her iPod was connected to a pair of desk speakers—our redneck stereo—and Adele was crooning softly in the gloom. The TV was off. Our router blinked at me from across the room. I'd demanded Wi-Fi to live, and had finally gotten my wish the day I turned thirteen. An odd-numbered birthday, so safe, and not unlucky at all. One of the few that had actually been pleasant.

Not that we paid for Internet service. There were dozens of tourist businesses in the valley. Nobody noticed a little stolen bandwidth. Mom and I usually swiped ours from the ski resort straight east. Even our cable was hooked up under-the-table, thanks to a friend.

Her door was closed. I imagined her crawling into bed a few

minutes ago, worried sick about me but worn out after another backbreaking twelve-hour shift.

My room was at the opposite end. I crept across the living room, wincing with every creak. The irony wasn't lost on me. Reaching my door, I paused to examine it. No bullet hole. The metal slats looked exactly as they always had.

I slid the door open. The track failed to squeak for the first time I could recall.

My heart skipped a beat. I rarely discovered mistakes.

Inside, my room was in perfect order. Bed made. Clothes neatly folded. Shoes in a haphazard pile under my desk. The carpet was clean. No damage to the closet, walls, or floor.

My fifth murder, erased.

Like it never happened.

A thump carried across the trailer. *Crap.* I shed my clothes and ruffled the covers, hoping Mom might think I was just getting up rather than just getting home.

I waited a minute, then yawned theatrically, opening my door and trudging to our shared bathroom. It didn't take long—the living room stretches only twenty feet. A seedy couch, a beanbag chair, and Mom's ancient rocker surrounded a coffee table where we ate every meal. Bookshelf. Floor lamp. Battered desk. We could pack up everything and move inside of an hour, though we'd probably just leave the stuff.

Her door stayed shut as I scrubbed my teeth while showering, washed my face, then ran a brush through straight black hair that barely reached my chin. I paused a moment, staring into the mirror. Saw the ghost of my mother, thirty years ago.

I looked away. Some things you don't want to see.

Crossing back to my room, I hurriedly got dressed—fresh jeans, *Walking Dead* tee, socks, sneaks, and a black zip-front hoodie. No one's ever accused me of being a fashion maven. I shoved books into a backpack and arrowed for the front door. The town had decided that school would remain open this week, and first bell was in thirty.

The knob was turning in my hand when my mother's door screeched open. Her head poked through the gap. One look, and I knew she wasn't fooled. Questions burned in her watery gray eyes, but she held them back.

"Promise me you'll be home for the Announcement."

Mom was short and slim like me, with long, stringy hair going white at the roots. Pale skin, pulled tight over birdlike features and a thin-lipped, frowning mouth. Everything about her seemed fragile and overused, like a wildflower that never got enough water.

I silently cursed the deadbeat father I'd never even met—a daily tradition upon seeing my mother's weathered face. Then I cursed myself. Because I just wanted out of there.

Try as I might, at moments like this I felt nothing more strongly than . . . distaste.

Disappointment. That my mother had allowed her life to reach this point. That the same could happen to me.

Shame blossomed inside me. Unfolded. Spread.

"I'll be home."

Mom's stare was unrelenting. "*Promise me*, Min. I don't know where you . . . and on your birthday, again . . . but . . ." She trailed off. Neither of us wanted to go there.

Her voice firmed like it used to years ago. "I'd like for us to be together, come what may. Please, Melinda."

"I'll be home," I repeated. "I promise." One foot over the threshold.

She nodded gravely, retreating back into her elevator-sized bedroom.

The screen door slammed as I hurried down the lane.

2

It's my birthday.

I'm wearing a pink taffeta dress with purple bows, the most beautiful piece of clothing I've ever owned. I love it. I want to dance around in front of our bathroom mirror, but Mom has a surprise for me. So we take a seemingly endless walk to the fairgrounds, at the edge of town, near the canyon.

My feet begin to hurt, but when we finally get there, it's so worth it.

A party. For ME. I squeal with excitement.

Mom leads me to a picnic table with a Mylar number eight balloon tied to one end. Thomas is there, and some other kids from school. Not all of them are my friends, but that's not her fault. I never tell Mom things like that. Only Thomas.

Big Things are going on across the field. Mom planned my party alongside a carnival that just pulled into town. I see rides. Games. A pony. Oh my God, a pony!

This is quickly becoming the best day of my life.

Mom is smiling, laughing as she passes out cups of juice and paper plates stacked with fruit. I love seeing her happy. Even as a brand-new eight-year-old, I know she normally isn't. I can tell by looking, just like I know Principal Myers doesn't like people staring at his leg, and that Thomas doesn't want to talk about his bruises.

Cake. Presents. A ride on the Tea Cups. Then I wait with Thomas while he barfs behind the Ring Toss tent. We both find it pretty funny. He hurries back to the picnic table to get a new shirt, but I don't follow.

Because the pony. It's RIGHT. THERE.

I race over to a bearded man who smells like leather. The pony's name is Princess, and I'm in love with her forever. I wish Mom was there to get a picture, but I'll tell her all about it when I'm done. When I ask her to buy Princess and keep her behind our trailer.

Too soon, my ride is over. I slip off the pony's back, hug her to death, and then skip back toward the picnic table.

A man appears and walks beside me. I look up, curious. Is he one of Mom's friends?

The man looks down at me. He's wearing a black suit, shiny black boots, and sunglasses.

Yes, he's a friend of my mother's. She's been looking for me.

And out of nowhere, cotton candy!

I take it with a squeal and chomp a mouthful, my free hand grabbing his automatically. The man misses a step, stumbling on nothing but flattened grass, but I don't tease him for clumsiness. In the fading light, he leads me across the field, toward a knot of trees overlooking the canyon.

I ask where we're going, sugar coating my lips and glazing my eyes.

To meet my mother. She has another surprise.

We reach the trees and weave through their round trunks, coming to the edge of the ravine. I stare down at the rapids, way far below. I've never been so close to the edge before.

The man breathes extra deep, then goes still. I can tell he's tense and wonder why.

"Is something wrong?" I ask.

He releases his grip. "I'm sorry."

I barely feel the push. Don't know what's happening.

I fall, not making a sound.

Not until the moment I hit the rocks.

I wake up in the woods. It's dark, and I'm alone.

I remember.

The man. The push. The jagged boulders. I begin to cry. Tears streak down my cheeks as I run my hands over my arms and legs.

I'm not hurt. My dress isn't even dirty.

I scream for anyone who might hear me, racing down the mountainside toward the distant glow of town. I find a path, a road, then a man walking a Yorkshire terrier. His eyes widen as he shouts for someone named Gail.

A blanket enfolds me. Flashing lights. A warm drink with marshmallows.

I get to ride in a police car! All the way home to the trailer park. Mom is there. She's been crying, hugs me so hard I can't breathe.

Everyone has questions. Mom. Neighbors. A police officer. Then a hefty man with a mustache appears, and everyone else moves aside. It's Sheriff Watson, here at our trailer, which means this is a Big Deal. He asks me to tell him what happened, real slow.

I tell about the man in the suit. Cotton candy by the canyon's rim.

Gasps, quickly covered. I see frightened glances among the adults, but I'm not supposed to notice, so I don't say anything. Instead I tell them about the fall. How the man pushed me over the edge, the rocks rushing up, and how everything went black.

Silence. Then Sheriff Watson asks me to repeat the last part.

So I tell it again. I keep going, adding details, even though I know my story is making the adults upset. I tell them about waking up alone in the forest. Running toward the lights.

Sheriff Watson turns his back and whispers something to the others. Heads begin to nod. My mother swoops in, crushing me to her chest, telling everyone I need rest. I've been traumatized, whatever that means. More nods. I'm hustled off to bed.

As Mom tucks me under the covers, I ask her the question that's been bugging me.

Who was the black-suited man? Did she see him? Does she know him?

The flinch is slight, but I catch it. She says no. Of course not. My imagination has gotten the best of me. Then she kisses me fiercely, fat tears leaking from her eyes.

Mom tells me not to be afraid. That I'm safe. That I need to sleep more than anything.

The light flicks off. She closes the door.

But I don't sleep.

I'm only eight, but I know lies when I hear them.

3

"Hey, Sleeping Beauty!"

My head jerked, and I nearly fell over sideways. I grabbed the post I'd been leaning against. Impossibly, I'd drifted off while waiting. Or maybe not so impossibly. Had I slept at all in the last twenty-four hours?

Thomas "Tack" Russo was marching toward me, a slight kid with unruly black hair and penetrating blue eyes. He wore a *Kickpuncher* sweatshirt and beige cargo pants, his camouflage backpack hooked over both shoulders.

"Out cold by the gate is not a good look." Tack shook his head. "You should've grabbed a spot by the Wilson fire. Looks like those guys had a killer campout."

"We're going to be late," I grumbled, stifling a yawn.

"No one'll care." His smirk slipped a fraction as he rubbed his arms, chasing away the morning chill. I spotted bags under his eyes as well. "Honestly, I wonder how many kids will even show up."

Pushing off the post. "Nobody actually *knows* anything. Not yet. And I doubt Principal Myers will suddenly learn to relax."

"Wait wait wait!" Tack swung his backpack around and unzipped it, pulling out a lumpy parcel wrapped in Sunday comics. Dropping to a knee, he held the ugly bundle aloft, head bowed like a knight swearing service. "Please accept this token as a symbol of my undying pleasure at your continuing to be alive for another year."

I blanched, my stomach abruptly churning.

Alive another year. Am I really?

Tack glanced up. Registered my discomfort, if not the cause. He rose quickly, cheeks reddening as he thrust the package into my hands. "Sorry. I tried to find you yesterday, but . . ." He trailed off with a wince.

Tack knew I hated birthdays. That I spent them alone when I could.

He just didn't know why.

Tack was my best friend, and utterly irreplaceable. One of the few things I liked about Fire Lake, other than the scenery. I couldn't risk our friendship by telling him the truth. Couldn't stand for *him* to think I was crazy, too.

"You shouldn't have bought me anything," I scolded. Every year I told him not to. And every year he did anyway.

Tack's grin returned. "If it makes you feel better, I didn't. I stole it."

My eyes rolled as I tore into the newsprint. After I'd ripped through a near-seamless ball of tape, a small cardboard box fell into my hands. Inside was a pair of vintage Ray-Ban sunglasses. Silver frame. Reflective lenses.

I slipped them on. They fit perfectly.

A stony visage crashed my thoughts. *He* wore shades like these.

I shoved that aside. Wouldn't let the evil bastard's shadow darken every moment of my life. Who cared if they were similar? I liked these damn glasses.

"See there!" Tack crowed triumphantly, slapping his hands together. "Perfect! Who's the dopest Bella now? Melinda Juilliard Wilder, that's who!"

"Shut it, dork. And don't triple name me today, or my mom'll get jealous."

Plus, I hated my middle name. It was the sole legacy of my father—being named after a prestigious performing arts conservatory on the other side of the country. Yet I couldn't dance. Or act. Or sing. I didn't even play an instrument. Another letdown courtesy of a man I never knew.

"What's Virginia worked up about this time?" Tack snatched the sunglasses from my nose and slipped them on. "Something from yesterday? Did you offend Jeebus at your private birthday shindig?"

"It was nothing." I began walking up the drive. I hated lying to Tack, but the conversation had strayed into dangerous territory. I wished I still had the shades to cover my eyes.

Tack fell in beside me. "You're right, we need to get moving." He handed back the glasses and hitched his pants. "Our classmates wouldn't know *what* to do if the prom king and queen were late on Announcement Day. They'd probably crap themselves."

I snorted. We hiked up to Quarry Road, then started into town. A light breeze was rippling the lake, which gleamed like a sapphire in the heart of the valley. We crossed a handful of quiet blocks before hanging a left onto Library Avenue. Street names in Fire Lake are pretty straightforward. The place never got big enough to require creativity.

"NASA really torpedoed business this month," Tack said, pointing to a cluster of vacant condos near the marina. "My dad's had zero work. No tourists clogging their toilets."

"People are staying home, I guess. Waiting. A trip to Fire Lake just isn't in the cards."

Tack raised both palms, rounding his eyes dramatically. "But *Outdoor Weekly* named us the best weekend getaway in the Rockies! What better place to spend your last days on Earth?"

"People can be so dumb, right?"

"The worst."

The hike to school usually takes twenty minutes, unless the weather is crappy. But that morning it was all sunshine and blue skies, with the temperature hovering around fifty-five degrees. A gorgeous day in the northern Idaho mountains. It felt like a prank.

As we moved deeper into town, unusual signs of neglect cropped up. A busted streetlight. Trash in the gutter. An Explorer was parked with its front two wheels on the curb, soaped letters on its windshield saying, "You can have it, Sheriff."

I was born in Fire Lake, knew it heart and soul. I'd never seen anything like it before. The disarray felt fundamentally wrong.

A tricked-out Wrangler rounded the corner, music thumping, a chrome gun rack welded to its rear. The top was down, and three shirtless boys were hanging over its sides.

"Oh, shucks." Tack sighed dejectedly as they tore up the

block. "We missed our ride! I really wanted to flash the guns today, too."

"I'd rather crawl on my stomach than hitch a ride with Ethan. New car or not."

Tack shook his head. "Lay off my dudes. We're going camping next week, gonna really bro-down. Probably get wasted. Kill something and eat it. It's gonna be lit."

"Lovely. I'll be at the spa with Jessica and the squad."

Ethan Fletcher is the one who gave Tack his nickname, though it didn't work out like he'd planned. During sixth grade, as a prank, Ethan and the Nolan twins fastened Thomas Russo to a bulletin board by his clothes using thumbtacks. They left him hanging there, miserable and humiliated, until he was found by Mr. Hardy. In the halls the next morning, the other boys began calling him Thumbtack.

When Thomas heard, he immediately adopted the name as his own, refusing to respond to anything but Tack. Adults. Teachers. Classmates. Not even when called on in class. He was Tack, and that was final. After a while Ethan even tried to get him to *stop*, and Tack took a beating for refusing. A boulder could take lessons in stubbornness from that kid.

"Man, talk about depressing." Tack paused beneath the awning of Valley Grounds, our favorite coffee shop. A hand-scrawled sign was taped to its front door.

Closed Until . . . God Bless

His shoulders hunched. "This end-of-the-world stuff is cramping my style. We might all be about to die, but that doesn't mean I don't need caffeine. They better reopen eventually, or it's gonna be a *long* wait until the big boom."

I knew he was kidding, but the snark soured my mood.

Forget next month. God, what will tomorrow *be like if the news is bad?*

"You're probably rooting for a direct strike," I said, trying to play it off. "No exams."

"But what of *us*, then?" Tack's eyes twinkled as he snatched my hand in his. "If the Anvil is destined to flatten Idaho, I want to spend my last moments with you, rolling down hills like we did as carefree children. Such precious memories! Like happy raindrops, double rainbows of—"

"Oh, shut up." I shouldered him lightly, pulling my fingers free. The bump triggered a dull ache in my shoulder. I rubbed the half-moon scar under my sleeve. It always stung after one of my "special" birthdays.

My thoughts darkened, snapshots of the attack I'd suffered strobing inside my head.

The world might be about to end, but what did I care?

My world ended all the time.

I stayed silent as we passed the library, reaching the school zone at the end of the street. Fire Lake has one large campus for all three divisions. The two lower schools flank the road, which dead-ends into the high school parking lot.

The spaces were mostly empty.

"Told you." Tack absently stroked a bruise on his chin. I knew where he got them from, and we didn't talk about *that*, either. "Half this stupid town is probably hiding under their beds right now." His expression darkened as he scuffed a ratty sneaker on the blacktop. "Maybe they're not so dumb. Why go to school if you're about to be sentenced to death?"

I flinched. Tack misread me. Slid an arm around my shoulder.

"Why don't we meet up after school?" His searching glance was thwarted by my new sunglasses. "We can watch the Announcement at Bedfellow's. If the news is thumbs-up, we can probably score some free drinks."

I shook my head. "I promised Mom I'd be home. She's been carrying around her mother's old Bible all week. You know how she gets. Virginia is dead certain the Anvil will smash directly through our roof."

"This *is* prime asteroid country," Tack said lightly as we cut through the parking lot. "Space rocks probably feel right at home in the Gem State. Our incinerated remains will provide a warm welcome."

I couldn't help but shudder. "There's a giant headline on CNN calling it a planet killer. They even made a freaking GIF of the world getting crushed. Who the hell wants to see that? If it strikes *anywhere* on Earth—"

"THE AGE OF HUMANS SHALL BE NO MORE!" Tack spread his arms wide, a thin smile curling his lips. But I noticed that his hands shook slightly. Even Tack Russo struggled to mock the legitimate prospect of annihilation. He was as scared as everyone else.

Everyone except me.

I'd tried to make the asteroid feel real. I knew the Anvil came from outside our solar system, a deadly ball of carbon, nickel, and iron twelve miles in diameter and traveling at an insane speed of 300 kilometers per second, and that an impact from such an object would deliver the kinetic force of more than a billion hydrogen bombs. First spotted three weeks ago, it was just now passing the outer planets. It would strike or slide by in just over a month.

Initial odds had been given as one-in-seven. A week later, that was revised negatively to two-out-of-five. In the last few days, some independent scientists online had moved to fifty-fifty, ratcheting global tension to a boiling point. Thus, the Announcement that evening—an official answer to the are-we-all-going-to-die question. Less than twelve hours, and counting.

Yet our little town had decided everything would go on like normal. School. Business. Public services. The leaders of Fire Lake had planted their heads firmly in the sand, and were inviting all citizens down there with them. Surprisingly, most were going along with it, even me. I guess pretending everything's okay is more comfortable than admitting things really, truly might not be.

Personally, I felt almost nothing. The concept of a world-destroying super-boulder was simply too abstract for me. Twenty-fours hours ago, a man had broken into my mobile home at dawn. He shot me through the shoulder and chest, then twice more in the head.

That was real. *That* was something to fear.

Wayward space rocks? I couldn't get there. Maybe I was in denial.

"How about we get together afterward?" Tack was refusing to take no for an answer. We'd reached the walkway to the courtyard, and would hit a crowd in moments. "Rain or shine. Come on! If it's bad news, we can hike out to the old miner's hut and discuss what to wear for 'death by interstellar debris.' Work on our hoarding strategies."

I took a deep breath. Nodded. "*If* I can slip away."

"It's a date!" Tack shouted, then charged up the walkway, arms thrust skyward as he continued yelling, "A date! A date! An end-of-the-world date!"

"Not a date, you moron!" But I laughed.

At least one resident of Fire Lake had something to cheer about.

4

I hurried to my locker before the bell rang.

Head down, I strode quickly down the hall with my arms crossed tightly over my chest. I'd never be described as outgoing, but that morning I was aiming for invisible.

One thing about me: I don't make friends easily. Ability to Trust seems to be a prerequisite for lasting relationships, and I'm usually short on that count. I rarely share things about myself, and that self-imposed isolation has consequences.

Being honest, it's probably more than just the murders. I know I see the world differently than others. I can be aloof. And at Fire Lake High School—where acceptance of quirks is always in short supply—that lands you on the outside looking in.

I'd become comfortable as an outcast. Relished it, almost.

So, *of course*, that morning I got cornered by the people I least wanted to see.

"Hey, Melinda!" Ethan called out, strolling down the hall in his letterman's jacket. He had close-cut blond hair and a sharp-nosed face that was gorgeous until you realized what a prick he was. His small mouth was bent in a smile. He loved using my full name, because I hated it. A handful of kids followed on his heels.

My gaze flicked from face to face. Ethan. Sarah Harden, and her cheerleading BFF Jessica Cale. The Nolan twins, with their flaming red hair. Noah Livingston. Charlie Bell, acne scars and all. Toby Albertsson.

A group I would charitably describe as Worst-Case Scenario.

I'd known Ethan since third grade, and we'd never gotten along. The others were okay individually—like it or not, we'd grown up in a giant puppy pile our whole lives—but they could be ugly when forming a mob. Which they were doing right now.

Ethan leaned against the locker next to mine. The others fanned out with varying degrees of interest. Sarah and Jessica barely spared me a glance, chattering nervously about the latest Announcement predictions. A school-wide beauty contest would rank them one and two, though they'd knife each other over who got top billing.

Noah hung back, scrolling his phone. A handsome boy with light brown hair and green eyes, he rarely spoke around me, or much at all. His father owned the ski resort on the northern slopes and was the richest man in town. The other four boys, however—Chris and Mike Nolan, Charlie, and Toby—gave me their undivided attention.

"Can I help you, Ethan?" In as neutral a tone as I could manage.

"I was just wondering about your disaster preparedness." His ice-blue eyes attempted an earnest look. "Is the trailer park ready for an Anvil strike?"

At mention of the asteroid, a wave of apprehension swept through the group—a subtle, dancing poltergeist of fear. I noticed little signs, things that most people might not pick up on but to me were practically shouts. Chris Nolan's eyelids tightened, while his brother shuffled his feet. Charlie's knuckles whitened on the textbook he was carrying. Sarah faltered in her gossiping, a hand shooting up to rake her strawberry-blond hair.

"Ready as anywhere," I replied dully, closing my locker. "Since it doesn't matter *where* the thing hits."

Toby snorted. Chris nodded, as if I'd scored a point.

"Mobile homes aren't really built for sturdiness," Ethan said matter-of-factly, toying with a nearby lock. "One good thing is, you won't lose much if it gets compacted."

Heat rose to my face. I glanced at Noah, who was frowning at his Apple Watch. Not joining in, but not lifting a finger to help me, either.

My gaze dropped. Why look to him? Noah was good-looking—tall and wiry, with the build of a swimmer, and sporting the best car, clothes, and lifestyle of anyone in Fire Lake—but he never took a side on anything. Or even much interest, as far as I could tell.

Yet something about him always stuck in my brain. Maybe it was sharing a birthday. All those times we were forced to stand side by side in elementary school, listening to the other kids mumble that lame song. Celebrating a day I'd come to dread.

Fire Lake High was the only upper school in town, with just 220 students. The fault lines were mostly about money and sports. Pretty girls could cheerlead a path to popularity, of course. A quarter of the school's parents employed the rest, a fact no one ever forgot. The fissures began appearing in middle school and never healed.

"Thanks for your concern," I said calmly, pushing through the circle. "It never occurred to me that trailers aren't built to survive asteroid impacts."

Ethan smiled as I retreated. "On the other hand, you could tow your place inside a cave or something. For safekeeping."

His joke drew a few chuckles, but I wasn't worth the trouble. Ethan allowed me to escape down the hall and turned away.

Then a voice rang out. "Of course, your place is probably *much* safer."

Tack was standing beside the door to first period. Ethan shot him an annoyed look. "Obviously, Thumbtack." Ethan's father owned the town's only grocery store, and they lived in swanky Hillside Gardens.

"Tack!" I tugged him toward the safety of class. "Don't sta—"

"No, no! That's not it." Tack pulled free of my grasp, his voice carrying so that others stopped to listen. "You see, God always favors the drunk and stupid. And your dad is blessed on both counts. So the Fletcher home is practically a safe haven."

Ethan blinked, his neck and cheeks flushing red. Then his face went still.

Sarah rolled her eyes. Jessica giggled, covering her mouth.

The bell rang, startling everyone.

"Catch ya later, E-Dawg." Tack slipped through the door. Ethan stared at the empty space, then looked at me, as if I were guilty by association. His smirk returned. "Tell your friend he made a mistake."

Inside the room, I scurried to where Tack was calmly arranging his things on the table we shared. The Nolan twins entered a beat later—Chris with a shoulder-length ponytail, Mike's red hair cut short and spiked with gel. Chris was a chatterbox who loved stirring the pot, although he wasn't a disaster by himself. Mike rarely spoke.

Chris chuckled, shaking his head as he sat. "You're ballsy, kid. I'll give you that much. But if I were you, I'd find a new route home after school."

"Thanks, Mike," Tack replied, knowing full well he was speaking to the other twin.

Chris snorted, unzipping his backpack. "Freaking death wish," I heard him mutter.

I wheeled on Tack. "Why'd you do that? Ethan's not gonna let it go."

Tack was digging through his bag, seemingly unperturbed. "Because I felt like it. And screw Ethan, he's a jackass. Maybe next time he'll think before he yaps."

"What he's *going* to do is beat the crap out of you."

Tack shrugged. "Wouldn't be the first time. I've taken worse." Unconsciously, his hand rose to the bruise on his face. We both fell silent. Maybe Tack *did* have a death wish.

Then I couldn't help but laugh. "You called his dad a stupid drunk."

"I sure did." Tack shot me an exhilarated glance. "He looked *really* mad, didn't he? Chris is right, I'd better dig a tunnel out of here this afternoon."

English passed uneventfully. At the bell, Tack fired out the door at warp speed. Our next class was directly across the hall, but no sense taking chances. I was following on his heels when my name boomed down the corridor.

"Min Wilder!"

I glanced left. Principal Myers was slowly emerging from the main office.

"Wonderful." Under my breath, as our school's fearless leader made his way toward me, his right knee locked and unbending, the result of a shrapnel wound he'd suffered in the first Iraq War. I would've hurried down to shorten the distance, but every student in Fire Lake knew you didn't acknowledge the principal's disability. Not unless you wanted a twenty-minute lecture on how little the injury affected him.

"Yes, Mr. Myers?"

"You have an appointment with Dr. Lowell today," he said sternly, a burly, broad-shouldered man in his mid-sixties, with thinning gray hair framing a round face. He wore pleated gray pants and a plaid button-down every single day. Leaning on his cane, Myers scrutinized me over the rims of bronze-framed bifocals.

"Yes, I know, sir."

He gave me a severe look. "Your special session is *not* canceled, despite all this Announcement hubbub and . . . and . . . whatnot. I was told to inform you of this specifically."

A sigh escaped before I could stifle it. "Yes, Mr. Myers."

"You had a birthday over the weekend, did you not?"

I stiffened in surprise. "I did." Cautious. *Why are you keeping track?*

Myers eyed me closely, as if expecting me to say more. I had zero intention of doing so. "Well," he said finally, his non-cane hand rising to scratch a wrinkled ear. "Okay, then. See to it you're on time."

"I will." Dismissed, I beat a hasty retreat into second period.

Tack was sitting at his desk, twirling a pen in his fingers. "That looked fun. What'd the Big Man want?"

"Just a friendly reminder to visit my psychiatrist." I collapsed into the seat beside him. We stuck together in our classes whenever possible.

"From our freaking principal. I hate this inbred town."

I nodded, more disturbed than I was letting on. Myers often seemed interested in my therapy sessions, and this wasn't the first time he'd delivered a message from Dr. Lowell. The connection didn't feel right. And why did he ask about my birthday?

"You think he'll try to go to college with us?" Tack asked.

An old joke, but I snorted anyway. Andrew E. Myers had been our principal-for-life, moving up through the system in lockstep with my class. The uncanny timing of his promotions meant I'd never had another administrator, despite attending three different schools.

Biology. Spanish. Then lunch. Tack wisely avoided the cafeteria, leaving me to eat by myself. Students bunched together in knots, whispering about the Announcement, each striving to outdo the last with how little they pretended to care.

But their laughter rang hollow, betrayed by tapping feet and dry-washed hands.

The afternoon proved more painful than the morning.

In Algebra II, Mr. Fumo assigned a worksheet we'd completed the week before, then spent the whole period refreshing his phone and glancing at the clock. In seventh period, Mrs. Cameron kept losing her place and repeating herself. After her third attempt to explain the siege of Acre, she gave up, blessed us all, and dismissed class.

I packed up quickly, hoping for a stealth sprint through the parking lot. I hadn't seen Tack since math—our schedules had Gym and Health flip-flopped, and Tack couldn't care less about European History, electing to take Home Economics instead.

But my hopes for a clean getaway were dashed. Exiting the main building, I heard laughter reverberate across the courtyard. A crowd was forming in the corner near the parking lot. *Crap.*

I sprinted over and wormed through the ring of onlookers. Ethan had levered one of Tack's arms behind his back and was forcing his face down toward the concrete. Flailing, my friend fought to free himself, but he was giving up at least fifty pounds. Toby and Chris were grinning, egging Ethan on, while Jessica and other members of the cheerleading squad pretended to protest. Sarah watched impassively, seemed bored. Beyond the circle, Noah was leaning against a walkway post, eyes drifting. The more Tack struggled, the more the mob swelled.

"Ethan, let him go!"

He glanced at me and smiled. "Oh, hey, Melinda. Glad you're here. Tack's about to sing 'Bad Blood' for us, and you shouldn't miss it."

Seeing me watching, Tack thrashed twice as hard, his eyes narrowing to slits in a way I'd seen many times before. "Let me go, you douchebag! I'm warning you!"

"Or what?" Ethan asked with a lilt. "You said some nasty things about my family, so now we're in a feud. I want you to sing about it. We all do, right?" Laughter erupted all around. Faces bore hungry expressions, as if seeking a violent release to the day's unbearable tension. This was getting ugly fast.

Ethan yanked Tack's arm higher, eliciting a painful yelp.

"Have any more funny jokes, Thomas? I'd love to hear them. Or maybe you're all tapped out for now."

"That's not what your mother said!" Tack kicked out a foot. Missed.

A low *ooh* rose from the spectators. Chris Nolan giggled. Toby danced and hooted.

Ethan's eyes went flat.

Damn it, Tack.

I seized Ethan's arm. Felt his muscles ripple. He looked down at my hand, then back up, blinking rapidly. For a split second, I wasn't sure he recognized me.

"Take it easy! Tack's just running his mouth, like always."

Ethan shook his head, shrugging off my hand. He spun Tack around and grabbed him by the shirt, pulling him close. "You can't talk to me like that, Thomas. Not ever."

"Kiss my ass!" Tack's head rocketed forward, catching Ethan across the nose.

Ethan's hold loosened and Tack wriggled free.

But he didn't run, the idiot. To everyone's astonishment, Tack leapt at Ethan and swung.

Damn it, Tack.

Ethan blocked instinctively, then slugged Tack full in the face.

A second, louder *ooh* rose from the crowd.

Tack dropped to the ground like a boneless chicken breast.

"Stop!" I jumped to stand between Ethan and my friend. "That's enough!"

Voices yelled for me to move. Chris and Toby were laughing, encouraging Ethan with cries of "Finish him!" and "There can only be one!"

Tack had pulled himself up against a post, hacking and spitting. "That all you got?" he wheezed, wiping the back of his hand across his mouth, then calmly regarding a red smear on his wrist. "You hit like a bitch."

"Don't!" I shouted at Ethan, arms shooting wide. "He's down! You won, okay?"

Ethan looked me in the eye. Blinked. Then he stepped around me and stomped on Tack's hand. My friend howled as Ethan squatted down to eye level. "Ready to channel Taylor Swift, Thomas? Warm up that pretty voice."

Hands balling into fists, I was about to do something stupid when a voice carried from beyond the circle. "Yo, Ethan!"

Ethan looked up, annoyed. He spotted Noah, who tapped his watch and pointed toward the parking lot. "Let's get out of here, man. I'm starving."

"But Tack hasn't sung yet."

Across the courtyard, a door swung open.

Principal Myers stepped outside. "What's going on out here?"

The crowd dissolved like smoke, Ethan and his friends hustling away with the others. In moments, the only people left were me, Tack, and our principal.

Myers trudged over and stared down at Tack, frown lines creasing his forehead. "Bit off more than you could chew again, didn't you, son?"

"Inner ear infection." Tack rose unsteadily to his feet. "I fall down a lot."

"Who did this?" Myers asked sharply.

Tack remained silent, eyes on his sneakers.

Myers grunted, then turned to me. "Ms. Wilder? Care to

share who just pummeled Mr. Russo? Although I bet I can guess."

I opened my mouth, then closed it. This was Tack's call.

"I see." Myers removed his glasses, began cleaning them with a handkerchief. "Well, normally we'd all go to my office until I had this sorted out, but today is not a normal day. If things go well tonight . . . assuming we get good news . . ." He shook his head testily, as if unsure how to continue. "We'll discuss it tomorrow."

Myers pierced me with the glare of a disappointed father. "Can you see that Mr. Russo's injuries are properly attended to? *Without* missing your appointment?"

"Of course." I scooped up our packs. Tack straightened his clothes with exaggerated dignity and began limping toward the parking lot. Myers watched us for a long moment before heading back inside.

I caught up with Tack by the curb. "Hey!"

He halted with his back to me. I put a hand on his shoulder. Felt him tense. Ignoring the reaction, I gently but firmly spun him around. "What the hell were you thinking?"

"That I was going to get my ass kicked anyway, so I might as well take the first shot."

"Well, mission accomplished. How's the hand?"

He flexed his fingers painfully. "I don't think anything broke. Hurts like hell, though. Got any Advil?"

I dug some from my bag, along with a package of tissues. As Tack downed three pills, I began dabbing his right eye, which was already swollen. His hand was a puffy mess.

Ethan had met my eye before delivering the stomp. That one was for me.

Inside, something snapped.

Ethan's smirk. His casual violence.

Or maybe yesterday had been one murder too many.

Releasing Tack, I spotted Ethan's Wrangler at the back of the parking lot, a dozen spots from the next closest vehicle. Everyone had fled on foot, probably down to the cafés on Main Street, intending to return for their cars after the smoke cleared.

We were all alone.

"Come on." I hurried toward the Wrangler.

Tack followed, confusion plain on his face. "What? Why?"

After checking to make sure the coast was clear, I reached inside and pulled the gas tank release. Circling to the passenger side, I spotted an oily rag and a can of WD-40 on the floor of the backseat.

"What are you doing?" Tack whispered. "Ethan loves this Jeep, maybe physically."

"He shouldn't have stomped your hand." I ripped the rag in two and doused the larger piece with oil. Then I unscrewed the gas cap and shoved it inside.

Tack's eyes nearly popped from his skull. He ducked behind the hood, eyes darting with new intensity. "Holy crap, Min! This may be a little out of proportion."

"So was crushing your fingers." I tapped my lips, stymied, ignoring the voice of reason screaming inside my head. Then I spotted a book of matches in Ethan's ashtray. *It's almost like he wants me to do it.*

Beads of sweat rolled down my back. I lit a match, used it to ignite the smaller rag. The oil-soaked cloth caught easily, orange tendrils curling and twisting like greedy fingers. Pivoting carefully, I held the flames under the larger rag hanging from the gas tank.

Poof.

Tack was bouncing on the balls of his feet. “Come on! We gotta bail!”

“Not too fast, though.” I rose, walked casually down the aisle. “Don’t attract attention.”

“Attention. Right.” He could barely keep from sprinting. “Wouldn’t want that.”

Thirty paces to the sidewalk. Ten more out of the parking lot. Roughly thirty seconds had passed, with no effect. As we crossed the street, I worried that my plan had failed and we’d have to go back and ditch the evidence.

A jarring boom. The ground shook. Glancing over my shoulder, I spotted a black plume billowing above the trees, angry shadows dancing just beneath.

Tack swallowed audibly. “Oh, man. We really did it this time. If Ethan ever finds out—”

“I almost hope he does.” Then I turned my back on the mounting inferno.

Here’s another thing about me.

I’m not afraid of much. Not after what I’ve been through.

And I forgive as little as I forget.

Hitching both our packs, I led Tack away down the street, my blood pumping mile-a-minute. Somewhere far off, a siren began to wail.

5

I hug the brand-new Fancy Farms Pony to my chest.

Rock it back and forth.

I love her. I love her piebald coat, like a checkerboard come to life. I love her flowing black mane, as soft as real hair. I love the slight bend to her right foreleg, as if she's ready to prance right across my lap and off the couch.

I name her Spirit. She's two feet tall, an exact replica of a real horse. I will cherish her forever.

It's my tenth birthday. Just Mom and me, tucked inside our trailer as a thunderstorm rages outside. The disturbing memory of two years ago has faded. It was just a bad dream, like they all said.

My presents aren't expensive, but I love them dearly. I know we don't have much money. Jessica told me so, one day after school. But I really, really wanted a horse to play with. Nothing as babyish as another My Little Pony—although, to be honest, I still play with the four I have. I wanted something lifelike. Something that felt as real as possible without a barn and hay and a jillion dollars.

And Mom found the perfect one.

I hop Spirit around the room while Mom readies my birthday cake. I'm overwhelmed with happiness. Everything I need is right here in our cozy mobile home. Why would I want all that other stuff Sarah and Jessica are constantly talking about? Tiaras and nail-styling kits and two-piece bathing suits. Seems so silly.

I wish Thomas was here, but I know not to bring it up again. A shadow crossed Mom's face when I asked why he wasn't coming. Something to do with his father. It's okay, though. I'll see him tomorrow.

There's a lull in the storm.

"Want to see the neighborhood, Spirit?" I carry her outside with both arms. Mom cautions me not to go far. I won't, I promise.

Some people like to make fun of our trailer park, but I know Spirit isn't like that. The packed-earth lanes and boxcar rows are perfect for a frisky pony.

The rain has let up, but the wind still howls, shaking the floodlight mounted on a post beside our unit. The sun has set, and it's very dark. The usual night sounds are missing, probably because of the storm. No crickets. No squawking birds. Not a single call of a hunting coyote. Suddenly, I don't want to be outside, not even in my own front yard.

As if in response, there's a crack of thunder. The sky opens up once more.

Before I can scurry back to the door, a wraithlike form steps into the light, throwing a long shadow that covers me head to toe. For a moment, I'm blind.

Then my eyes adjust and I see him.

The black-suited man.

He's here, standing across from me in the pelting rain.

The nightmare of two years ago explodes in my brain. Cotton candy. The chasm. A push in the back and a long, long fall. The man looks exactly the same as on that day.

I scream, but the sound is swallowed by the storm. Dropping Spirit in the mud, I dart for my front door, but the monster is quicker. So I whirl and bolt down the rain-soaked lane, then up a narrow alley between neighboring units.

Heavy boots slosh through puddles behind me. Fighting panic, I double back along the rear fence, hoping to swing behind our trailer and pound on the window. Mom has to be wondering why I'm not back inside by now.

Lightning knifes across the inky-black sky.

I freeze. The man is ahead of me, blocking my path. I dive into the scraggly bushes lining the fence. There's a hole in the chain-link nearby. Thomas and I use it all the time.

Branches snap a yard from where I'm crawling through the mud. I can sense the man straining to reach me, hindered by the grasping thorns. Slithering on my belly, I find the gap and scramble through it, a thousand tiny needles ripping at my skin.

I stand, run, pitch headfirst into a flooded gully. Without a plan, I struggle down the swollen creek bed, thinking only of escape.

A splash behind me. Pebbles rocket past, as if kicked.

He's close, and closing.

I claw up a muddy bank, then dash blindly into the forest, smashing through spiderwebs and sodden shrubs. Seconds later the ground disappears and I fly forward, tumbling down a scree-covered slope toward a raging creek. My hand shoots out and snags a tree root, arresting my fall so that I'm hanging over the drop. Looking down, I see the grinding teeth of rapids gone berserk.

I hear leaves thrashing. Look up. The black-suited man is watching me from the edge of the bluff, thick raindrops running down his cheeks. He's still wearing his sunglasses despite the near total darkness. Then, slowly, deliberately, he climbs down, stopping just a few feet above where I cling to the cliff side.

A terrified whimper escapes my lips. I'm trapped. How could this be happening again?

The man stares at me. Rainwater seeps from his soaked business suit. His face is as blank as Death himself.

"I'm sorry."

A shiny black boot smashes down on my fingers. I gasp in pain as my left hand loses its grip. I swing wildly, on the verge of plummeting to the white water below.

"Please!" I beg. "Don't!"

The foot stomps on my right hand.

Snapping bones. A rush of air. Then I'm underwater, tumbling and spinning. Liquid fills my nose. My mouth. My ears. Something slams into my side, and ropes of agony shoot down my left arm. That hand refuses to respond. I kick back to the surface, organs throbbing in distress.

Breathe.

I struggle against the current as I'm swept downstream. My lungs burn. My vision blurs. I see fiery lines and twinkling stars. A chaotic, tinny pounding fills my ears. I can't hear my own shrieks.

I feel it before I see it. Vibrations down to my bones. Then a rumbling, grinding noise, like a dragon's growl. I fight to stay afloat as the current accelerates.

Thirty yards downstream, the water is disappearing.

I don't have time to scream. I slip over the falls, dropping twenty feet to a rocky pool below. Something dark and huge appears in front of me. My heart flutters as I streak directly toward it.

Pain explodes at my temple.

I see and feel nothing more.

I'm lying on my back.

It's dark.

I'm in a clearing in the woods. The same one as before, I'm sure of it.

I lift my left arm. Examine it closely.

No scrapes, cuts, or broken bones. My clothes are dry and undamaged.

I run all the way home, stopping for nothing.

Flashing lights surround my trailer. I shout for Mom. Adults come running.

My mother crushes me in a hug, then thrusts me out to arm's length, running her hands over my body, making sure I'm okay. It's the same night. I see Spirit lying in the mud, and for some reason this is what makes me cry.

The questions begin. I tell the truth. To Mom. Officer Somebody. Sheriff Watson, having arrived late and out of uniform in his off-duty Ford pickup.

When I'm done, glances are exchanged. The atmosphere isn't the same as last time. Sheriff Watson makes a call on his cell phone, then goes to sit in his truck. Twenty minutes later a short man in a tweed jacket arrives.

He smiles at me. Introduces himself as Dr. Lowell. Says he'd like to talk to me about my experience. Would that be okay?

I shrug, wrapped in my mother's protective embrace, as I wipe dirt from Spirit's mane and fuzzy coat. I look to Mom. She nods slowly, her eyes never leaving the stranger.

Okay, sure.

Dr. Lowell asks my mother if he and I can speak privately. Mom tenses, but then rises and smooths her skirt. Once alone, he pulls the rocker over and sits across from me. Smiles. Asks me to tell him everything, starting with what happened tonight.

I do. Cautiously at first, but soon the words pour out like a confession. Dr. Lowell smiles and nods, never interrupting. I like talking to him. He listens better than anyone. Before I know it, I'm telling him about the last time, too.

When I finish, he thanks me for being so brave. He's totally calm, which strikes me as weird, given my horrible stories. Dr. Lowell has lots of answers, but they seem almost rehearsed. I can tell he's watching me intently.

Suddenly, I like him a lot less than before.

Dr. Lowell explains what really happened to me, and why.

The things I experienced aren't real. I have something called a dissociative disorder, which makes me believe scary things happened when they really didn't.

When he's finished talking, I nod, not knowing what else to do. Mom clearly wants me to speak with this person, so I have to play along. Then Dr. Lowell reaches into his pocket and pulls out an unmarked bottle.

He shakes a single blue pill into his palm. Holds it up so I can see.

This is medicine, he explains. Made for people like me. If I swallow one pill every day, the chemicals inside will help keep bad thoughts away. Will I take it?

I stare at the pill for a long moment. Even at ten, I understand what it means. Know now what the adults had been whispering. No one believes me. They think I'm a freak.

Dr. Lowell leans forward. Softly repeats his request.

Will I take the medicine?

Yes, I will.

But I'll never share what happens to me.

Not ever again.

6

I sat in Dr. Lowell's drab waiting room, thumbing through an old *Us Weekly*.

Tack had gone home. He'd promised to come by my trailer after the Announcement, whatever the verdict might be. I'd watched him hurry away down the sidewalk, scanning cross streets, still jittery about what we'd done to Ethan's Jeep.

I could scarcely believe it.

Slouching in one of Lowell's uncomfortable lobby chairs—sixty minutes after the fireball, my initial rage having long since burned off—I was growing more and more stunned by my actions. What had I been thinking? *Blow up his freaking car?* That's juvenile-prison-level madness.

What would my mother say? What would Tack's father do?

I shivered, and not from the arctic-level temperature Lowell maintained in the building. Destroying Ethan's Wrangler was the most reckless thing I'd ever done. I truly, deeply, seriously hoped Tack and I hadn't been seen. The alternative was too awful to contemplate.

We TORCHED his JEEP. In the high school parking lot!

Was I as crazy as everyone thought?

A door opened, and Dr. Lowell stuck his head out. He didn't have a secretary or assistant of any kind. I guess he didn't have enough clients to justify the expense.

"Ah! Min. Right on time."

Smiling, he eased the door open and swept a hand inside. Beneath a thatch of red hair were flinty green eyes and a smooth, pale face dotted with freckles. Lowell wore his typically inoffensive, shrink-on-the-job garb—corduroy pants and a light blue sweater.

"Please come in. Would you like a soda? Water?"

"I'm fine." Same offer, same response. Every time.

Lowell nodded amicably. "Okay, then. Please sit wherever you like."

I took the same spot as always, a leather fainting couch beneath the windows overlooking the lake. As far from him as I could manage in the snug, wood-paneled office.

On script, Lowell spun a recliner to face me and sank into its depths. A notebook sat on a table to his right, untouched. He never wrote anything during our sessions, though a few times, returning soon afterward for a forgotten jacket or misplaced backpack, I'd caught him scribbling away like mad in its pages.

Lowell had seemed almost embarrassed on those occasions—quickly locating my belongings, asking if I needed anything else, then ushering me out with a hearty grin—as if I'd caught him doing something naughty. Who knows? Maybe I had.

I slumped down, eyes traveling the room. Bookshelves lined the walls, displaying various scientific tomes, objects full of psychological importance, and pictures of Lowell on his travels. He didn't seem to have a family—no shots of a loving wife or kids, not even a slobbering Doberman. Landscape art filled in the blanks, bland and forgettable, probably rated "not likely to incite violence" by the Idaho State Board of Psychiatry.

A bulky, antique-looking wooden cabinet sat in the corner—banded with bronze, lacquered to a shine, and never opened during my visits. A MacBook Air was the only thing on his desktop.

"So," Lowell began, hands folded, one foot resting on the opposite knee as he fixed me with his patented "I'm your friend" look. At first he'd tried to get me to call him Gerald, but I'd flatly refused. "How has your week been since our last visit?"

Visit. Always a visit, and never a session. My shrink didn't want me to feel *forced* to be there, even though I was.

I shrugged. "Fine. Principal Myers said you wanted to meet today instead of Wednesday."

"Sunday was your birthday," he supplied, his relaxed bearing not shifting an inch. Dr. Lowell had a gift for stillness, to the point it was unnerving. "We always meet the day after your birthdays, just in case you feel a need to talk. To share."

"I'm good." Glancing out the window. "Nothing to report."

Gunshots echoed in my head. I felt the sting of white-hot slugs tearing into me.

I drew my knees up to my chest. Could feel Lowell's eyes. Observing. Assessing. Taking my measure.

A glance at the clock. Forty-five minutes to go.

He didn't miss my reluctance. "Min," he said softly, his voice heavy with compassion, "I hope I don't need to remind you that you can trust me. Anything we say in this room will never be shared outside of it. I'm here to help. If something is bothering you, talking about it in a safe environment will almost certainly make you feel better. I promise."

Is that what this is? A "safe environment"?

I didn't know what to say. So, a lie. "Yeah. But nothing happened."

My response sounded unconvincing, even to me. Too strident, as if by overselling a denial I'd confirmed the opposite.

"I'm not entirely persuaded, Min." Dr. Lowell's tone remained light and conversational, almost apologetic. "I think there's something you're not telling me."

Not a question, so I didn't answer. Though my flaming cheeks might've spoken for me.

Uncrossing his legs, my psychiatrist leaned forward, his face growing serious. A twinge of frustration had crept into his eyes.

"We've been having these visits for six years now, Min." His voice was calm, but carried an undercurrent I couldn't decipher. "I like to think I've gotten to know you well." He paused, as if considering, creating an awkward moment I did nothing to disturb. Finally, "I sense that you're holding back today. I'd like to know why."

I hugged my knees closer, stalling for time. In all our "visits," I couldn't recall Lowell ever pushing me like this before. He rarely pried, and never directly called me out. I was always allowed to steer the conversation, or at least given the illusion of such control.

Say something, *at least.*

"Sorry." Not meeting his eye. "Yesterday was boring. I hung out by myself while Mom worked, and then . . ." I trailed off, but the silence stretched, and I knew I'd have to break it this time. "I just wanted to be alone. So I was."

His corduroy pants squeaked as he straightened. "Nothing unusual happened? No . . . bad memories? No lost time, or unexplained events?"

My feet hit the floor, defensive walls slamming into place. "No, Dr. Lowell. I didn't have a psychotic episode yesterday. Is that what you want to know?"

Lowell leaned back in his chair. He schooled his body to stillness, but his entire being radiated . . . disappointment.

Uneasiness roiled my gut. Did he *know* something happened?

"Are you taking your medication?" Dr. Lowell asked abruptly.

The question caught me off guard. "What? Oh, yes." Except for that morning. In my rush to make it to school on time, I hadn't swallowed my little blue pill.

"You need to take it *every day*, Min." As if he'd read my mind. "It doesn't work properly otherwise." His eyes crimped slightly at the corners. *He's angry. And hiding it.*

The strange behavior made me bold. "What *is* the pill, Doctor?" In an inquisitive voice, wearing an expression of harmless curiosity. "I mean, what's it made of? What's it supposed to do?" In all our sessions, I'd never really asked before.

A slight tic, swiftly covered. But I saw.

"Neurotandal is a psychotropic compound used to treat patients who have mild-to-severe dissociative disorders of a complex nature," he said smoothly. "But you know that. You've been taking this prescription since you were ten."

I crossed my legs casually, leaning back against the wall and feigning nonchalance. We were wading into the deep end, broaching a subject that had bothered me for years. I knew I had to swim carefully.

"It's just, I can only get the medication from you. It's not at the pharmacy, or anywhere else I know of. I Googled it once and got zero hits, which never happens. I was just wondering . . . you know . . . why."

Lowell answered effortlessly, as if reading from a manual. "Neurotandal is an experimental drug, which means it's still stuck in the quagmire of FDA approval and therefore not publicly available. That's why your mother had to provide written permission when you were little. We'd hoped that it would be right for you, and, thankfully, it has been."

Then why do I keep seeing the black-suited man? Why do I still die?

Lowell was watching me steadily. Gauging my reaction to his words. This "visit" clearly hadn't gone as he'd wished.

Did he sense I was covering up an attack?

He shouldn't, because I'd done it before.

My deaths at twelve and fourteen? I'd never said a word about them. I'd had sessions just like this one after both days, but on those occasions he'd accepted my deflections. So why was today different?

Because he knows.

My instincts spoke with bone-deep certainty. I was suddenly sure Lowell knew things he shouldn't. The notion more than unnerved me. I wanted out of his office immediately.

No. Don't run. Set a trap instead.

"Honestly, this morning was way more eventful than yesterday."

"Oh?" Lowell's head tilted, warm lamplight reflecting in his eyes. "Something at home?"

Careful.

Frowning, I ran fingers through my hair. Scratched at my cheek. My very best Normal Sullen Min impersonation. "Mom barely noticed me come in, and didn't say a word until I was half-way back out the door. Sometimes I think she's given up on me."

"Your mother works very hard," Lowell said gently, "but she's always in your corner. During stressful moments parents can be just as tongue-tied and out of answers as their children. But it doesn't mean they've given up, or love them any less."

I nodded, not trusting myself to speak.

My slipup had been plain, yet Lowell hadn't blinked.

He didn't ask where I was coming from. Or why I'd been out in the first place.

The omission might seem innocuous—that he'd simply mis-understood what I'd said—but I knew better. Dr. Lowell *never* missed things like that. Six years of therapy had left me with little doubt on that account.

My mouth went dry. The implications were staggering. I needed out of there, *now*, but the hour was barely halfway gone. So I gritted my teeth and mentally closed ranks, determined to give as little as possible.

The rest of the session was brutal: Lowell asked questions, I gave terse answers, and neither of us was satisfied. Finally, he glanced at his watch. "It seems we're out of time. I look forward to seeing you on our next visit."

I grabbed my pack and beelined for the door. Through the lobby and out onto High Street, streaking away as fast as possible without drawing eyes. I glanced down toward the lake. Flashing lights illuminated the school parking lot. I saw the town's fire engine and two of our three squad cars. Despite everything, the sight warmed my heart.

Like punching people now, tough guy?

I was hustling home as fast as I could—satisfied or not, I didn't want to run into Ethan any more than Tack did—when a thought surprised me so much, I stopped in my tracks.

Lowell had peppered me with questions for nearly an hour. But never, not *once* during the eternity I was trapped inside his domain, had he mentioned the Anvil.

I stood in the middle of a crosswalk, face scrunched in disbelief. *The potential end of the freaking world isn't on my shrink's radar?* How was that possible? That wasn't relevant to my mental health?

A horn beeped, and I jumped. Hurried to the sidewalk. Talking to myself wouldn't yield any answers, and I was the perpetrator of a recent felony.

I needed to get my butt off the streets.

7

My body locks up with fear.

It's the morning of my twelfth birthday, and I dread what's coming. I'm certain I won't survive this time.

I struggle to reassure myself. My eleventh passed without incident. I spent the whole day locked in my room, refusing to speak to anyone, not even Mom. She called Dr. Lowell, who came by the trailer and tried to coax me out.

Nothing will happen, he said. The past experiences are all in your head.

But I didn't budge. I took my medication that morning, but with zero faith it would work. A pill can't stop a killer. Can't hold back my personal angel of death.

But it did.

Nothing happened that day. The black-suited man never appeared.

No fleeing. Or falling. Or dying. No waking up in the woods, cold and alone.

Maybe the medicine really did work, and the murders were delusions after all.

A knock on my door. Mom. She takes one look at me and sighs. "Now, Min." Sitting on the edge of my bed, she brushes damp hair from my eyes. "You're going to school today, and that's a fact. I've already spoken with Principal Myers, and he's expecting you."

"You called the principal!?" Aghast. If the others find out my mother trades phone calls with Peg-Leg Myers . . .

"And Dr. Lowell," Mom confirms, each word a dagger. "Everyone understands why you're upset, but we've got to put that behind us. Today is going to be a normal, happy birthday, and it starts with school." She forces a smile. "There'll be a party for you and Noah Livingston. Isn't that nice?"

"Right. Nice." She has no idea.

I can picture it now: standing in front of the firing squad beside Noah—the cutest, richest, shyest boy in my grade—while his friends snicker and make fun of us, taunting him about his "girlfriend." He'll turn red and edge away, leaving me up there alone like a freak.

Mom snaps open the blinds, then clucks audibly. "Well, there goes the bus. You'll have to walk in. I'll let them know you'll be a few minutes late." She looks over, sees my pained expression. "I'm sorry, Min, but I have to be at work in thirty minutes, and not showering again won't do. Thomas must've thought you weren't coming. He got on."

"It's Tack now." Of course he thought that. I told him so myself, yesterday.

Moaning piteously, I gather my things. Begin trudging down the dusty lane toward the gate. The sky is leaden gray, as dark as my mood.

The road into town is strangely empty. Down in the valley, the lake is stirring and roiling. Though I can't feel them yet, I know heavy winds must be sweeping its surface. A light mist creeps over the surrounding woods, punctuated by bursts of rain. Dully, I try to imagine more ominous weather for me to be out walking alone in. I guess it could be sleeting. At midnight.

High beams knife through the thickening fog. I move to the shoulder and wait for the car to pass—a dark, late-model sedan of some kind, moving fast. Idly, I wonder who was that far up Quarry Road this morning in anything less than a pickup.

The car snakes around a bend.

Something about it. I edge farther back onto the shoulder, but the drop-off is steep and slippery from the rain.

The engine revs. I catch a glimpse of the driver.

Sunglasses. Dark suit.

I scream, but it's far, far too late.

The car swerves, its hood ornament zeroing in on my chest.

A flash of agony. The sensation of flying.

Colors explode, and the world disappears.

I stir well after nightfall. Pitch black, but I know where I am.

My brain shuts down. For a time I just sit there, unable to process.

I see his face through the windshield, an instant before impact. Feel the car slam into my side, crushing bones and tossing me through the air like a rag doll.

It didn't stop. It's never going to stop.

My leg brushes something and I recoil. But it's only my backpack, fully zipped and undamaged. Of course. With nothing else to do or say, I stumble home.

My mother grabs me the moment I enter our trailer, her tired features twisted in a manic combination of anger and relief. A wave of déjà vu engulfs me. "Where have you been?!" Tears spill from her red-rimmed eyes.

Movement in the corner. Dr. Lowell is sitting in my mother's rocker, drinking from a teacup. "Now, now, Virginia. Please. Let's talk to Min calmly. I'm sure she's just as frightened as you are."

My hackles rise. What's he doing here?

"I took the pill," I blurt automatically. Then I regret speaking at all.

"I believe you." Lowell's voice is soothing. "Please, sit. Everything is going to be all right. Your mother did the right thing to call me when you failed to show up at school."

Mom releases me, and I do as instructed.

Dr. Lowell assumes his "counselor" posture. His clothes are neat and dry, his red hair only slightly ruffled. It occurs to me that he's been here, alone in the trailer with my mother, for quite some time. "Please tell us what happened today. In your own words. Take as much time as you need." He smiles encouragingly, ghostly pale in the low light.

I don't respond, hateful memories roaring back to life.

"This is a safe place, Min." Dr. Lowell's pleasant affect never wavers. "You're home, with only your mother and me listening, and we both have your best interests at heart. I want you to treat this like one of our regular office visits."

Something about the way he's sitting. The false ease. A sharpness to his gaze.

His tone. There's a hidden eagerness I don't like.

So for the first time, I lie.

"I skipped school." Eyes on our cheap carpet. "I didn't want a party with Noah, or anyone else. So I hiked into the woods and hid. Read

a book. But then I accidentally fell asleep, and woke up in the dark. Ran home."

My mother slaps her thigh. "Melinda! How coul—"

"Let's not judge, Virginia," Dr. Lowell chides gently, one leg still resting comfortably across the other. "Min has had some very difficult birthdays in the past. It's understandable she might not want to celebrate their anniversary." He studies me thoughtfully, and though his bearing never changes, I feel added weight to his next words. "Is that what happened, Min? Is there anything else you want to tell me? Anything at all?"

I shiver, as if sinking to the bottom of a deep, dark pool.

But I made up my mind a long time ago. So I meet his eye. Shake my head.

"I have nothing else to say."

8

The Announcement was set to begin in three minutes.

I flipped a few channels. The presidential seal filled each one. For the first time in history, Uncle Sam was preempting every station and network. If you wanted *Game of Thrones*, you were simply out of luck.

I tried Twitter, but couldn't get a signal. Everyone in America must've been clogging the towers. Mom was pacing our kitchenette, wiping dishes that were already dry. Her hands shook. I worried she'd drop one and cut herself.

I rose and walked to her side. Gently took the rag away. She tensed, eyes squeezing shut as her chin dropped. "I'm fine . . . Everything is . . ." She shook her head, as if clearing it. "It's just not fair to *you*. To young people. You don't deserve to have your lives snuffed out before you can even—"

"Why don't we sit?" I guided Mom to her rocking chair, then dropped onto the couch beside it. Her pessimism rattled me, but I was determined not to show it. "Let's wait and see what NASA has to say first, okay? Who knows? Maybe the Anvil is made out of toilet paper."

My mother snorted wetly, dabbing her eyes with a tissue. She got a faraway look. "Did you know, when the preschool tested you as a toddler, your IQ was through the roof? Highest number they'd seen in years, the lady said. I don't remember what it was, but it was *very* good." Then her frown returned. A beat later she surged forward, grabbing my hand.

"I want you to know something. And I want you to remember it. Always."

"Okay." I swallowed. "What is it?"

"Everything I've done. All the . . . hard . . . all the . . . *hateful* choices I've had to make." Mom paused, as if searching for an inner strength that had clearly fled. "I did what I thought was best," she finished, releasing my hand. "Always that."

She looked away. I released a breath I hadn't realized I was holding.

"It's okay, Mom." Though I wished she wasn't doing this now. "I know what—"

"No!" Her eyes closed. "You do *not*. But there was no other way. I believe that, at least."

I stared, baffled. But at that moment a voice blared from the TV.

"Please stand by for the president of the United States."

The Announcement was beginning. All other thoughts flew from my head.

Am I about to be told the exact moment of my death?

The seal disappeared, replaced by a live shot of the Oval

Office. The commander in chief was sitting behind her desk, a grave expression on her face. Without preamble, she said, "I've just been informed that NASA, seconds ago, completed its final calculations regarding the path of Asteroid 152660-GR4, more commonly known as the Anvil. Neither I nor anyone on my staff has yet heard their conclusions. Therefore, we go live to NASA headquarters in Houston."

I sat forward on the couch.

A lonely podium on a simple black stage, in what could have been any auditorium in the country. A breathless man in a white lab coat practically sprinted toward the microphone.

Adrenaline flooded my system. This was it. The moment.

The gangly scientist seemed barely able to speak. "It's going to miss!" he finally wheezed, then shouted full-throat into the mike. "The Anvil will bypass Earth at a range of thirteen thousand, eight hundred, and twenty-seven miles!"

Pandemonium. The auditorium erupted in thunderous cheers. Flashes strobed. People were hugging and screaming with joy. The feed cut briefly to a network studio, where the lead anchor was shaking uncontrollably in his seat, gasping in relief.

My mother slid from her chair to the floor.

I dropped to my knees beside her and grabbed her hand. "Mom? Mom?!"

"Praise God!" she mumbled, rolling to her back to stare at the ceiling. "This wasn't it. It's not time yet. I was so sure . . . so convinced . . ."

I pulled her upright, my heart nearly beating out of my chest. "It's going to miss, Mommy! We're okay! Everything is okay!"

She tensed so abruptly, I released her in surprise. Sadness

crept back into her eyes, but this time Mom tried to cover it. She patted my hand. "That's right, Melinda J., that's right. God is good. Everything is going to be okay." But the raw honesty was gone. I was disappointed by her clumsy attempt at placating me.

The president reappeared onscreen, smiling broadly, but I couldn't hear her words. Outside, explosions began echoing up and down the valley. I ran to the window. Fireworks were lighting up the night sky, punctuated by sharp pops and booms that could only be gunshots. I heard exultant screams and shouts. Running feet and raucous laughter. Fire Lake had been given a death-row pardon, and its people were celebrating. Hard.

"Get away from there!" my mother admonished, regaining her composure. "Damn fools firing their rifles into the air! Liquored up to boot. People are going to get hurt tonight, mark my words."

I stepped back from the glass. News coverage had switched to live shots of major cities. People were pouring into the streets, dancing, as if everyone had won a championship at once. I checked my phone again, but still couldn't get a signal.

I was surprised to discover that I didn't share the euphoria. Couldn't connect to the wild celebrations. Why not? Did I *want* an asteroid to kill the planet?

"I'm going outside. Need some air."

Mom's head whipped to face me. "Not a step into town, though. People will be off their rockers tonight."

Nodding, I stepped out into the cool evening. Barely made it three steps.

Blood rushed to my head. The ground tilted. I staggered,

dropped into a lawn chair beside our fire pit. Dark thoughts were choking me. Paralyzing me.

The planet wasn't going to explode after all. My life would continue as before.

And in two years, it would happen again.

A hand rose to cover my face. Ran its length. The weight of thc world resettled onto my shoulders. The madness would continue, and I didn't even know what was real.

My eyes popped open.

Proof.

There had to be something. Here. At my house. Some tiny piece of confirmation that the black-suited man *existed*—if only for my own sanity.

I rose, reconstructing the event in my mind. He would've assumed I was inside when he arrived. It'd been early, on a weekend. But did he check to make sure? How would he do that?

I began circling the trailer, looking for the slightest indication someone else had done the same. I rounded one corner, then another, reaching the outside of my grimy bedroom window.

My breath caught.

There. In the mud.

I dropped to my knees to be sure.

A single boot print. Low-heeled, with a waffle tread.

Images flickered in my mind. Me, sprawled on my bedroom carpet. A smoking hole in the door. The searing brightness of my fluorescent lights. The black-suited man, standing over me, his boot inches from my face.

Shiny. Black. Low heel. Waffle tread.

This was *evidence*. Undeniable, concrete fact.

A shallow boot print wouldn't convince Mom. Or Lowell. Not Sheriff Watson and the Fire Lake PD, all of whom knew about my two previous "adventures" as a little girl. It wouldn't persuade a single solitary soul that I'd recently been murdered.

But it was enough for me.

Hot tears streaked down my cheeks, falling like raindrops from my chin.

I'm not crazy. The black-suited man exists.

He wore heeled boots, left footprints, and had prowled the perimeter of my trailer before shooting me to death. I stumbled back to the chair and collapsed into it.

The murders were not delusions.

But . . . then . . . what *were* they? How did I die and come back to life?

Why that clearing? How did I get there? Where was I during the time in between?

I'd spent a lifetime avoiding these questions, part of me secretly convinced I really *was* insane. It was the only answer that truly made sense.

No more. My experiences were real. Mud doesn't lie.

So what the hell am I supposed to do now?

Pine straw crunched. I flew from my seat as something large pushed through the hedges behind me. "Easy there, Rousey." Laughter played on Tack's lips as he brushed leaves from his long-sleeved Black Keys T-shirt. "Since when did you learn how to box?"

I glanced down. Discovered my hands were curled into fists. I released them, wiping my eyes, face reddening in embarrassment.

Tack misunderstood. "Hey, hey!" He swooped over and gave me a hug. "It's cool! We're okay. The Anvil was just a huge boogeyman after all, like you said."

I nodded, shivering. Automatic gunfire sounded in the distance, followed by several loud booms. The front door to my trailer flew open and Mom's head poked out. Tack released me and dropped into a lawn chair.

Mom pursed her lips. "Those idiots in the liberty camp are gonna shoot each other full of holes tonight. Can't say I'll miss them." She nodded to my friend. "Evening, Tack. Looks like I'll be seeing more of you around."

"Yes, ma'am. My asteroid deflector sure did the trick."

Mom chuckled. "I'll let the neighbors know who to thank. You two stay close."

"Actually," Tack said, popping to his feet, "we were thinking of heading up to Tip-Top Grove. It's like a dozen Fourth of Julys down by the lake, and I want to see the show. From a safe distance," he added hastily.

Tack shot me a wink. *Whatever.* I had to admit, watching the shenanigans taking place around the valley would be more interesting than sitting here beside a cold fire pit. *I could use a distraction.*

Mom gave me a stern look. "You two stay this side of Quarry Road. Folks in town will be blowing off steam for God-knows-how-long. There'll be trouble, I'm sure of it. Tomorrow's gonna be an asylum at work."

"Don't worry." I started after Tack, who was already skipping down the row like a six-year-old. Mom flashed the rueful smile she reserved just for him before disappearing back inside.

"Yo, Doofus! Slow your roll. Why do you want to visit Tip-Top?"

Tack waited on the common that divided our trailer park. "I was telling the truth, actually. Crazy stuff might be jumping off in the village, and I want a good view of the mayhem. Who knows? Maybe someone will accidentally blast Ethan before he can kill us."

With a sharp shock, I remembered the crime we'd committed that afternoon.

Jesus. What had I been thinking?

Exiting the gate, we took a rough trail to the base of Miner's Peak, a towering stone monolith that conveniently blocked our neighborhood from view. If it hadn't existed naturally, Fire Lake's citizens would probably have had it built. Tip-Top Grove was a glade of evergreens crowning its rocky point, a ten-minute, mostly vertical hike from the trailer park. From there you could see downtown, the lake, pretty much everywhere in the valley. I was puffing hard by the time we reached the summit.

The Grove is a popular hookup destination, but we found it blessedly empty. I was about to sit down when Tack slapped the trunk of the one giant oak. "Let's go old-school." He stared up into its tangle of thick limbs. "How high do you think we can climb?"

"Seriously?" Then I thought, *Why not? I'm not too cool to climb a tree.* I reached out and rubbed the gnarly bark. Childhood memories flooded back. "As high as it goes, of course."

Tack grinned and hoisted himself into the lower branches. He lowered a hand to pull me up, but I slapped it aside disdainfully. "Keep moving."

"Ho ho!" Tack chortled. "Sorry, Katniss! Forgot you were a hard-core survivalist."

"Damn right." Drawing level with Tack, I selected an alternate route and shot past him. "I bet we can still reach the Ski Lift."

Twenty feet up, a group of intersecting branches formed a comfortable basket. I hadn't thought of it in years. We settled in. The valley spread out below us like a picture book.

A smile split my face. I had to hand it to Tack—this was a good idea.

Moments later, fireworks exploded in rapid succession, blooming like molten flowers before sizzling into the lake. A round of pops carried across the water. "The libertarians are expressing their right to bear arms," Tack noted drily, pointing to a cluster of lights just visible on the far side, "even though it's a crime to fire live rounds so close."

"That whole camp is illegal." The unsettling bangs and snaps continued for a few minutes before petering out. "Mom says Sheriff Watson doesn't have the guts to clear out the squatters."

"The Plank is quiet, at least." Tack was peering in the opposite direction, at the narrow suspension bridge spanning Gullet Chasm. Fog filled the ravine below it, obscuring the bottom and giving the crossing a ghostly feel.

"Hard to believe that's the only way in or out," I said, eyeing the delicate lattice of metal cables. "What happens if the bridge fails?"

"It did, once." Tack propped his feet on a knotty branch, visibly pleased to know something I didn't. "In the sixties. My granddad said it was a huge mess. About half as many people lived up here, but they were trapped in the valley for something like two months. The National Guard had to airlift supplies."

My eyebrows rose. "How'd they finally rebuild it?"

"With metal and concrete. Duh."

I laughed, settling back against the trunk. I was glad to be there with him. This little trip had rescued me from a miserable night of anger and paranoia. I could always count on Tack to make me feel better.

So why not tell him everything?

The impulse was so powerful, I inadvertently relaxed my grip, wobbling a moment before steadying myself.

Why *not* tell Tack? I needed to trust someone, didn't I?

But will he believe?

Inexplicably, Noah Livingston's face popped into my head. I pictured him sitting in the tree next to me, gazing out over the valley. Which was nuts, since we'd never done anything like this together. So why did I think of him now?

I realized Tack was watching me. "Something wrong?" he asked.

Tell him. Do it. You'll feel so much better.

High beams scythed through the branches like a scalpel, nearly blinding me. I glanced down, blinking, as a line of xenon headlights appeared at the far end of the bridge.

"What the hell?" Tack rose up, craning for a better look. "You seeing this? There must be forty trucks crossing to our side!"

Tack was right. A tightly packed convoy was traversing the Plank and continuing toward downtown. Vans. Jeeps. SUVs and Humvees. All were an unobtrusive gray, manned by soldiers in uniforms.

"Who in the world . . ." Tack was leaning farther out than I liked, legs wrapped around a quivering limb as he snapped pics on his phone. I doubted he could get a decent shot from this distance. "See those big rigs?" He pointed to a pair of eighteen-wheel trucks rolling along in the center of the formation. "What's that painted on their sides?"

Squinting, I could barely make it out in the darkness. "Looks like . . . black triangles. Maybe a starburst? I can't see from here."

Tack sat back and zoomed the images. "These jokers *have* to be military, but I've never seen that unit marking before. Which is kinda nuts, because I'm good with this stuff."

I trusted him. Tack's father had been Special Forces before being discharged for an incident in Afghanistan. We never talked about it, but, judging from the look on Mom's face whenever the subject came up, it hadn't been an honorable end to his service.

The motorcade snaked through town—never pausing, despite quite a few gawkers and drunken catcalls—exiting the opposite end and swinging onto Old Fort Run, a little-used dirt road that dead-ended on the eastern side of the valley.

"Oh, wow!" Tack glanced at me. "Only one thing over there."

"Yep." I watched the formation slip from the village lights. "Supposedly nothing."

Like everyone else in Fire Lake, I'd heard rumors about the government land. An old internment camp. A defunct nuclear testing facility. Training grounds for Seal Team Six. Plenty of speculation. But the property had been abandoned since before I was born, with only a chain-link fence and a few warning signs. Keep Out.

We watched the convoy disappear into those woods. When it

failed to emerge over the next few minutes, the answer was clear.

Tack slapped his leg. "Something's up. That's *never* happened before."

"Maybe it has. It's late. What if they always move around at night?"

Tack shook his head firmly. "I'd have heard. My dad wouldn't have missed something like this, I'm sure of it."

I held my tongue. Though an ace mechanic, Wendell Russo wasn't considered "reliable" by most in town, unless you were Mr. Kappel at the liquor store. But despite the rough treatment he received at his father's hands, Tack revered his old man.

"Let's head home." Tack was suddenly energized. "My phone isn't getting a signal, and I want to Google that symbol. What do you think is back there, anyway? Looked like a lot of soldiers in those trucks. Where are they all going to sleep?"

Tack dropped to a lower branch, then stopped short, peering back up at me. "Wait, did you want to say something earlier?"

I took a breath. Shifted so he couldn't see my face. "No. I'm good."

An hour later, I was alone in my bedroom. Mom was already asleep.

When Tack had finally been able to connect, image searches had turned up nothing. Which he couldn't believe. I could sense an obsession forming in his mind, but this time I was just as curious.

Something didn't smell right.

The timing.

An unidentifiable military unit arriving in our sleepy valley on the same night the Anvil news went public? I don't like coincidences, and that felt like a big one.

But to what end? The Anvil will miss, so why does it matter?

I slipped into an old tee and boy shorts. Drank a glass of water. Brushed my teeth and washed my face. Then I saw it. There, on my nightstand.

The little blue pills.

I'd taken one every day for the last six years.

I stared at the bottle. Then I walked to the bathroom and turned it upside down over the toilet. Flushed. I trashed the container and hopped into bed.

Dr. Lowell.

He'd fed me a story of delusions and disorders.

But I saw a footprint.

Weighing courses of action, I settled on a plan.

Dr. Lowell must keep records. About me. About my treatment.

I was going to find them.

9

My back presses against a row of lime-green lockers.

Two men in uniforms stride by, their tightly laced boots drumming the yellow-and-white checkerboard floor.

Mrs. Thompson squeezes my shoulder. Says soothing words, but I barely hear. What are they doing in our school? Why are all the teachers wearing those big, fake smiles that mean something's wrong?

Principal Myers hobbles by, frowning at nothing. He's not pretending like the others. I know that's bad. Adults always pretend if they can.

Mrs. Thompson gathers the kindergarten class together. I stand next to Thomas and we lock our fingers. Noah edges close on my other side. He's breathing hard, eyes round as dinner plates. I take his hand, too. I don't want him to be scared either.

He seems surprised. We haven't spoken since our class party yesterday, when he couldn't blow out his half of the candles and I had to finish them. But he doesn't let go.

"Remember what we talked about, children," Mrs. Thompson

says. "Some unhealthy chemicals were spilled nearby, on the other side of the valley. Things that would make us sick. And we don't want that, do we?"

We shake our heads like tiny robots.

"That's right. So some nice people are here from . . . from . . ." Her eyes tighten before she continues, "—from the government, and they're going to give us very special medicine to make sure that doesn't happen."

A hand goes up. Toby. "My daddy said someone spilled pesticides over by Rock Creek," he whispers, wide-eyed, "and we're all gonna get cancer, and that it's the president's fault."

Mrs. Thompson makes her patient face. "No one's getting cancer, Toby, and the president has nothing to do with this." She shifts to address the entire group. "Something called a pathogen was accidentally released into the environment. Now, does everyone remember talking about germs last week? Why we wash our hands before we eat?"

Solemn nods.

"Well, a pathogen is a really bad germ. This particular one is experimental, which means it's still being tested to make sure it's safe."

"Safe for what?" Thomas asks, never one to raise his hand.

"To use on the crops we eat, to keep bugs away." She runs a fluttery hand through her hair. "But it could be harmful to people, so we have to take extra-special care to make sure no one gets sick."

Toby nods. "Cancer. Like my grandpap."

Noah squeezes my hand tighter. His palm is sweaty, but I don't let go.

Mrs. Thompson releases a sigh. "Not cancer, Toby. I really wish you'd stop saying that."

Two women in white lab coats hurry past us. Both have surgical masks covering their faces. Mrs. Thompson watches them all the way down the hallway.

"Why don't we get masks?" Thomas asks.

"We obviously don't need them," Mrs. Thompson replies cheerily, but sharper than before. Then a voice rings out, making everyone jump.

"Kindergarten!"

A man with a notebook is striding down the corridor. White coat. Mask. White paper cap on his head. "Follow me," he orders. Not nice.

Mrs. Thompson glares at him, but he doesn't react. She turns back to face us. "Everyone have a buddy? Okay, good. Stay in line and follow me, please." She sets off down the hall without another glance at the man with the notebook.

Thomas gets caught in the shuffle and ends up stuck next to Jessica. Noah and I are still holding hands. "Be my buddy?" he asks in a shaky voice.

"Okay." I don't usually play with Noah, but I can tell he's afraid. I won't ditch him now. Thomas sulks at the back of the line. I mouth him a quick "Sorry."

We troop down the hallway, heading for the double doors to the gymnasium. The man with the notebook asks us to stop and wait. As he slips inside, my eyes drift down the corridor. A door has been wedged open. I can see inside, all the way to the principal's office.

People are gathered. Principal Myers, of course. And the big mustache-wearing man is Sheriff Watson—I recognize him from the sign on my neighbor's lawn. Two other men in suits are standing beside the desk. They're all looking at something rolled open on its surface, faces super-serious.

Principal Myers straightens, points directly at one of the unknown men.

"You don't know, do you? About any of this! You don't know a damn thing!"

I jump in surprise. The movement catches his eye. Seeing me watching, Myers growls like a grizzly bear. "For God's sake!"

My eyes dart away, but it's too late. Myers barks something else, and the door slams shut.

My stomach does a flip. I could get in trouble.

Noah is staring at me, his face pale. Did he see, too?

Before I can ask, a gym door swings open. "Enter, please," Notebook Man instructs. It seems like the rest of the school is already in there. Older kids exit on the left, grumbling and rubbing their shoulders.

"Oh no, it's a shot!" Toby moans. A spike of fear travels the group.

Noah squeezes my hand. I squeeze back.

Mrs. Thompson doesn't respond, which all but assures it's true. We reluctantly follow her to a folding table, where a stern-faced woman with thick glasses sits. Eight white tents have been erected on the basketball court. First graders trickle out slowly from them, massaging their upper arms.

"Needles," Mike and Chris hiss in unison, our worst nightmare confirmed.

Notebook Man stands at the front of the line. "Arrange yourselves in alphabetical order. When your name is called, come forward and answer Dr. Parker's questions."

This takes a few minutes, Mrs. Thompson grumbling the whole time. Knowing we won't be close in line, I let go of Noah's hand. He holds on a little longer, then releases me, wiping his slick fingers on his shirt. "Sorry."

"S'okay." I dry off my hand behind my back, so he doesn't see.

"Albertsson, Tobias."

Toby slinks forward, legs shaking. I can't hear what the woman asks him. I'm a W, practically last in line. One by one, the others are called to the front, answer questions, and then disappear into one of the white tents. Finally, my name is called.

"Wilder, Melinda."

I approach the table.

"Age?" the woman asks in a dull monotone.

"Six," I answer, eyes darting to Mrs. Thompson. My teacher has a weird expression on her face, but she smiles encouragingly.

"Date of birth?"

"September seventeenth."

The questions go on for several minutes. I do my best, but I don't know all the answers. The woman frowns each time I come up short. I catch one muttered comment from Mrs. Thompson—how would a six-year-old know her medical history?—before it finally ends. The doctor stamps some papers, closes a file, and then points to the last tent on the right. "Please report to Bay F."

I trudge across the gym and slip through the white curtain. Inside is a chair like at the dentist's office, and a small cabinet with medical stuff. I see a box of needles and an orange bin covered in loud printed warnings.

My heart drops into my shoes.

A white-coated man enters through the back. He's thin and gray-haired, with twinkling blue eyes floating above a white mask. Dropping his clipboard onto the cabinet, he pulls the mask down and smiles. "Hello, there!"

"Hello." Hugging my arms to my chest.

“Come, come!” The man squats down on his heels so we’re eye to eye. “There’s nothing to be afraid of”—popping up to glance at the clipboard—“Ms. Melinda. I’m Doctor Harris.”

“Min,” I mumble.

His smile grows. “What’s that?”

“Min.” A little louder. This one seems nicer than the others. “My name is Min. I hate being called Melinda.”

“Well then, we won’t make that mistake again.” With exaggerated strokes, he crosses something off on the clipboard and writes. “Name: Min, and definitely not *Melinda. There we are! All better now.”*

His grin is contagious. I smile back.

“Now, Min,” he begins, “would you mind climbing up into my whirly chair for a tick? I promise we’ll go through this step by step, okay?”

I tense, but do what he asks, clambering up onto the seat.

Dr. Harris plops down onto a tiny, wheeled stool. “I’m sure you’re a little worried about what we’re doing today.”

I nod slowly. He nods back.

“Well, don’t fret.” He taps the clipboard. “This examination is purely precautionary. We just need to make sure you stay safe and well. Are you okay with that?”

“Yes.”

“I thank you, Min. Now let’s get these silly tests out of the way.”

Over the next twenty minutes, I am weighed, measured, poked, prodded, and generally inspected. Dr. Harris is very polite, explaining all the procedures beforehand and always asking for permission. He jots down notes after each one.

Finally, Dr. Harris hunches back on his stool. “Only two more things, then we're done. Unfortunately, you're not going to love either one."

"What things?"

"I need to take a teeny-tiny blood sample, and then . . . I must give you . . ." His voice drops to a whisper, his eyes popping to a clownish degree, "—a SHOT."

The doctor's face is so funny, I giggle. I can't help it.

"That's the spirit!" Dr. Harris offers a high five, and I meet it. I'm not as scared as I was. He swivels, slides open the cabinet, and removes a tiny kit. "Let's just get it over with. What do you say?"

I swallow. Nod.

He beams at me. "Good girl. I thank you."

The first needle isn't so bad. Dr. Harris tells me to look away—so that I don't have to see my own blood—but I watch it fill up the tube instead. He tells me how brave I am.

The second needle stings. It's larger and longer, and I feel it bite into my shoulder. I whimper slightly, but Dr. Harris pats my back, speaking soft encouragements as he presses the plunger. In moments it's over. The doctor quickly applies a bandage, leaving nothing behind but a slight itch.

"Excellent, Min!" Dr. Harris puts my blood into his kit, then scribbles a few more notes onto his clipboard. "Only one moment more, and then you can go back to class." He carries the kit out the back of the tent.

I notice his clipboard is still sitting on the cabinet.

Hopping down, I walk over for a look. The doctor's handwriting is small and squiggly, but two words are stamped in red at the bottom of the page. Project Nemesis.

• • •

An hour later I'm back in Mrs. Thompson's room, playing with the magnetic letters. Everyone is rubbing their shoulders. Jessica and a few others have been sniffling since we returned, but most are excited. They think we've had an adventure, like the adults keep saying.

The soldiers are gone, which clearly makes Mrs. Thompson happy. I wonder if the men in suits left with them. Is Principal Myers still mad? Did he have to get a shot, too?

A knock on the door.

I look over, then freeze.

Principal Myers has entered the room, but that's not what surprised me. Standing beside him is Dr. Harris. Spotting me, he smiles and waves. Caught out, I wave back.

"This is not what was discussed," Mrs. Thompson is saying, looking upset. "The permission slips only cover school-based physicals and inoculations. I can't let you take students away from here simply because this man—"

Principal Myers cuts her off. "I'm aware of your objections, Agnes. But I don't need to remind you who runs this school. I'll be along to supervise."

Mrs. Thompson's shoulders droop. "Their parents, surely—"

"Will be informed, of course. Now please call the students forward."

Mrs. Thompson stares at Myers as if seeing something for the first time, then looks over at me. Our eyes meet, and she flinches. Then puts on her big fake smile. "Min? And Noah? Could you both come to the front, please?"

I stand up slowly. Walk to her desk. I hear Noah following on my heels. If Dr. Harris wasn't smiling so encouragingly, I'm not sure I'd do it.

Dr. Harris drops to a knee before the two of us. Noah's legs tremble as we stand side by side. "Min, hello again. Noah, my name is Dr. Harris. I have something very special to tell you. We're going on a trip!"

His eyes twinkle in the fluorescent light. "Won't that be fun?"

10

I woke up sweaty and breathless.

My shoulder was cramping, right beneath the old inoculation scar. I rubbed it fitfully, trying to clear my head.

The doctor's face was burned into my retinas.

I reached out blindly, hand-locating the clock and spinning it to face me.

Six a.m. I knew more rest wasn't coming.

I sat up, blinking in the darkness. The kindergarten memory was like a scab picked open. *Dr. Harris. I'd forgotten his name was Harris.*

I hadn't thought of that day in years. I remembered being ushered into a van with Noah. The doors had shut and we'd been driven somewhere miles away. But not over the bridge—even at six I'd known to listen for the *thump-thump, thump-thump* of wheels crossing partitions.

We'd gone the other direction—into the eastern woods.

I stiffened.

Where the convoy went last night. Is that what made me think of it?

I could recall little else of that afternoon. Dr. Harris led us inside an unfamiliar building. Noah and I were separated. The lights were bright. Soldiers and people in lab coats filled the halls, some eyeing me curiously. Harris took me to a room equipped like the tent from school. The door closed, and then . . . then . . .

Nothing.

I remembered nothing else. I'd woken up at home.

Mom had listened to my story, holding my hand and stroking my hair. She'd given me a cherry Popsicle, then stormed to the telephone. Mom had begun yelling almost immediately, and I'd heard her say the name Andy, which is what some adults called Principal Myers. Then she'd hung up and sat still a moment, holding her head in her hands. Seconds later she'd put one of my DVDs into the player, told me to stay put, and then hurried from our trailer.

I pushed my sheets away and stood, a statue in the darkness. Details were flooding back faster than I could process them. Why hadn't I thought harder about this before? Where had I been taken? Why? By whom?

My mother hadn't come back for two hours, and never explained. She'd even given me a second Popsicle, which *never* happened. Mom had hugged me close, telling me not to worry about that afternoon. I wasn't supposed to talk about it. The other kids wouldn't understand and might tease me. I was to keep the whole thing secret.

I was a kid. Six years old, with a second cherry Popsicle. So that's what I did.

But I'm not six anymore. I'm sixteen, under attack by a serial killer, and nothing my mother did that day makes sense.

We never learned more about the spill, yet we'd had blood tests at school every year since. Supposedly they were still checking for pathogens. The samples were always taken by the same company, but the results were never shared. As far as I knew, nobody else had been driven onto the government land like Noah and me. Others could've been told to keep it secret, too, but Fire Lake is a small town. I'm sure I would've heard something.

Noah. I'd never once talked about it with Noah. How was that possible?

Because we don't talk at all.

What did they tell my mother? Why had she never mentioned it?

A dark suspicion took hold.

My mother knew things she didn't share. I'd sensed that for years. Same with Lowell, and maybe Principal Myers too. How far back did it go? Was there really ever a chemical spill?

I stood frozen in the darkness, mind running wild.

A lunatic hunts and kills me every two years, yet I come back to life.

The adults surrounding me are hiding things.

Those facts have to be connected. Or am I really crazy after all?

I waited for Tack by the gatepost, breath misting in the brisk morning air.

He was on time, though yawning every second. A Hollywood-quality black eye offset the purple splotches blossoming along his chin. I almost asked what his father had said, but knew the answer. No way had Wendell been awake this morning.

A yawn escaped my own lips. I hadn't been able to fall back

asleep. So I'd dressed quickly in an old sweater and jeans, then snuck into the living room to watch CNN and witness the world's hangover.

Twitter was alive with crazy hashtags—things like #TakeYourSecondChance and #followingdreams—the usual sparkly crap people spouted after a major scare. Stuff that would be forgotten by this time next week.

"So we're going to live!" Tack quipped, never breaking stride. He wore cargo shorts and a red *Machete Kills* tee over a long-sleeved thermal. Somehow he never got cold. I fell in beside him and we headed up the rise. "Just long enough for Ethan to strangle us."

"Not my brightest idea."

"Relax." Though Tack didn't appear to be following his own advice. "There's no way he can prove it was us. And who'd believe we'd really do that? *I* don't even believe it."

We hit pavement and began descending. The lake sparkled in the heart of the valley, unconcerned by mankind's problems.

"The news said half of Reno nearly burned down," I grumbled. "People lost their minds."

"No doubt." Tack pointed to where smoke was rising from the old paper mill. Flashing lights announced the fire truck's presence. "Some idiots did *crazy* stuff last night, just happy to be alive." He tossed me a significant glance. "Like, say, torching a shiny new Jeep in the high school parking lot."

I pursed my lips. "Interesting."

The timeline didn't work—the Wrangler's smoldering remains had been found well before the Announcement—but countless other acts of vandalism had likely occurred. The entire

Fire Lake police force consisted of eight dopey officers—no way they'd investigate everything. If we were lucky, my mad impulse would get swept under the rug with all the rest.

When have I ever been lucky?

Reaching the village proper, we found evidence to support our hopes. Windows were smashed up and down the block. Someone had looted the display items from Buford's Hardware. A police deputy was squawking into his radio as he stood over a fat, shirtless dude snoring in the gutter. It had been a big night.

We reached the school parking lot. I tried not to eyeball the crime scene, but my head swiveled on its own volition. Joey Alcorn, who operated the junkyard, was just then securing the scorched ruin of Ethan's Jeep to the back of his flatbed wrecker. He waved a filthy hand; we guiltily returned the gesture. The Wrangler was a total loss, an acrid-smelling skeleton of blackened metal and melted fiberglass.

"Ho, boy," Tack breathed.

"Yep."

Joey popped into his truck and pulled away, leaving nothing behind but a charred smear on the pavement. A spasm ran through me. *If anyone ever finds out . . .*

"Listen to that!" Tack pulled me toward the walkway. Music was thumping from the courtyard. "Who's having a dance party without me?"

Everyone in school was outside, hugging and high-fiving, hands in the air as they bounced to the beat. Juniors and seniors swarmed the low-walled stone patio—unofficially off-limits to underclassmen—while sophomores surrounded the flagpole where the youth group usually held morning convocation. "Turn

Down for What" was blasting from a speaker propped on a Nolan twin's backpack. Principal Myers was going to have a heart attack.

"That's my kind of prayer circle," Tack said. "Hopefully this is a permanent change."

We'd never actually joined the showy student devotional that took place before first bell. Most of the group spent the entire silent minute with their eyes cracked, keeping track of how many classmates were witnessing their piety. Few got anything spiritual from it, I suspected, although Hector Quino did his best to keep the mood solemn.

But today everyone seemed jacked up on Red Bull. Bro-hugs were rampant. Relieved smiles were paired with machine-gun bursts of laughter. Boys were chasing girls, who screamed prissily before allowing themselves to be caught. No one seemed to care about class.

Derrick Morris, skyscraper tall and one of the four black kids in our grade—we all knew the count; welcome to northern Idaho—had his shirt off despite the chill. He reared back and howled, "I'm alive!" while extending both middle fingers skyward. Toby snuck over and lifted him up from behind. They both started laughing and jumping up and down, chanting something I couldn't make out but had to be stupid. As they broke apart, I saw Toby swig something hidden inside his jacket.

"We should get inside." I was already crossing to the main building. "Last thing we need is—"

"Hey! HEY!"

Too late. Ethan came storming over, half our class at his back. I saw gleeful eyes and hurried whispers. Bile rose in my throat.

Tack inched closer to my side. "Just relax. I'll say we—"

"*Don't say a single word, Tack!*" I stepped in front of him, mind racing.

Ethan charged to within a foot of where I stood, his gaze lasering over my shoulder at Tack, who glared back defiantly despite his trembling arms. Ethan's face was flushed. There was a glassy aspect to his eyes I didn't like. I suspected he'd been trading sips with Toby.

"You torched my Wrangler, didn't you?" Ethan's voice was soft, almost monotone. He pointed a finger at Tack. "I know it was you."

"That was your *Jeep*?" Tack replied, all choirboy innocence. "I thought Spencer's dad had dropped by for a cookout."

Scattered snickers. Spence Coleman's father ran Pig House BBQ, and threw massive tailgates for every Boise State football game. His half-ton outdoor grill was legendary—wheeled, monstrous, and smoke-stained jet-black by hundreds of hours of use.

Ethan smiled unnaturally. "A joke! Like your life, only less sad."

More chuckles. The crowd was enjoying Round Two. I spotted Chris Nolan whispering with Sarah and Jessica while his brother, Mike, watched silently. Noah was slouching behind them, oblivious. He squinted over at us for a beat, then looked down at his phone.

A flash of disgust. Why had I been thinking of Noah lately? He was useless.

"Nice face!" Toby called, rubbing his cheek where Tack's was a bruised mess.

"Still prettier than you," Tack shot back. Toby laughed.

"I had that Jeep for two weeks," Ethan said matter-of-factly, but a pink stain was creeping up his neck. "*Two*. My golf clubs were in it." He shifted to include me. "You guys destroyed it. I know you did. Nobody else would dare."

Play dumb. It's the only way.

"Someone lit your Wrangler on fire?" I asked in a startled tone.

"You know someone did."

I crossed my arms. "Why would we burn your car, Ethan? And how?"

"I don't know how. Or care. But it's not hard to figure out *why*. I kicked Thumbtack's ass and he couldn't handle it."

I spoke calmly, but made my voice carry. "You're being ridiculous. Tack and I didn't blow up your Jeep in the school parking lot, in broad daylight. Because that's *insane*. We're not Navy Seals." *Gulp*. Then inspiration struck. "There were electrical storms up and down the canyon yesterday. Maybe your Jeep caught a stray bolt. Probably because of that ridiculous gun rack you screwed to it like a lightning rod."

The last bit seemed to do the trick. I saw nods in the crowd. Whispers of agreement. Doubt even crept into Ethan's eyes.

"Told you they didn't have the balls," Chris muttered to his brother, who shrugged.

"Somebody would've seen," Toby agreed with a hiccup. "Plus, Tack's too much of a wuss."

I stepped on Tack's foot to keep him from mouthing back. Ethan was still watching.

I met his eyes. Hoped he couldn't see the lie in mine.

Ethan grinned without a hint of warmth. "If I find out you had anything to do with it . . ." Then, unwilling to simply let us go, he changed gears. "Why aren't you guys happier, huh? I saw you lurking over here by yourselves, all emo and sad. Did you want the Anvil to kill everyone?"

"I was hoping *you'd* die," Tack deadpanned. "Does that count?"

Ethan tensed, but then his gaze slid left. Principal Myers was hobbling into the courtyard.

"To be continued," Ethan promised. He snatched up his bag from the grass near the flagpole and hurried toward C building. The crowd evaporated.

Myers looked like he hadn't slept a wink. If he was overjoyed mankind wasn't going to perish in a rain of hellfire, you couldn't see it. "Get to class," he ordered, leaning more heavily on his cane than usual. But the bell rang as he spoke, making us tardy. Myers turned and began limping toward the door. "Come along, then, and get a note."

Mrs. Ferguson was sorting permission slips at the counter in the office, her graying black hair organized in a tight bun. Myers waved us into hard plastic chairs. "Delia, please write these two passes into class. No punishment this time."

"Yes, sir, Mr. Myers. You need coffee this morning?"

He forced a smile as he eased past her. "Bring the whole pot. But give me ten minutes."

"I'll make a fresh one." She turned to regard us as Myers disappeared down the corridor to his office. "Tack and Min. Min and Tack. Always the pair, like a couple a' bad pennies. What you done this time?"

"We cured cancer," Tack said. "We're supposed to get an award. It's named after you."

She chuckled low and deep. "Oh, I'm sure." Then her voice hardened. "You wouldn't know anything about the act of terrorism that took place in our parking lot yesterday, would you, Mr. Russo?"

Tack's eyebrows rose. "I was at the opera, milady."

I covered my eyes, but Mrs. Ferguson snorted. "Enough cheek to mold a newborn baby. You'll have to wait while I get this brew going. That man is running himself ragged these days." With a loud *tsk*, she walked into the break room.

"Think she bought it?" Tack whispered.w

Rolling my eyes, I rose, began pacing the waiting area. Being this near the principal's office stirred memories of my dream the night before. Myers, huddled with Sheriff Watson and those strangers in suits, poring over documents in our elementary school. Myers, ordering Mrs. Thompson to release Noah and me into some doctor's custody.

What had he said to my mother that afternoon? Could I trust him now?

Was he a part of what happened to me on my birthdays?

I stopped pacing. Myers's office was in the rear of the administrative suite, around a corner from the front counter. On impulse, I pushed through the swinging door. I could hear Mrs. Ferguson humming as she fumbled with coffee filters in the break room.

Tack watched me curiously, a question on his face.

I snuck around the corner. Peered down toward the principal's office.

My breath caught. Myers's upper body was slumped across his desk. His shoulders shook. I was certain he was crying.

I stepped back, desperate to escape the awkward moment.

My heel clipped the wall.

His head snapped up. Myers pierced me with a watery gaze.

For several heartbeats, we stared at each other. Then his landline rang and he leapt to answer it, as if he'd been waiting for a call. "Myers! Yes, I'm here, damn it! Patch me through." When he glanced back at me, it was like he'd forgotten I was there. With a grunt, he reached out and slammed the door shut.

I scurried back to the lobby. Tack shot me a look, but I waved him off, dropping into a seat as Mrs. Ferguson reappeared. My mind was racing as she wrote our passes.

Myers hadn't stormed out to chastise me. Would he let me walk away without a word, after seeing him like that?

A door opened inside the suite. Cringing, I prepared to have my skin peeled off, but instead I heard another door open and close. I glanced at the office phone on the counter. Line One was blinking, then went solid. Myers had placed his call on hold, then picked it up somewhere else.

The conference room? That was the only logical space back there.

My instincts blared in warning. The world might've been "saved" last night, but that didn't satisfy Principal Myers. What could still be bothering him so much? *Who's on the phone?*

"No side trips, you hear? Those passes are good for five minutes."

We nodded. But out in the hall, I turned left instead of right, following the wall twenty yards down.

"Min? What are you—"

I shushed him, examining a door. The conference room was on the other side.

A hasty scan of the hall, then I pressed an ear to the wood.

Tack began stroking his chin. "I see. You've lost your mind."

"*Shh.*" I could hear Myers talking, but couldn't make out the words. I listened intently for a few seconds, then dropped to my stomach, flattening on the ground and pressing my ear to the gap at the base of the door. Suddenly, his voice became less muddled.

"It's happening soon," Myers said curtly. "A matter of days. We're done here, and there's nothing more to say." A short pause, then Myers clearly interrupted. "I won't. I won't do it. It's sink-or-swim time. That's all there is to it."

The hair on my arms stood. What was he talking about?

A longer pause. When Myers spoke next, his tone was low and dangerous. "Then let me make *myself* clear, General. I won't allow a single Nemesis man on campus. Watson will back me on this. The project is nearly complete. Everything is in motion. I won't rattle the cage right at the end."

A voice boomed from somewhere behind me. "What are you two doing?"

I scrambled to my feet. Mrs. Garcia was striding toward us, arms laden with exam books. "Min Wilder! Why are you lying on the floor?" She glanced at Tack, who waved inanely.

"Sorry!" I hitched my backpack, nearly tumbling in the process. "Dropped my necklace."

"Well?"

I swallowed. "Well what?"

"Did you find it?" As if speaking to a child.

Nodding like a bobblehead, I grabbed Tack's arm and dragged him down the hall. "Oh! Yes, thank you! *Gracias*. Sorry, I mean. For the confusion. *Lo siento. Adios!*"

Reaching class, we slipped inside. "What was *that* about?" Tack insisted, but the lesson had already begun. We held up the passes, but Mr. Hayles just waved us to our table. He looked awful—a red-eyed, unshaven mess—but was gushing about Alfred, Lord Tennyson and the exhilaration of eluding certain death.

I didn't pay attention. Ignored Tack's impatient glances. My mind was still on tilt.

Nemesis.

That word again, after all these years.

The shots. The tests. My secret ride into the woods.

This wasn't about some pesticide spill. It never had been.

Something big was going on. So big the Anvil didn't enter the equation.

Myers said the project was happening now. Here. In Fire Lake.

We were sitting in the crosshairs.

11

I have a plan.

I'm crouched on the southern shore of the lake, lurking behind one of the summer camp's wooden outbuildings. I've been thinking about dying since the moment I woke up.

Happy fourteenth.

All morning I stayed glued to Mom's side. I made her walk me to the bus, then sat next to Tack and covertly held his hand all the way to school. He didn't understand, but didn't break my grip, either. Three periods later, I snuck out the back door.

Starlight's Edge Fellowship Camp. The tired old facility is closed until next month. I've never been on the grounds before, but that's the point. The black-suited man can't possibly know to find me here.

And if he can't find me, he can't kill me. I could still make the party.

I've given up trying to figure out why, but Sarah and Jessica included me in their plans for Noah's birthday celebration. Cake. Bowling. They even rented out the back room so we can dance afterward. Everyone in our class is going, and, incredibly, it's half for me.

The invitation says "Min Wilder" right on the front. It's a miracle.

Hide here until nightfall, then straight to the Seven-Ten. This can work. It will *work.*

Leaves crackle behind me. My whole body tenses as I whirl. A doe steps from the trees, regards me cautiously. She nibbles a patch of clover at the edge of the woods.

My eyes close. I take a breath. Suddenly, I worry I've miscalculated. I could've planted myself at Dale's Diner, or the public library. Lots of people at both. Too public for an execution.

But I'd have had to move eventually. Mom might've tracked me down. Or Tack. Principal Myers could've gone looking for a truant. Our town is too small to hide in plain sight.

This way is better. No one knows where I am.

Engine noises. Tires on gravel. Creeping to the corner, I peek around. A mud-splattered SUV is sending up clouds of dust as it barrels along the lakefront road.

It abruptly slows. Stops. Tinted glass, so I can't see inside. The vehicle idles fifty yards from where I'm hiding.

The driver-side door opens.

The black-suited man steps out.

Turn. Run.

I'm in the trees before my next breath, clawing up the mountainside like an animal. No plan. Nerves flailing like downed power lines. A single question burning in my brain.

How?

How did he find me here, in the middle of nowhere?

There's no path. No houses for miles. I chose this spot because of its isolation, and that may be my downfall.

I bomb through a copse of prickly cedars, then pause a beat, listening.

Pebbles scatter not far below.

I heave myself over a boulder, throwing caution to the wind in a blind panic to escape. This section of mountainside is exposed, the ground broken and uneven. Scree tumbles downhill behind me, giving away my position.

I can't calm down. Can't think. I don't want to die again.

The slope steepens. A voice in my head is screaming that there's no escape this way. Soon I'll reach the top—a granite ridge overlooking the chasm. Nowhere to run from there.

The voice finally breaks through. I stop, gasping, desperate.

Hide. Hope he's unfamiliar with the terrain. Then slip past him, back down to the lake. His car will still be there.

I frantically scan for a good place.

There. Thirty feet up, a stone ledge juts from the mountainside. If I can get onto that shelf, the bastard can't reach me. I could bash his head in from above if he tries.

I begin to ascend, trying to remember everything I know about rock climbing.

Reach. Hold. Extend. Gather. Reach. Use your legs. Breathe.

I cover the first ten feet easily, then the second. But the last pitch is trickier. I'm digging my fingers into a shallow crease when shards of rock explode beside my face.

I shout, nearly lose my grip. My head whips around.

The man is directly beneath me, holding a fist-sized chunk of stone. His suit is ripped and he's breathing hard, though his sunglasses remain in place. As I watch, horrified, he rears back and throws again.

This one strikes me in the back. One toehold slips. The other. I grunt, shoulders straining as I cling to the cliff face, muscles stretched to their breaking point.

His third volley smashes my hand, and I'm falling, scrambling uselessly for purchase as I plummet to the boulders below. I land on my back and feel something snap.

A tidal wave of pain, then . . . nothing. Numbness. Lack.

I try to rise, but have no feeling in either leg.

A shadow falls across my face.

Woozy, I don't even try to crawl away. Instead, I peer up at my killer.

"Why are you doing this to me?"

No answer.

"Who are you?" Slurred. I'm fading, my mind swirling through black-lined vortexes.

Time slows. I hear an eagle call. A breeze stirs my sweat-soaked hair, granting me a last moment of comfort. "I hate you," I whisper.

The man steps out of my field of vision. Returns with a larger stone.

"I'm sorry."

Sunlight glints off his sunglasses.

His arms come down, and everything goes black.

Darkness. The clearing. Another tear-streaked walk home.

Something buzzes in my pocket and I yelp. Then feel stupid, remembering my new phone.

It hits me.

"No, no, no." But Jessica's text says it all.

"We include u & u don't even show? Lose my #. Sarah says the same."

My head drops. I don't write back. What's the point? The girls let me in for once, and I stood them up. They'll never talk to me again. What will Noah think?

My mother is waiting outside in a lawn chair. Knitting. Looking a thousand years old.

I catch her sigh of relief at my approach.

I stop and stare at my shoes, too exhausted to even lie.

Mom watches me for a long moment. Then she rises without speaking and shuffles to the front door. Opening it, she gestures me inside.

I slip past her, straight to my room, and lock the door.

She doesn't ask where I've been.

I don't tell her.

12

The sensation of falling.

Then a sharp smack as my face struck the desktop.

My head rocketed back up. Snickers erupted all around me, but thankfully Mr. Anderson hadn't noticed. Cheeks flushing scarlet, I lowered my head and made myself busy.

My fourth murder, two years ago. As unpleasant a memory as I possessed. I squirmed in my seat, trying to shake the horror of the heavy rock that ended things.

The fallout at school had been devastating. Never popular, I'd been completely frozen out after missing the bowling party. The girls even spread nasty rumors about my "runaways" as a kid.

I was a freak. A head case. A drama queen.

I didn't put up a fight.

The bell rang. Students began gathering their things.

I didn't move. Not even when Tack tugged on my arm.

"Min?" He dropped into a crouch, bringing his bruised face level with mine. "You okay?"

I rounded on him. "You up for a mission tonight? Something dangerous and stupid that will probably get us both in trouble?"

He flared an eyebrow, dropping his voice to a dramatic whisper. "Are we kidnapping someone? Is it Mr. Anderson? Do I need to burn off my fingerprints?"

I pushed his head aside, rising. "This is serious, Tack. I need to check on something, and I can only do it by breaking and entering. Tonight. Late."

Tack's other brow lifted. He crossed his arms, eyeing me with a new level of curiosity. "Okay, my bad. What's the target? What are we looking for?"

Now that we'd come to it, I hesitated.

Tack must've sensed my reluctance. "Uh-uh." He tapped the desktop with his finger. "Too late for second thoughts, Melinda. Whatever you're planning, I'm in. I'll sleep outside your trailer tonight if I have to. Done it before."

I couldn't help but smile. "Fine. Dork." I headed for the door, forcing him to scamper after me. "First, let's just get through the rest of the day."

"Wait!" he whined with impatience. "What's the mission? Where are we invading?"

I stepped into the hall. Principal Myers was laboring down the corridor, his cane tapping a steady beat on the linoleum. He glanced at me, then looked away. Struck immobile, I followed his progress as he grunted toward whatever task he'd set for himself.

Not yet, Mr. Lifetime Principal. But you're on my list.

Tack chucked my shoulder with his like we did as kids. "Hello? Come on, don't leave me in suspense! Whose privacy are we violating?"

Deep breath.

"Dr. Lowell's."

Needles gouged my back, but I ignored them. Couldn't make a sound.

Tack and I were hiding in a clump of bushes overlooking Lowell's office. If discovered, there was no way to play this off. It was late. We were quite clearly spying.

"What's he *doing* in there?" Tack grumbled, his scrawny legs pressed against mine. He shifted, raking more prickers across my spine. I punched his shoulder in retribution, then shook my head. I was as perplexed as he was.

My watch read 2:00 a.m., yet a light still burned. I couldn't think of a single reason for him to be working so late—I knew he didn't have more than a dozen or so patients. Frankly, I sometimes wondered how he stayed in business.

Tack squirmed again. He hated tight spaces, but this was the only vantage point from which we could stake out the exit. "Man, if that jackass left his lights on and went home early, I'm gonna—"

"*Shh.*" My fingers dug into his forearm. The glow in Lowell's window had vanished.

We waited, literally on pins and needles, as the door swung open and Lowell emerged carrying his briefcase. He locked up behind him, then strode to his BMW and climbed inside. Headlights blazed and he was gone, cruising toward his home in Lakeshore Estates.

"Did he activate an alarm?" Tack whispered.

"Nope. Come on."

I swallowed, thankful Tack couldn't sense my nerves in the dark. Moving as silently as possible, we crept across the parking lot. I was about to try the door when Tack shook his head. "Trust me," he whispered.

I followed him along the wall until we reached the windows. Barely breathing, I scanned the block for any movement. Saw none. I doubted another soul was up and about on High Street at this time of night.

Tack reached into his pocket and pulled out his student ID. Working carefully, he wedged the card into the gap where the upper and lower windows met, next to the latch, then jerked it sideways. There was a soft click. Tack grinned, flattened his palms against the glass, and pushed upward. The lower pane rose.

We scrambled through and hastily shut the window behind us. I pulled the curtains for good measure. Then I located Lowell's desk and turned on the floor lamp beside it. Enough light to see by, but the drapes would mask our presence.

Looking pleased with himself, Tack dropped onto the fainting couch. "Old windows. Nothing to the lock—that kind slides right open unless you add a latch stopper. I helped my dad install a few when he was still working at Buford's."

Yet another job his father held briefly before getting fired. I remembered that summer well. Tack had done more than just "help"—he'd done most of his father's work for a solid week, trying to keep his old man's latest bender under wraps. I'd never been angrier at Wendell Russo, except for Tack's bruises. But I was grateful for my friend's experience at the moment. I couldn't believe how easily we'd gotten inside.

Tack sat up, perhaps having cycled through the same unpleasant memories. "So. You ready to explain why we're here?"

I stood in the center of the room, chewing my lip. Having completed the break-in, I wasn't sure exactly how to proceed. "I'm looking for information," I said slowly. "Anything that involves my treatment. I need to know what Lowell's been writing about me."

Tack ruffled his hair, a nervous habit. "What are you worried about?"

I hedged. "In my last session, Lowell was super-weird. He kept asking questions that didn't make sense." I looked away, pretending to survey an office I knew intimately. "I want to know what he was after."

Tack seemed mollified. Even amused. "Well, you've certainly upped your risk tolerance. Breaking in just to look at his notes? That's *nuts*, girlfriend. I can't believe we're doing it."

"Then help me search, so we can leave." I rapped my knuckles on Lowell's mahogany desk. Tack nodded, rising and joining me. We tried all four drawers, but they wouldn't budge. "Do your talents extend to locks as well?" I asked hopefully. Tack had ordered a set of picks a few years back, informing me of his intention to become a gentleman spy. I'd never heard another word about it.

He shook his head with a wince. "Never got that far. My dad intercepted the tools in the mail and tossed them. Tanned my hide, too." He plastered on a smile. "I'm pretty skilled at smashing things with a hammer, though. We could bust these suckers open. Make it look like a robbery?"

Tempting, but I had another thought. I swiveled, located a

porcelain dish on the shelf behind Lowell's chair. Found a small brass key ring inside. "How about we use these?"

Tack gave me a slow clap. "Oh, well done!"

"Lowell's always fiddling with that dish. Had to be keys or candy."

"Still, this quack is making it easy." Tack frowned, as if he didn't trust anything that came without a fight. "Not exactly Homeland Security, is he?"

"Don't look a gift horse in the mouth." I knelt before the right-hand drawers and started trying keys. There were three on the ring—two similar, the last of vastly different make.

"Why not?" Tack asked abruptly.

"Huh?" The first key didn't fit, and the second failed to turn.

"Why can't I look at its mouth?" Tack was squinting down at me. "Do people hide things in the jaws of free horses? Like a Trojan horse? Because I don't get it. Before hearing that phrase, I can't think of a single reason why I'd have checked my sweet new horse's mouth, but now I *definitely* would. Like, first thing."

I paused. "It's about the teeth. They might be bad. I think."

He stared back blankly.

I rolled my eyes, slotting the last key. "The *point* is that the horse you're getting is free, so it doesn't matter if its teeth are bad because you didn't pay anything. So you should just take your bonus horse and be happy. Don't be a jerk and look for flaws."

Tack nodded sharply. "These keys are like bad horse teeth. We shouldn't look at them."

"No, that's not at *all* what—"

I broke off. The lock had turned, and the top drawer slid open.

Tack pressed close behind me as I rifled its contents. Pens. Post-its. A stapler. A ruler. With a huff, I closed the drawer and tugged the larger one underneath. It opened smoothly, apparently connected to the same locking system. It was nearly empty, just a few hanging folders pushed to one side. I began thumbing through them as Tack moved to the opposite end of the desk. Those drawers were locked as well, so I tossed him the ring. The second key worked, and he began rooting inside.

"Anything?" he asked, not looking up.

I shook my head. "Nothing of interest."

The folders had printed tabs, and were the definition of boring. Journal articles. Tax returns. Restaurant takeout menus. I was about to move on when the last file caught my eye.

"Wait."

Two letters were scrawled on its tab: *P.N.*

I removed the folder. Thin and light, it held no more than a dozen pages. I scanned the top sheet inside. My blood ran cold.

I was holding a detailed list of expenses. Pencils. Paper. Toner. Data storage. Innocuous professional items, their tally running half the page. The form appeared to have been compiled by Dr. Lowell and submitted to something called "DoD-DARPA. Advance Research Group P.N." Someone named "LTG William P. Garfield" had signed the bottom and stamped APPROVED in bold black letters.

Bland as bland could be. Two days ago, I wouldn't have given this unexceptional bit of paperwork a second glance. Had no interest in how Dr. Lowell underwrote his highlighter costs.

But my eyes were riveted to the top of the form.

The expenses had been submitted under a specific heading.

Project: Nemesis. Status: Classified—Top Secret.

The folder almost slipped from my fingers.

"Min?" Tack had paused his search on the other side of the desk. "You okay?"

I didn't answer. Setting aside the first sheet, I examined the next. Identical, except dated a month later. I pawed through the stack. Eight expense forms altogether, one for each month of the current year. Their contents barely varied. All were labeled Project Nemesis and approved by the same William Garfield. All were rated top secret.

Tack reached over and took one from the folder, his eyes rounding in surprise. "Why are these marked classified? And what's Project Nemesis?"

I ran a hand across my slick forehead. "I don't know."

"You know something." He was studying me, and it wasn't a question.

I looked at Tack. Could tell he wasn't going to let the matter drop. "The name," I said carefully, placing the documents on the desktop. "Project Nemesis. I've seen it before."

Tack nodded. "From Dr. Lowell?"

I shook my head. "On some paperwork I saw years ago, at school. The day we got those shots because of the chemical leak."

"Oh." Tack relaxed. "So Lowell's still charging the military expenses for a decade-old cleanup? Slick. I wouldn't have given him that much credit."

"No. That's not—" I paused, gathering my thoughts. Deciding how much I'd reveal. "I heard that name again this morning, in the hall outside Principal Myers's office. He mentioned Project Nemesis to someone on the phone."

Tack bumped a fist against his chin, considering. "That's weird. After all these years, the pesticide spill is still a thing? And why call an inoculation program Project Nemesis? That seems a bit, I don't know . . . dark."

I wasn't going to reply, but then something he'd said jumped out at me. "Why'd you say Lowell is dealing with the military?"

He tapped the top of the form. "DARPA. That stands for 'Defense Advanced Research Projects Agency.' It's responsible for developing new technology for the Department of Defense. Conspiracy nuts are always going on about it. That's who this Garfield guy must work for. 'LTG' means 'Lieutenant General,' FYI, so he's no slouch. That's three stars. Seems weird for an environmental disaster, but that must be why the project is classified. Everything they do is."

I barely heard his last words. My mind was racing.

A general. The Department of Defense.

Project Nemesis *was* a secret government program.

Principal Myers had been involved in Nemesis for years, as far back as the shots when we were six. Had Dr. Lowell been with the project that long as well?

Glancing down at the folder, I finally noticed the last two pages inside it. They'd been stapled directly to the back of the file.

"What are those?" Tack asked.

"Consent forms, it looks like. They don't have the same header as the expenses, but—"

I gasped. A hand flew to my mouth.

"Min? What's the matter?" Tack waited a beat, then snatched

the folder and read silently. He shot me a startled glance. "Your *mother*? She signed this, Min! Right here, at the bottom. It's dated ten years ago!"

As if I hadn't seen.

Ten years. A decade. I was six.

"What's it for?" Tack flipped the page up. The back was blank—as documents went, this one was short and boring. He started reading the form stapled behind mine, but I held out a hand.

When he hesitated, I snapped my fingers impatiently. Tack flinched, then handed me the file. Heart hammering, I examined the document my mother had signed, line by line.

The language was largely boilerplate. I was listed as the patient. Dr. Lowell as my treating physician. My mother was agreeing to "various procedures, as discussed during the in-person consultation." The middle three sections were blacked out. Legal mumbo-jumbo made up the last paragraph, but nothing that seemed particularly sinister. If a stranger found this on the street, it wouldn't provoke the slightest interest.

But to me, it was a series of land mines.

What "consultation" had my mother had with Dr. Lowell when I was six? What "procedures" had they discussed? Why was this form stapled into a Project Nemesis folder?

Then the date beside my mother's signature registered.

September 18, 2007. The day after my sixth birthday.

The day of the inoculations. The day I was taken somewhere by Dr. Harris, and can't remember what happened next.

Mom knew.

She'd consented, that afternoon, to some sort of relationship with Dr. Lowell. It must've happened after she stormed out to confront Myers and left me alone.

But what had she agreed to about me?

Therapy? Medication? I didn't know. Then I experienced another electric shock.

Lowell didn't start treating me when I was six.

We met on my *tenth* birthday, the night of my second murder. Yet I was holding proof that Mom and Lowell had decided something *four years* before I was ever introduced to him.

And they never told me. Neither one. Not ever.

The room spun. I sat heavily in Lowell's chair, unable to breathe.

"Min?" Tack's hand found my shoulder. "What is it? What's wrong?"

Lowell. Myers. The Department of Defense.

What had Mom given these people permission to do?

My vision blurred. Suddenly, I was back in our trailer, lying on my floor, blood gushing from a burning hole in my chest. The black-suited man stood over me. For a terrifying moment, he wore Dr. Lowell's face. Then Principal Myers's. Then my mother's.

It was all I could do not to scream.

13

Nemesis.

I considered the word.

The inescapable agent of someone's downfall.

A long-standing rival; an archenemy.

I thought of the murders I'd endured. Deaths that made me question my sanity, even the fabric of reality itself.

Yet here, on this familiar desk, in this comfortable office, at the heart of the sleepy little town I'd called home every day of my life, was a decade-old contract linking my mother and my psychiatrist in some sort of secret agreement about me.

And I've had a nemesis ever since.

"Min?" Tack repeated, but I still didn't respond. I was paralyzed.

With an irritated grunt, Tack spun Lowell's chair so that I faced him, worry lines creasing his forehead. "Yo, Melinda J. What's up?"

I looked away. Couldn't explain. Not without telling him everything.

Pull yourself together.

"It's nothing." My voice shook. I covered it with a cough, grateful for the dim lighting. "Let's see what else we can find."

Tack's gaze lingered, blue eyes glinting in the lamplight. Then he pointed to his side of Lowell's desk. "I only checked the top drawer so far. Nothing worth discussing." He yanked the bottom one open. A single object rested inside.

"Bingo." Tack removed a MacBook and placed it on the desk. "Think we should steal it?" He drummed the laptop with his thumbs. "We could visit a tech-geek message board, maybe find a friendly hacker. Isn't that what Anonymous does?"

"No need. I know the password."

"Seriously? How?"

Despite everything, I grinned. "Dr. Lowell mumbles when he types. I pay attention."

I fired up the laptop and a pop-up box appeared. I typed out eight simple letters. I even knew what the keystrokes *sounded* like. "Stanford. He went to school there."

"That's his password?" Tack snorted. "I'm pretty sure your shrink failed Data Encryption 101. Nice job, Stanford."

I tucked my hair behind my ears as the system loaded. "He obviously doesn't stress about security."

"Then we're teaching him a valuable lesson." Tack leaned in so he could read over my shoulder. I felt his breath on my cheek as a satellite photo of Earth filled the monitor, followed by an assortment of icons. Tack pointed to a folder in the corner. "Case files. That looks promising. Click there."

Inside were subfolders sorted by name. A few surprised me. "Mr. Fumo? I wonder what he sees Lowell about."

"Napoleon complex," Tack said confidently. "He's as short as I am. Or maybe he thinks he's a Viking god trapped in a math teacher's body. Let's find out. Open sesame."

"I will *not*." Indignant. And slightly ashamed for sharing the impulse. "We didn't come here to violate people's privacy. I only want to see *my* file."

Tack rolled his eyes. "*Bo-ring*. Fine. But your name isn't listed here."

I double-checked, and he was right. Then a different name popped into my head—my terrified partner on that ride with Dr. Harris ten years ago. I rescanned the list, but Noah wasn't there either.

I closed out and examined the rest of Lowell's home screen. Everything else seemed innocuous. Program links. A folder labeled "Personal" that was largely empty. Some journal articles. A PowerPoint labeled "Northern Idaho Psychiatric Retreat—Presentation, 2016." My doctor's hard drive was as dull as his office.

I sat back, stymied. Experienced a moment of doubt. What did I really expect to find? A cache of top-secret military documents? Orders from the Joint Chiefs, in PDF format?

Tack stretched his arms over his head. "Well? We done here?"

I glanced at a nearby shelf. Lowell stared back at me, hoisting a smallmouth bass with a wry smile on his face. *Is that fish me, Doc? Did I take the bait?*

"No." Sitting forward, I selected "All My Files." Over the next five minutes I scrutinized the complete list, but my name didn't appear anywhere.

"Welp." Tack was chewing a thumbnail, plainly ready to give

up but trying to hide it. "Maybe you're just really, really boring. Like, his dullest, least interesting case. A total snooze."

"Let's try running searches."

Melinda Wilder. Min. My birth date. My Social Security number. My mother's name.

Nothing. On this laptop, I didn't exist.

Tack straightened and stepped away, yawning into his fist. "Guess your file is somewhere else. Maybe because you're a minor?"

I was about to agree. Froze instead.

Without responding, I searched the one thing I hadn't tried.

Nemesis.

The screen blanked. Planet Earth disappeared as the laptop hummed with renewed purpose. A new home screen sprang up, backed by a high-res satellite image of the sun. A single, unlabeled folder sat in one corner.

"Oh, snap!" Tack's eyes widened in delight. "A second desktop. Here we go!"

Taking a deep breath, I clicked the folder. A short list of files appeared. Tack swore.

Melinda Juilliard Wilder.

My name was the very first one.

"What does this mean?" Tack pointed to the metadata beside my file. "The subheading for your document is Beta Run—Test Patient A. Not gonna lie—I don't like the sound of that."

Abruptly, I wished I were alone. If Tack read Lowell's notes about me—even just the highlights—he'd learn my darkest secret. I wasn't ready for that, but banishing him now would be unfair. He'd shared the risk of getting me in here. I owed him.

So I steeled myself for whatever came next. "Only one way to find out."

I selected my file. A new password box opened. I entered "Stanford," but was denied. Frustrated, I typed the word again, more slowly. Same result.

"Well, fart." Tack had a way with words.

"*Come on come on come on.*" I thought for a moment, then tried "Nemesis."

The box disappeared with a beep.

"Nice!" Tack crowed, but then a red stop sign flashed on-screen.

"Shit! I'm locked out. Too many incorrect entries."

Tack shifted uncomfortably. "Will Lowell see that?"

I shrugged helplessly, then minimized the warning and checked the folder. A red key icon had appeared next to my file name.

My stomach twisted in knots. "Damn it. I think Lowell has to reset his password or something. He'll know someone tried to access my file."

Tack narrowed his eyes at the monitor, thinking hard. Finally, "Lock out *all* the files, one by one. We can't do anything about yours, but if we jam the entire folder, at least he won't know which document was the original target."

"Brilliant!" I squeezed his hand, then clicked the next file before its name penetrated my brain. "Oh God. Tack, look."

Noah Charles Livingston.

"That jackass?" Tack sniffed. "I wonder what *his* problem is. Affluenza? Trust fund guilt?" He tapped the screen. "Check out the metadata."

Noah's subheading was similar to mine: Beta Run—Test Patient B.

I held his hand before the shots. He was so scared.

My mind was galloping in circles. They'd taken us both to that facility.

Melinda Julliard Wilder. Noah Charles Livingston.

Test Patient A. Test Patient B.

Were his sessions like mine? I thought of Lowell's droning. The blue pills. I tried to imagine *Noah freaking Livingston* in my place on that stupid couch, evading Lowell's questions, doubting himself, a ball of frustration and suspicion like me.

I couldn't get there. But then the real question hit me, and I nearly threw up.

The murders.

The black-suited man.

Is it happening to Noah, too?

The idea that another person might be sharing my wretched experiences had never occurred to me. I didn't want it—wouldn't wish that on *anyone*—even as the notion gave me a wild surge of . . . relief.

"Weird," Tack muttered, focused on the laptop. "There aren't any other patient-named files here. The rest aren't even words—just letters and numbers." He blew out his cheeks. "Only you and Noah. I didn't even know that douche was in therapy."

Neither did I.

But suddenly, everything had changed.

Maybe I wasn't alone. Maybe Noah was just like me.

My energy level surged, despite the hour. I thumped out wrong passwords for each file, proceeding down the list as fast as I could. Angry red keys appeared in a row. I was halfway done when Tack popped up and plucked the Nemesis folder off the desk. He flipped over my consent form to examine the one beneath it. Then, clicking his tongue, he thrust the document in front of me. The second patient consented for was Noah C. Livingston.

"His mother signed." Tack tilted his head. "Didn't she die when we were little?"

"First grade." I traced her signature with my eyes. "I remember because we turned seven that year, but his mom didn't come to the class party like usual, and I got shushed for asking about it. Then a few months later another woman was dropping him off at school."

Turning back, I clicked the last document. Did a double take. "Yo, Tack!"

He dropped the stapled forms. "What?"

"This file is actually a folder, and check out the title." My finger jabbed the monitor. "VHG Federal Land Reserve. That's the name of the government property on Old Fort Run!"

"Where the convoy disappeared last night." Tack actually clapped. "Open it!"

At first the contents were disappointing: a few hundred files with indecipherable names, each consisting of three letters followed by six numbers. I could tell they were password-protected like the others. Another dead end.

But then something jumped out at me. The three-letter codes seemed to repeat every dozen files or so, while the last two numbers stayed the same for long intervals. But the middle four digits always changed.

The answer came in a flash. "These numbers are dates. Look at the bottom section. They all end in seventeen. Those must be from this year."

Tack nodded. "But what are the letters?"

One sequence was demanding my attention. VGW.

I knew those letters.

A tear spilled onto my cheek. I tried to hold it back, but couldn't.

"Initials," I said in an unsteady voice. "I think these are reports of some kind."

I moused over the last VGW file. Metadata appeared.

PN_FIELD_OBSERVATION_REPORT_SUBMITTED/FILED/091817

09.18.17. The day after my birthday. Yesterday.

Tack was silent a moment, then squinted over at me. "What's going on, Min? Seriously. No more holding back. You persuade me to break into your shrink's office in the middle of the night, and we discover you're part of some classified military project." He exhaled in disbelief. "Noah too, of all people. There are files calling you a 'beta run,' and now we've got the out-of-bounds woods popping up only hours after we see an armored caravan drive into them, for the first time in, like . . . I don't know . . . *forever*." He hesitated, then said the words aloud and made it real. "Are those really your mom's initials?"

I cleared my throat, stalling, and not very well. I wanted to crawl away and hide.

"We need to talk to Noah," I said finally.

Tack's jaw tightened. "How's *he* gonna help? By asking his daddy to handle it?"

I understood his reluctance, but I couldn't ignore this lead.

Noah was involved with Project Nemesis. He might know things I didn't.

"I need you to trust me on this."

Tack seemed about to argue, then shrugged instead. "Whatever." He forced a lightness into his voice I knew he didn't feel. "If you want that dope slowing us down, it's your call. I'll get him a bike helmet to wear for safety."

He glanced at his watch. "Two thirty."

I nodded, closing everything. Hopefully Lowell would think the password issue was some kind of software glitch, and ignore it. He seemed the type. I shut down the laptop and put everything back how we found it, then relocked the desk.

I wouldn't think about my mother and field reports. Not yet.

I was returning the keys to their dish when the third one caught my eye. Burnished brass. Longer and thinner than the other two. Plainly designed for some other type of lock.

I turned around. Eyeballed the antique cabinet across the room.

Its lower doors were closed. There was a keyhole.

"What?" Tack swiveled to follow my line of sight. "*Ah*. Sure, why not?"

I crossed the shadowy office and knelt before the wooden panels. Inserted the key. It turned easily, and the carved doors swung open. Inside were two plastic document boxes filled with manila folders.

I dragged a box from the cabinet. Selected a folder at random.

"'Tobias G. Albertsson—4/5/2002.' Hey, that's Toby!" Startled, I pulled another file. "'Sally D. Hillman—6/24/2001.' She was in our grade too, remember? But her family moved to Lewiston four years ago." Then I noticed a red line slicing through her name on the tab.

Tack grabbed the other box and dug in with both hands. It held similar files, each labeled by name and date. All were former or current classmates. Tack counted thirty-three folders in his container. "I bet everyone in our grade is in these."

"But why? Lowell obviously doesn't treat the whole class."

"Alphabetical." Tack riffled through his box, a strange excitement in his voice. "This set starts with *L*. And . . . *boom*. Here's me! Thomas 'The Dark Knight' Russo. This one's gonna be tasty, folks. FYI, those are birth dates on the labels, although I imagine you guessed that already."

He read silently. Then his back stiffened, eyes rounding as he pawed through the stack of pages inside. Finally, he slapped the folder shut and flung it across the room, staring after it like the contents might bite him.

"How in the—" Tack cut off, his mouth hanging open. Then he looked at me fixedly, with no humor in his eyes. "What the *hell* is going on, Min? Why does your wacko shrink have a Nemesis file on *me*? One that includes everything I've ever done!"

"A Nemesis file? How do you know that?"

Tack shook his head, uncharacteristically silent. Alarmed, I pulled another folder from the box in front of me. Jessica L. Cale—1/14/2002. Not my favorite person. The first page was a basic worksheet. Name. Address. Age. The usual particulars, typical of any intake form or official registration. Typical, until you noticed TOP SECRET stamped at the top and General Garfield's signature scrawled across the bottom.

The breadth of information was staggering, as was the level of detail. Medical files. Report cards. Newspaper clippings from when Jessica won the Junior Miss Idaho pageant at twelve. There were printouts of her Facebook and Pinterest pages, her Instagrams, even Snapchats. Xeroxed school pictures. An analysis of her Twitter feed. At the back I found a Google Earth image of her house, clipped to a spreadsheet documenting her parents' work histories and criminal records. There was even a roster of household pets.

I dropped Jessica's file—having learned more about her in the last two minutes than during a lifetime of going to school together—and pulled another. Harrison S. Finch—a freckly boy I vaguely remembered from middle school. He'd broken his arm once, goofing around on the jungle gym before first bell. Then his family had up and moved, to where, I'd never learned. Inside his folder were the same types of documents, but the data collection ended in 2013, the same year he'd left town (for Billings, I now saw). Nothing in his file was more current.

I rechecked the tab. Noticed a red line through his name.

I grabbed more files. Casey F. Beam. Gregory Kozowitz. Lauren J. Decker.

All classmates. All with identical workups.

"These are like FBI dossiers!" Tack sputtered, his usual cool completely blown. "But get this—*only* sophomores. I checked my entire box. No juniors. No seniors. No freshmen. Just *our* grade. Do you know how creepy that is? Why would Lowell have this stuff? Who gave it to him? Why only our class?"

"This can't be legal." I waved a file to make my point. "Here are twenty pages of Cash Eaton's medical records, about his irregular heartbeat. That kind of information is protected by law. You can't just Google it and make copies."

"Where's your file?" Tack asked suddenly, eyeing the pile of folders spreading across the carpet. "The *W*s should be in my box, but I didn't see your name."

"My group is *A* through *K*." I thumbed through them anyway to be sure. "I'm not in here."

Tack quickly searched the other container. "Noah's missing, too."

"There were thirty-eight files in this box. That makes seventy-one altogether."

"One for everyone!" Tack swept a hand like a bitter game-show host. "We're being spied on and charted like terrorists, by a shady head doctor neck-deep in a government conspiracy. Which is code-named *Nemesis*, by the way. Nothing terrifying about that! Good times. Super. I'm excited to be a part of this."

I felt a twinge in my scar. Gunshots echoed in my head.

You don't know the half of it.

Beta Run. Test Patient A. Test Patient B.

Yet this was bigger than just Noah and me. No denying it now.

"Did you notice some of the names are scratched out?" Tack said.

I nodded. "Six in my box. All kids who *used to* go to school with us, but don't anymore."

"Five in mine." Tack dug up a red-lined file. His voice dropped. "This one's for Peter Merchant. And I saw another earlier on Mary Roke."

I got a chill. Petey Merchant had drowned when we were

ten. His canoe capsized during a summer squall, way out on the lake, and he'd never been a strong swimmer. His family moved away soon afterward.

Mary Roke died when we were thirteen. Bee stings. No one knew she was allergic.

I did a quick calculation. "That leaves sixty with names that aren't marked through."

"Close to the exact number of kids in our class. We've been sixty-four strong for two years now, and these boxes don't include you and Noah."

"And two others. I wonder who else?"

I surveyed the files fanning out across Lowell's carpet. To figure out who was missing, we'd have to make a list. "Let's takc pictures of everything." I dug into my pocket for my cell. "Then we'll have proof. I'll email them to myself to be safe." But my iPhone quit the moment I pressed the home button, a victim of our late-night stakeout. I glanced at Tack, but he shook his head. "Mine died before we left the bushes."

"Damn it." My eyes traveled the room, hunting for another option.

I noticed a splash of yellow buried in the mass of folders. Pulled it from the pile. A single sheet. The document wasn't part of anyone's personal workup—it must've been wedged inside a box between the files.

From the Desk of General W. P. Garfield.

"What's that?" Tack asked.

"A memo to Project Nemesis." I scanned as I spoke. "The general is thanking everyone for their service and dedication. He's proud of everyone for 'seeing things through to the bitter end,' whatever that means." Then my heart sped up. "Listen to this: 'Final preparations are in place. Over the next ten days, we must remain steadfast and complete our objective. Godspeed.'"

Tack spread his hands. "What the hell does that mean?"

"No idea. This is dated two days ago. Lowell was supposed to destroy the message—it says so right here on the page. I wonder why he didn't?"

When I looked up, I found Tack watching me intently. The bruises on his face gave him a ghoulish affect in the murky half-light. The wall clock ticked on, uncaring, as we sat on the floor, each a momentary prisoner of our own thoughts.

"What's going on, Min?" Tack asked again, in a small voice. "What is Project Nemesis?"

I had no answer.

Not that we had time for one.

Outside, tires screeched in the parking lot, followed by slamming doors.

PART TWO

NOAH

14

My heart stops beating.

I freeze, trash bag in hand, the only illumination a streetlamp half a block away.

It's my fault, really.

I lie down. Close my eyes. Only for a second, but that's all it takes.

Someone is here. In the shadows at the foot of the driveway.

My executioner.

Such a mundane thing to dream about. Taking out the garbage? Boring, honestly, except for what's about to happen next.

Steady footfalls as the man climbs the hill. The trash bag slips from my fingers.

I close my eyes.

Pretending it was a normal day didn't work. Nothing ever works, not on the even years. This was always going to happen, so I might as well accept it. Get it over with. I don't remember falling asleep, but then, I never do.

I open my eyes.

A spark of red, quickly extinguished. Cell phone? Lighter? Does my darkest nightmare now smoke cigarettes?

I can't move. Can't breathe.

Again.

Two years since our last meeting, but again.

He walks slowly. Deliberately. He thinks I'll run, but I won't.

I can't escape. It doesn't work. This is all in my head. How can I run from myself?

I close my eyes.

"You aren't real."

My voice shakes, but I repeat the words. Louder this time.

"You aren't real!"

He reaches my side. I feel him watching me. My heart pounds so loud, he must hear it.

I open my eyes.

Stone-carved face. Black suit. Boots. Silver sunglasses, despite the darkness.

Identical, in every detail. Except he is *smoking. He's never done that before. He's never done* anything *before. Except what comes next.*

The man drops the cigarette. Grinds it with his heel. He's acting strangely. Less robotic. I could swear he's tired, though I don't know how I can tell.

Of course I can tell. He's part of me. Somehow.

The black-suited man reaches into his jacket. Withdraws a serrated knife.

"This is the last time."

My head jerks back. He's never said anything before.

"The last time?" I stammer, tears gathering in my eyes. "Are you sure? How can you know?"

"I know."

It's hard, but I smile, heaving a sob of relief. "Thank you. Oh God, thank you so much." The tears spill out and run down my cheeks. "I just want this to be over."

His face twitches. "Never thank me."

I nod anxiously. I have more to say—more to ask myself—but I don't dare. If by some miracle my lifelong nightmare is truly ending, I can't risk anything that might jeopardize that.

I close my eyes.

"Do it, then."

A beat. A long breath.

The knife slams into my chest.

A spike of agony. This might not be real, but it hurts just the same.

Faint words, whispered close to my ear. "I'm sorry."

He withdraws the knife. I fall.

Blood pumps onto the pavement. Slides down the hill.

Cold.

Blackness.

Nothing.

Thank God.

It's finally over.

15

My head snapped up.

I jerked awake, an instant from sliding to the floor. Adrenaline hit me like a kick in the balls. So much for staying alert.

It took a moment to get my bearings. Dr. Lowell's depressing lobby. The world's least comfortable chair.

I rubbed my eyes. Turned, spat in the wastebasket. My brain shifted from reliving the nightmare to full-on panicking about it. God, what was taking him so long? Lowell was the only person I could be real with.

A twenty-minute wait. I'd drifted off. Hadn't slept well in days.

Years? Ever?

Not without my medication. My prescription always ran out on my birthday. Lowell was the only place to get more. And I needed those pills. Needed to sleep again, without fear.

I glanced at the clock: 6:10 a.m. *Come on!*

He cancels my appointment, can't see me for two excruciating days, and now he's late.

I rose, began pacing. Man, I didn't need this. Changing the routine, right when he knew I needed him most. It's not like I was looking forward to it.

My birthday session, on a bad year.

Time to admit I'm still crazy. Hooray. Shit.

Finally I couldn't take it any longer. I strode to his office door and yanked it open, knocking only as I stepped inside.

"Dr. Lowell? It's Noah Livingston. We have an appointment right now, and I really—"

I halted midstep. Lowell was on his hands and knees before his old wooden cabinet. He twisted around in surprise, a stack of folders clutched in his arms.

"Stop right there!" he shouted, glaring. "What are you doing, just barging in?" Lowell hastily shoved the files into the cabinet and slammed its door. Locked it. Then he lurched to his feet, anger clouding his pale features.

I stepped back, stunned. In all the years I'd known him, he'd never once raised his voice. I didn't even know he was capable of it.

Dr. Lowell took a deep breath. When he spoke next, he'd recovered his normal soothing tenor. "What are you doing here, Noah?"

I gave him a troubled look. "We were supposed to meet. You canceled my special visit on Monday, and weren't able to see me yesterday."

Lowell closed his eyes. "Of course. I'm so sorry, Noah. This week has been . . . chaotic. Please sit down. I'll be with you in a moment."

I took my usual seat in a recliner and waited anxiously. This was almost too much. I'd been living with crushing anxiety for two days, had gone off my meds, and now my psychiatrist was acting like a totally different person.

"You got my calls? I tried to reach you from the cave, but there was no reception. Then when you canceled our appointment, I . . . I didn't know what . . ." My voice choked off. Dr. Lowell had never postponed a visit before.

"It's been a trying week. That's no excuse—I know you rely on me, and I've let you down." Lowell reached into his jacket and removed a medicine bottle. "Have you run out of your prescription?"

I nearly snatched the bottle from his fingers. Nodding tightly, I waited for him to hand over the pills, then swallowed one dry before he was able to continue.

"Why don't you tell me what happened?"

"In the dream, or the cave?"

"Let's start with the dream."

I told him about my nightmare. Every nauseating detail. Stabbed in the heart this time—I couldn't wait to hear the explanation for *that* one. What the knife "symbolized," or whatever. What Black Suit actually speaking to me might mean.

But Lowell merely nodded, so I kept going. Admitted the rest.

The cycle was always the same: a sleepwalking dream I couldn't distinguish from reality, followed by waking up in the cave. It wasn't even a *cool* cave, just a random crack in the western canyon wall, bordering a pond. It's a miracle I'd never stumbled into the water and drowned, or fallen into the gorge.

This was the fifth time I'd blacked out. Always on my birthdays, even years only.

Nuts. I'm freaking nuts.

It was terrifying. Humiliating. Getting worse.

The entire awful story spilled out, including the aftermath. Opening my eyes in the gloom. My hands flying to my chest, where no wound existed. Shame setting in. Crying, huddled on the stone floor, unable to make myself move. *A tough guy, that's me.*

Tears stung my eyes, but I forced them back. "I'm just so tired of this. I'd been doing well these last two years. I accepted the truth of my problem, and I mask my feelings every day, like you taught me. I . . . I work as hard as I can to be normal."

Lowell nodded. "How is the anxiety?"

"I try to compartmentalize. I can make it through most days without a problem if I stay detached. But without my pills I can't sleep."

He frowned. "That's odd. You've been off them for how many days now?"

"Only two. I tried to come in yesterday, but—"

"I know. It couldn't be helped. Just be sure not to miss another dose this week."

"But why didn't it work?" I could hear the tension in my own voice. "What's wrong with me?"

"You experienced a regression," Lowell said calmly. "A minor setback, nothing more. I don't want you to worry, Noah. We'll get to the bottom of it together, I promise."

I shook my head. "It's not *fair.* I've been taking my pills. Every damn day!"

"That's only part of the work, Noah. A big part, of course, but our time speaking together is just as vital."

"But why did the dream come back? Why can't I ever remember falling asleep?" In a fit of pique, I jerked up my sleeve and thrust my shoulder forward. "Why does this stupid scar burn every time?"

I was panting, had risen halfway from my seat. The last two days had been the worst of my life. I felt broken and alone. I'd kept my head down at school, avoiding people, wishing everything and everyone would just go away. But nothing I did made me feel better, and now my shrink couldn't help either.

"Let's go through the rest of that morning. Step by step. Tell me exactly what happened." Lifting his notebook, he looked at me expectantly, pen in hand.

I dropped back into my chair, embarrassed. Took a breath. Ordered my thoughts like he'd trained me. "I woke up in the same place, then snuck home like always. No one saw me slip back into the house—Rosalita was still in her quarters, and the cook never shows up before eleven. Our property takes up most of the block, so I know the neighbors didn't see."

Not that they'd have said anything. Winding Oaks is the most exclusive address in Fire Lake—tucked in the southwestern corner of the valley, its steep streets rising in tiers that provide spectacular views of the lake. Our place sits practically alone at the top. Dad likes looking down on people. No one bothers him if they can avoid it.

His name alone had gotten me out of a few jams growing up. Which is good, since I hate conflict and try desperately to avoid it.

If they only knew how little my father cared about me.

How much of a disappointment I was to that ruthless old shark.

"So you're *sure* no one noticed you'd been missing overnight?" Lowell seemed strangely intent on the question. "Not even your father?"

I snorted. "Dad ghosted four days ago for a wine-tasting holiday with Mandy. One last trip to Italy, in case the worst was about to happen. He left me a birthday check on the coffee table."

"I see."

"I went to school that morning, just in time for the Announcement hysteria. People were fighting, and our teachers acted like we were all going to die. Did you know someone blew up Ethan Fletcher's Jeep in the parking lot?"

"I heard." Lowell glanced at his watch. I blinked. He *never* did that. "It must've been a huge relief when they announced the miss."

"Well, yeah, obviously. But then I got dragged around to a bunch of parties. People were acting like lunatics, while I was barely holding it together." I swallowed. "It happened *again*, Dr. Lowell. I . . . I need it to stop."

"I understand, Noah. Believe me, I do. Tell me about your friends."

I hesitated. "Same as always. Sometimes I'm not even sure they like me."

"That's not true, Noah. You're highly regarded by your peers. The problem you're having—the problem you've always had—is that *you* don't like you. We must continue to work on that."

I didn't respond. About this, Lowell simply didn't understand.

But he wouldn't drop it. "The accumulated stress of your sleepwalking experiences has manifested in an acute insecurity. We need to delve into those feelings. Unpack them individually, and shove them into the light of day. Because they aren't accurate, Noah. You're a special, talented young man."

"I'm a coward."

Lowell *tsk*ed. "You have a generalized anxiety disorder. A medical condition doesn't make you a coward."

"Tell that to my father." My fingers made air quotes. "He says 'mental illness' is a crutch for the weak-minded. That psychiatry is a scam to separate suckers from their money."

Lowell's voice hardened. "Then he's a fool."

"No argument here."

But in some ways, my father was right. Lowell might give fancy names to my problems, but the facts remained the same. I *was* weak. I was afraid of my own damn shadow. I ran to my shrink every week and prayed he could fix me.

Lowell glanced at his watch again. I felt sick. He wanted rid of me.

Suddenly, the room began to vibrate. Lowell's green eyes rounded in surprise.

He shot to his desk. I gripped my armrests as the shaking increased, watched a dolphin figurine shimmy across a shelf before dropping to the carpet.

Lowell had spun his laptop to face us and was opening his web browser.

The tremors ceased.

Lowell was breathing hard as he navigated to CNN and opened the live stream.

"*—at Yellowstone National Park just minutes ago. Officials estimate the initial quake was somewhere in the low sevens on the Richter scale, causing damage throughout—*"

I lost the thread. Was watching my psychiatrist wheeze, red-faced, his hands locked onto the sides of his computer. Lowell's forehead was damp with sweat.

"Doctor? You okay? Sounds like a minor earthqu—"

"Go." Lowell pointed to the door without looking up. "*Now* please, Noah. We'll, uh, resume where we left off tomorrow. Or perhaps the next day. I'll be in touch."

"Okay. No problem." Unnerved. This whole visit had been a disaster.

Trudging toward the exit, I stopped to gather a few books that had fallen.

"Leave them!" Lowell ordered. "Thank you, Noah, but I'll clean up. Off you go now."

I retreated into the lobby, shaking my head. Earthquakes are scary, no doubt, but that one had barely rattled a teacup.

What was he so afraid of?

16

PROJECT NEMESIS

File: INTERVIEW TRANSCRIPT: NOAH C. LIVINGSTON ("NL")

Date: OCTOBER 21, 2016

Specialist: DR. GERALD LOWELL ("GL")

Subject: TEST PATIENT B, BETA RUN, SESSION 14-J3

GL: Take me through what you remember, Noah. Step by step.

NL: Do I have to?

GL: The direction of our conversation is always up to you. But it's important for us to talk about your experiences, even the older ones. By discussing painful memories, we can draw some of the sting from them. Take away their power over you.

NL: [PAUSE] That one is . . . hard. It was the first.

GL: Do you remember falling asleep?

NL: [SUBJECT SHAKES HEAD] But I remember that day like it was yesterday. I . . . I . . .

GL: Relax, Noah. Remember, this is your safe place. It's just you and me here. Nothing can hurt you while we talk.

NL: [PAUSE] It was my eighth birthday. I was at soccer practice. No, wait—it was a game. I remember because my team wasn't good that year, but we were winning. I set up Chris for an easy one, and I stopped Cash from tying it up.

GL: Who was there with you?

NL: Lupe, my nanny. Plus my first stepmother, Janice. Lupe was cheering for me, but she upset Janice by being too loud. So Janice sent her to get more ice from the car. Janice always brought a squeeze bottle to my activities, and she'd usually finish it a couple times while I played.

GL: But Janice was watching you?

NL: Not a chance. She had her magazine and her cup, and never looked up from either one. I think she actually wobbled to the bathroom right before . . . before . . .

GL: Go on, Noah. I know it's hard, but this will help in the long run. I promise.

NL: [PAUSE] I must've fallen asleep on the sideline, or . . . maybe . . . I don't know. But suddenly the game is over and he's standing there. Black suit. Sunglasses. I . . . I . . . it seems so real when I talk about it . . .

GL: I know it does. That's part of your condition. These dreams are so powerful in your mind that you struggle to differentiate them from reality. The sleepwalking component only reinforces this confusion. But they *aren't* real, Noah.

NL: Then why do we have to do this? Why can't I just try to forget?

GL: It helps. Do you trust me?

NL: [SUBJECT NODS]

GL: Then please, continue when you're ready.

NL: [PAUSE] I walked into the woods next to the field, to retrieve a ball. There's nothing back there. And . . . and . . .

GL: What happened, Noah?

NL: [SUBJECT SHIFTS] A bag dropped over my head. I . . . I couldn't breathe . . . I was screaming, but . . . no one came . . . I couldn't get it off, or break through it . . . Then it was so hot, so dark . . .

GL: [PAUSE] Noah? Do you need a minute?

NL: [SUBJECT SHAKES HEAD] That's it. I woke up in the cave for the first time.

GL: That must've been very traumatic. What did you do next?

NL: I ran home crying. When I got back, Janice ripped me a new one, even though she could barely stand up straight. Losing me would've gotten her in trouble with Dad. Worst part was, she'd fired Lupe and was blaming everything on her.

GL: Did you tell anyone?

NL: No. What was I going to say? I had no idea what had happened. I was in the park, then suddenly I was miles away in a cave. I wanted to talk about it even less than she did.

GL: You seem upset about Lupe. Did you like your nanny?

NL: I *loved* her. She'd been living with us for years, way longer than Janice. I found out later she was out looking for me while I was missing, even after getting canned. [PAUSE] She was the only person in the house who actually cared about me.

GL: That's not true, Noah.

NL: [SUBJECT SNORTS] To Janice, I was this weird little troll attached to my father. I overheard her say I should be sent to boarding school right after they got married. She didn't last much longer than Lupe. They divorced a year later.

GL: Janice was a narcissist. That much is clear. But your father cared for you. *Cares* for you.

NL: Sure.

GL: He *does*, Noah. You're his only child. He loves you. Why would you doubt that?

NL: Know where my father was during all this?

GL: [SPECIALIST SHAKES HEAD]

NL: Out of town. As usual.

17

I felt the knife plunge into my heart.

My eyes snapped open. I hadn't been asleep, but every time my lids closed, the dream came back to haunt me.

Black Suit was always there, lurking in my mind.

Promising relief this time, even as he executed me.

I was sitting in a small copse of cedars bordering the gym, my back against one of the gnarly trunks. My eyes felt itchy and grainy, allergic to the sun. My whole body ached. I'd have traded my trust fund for eight good hours of sleep, but I didn't dare risk it. I'd taken my pill only an hour earlier in Lowell's office.

Who was this killer I'd created? Lowell never got into that. As I thought more about it, the things my psychiatrist *didn't* ask me about made less sense. But I was too wiped to think straight.

I'd watched the Announcement by myself. Scared to death. My dad had sent me a single text message from Rome, telling me to adjust the sprinklers for fall. Insisting that all the asteroid hysteria was "total BS."

And he'd been right. Which kinda pissed me off, as crazy as

that sounds. A busted clock having the correct time by accident. Then the Nolans figured out my dad was gone, and the whole crew showed up at my door.

I couldn't say no. It wasn't worth the fight.

Which wasn't *all* bad. It had been nice having company after being alone. Ethan and I played ping-pong while the girls watched Dubsmash videos. Toby told a bunch of crazy stories about the liberty camp while gorging on my chips. But then some of the others got rowdy and loud. I'd seriously considered slipping away from my own house.

I rubbed my face, wondered briefly whether I could get up if I wanted to.

What would happen if I just slept here?

The Nolan brothers had broken into my dad's liquor cabinet, and before long half the group was tanked. Ethan had gotten colder by the minute, swearing he'd find out what happened to his Jeep. Then Sarah had stalked me like a carnival prize, as if our breakup the year before never happened. She'd suggested we take a walk down to the waterfront. I'd played as dumb as possible, even hiding in the bathroom at one point. She was still gorgeous, but something about her scared the crap out of me. There was a reason we'd only lasted two months.

When the fireworks started, we'd piled into the Nolans' disgusting van and drove from place to place like circus morons. Toby and Mike started breaking anything within reach. It'd taken twenty minutes to convince Ethan that buzzing the trailer park was a terrible idea. I'd been stuck with them for hours. Yesterday had been just as bad. People too jacked up, right when I needed things to calm down.

An earthquake sure didn't help. Thanks a lot, Mother Nature.

I closed my eyes again. Debated whether I'd even go to class. Nobody would say anything, except maybe Myers. But who was he going to tell? My father was busy getting loaded in another hemisphere.

I had the sudden impression of being watched. Opening my eyes, I spotted Min Wilder striding across the parking lot.

"Hey! Noah!"

What?

I scrambled to my feet, then felt foolish for doing so. Tried to act natural. Which was difficult, since the two of us talking wasn't natural. Min didn't mix with me and my friends these days at all. Not after the birthday party fiasco two years ago, when for some crazy reason I'd talked the girls into including her and then she didn't even bother showing up.

Her gray eyes sparkled with intensity. I didn't get a friendly vibe.

I yawned into my fist, a nervous habit I was powerless to prevent. Min always made me uncomfortable. I don't know why, but I felt like she could see right through me. Her gaze had a penetrating quality that made me feel like a fraud.

Which I was. Which is why I avoided her. Which wasn't possible right then.

"We need to talk."

I answered without thinking. "We never talk."

"Thanks for the tip." Min ran a hand through her glossy black hair, then briefly pinched the bridge of her nose. *She's exhausted.* The last few days had been rough on everyone, I guess.

There was an awkward pause.

"What's up?" I blurted. Then wanted to kick myself for sounding like a jackass.

"You're a patient of Dr. Lowell's, right?"

I nearly jumped. I don't know what I'd been expecting, but it wasn't that.

"I don't know who told you whatever, but I'm not supposed—"

"I *know* you see him, Noah. It's a small town."

I hesitated. "So what if I do?"

"Say 'yes,' for starters." Her stormy eyes dug into mine. I could swear she was taking my measure, and I was coming up short.

I gave in. "Fine. Yes. Dr. Lowell is my psychiatrist."

Min nodded, like an interrogator who'd forced a key admission. "I see him, too."

That surprised me. Why would Min see a shrink? I remembered something vague about her running away when we were little, but didn't know the details.

Another pause. My shoulders tensed. "Are you having problems with Lowell?" I asked, before I'd thought better of it.

Where'd that *come from? I don't want to have this conversation.*

But my question broke the spell. "Do you trust him?" Min asked, eyeing me intently.

"Of course." Flustered. "Why ask that?"

"Because *I* don't." She closed the distance between us. "I've been his patient since I was ten, and I don't think I've *ever* trusted him."

I was reeling. I'd been seeing Lowell for almost the exact same amount of time.

And trusted him completely.

"Why are you telling me this?" Her presence was everywhere. Piercing eyes. Shampoo smell. The delicate curve of her neck. I began to sweat.

"I found something." Min glanced around to make sure we weren't being overheard. It should've been comical, but it wasn't. "Last night in Lowell's office. There are things you need to see. Something big is going on, and you and I are part of it. Maybe the whole town."

I stared, unable to respond. My mind flashed back to that morning. Dr. Lowell, angry and off his game, shoveling files into his cabinet. Deep inside me, a voice was shouting in agreement. With a shock, I realized it had been there for years.

Min was standing close. Waiting. Needing something from me.

A connection was forming. I just needed to embrace it. Be as brave as she was.

But I never had the chance.

"There you are."

Our heads whipped as one. Tack stepped onto the curb. Deep purple bruises ringed a black eye so complete it looked like a Halloween gag. "Missed you at the gate, Min. You walk in?"

"Sorry. I was in a hurry and couldn't wait."

"To see Noah, it looks like." Spoken with a slight edge.

Her lips quirked. "That a problem?"

"Of course not. I just—" Tack looked at me, then changed what he'd been going to say. "We never discussed our next move." Talking around me, but I was too confused to be offended.

"I said I was going to talk to Noah. I'm doing it right now."

Something passed between them. Tack nodded tightly.

All my insecurities came crashing back. What did these two want with me?

A dark blur fluttered by my ear. Tack's head jerked back an instant before something struck him in the face. He staggered back as howls of laughter erupted behind me.

I spun, winced inwardly. Ethan and some of the others were cutting through the parking lot.

"You can borrow that!" Toby pointed to his copy of *The Count of Monte Cristo*, now lying in the grass. "Actually, read it and tell me what happens. I thought we were asteroid meat and never bothered."

Chris Nolan laughed, elbowing his twin brother, but Ethan remained uncharacteristically silent. His gaze bounced from Min, to Tack, to me. I looked away.

Great. The last thing I need.

"Noah?" Ethan said quietly.

"Yeah?"

"What are you doing over there?" He was staring a hole through my head. And not just him—Sarah was watching me as she chatted with Jessica and Derrick a few yards up the walkway.

Unconsciously, my shoulders hunched. "I was sitting under a tree. They came over to ask me something."

Ethan glanced at Min. "Well? Why do you want Noah? Looking for arson tips?"

Looks were exchanged behind Ethan's back. No one seriously

thought Min and Tack had firebombed his Wrangler, but Ethan wanted it to be true. So to him, it was.

And yet . . . I actually didn't know. I'd been there when Ethan punched Tack in the courtyard. I'd even tried to stop that nonsense, hoping to distract Ethan from going in for more damage. Thankfully, Myers had taken care of it.

Min had been *furious* with Ethan. I'd met her eye once, during the fight. As crazy as it sounds, part of me thought Ethan might be right. Min struck me as a person who'd get revenge without needing to take credit for it.

Not that I was going to voice that opinion. The *hell* I was getting involved. I spent my days avoiding exactly these types of situations.

"Did your fortune-teller say we did it?" Tack said. "You should've asked if your Jeep was in danger in the first place. Headed things off at the pass." That kid never knew when to shut up.

Min winced. She knew it, too.

Ethan's whole body went still, a bad sign. "Did you say something, Tack?"

Min intervened before he could answer. "Enough, Ethan. Go after him again and I'll tell Myers. Tack covered for you last time, but I'm sick of it. Bullying is so lame. Nobody's impressed."

"You'll tell the principal? Talk about not impressed."

This was so tired. I glanced at Chris. He shook his head sharply. *Don't get involved.*

When I looked back, Min was staring at me. Unnerved, I dropped my gaze.

Ethan didn't miss the exchange. "What, you think Noah is

going to rescue you? Is that what you want?" He slugged my shoulder, flashing a crooked smile. "Sorry, Trailer Park, but you're reaching above your pay grade."

Min's face burned. She glanced at me again, this time with contempt.

I opened my mouth, but nothing came out.

"Come on, Tack." Min grabbed her friend's arm and pulled him toward the courtyard.

"See you guys later!" Ethan called. "Save me a spot in the far corner!"

The others laughed dutifully. Even me. Then Sarah snaked my arm. Flashing white teeth, she guided me up the walkway. "Hey, Noah. What's new?"

"What? Oh. Nothing." My pulse accelerated, and not in a good way. "You?"

"Not much." A few classmates were loitering by the flagpole, but most had gone inside. Yet Sarah leaned close and spoke conspiratorially. "I was thinking of going to the park after school, just to hang out for a while. Do you want to come with me?"

I strolled along beside her, playing it casual, secretly as uncomfortable as I'd ever been. I felt like a surfer who'd spotted a dorsal fin in the waves, then lost sight of it. I didn't know how to discourage this new attention.

"Who's going?" Stalling. We were ten yards from the door, where I could pull away without looking like a prick. "Jessica and everyone?"

Sarah flashed her flirty smile. "I haven't asked anyone else. We never do stuff alone anymore."

Red alert! I could feel the noose tightening. Groped desperately for an escape.

"I'd hate to leave the others out. They always include us." Before she could object, I pivoted, called out to the first people I saw. "Chris! Toby! You guys want to hit the park after school? A bunch of us are going, I think."

The two boys looked at each other, then shrugged, nodding in mild surprise. I was never the one to make plans. I glanced back at Sarah and nearly missed a step. Anger flashed in her eyes before disappearing behind a plastic smile. "I guess that settles it." She released me abruptly and went inside.

All I felt was relief. I was sorry to hurt her feelings—and, frankly, a little worried about what she might do—but I wasn't interested. Sarah was gorgeous and smart, the only daughter of two doctors, but she was also cold and manipulative. When we'd been dating, I'd watched her slyly orchestrate fights among the girls. Potent words dropped here and there, untraceable, that caused major rifts down the road.

Min crashed my thoughts. She was completely different. A raging fire where Sarah was ice. *Why am I comparing them?*

"Hey, space cadet!"

I spun. Ethan waved me over to where he was huddled with Toby and the guys. Charlie seemed worked up about something. "You heard?" he asked excitedly, scratching at his pimply cheeks. I shook my head along with the rest. I'd come straight from Lowell's office and hadn't checked my phone.

"The earthquake?" Ethan said dismissively. "Who cares? It was in Wyoming. I barely woke up."

Charlie puffed, excited to share fresh gossip. "That was just the start. There've been six more since then!"

"They're called aftershocks," I corrected absently. "They couldn't have been much if we didn't feel them."

Charlie's head wagged. "No! Six more *earthquakes*. The biggest was in South America—it set off some volcano in Peru. The news guys can't explain it."

"Like the bees," Toby chimed in.

Derrick squinted his way. "What?"

Toby ran a hand over his shaved scalp. "Something like a million bees in Tennessee all dropped dead at once. It might even be a billion. One second, they're buzzing around, stinging people like a bunch of jerks, then *boom*. All dead." He shrugged. "Apparently that's bad."

Chris laughed. "Nobody believes those conspiracy sites, man. The Anvil is gonna miss, so now they need a new problem to geek out about. You liberty campers are freaking gullible."

Toby shot him a wounded look. "That story was on Buzzfeed, bro. My mom's Facebook timeline, too. Real enough for you?"

First bell rang. Ethan rolled his eyes. "How many more years of this? I swear, working at the grocery store is less painful."

Toby grunted in agreement as we trudged inside. "Graduation can't come fast enough."

Sarah reappeared in the hallway, and my anxiety spiked. I felt my chest constrict for no reason. I stumbled on my feet, suddenly unable to control my breathing. Derrick gave me an odd look, but I played it off, testing my shoe on the floor. Then I ducked into a bathroom when no one was looking.

Alone, I splashed water on my face. Things were always bad after one of my dreams—plus I'd missed two pills—but this was the worst I could remember. I couldn't shake a feeling of dread. The scar on my shoulder was aching. I was a mess.

"Go away," I whispered to the mirror, embarrassed by what I saw there.

"Whatever this is, please go away."

18

PROJECT NEMESIS

File: INTERVIEW TRANSCRIPT: NOAH C. LIVINGSTON ("NL")

Date: JANUARY 4, 2017

Specialist: DR. GERALD LOWELL ("GL")

Subject: TEST PATIENT B, BETA RUN, SESSION 15-A1

NL: I . . . I think . . . it was the worst.

GL: That's understandable. You were only ten years old. You'd dreamed of this man before. You feared him.

NL: [SUBJECT RISES, BEGINS PACING]

GL: How did the day begin?

NL: [SUBJECT PACES] The neighborhood park. I walked there by myself.

GL: You were alone?

NL: [SUBJECT NODS] We were between housekeepers at the time, and my father had divorced again. Tiffany barely lasted six months.

GL: How was your relationship with your father?

NL: Relationship? I barely saw him. [PAUSE] [SUBJECT RETAKES HIS SEAT] It got worse after Tiff left. Dad drank a lot, and the house went to crap after he fired the staff.

No food. The yard was a jungle. We never had clean laundry until I learned how to do it. He'd skip weeks of work, traveling by himself. Or just sitting in the media room, watching movies in the dark.

GL: How was he the morning of your birthday?

NL: [SUBJECT SNORTS] He forgot. I don't think he came out of his bedroom the whole day. Honestly, that was a gift all by itself.

GL: Your father was going through a difficult time. His wife had left him.

NL: Second wife. That's what happens when you treat people like possessions.

GL: Let's move forward in your day. Tell me about the park.

NL: Not much to tell. It's three blocks from my house, down the hill like everything else. I hung out by the swings and played with my Transformers. [PAUSE] The weather was nice. I remember . . . having fun. It was a good morning for me. Until . . .

GL: You saw him.

NL: [SUBJECT NODS]

GL: Where?

NL: On the . . . Walking home. I was heading up Palisade, which is pretty steep. I wasn't looking around, because I had toys in both hands and didn't want to drop them. The next . . . he was at the corner . . . [PAUSE] [SUBJECT SOBS]

GL: Noah, we can . . .

NL: He was sitting in a black car. Watching me. No expression on his face. I . . . I just froze. I couldn't believe it.

GL: Do you have any idea when you fell asleep?

NL: [SUBJECT SHAKES HEAD VIOLENTLY] None. I don't remember lying down, or resting, or anything. It must've been at the park, but the memory is seamless. I don't understand how—

GL: Your brain seems to erase the moment you fall asleep. That brief period of time before powering down and falling into a dream state. A low-level narcolepsy, perhaps, not uncommon in these situations. The main problem lies in your body not shutting down its higher functions, such as movement. For some reason you remain active on a subconscious level, and sleepwalk.

NL: It doesn't feel subconscious. Everything about it seems real.

GL: Tell me what happened next.

NL: He . . . he got out of the car. I tried to run, but he was already too close. He grabbed the back of my shirt. I spun . . . begged him not to . . . He tossed me down. [PAUSE] I rolled . . . tried to run again. Something hit the back of my head. I remember how much it hurt. I . . . If I close my eyes right now, I can *still* feel . . . I can *hear* my skull cracking—

GL: Noah. Calm your breathing.

NL:—my *head* caving in! But I didn't die right away. I struggled, but my arms wouldn't move! Then he hit me again—

GL: That's enough, Noah. Look at me. Noah, *look* at me! [SPECIALIST PLACES HIS HANDS ON SUBJECT] You're safe. We're in my office. It was all just a dream. Understand?

NL: [PAUSE] [SUBJECT NODS]

GL: Let's take a break. Would you like something to drink?

[SESSION SUSPENDED—4:36 PM]

[SESSION RESUMED—4:48 PM]

GL: What happened when you regained consciousness?

NL: [SUBJECT SHRUGS] Nothing, really. I woke up in the cave. Ran home again. [PAUSE] And then you were there, Doctor. Waiting for me in my house.

GL: That's right, Noah. You didn't know, but Tiffany had asked that I visit you on your birthday. No one answered the door when I arrived, but it was open. I wanted to make sure everything was okay, and you walked in the second after I stepped inside. A most fortuitous coincidence, since you clearly needed help.

NL: Tiff. [PAUSE] It's still so weird. I barely knew her, to be honest, and she'd been gone for almost a month. How did she know to make an appointment for me? I never told her anything, and I'd only been your patient for a few weeks.

GL: She must've sensed you needed help, if not exactly why. As for that afternoon? Sometimes we just get lucky. I'm thankful for her intercession every day.

NL: You told me everything was going to be okay if I started taking the pills.

GL: Everything is okay, Noah.

NL: But the dreams haven't stopped. I still sleepwalk.

GL: The important thing is that you know it isn't real. We're taking steps. By talking through your dreams like this, we'll discover the key to controlling them. Trust me.

NL: I do trust you. [PAUSE] You're the only one I trust. You didn't tell my father what happened that day. I . . . I never thanked you.

GL: No thanks are necessary. You can always trust me, Noah. I'm here for you.

19

I picked myself up off the blacktop.

Ethan trotted to the top of the key and held up his hand for the ball. Derrick tossed it to him, his brown skin gleaming in the afternoon sunlight. Toby stood beneath the basket, pale, pudgy, and annoyed at having to play on the "skins" team in front of the girls. His bald head only came up to Derrick's shoulders, but he was trying to guard him anyway.

"Get your head right, Livingston." Ethan set the ball on the ground, panting slightly as he tugged on his shorts. "It's game point. You're going down this time."

"That was a moving pick," Chris complained, tucking sweat-drenched red hair behind his ears. "You leveled Noah. That should be our ball."

Ethan rolled his eyes. "Quit being a pansy. This is pickup basketball, not synchronized swimming." Glancing at me, he adopted a singsong voice as he picked up the ball. "Did I foul you, Noah-bear? Are your feelings hurt?"

I shook my head. Ethan grinned, then fired the ball into my stomach. "Good. Check."

I tossed it back just as hard. "Check."

"Oh ho! Looks like somebody finally woke up!" Then he darted right, trying to muscle past me to the basket. Derrick and Mike backpedaled to give him room—it was clear he didn't intend to pass.

Ethan is strong, but I'm quicker. We both knew I was the better player, but in the park I usually dialed it down. Ethan could be super-competitive, and these games meant nothing to me. I didn't see the point in trying too hard.

But he was going at me harder than usual. I'd hit the deck three times, all courtesy of him. My competitive flame is slow to ignite, but that last forearm shiver had flipped a switch.

I snaked sideways and cut off Ethan's drive. He tried to reverse his dribble, but I poked the ball away. Gathering it behind the three-point linc, I turned to shoot.

Red-faced, Ethan lunged to block my shot. I head-faked and took a bounce to my left. Watched him fly by. Then I pulled up. Swish. The minute the ball zipped through the net, I knew it was a mistake.

"Game!" Toby shouted, slapping five with Chris before rushing over to me. He crouched down and tried to lift me up. "Noah schools Ethan for the win!"

Ugh. Thanks for nothing, Toby.

Ethan spat on the blacktop. "He traveled!"

Everyone looked away. I clearly hadn't.

"No way, bro." Chris was already walking toward the bench. "Game over."

Mike followed his brother, ripping his shirt off and wiping his spiky red hair. He shot me a glance. *Not smart.* And he was right.

Derrick and Toby also drifted off the court, a subtle rejection of Ethan's claim. Sensing he wasn't going to get his way, Ethan turned and kicked the ball into the playground. "Cheaters can chase."

I sighed inwardly. Walked after my ball. Ethan was exhausting sometimes.

I snagged it from under a jungle gym and trudged back to the group, thinking of ways to salve Ethan's pride. At times like this, I honestly wasn't sure we were really friends.

We were in the park beside town square. Everyone was playing it cool, like the Anvil scare never happened. The girls had shown up midway through the first game and were sitting in the grass, gossiping, voicing the occasional cheer when someone scored. Sarah had whistled for me after three made baskets. Ethan's face got redder each time.

Reaching the bench, I was relieved to see Toby and Derrick taking off their basketball shoes. We wouldn't be running it back. "I say we cruise by the trailer park," Ethan said abruptly. "Noah can visit his girlfriend, and my good friend Tack might have more funny comments."

This again? Ethan was obsessed. But I kept my mouth shut and let the jab slide, shoving the ball into my duffel bag.

"Had enough?" Ethan said. "Taking your ball and going home?"

Kind of stupid, since we were clearly done. Mike and Chris had changed into fresh tees, and Toby was slipping on his sandals.

But I nodded anyway, grinning sheepishly. "Gotta quit before my luck runs out. You almost broke me in half."

Ethan rolled his eyes, but chuckled. "Nice shot, by the way. I almost flew to Spokane."

We bumped fists, and I relaxed. Collapsed on the bench. The air was crisp on my bare skin, just a shade north of chilly. I glanced at my phone. Nothing from Dad. The time was 4:14. With any luck, I could be home in twenty minutes.

Although . . . if we did *go by the trailer park, I might see Min.*

I'd been thinking about our encounter all day.

What had she wanted to tell me? A reason I shouldn't trust Lowell?

Something about her had gotten under my skin. When the guys got Neanderthal drunk and started rating the hottest girls in school, Min's name never came up. I thought that was crazy.

Am I the only one who sees it?

She'd shown guts defending Tack. Min didn't back down from Ethan like everyone else. She definitely had more balls than me. *Just like when we were little. When that weird doctor took us away from school.*

I sat up straight. Where had *that* come from?

I ran a hand over my eyes, sweating anew as memories came roaring back.

The questions. Shots. Min had held my hand that day. Had been my buddy.

Principal Myers had ushered us into an SUV and shut the door, then argued with that doctor in the parking lot. The doctor had shoved two pieces of paper into his hands. Myers had yelled something at him, nose to nose, before limping back inside.

Then the ride. We'd gone to some building in the land reserve, and then . . . then . . .

I don't remember what happened next.

How can that be?

My heart began to pound. Min said we might be involved in some weird project. She'd learned something important. *And now she's pissed at me.*

I shot a hooded glance at Ethan. At times I almost hated him, despite how hard I tried to get him to like me. Then I blinked. Ducked my head.

You've got your own issues. Don't go looking for more.

I never did. I might hate the cowardly voice in my head, but I always listened. It occurred to me that it sounded a lot like Dr. Lowell.

"Well, Noah?" Ethan boomed.

I started. The others were looking at me, wearing their typical Noah-zoned-out-again expressions. Chris seemed amused as he zipped up his bag, while Toby crossed his eyes. Derrick shook his head, muttering something about ADHD.

"Sorry," I said, quickly pulling on a clean shirt. "What'd you say?"

Ethan closed his eyes, shook his head with exaggerated slowness. "What color is the sky in your world, Noah?" I forced a laugh with the others. "We want to hang out at your place," he continued, obviously repeating what I'd missed. "Your dad's still gone, so it's cool, right?"

"When's he getting back, anyway?" Derrick yawned, stretching all six and a half feet of his lean frame. "He's been gone awhile, right?"

I shrugged. "Whenever he feels like it. Two weeks. Tomorrow. Who knows?"

Derrick sighed wistfully. "Man, you've got it good. Wish *my* parents would take off for a week. I'd throw a party every night."

Chris bumped fists with Derrick. "Noah's dad is in Italy right now, with a model half his age. Drinking wine and doing whatever the hell he wants. That guy is the *man*!"

Yeah. He's great.

"So?" Ethan threw his bag over his shoulder. "Come on, Livingston. Let's go to your place. I want to shoot pool."

I tried to think of a way out. Blanked. "Sure. Okay."

"Good." As if he'd never considered I might refuse. Cupping his hands, he yelled across the park. "Hey, ladies! We're all going to Noah's house. Meet us there in twenty." Jessica waved as the girls began gathering their things.

Irritation sparked. Typical Ethan, calling the shots, even when they weren't his to call. My anger was so hot and unexpected, I gave voice to it before I thought better. "Is it your house or mine? Hard to tell."

Ethan halted, surprised, then amused. "You got a problem with—"

He never finished.

The earth beneath our feet leapt. Everyone went tumbling as a groan echoed across the valley. Toby careened into the bench, opening a gash on his forehead. The others scrambled around like crabs, faces terrified as the ground shook like a living thing.

"Earthquake!" Chris shouted needlessly. His brother staggered over and threw an arm around him. I watched with sick fascination as a swing set shook off its moorings. There was an explosion somewhere up the block. Car alarms screamed as glass shattered all along Main Street. The lake roiled and hissed.

The vibrations stopped. I rose unsteadily, overwhelmed by all the alarms going off at once. The girls streaked over to where Derrick was examining Toby's cut. Jessica was crying, holding her elbow. Everyone else seemed okay.

"Yo, look at that!" Chris pointed to black smoke rising from the docks. "Is that coming from the marina?"

Mike shook his head, jarred into actually speaking. "Mechanic's shop next door. Oil drums, I bet."

Toby winced as Derrick pressed a sock to his scalp. "They better get on that blaze, or the whole waterfront might go up," Derrick said. As if in response, a siren joined the clamor.

"Busy week for those guys," Chris joked. Ethan glared at him, and the smile vanished.

Commotion down the block. People had gathered in front of a broken store window, their backs to us as they mobbed something we couldn't see. Cries erupted from the group. A woman spun away, hands covering her mouth.

"What's going on?" I whispered.

"I don't want to know," Jessica whined, hugging her body tight. I was surprised to discover I felt the same. I was past my stress limit. I wanted to go home and hide in my room.

Ethan began jogging across the square. After a slight hesitation, we all followed. Approaching the storefront, I swallowed hard, certain we were about to see something horrible. A crushed body, or some poor sap impaled by a lamppost.

But it was much, much worse.

Valley Home Entertainment Specialists is a tech shop owned

by Charlie Bell's mom. Half the display screens were busted, but a 65-incher still worked, tuned to CNN. Onscreen, in vivid 4K OLED, was a nightmare.

"*The devastation in Portland defies comprehension*," a shaky voice said as a helicopter flyover filled the screen. "*Officials believe the epicenter of the massive 9.2 earthquake was twenty miles offshore, along the long-dormant Cascadia subduction zone. As you can see, very little of downtown remains standing. After the initial destruction, a tsunami swept in from the coast, washing all the way to the I–5 corridor. It's already being called the worst natural disaster in the history of North America. Fires are burning in the neighborhoods of—*"

A second voice broke in as the feed cut to another city. *Seattle*, people whispered, their faces slack with shock. A helicopter zoomed in on the remains of the Space Needle, which had snapped in half like a chopstick and lay in ruins on the streets below. The rest of the city looked like a war zone. In hushed tones, the narrator reported similar scenes of destruction in Tacoma, Vancouver, Astoria, and a dozen other places, with tens of thousands feared dead, drowned, or trapped beneath the rubble.

"Holy crap." Toby was staring, wide-eyed. "The Pacific Northwest just got smashed."

I didn't want to see any more. A familiar panic was rising in my chest, squeezing the breath from my lungs. I slipped to the back of the crowd, then ducked down an alley toward the lakefront.

Smoke billowed along the wharf as the fire department battled near the marina. Thankfully the fire appeared small, and the millions of gallons of available lake water gave our volunteers the upper hand. I walked west for three blocks, then turned back uphill, planning to bolt home. I'd lock myself in, and if the others came by, I'd pretend I wasn't there.

Instead, I stopped dead.

Stared.

Halfway up the alley, Principal Myers was huddled with Sheriff Watson. The two were arguing heatedly, Myers pounding a fist into his open palm as he made some point. Then a shift in the breeze cleared more smoke, revealing several others.

Dr. Lowell was standing beside Myers, frowning with his arms crossed. Beside him loomed a tall, thin-faced man in a bow tie—Dr. Fanelli, the town's other psychiatrist. The two shrinks were rumored to dislike each other, and I'd never seen them together before.

Myers cut off abruptly as another man raised a hand. Though his back was to me, I could tell he was wearing a military uniform. The others listened with varying degrees of impatience as he spoke. When he finished, everyone started talking at once.

My instincts warned me not to be seen. I was witnessing a conference no one was supposed to know about, I was sure. So I slunk back to the corner and took cover, then peeked around again. Min's warning echoed in my head.

A cell rang. The officer removed a phone from his vest, listened a moment, then hung up. "We need to wait. He's coming now."

I stared, torn between curiosity and a deep impulse to leave and forget the whole thing. Why get involved in something I could avoid? I hesitated, unable to get my feet to move. Then another man joined the circle, and my world collapsed around me.

Polished boots. Silver sunglasses.

Black Suit strode from the whirling smoke, a nightmare come to life.

He was here. He was real. He was speaking to my goddamn psychiatrist.

I'm not asleep. God help me, but I'm really not this time.

I collapsed to the curb, then scrambled out of sight. My stomach heaved and I vomited on the pavement. Dazed, I rolled over and lay there, staring up at the char-stained sky.

I was never asleep. Not for any of it.

Everything Lowell told me was a lie.

Then another thought exploded in my head.

GET OUT OF HERE NOW OR HE'LL KILL YOU AGAIN.

Staggering to my feet, I ran as fast as I could.

20

PROJECT NEMESIS

File: INTERVIEW TRANSCRIPT: NOAH C. LIVINGSTON ("NL")

Date: MARCH 30, 2017

Specialist: DR. GERALD LOWELL ("GL")

Subject: TEST PATIENT B, BETA RUN, SESSION 15-C4

NL: I was so desperate not to fall asleep.

GL: Understandable, given your previous dreams. I know you don't like talking about your twelfth birthday, Noah, but we must treat that dream the same as the others.

NL: [SUBJECT SHUDDERS] It was so . . . surreal. [PAUSE] I was home, but not alone. Carol was there, my father's third wife. She was downstairs the whole time. At least, I think she was. How could I have gotten past her in my sleep? How did I dry off, or get my clothes on?

GL: Take me through what you remember.

NL: [SUBJECT SIGHS] I was upstairs, watching movies. All I could think about was bedtime. Being alone in my room, with the dream coming. I planned to stay awake all night. It was already dark out, but not late, maybe an hour past dinner.

GL: Your father?

NL: Working. The new housekeeper was in her room. I thought Carol was downstairs watching *Real Housewives*.

GL: How did you feel about Carol?

NL: About her? I felt nothing, really. She was my dad's third wife after Mom died. I was numb to the process by then. Carol was just a lady living in my house.

GL: I see. Please continue.

NL: For some reason, I decided to take a bath. [SUBJECT SHAKES HEAD] So, so stupid. Of course I passed out. That's what baths do to you.

GL: Do you remember falling asleep?

NL: [SUBJECT SHAKES HEAD] I closed my eyes a few times, but thought I stayed awake. I had music blaring and all the lights on. Obviously I didn't, because suddenly I was looking up and . . . and . . . he was there. In the bathroom. Standing over the tub, with no place for me to run.

GL: You knew by then that the man wasn't real. How did you react?

NL: I squeezed my eyes shut. Told myself I was dreaming. But when I opened them again, he was still there. I remember his sunglasses fogging in the steam. The damn black suit. Nothing different about him, not a single detail.

GL: What did you do next?

NL: Nothing. I . . . I just sat there. I didn't move. Or scream, or run, or fight back. [SUBJECT PAUSES] I knew he was there to kill me, but I just waited for it. I made it easy for him.

GL: It's okay, Noah. Remember, the experience wasn't real.

NL: It felt real, okay!?

GL: Yes it did, and does. I know that. Would you like to stop for a minute?

NL: [SUBJECT LAUGHS HARSHLY] Not much else to tell. Something dropped from his sleeve into his hand. A black metal rod. He stuck one end in the water and pressed a button. Who knows how many volts I dreamed up? Enough to kill me fast! I guess I should thank myself for that.

GL: Anything else?

NL: I might've yelled for Carol at the last minute. Didn't matter, though. Only difference this time was, everything went white instead of black. Something new for your notes.

GL: Does it bother you that I record details? I hope you know by now what I seek to accomplish by reviewing these dreams now that you've reached adolescence.

NL: [SUBJECT WAVES A HAND] I woke up in the cave. I was dry, with clean clothes on, so add sleep-getting-dressed to my subconscious skill set. But this time my father caught me sneaking in from the yard. Carol was crying, but she went upstairs when he started yelling. That was the first time I realized he knew I was crazy.

GL: I've never shared our conversations with him, Noah. Please believe me when I say that. I'm bound by ethics to never discuss what we talk about, not even with your father. When we first began treatment, I gave him a broad diagnosis and told him you and I needed to meet regularly in order to work on the underlying issues. He was made aware of your sleepwalking, but that was a safety concern I couldn't withhold from your legal guardian.

But I haven't shared any details of your dreams. Not the murders. Not Black Suit. Not any of it.

NL: Well, he knew enough. Dad ripped into me. Called me a coward. A "mental defective."

GL: That's terrible. Those words must've been very painful to hear.

NL: He said I wasn't a "Livingston man," whatever the hell that is. Drunk a-hole seems closest.

GL: I'm sorry he said those things. Did you respond?

NL: I ran up to my room and locked the door. Downed my pill. Then I called you. I remember you answered on the first ring. I was so grateful.

GL: I'm glad you made that call. Truly.

NL: Happy birthday, right? Twelve years old, and a lunatic.

21

The doors were locked.

Security system activated. I sat behind my father's desk, staring at a computer monitor.

I didn't want to think about earthquakes, tsunamis, Portland, or any of that awful stuff. Instead I was watching video feeds from fourteen different cameras positioned in and around my house. A loaded Beretta M9 pistol was resting on my lap.

I couldn't remember how long I'd been sitting there. Hours, at least. The sun had gone down, and all the lights in the house were off. I wanted it to look like no one was home. Only the greenish glow of the screen betrayed my presence.

He's real.

My mind cringed every time I thought it, but the truth was inescapable.

I *saw* him. In broad daylight, on a Wednesday, in the middle of freaking town.

How can that be? If the murders aren't dreams, how am I still alive?

I laughed out loud. Found I couldn't stop. A part of me knew I was barely holding on—one small slip from really losing it—but I didn't know what else to do. I couldn't process Black Suit as a living, breathing person.

Was he coming for me again? He'd said it was the last time.

I shivered, realizing that conversation had actually taken place, out in my driveway three nights before. I didn't remember falling asleep because I hadn't. Not then, or any time before.

A stranger has been killing me over and over and over. How? Why?

A dog barked and I shot to my feet, the Beretta tumbling to the floor. I grabbed it and set it on the desk. The gun was my father's, one of many he kept in a case. He thought I didn't know the combination, but of course I did.

With a moan, I dropped into the soft leather desk chair. Thought about popping a dozen blue pills, then angrily dismissed the idea.

The pills came from Lowell. Lowell was a goddamn liar.

I wasn't crazy. I was being played.

But wasn't that even worse? *At least crazy made sense.*

"Stop," I said aloud in the dark, empty office. I liked the feeling of control it gave me, so I kept it up. "Don't panic. Think."

The truth was overwhelming. A man who regularly slaughtered me just had a secret meeting with my principal, my psychiatrist, and the head of law enforcement in my county.

I wiped a hand across my face.

Was I really sure?

The whole thing was impossible. The assassin of my nightmares was a living, breathing person, and spent his time in a secret conspiracy with a bunch of local nobodies? Oh yeah, side note—apparently I couldn't die. *Come on.*

Did I imagine the whole thing? A new level of regression?

My eyes shot to my cell phone, charging by the door. I was seeing things that weren't possible. Dr. Lowell would have answers. He'd know what was wrong and tell me what to do. Maybe he had another pill I needed.

Lowell could make it all go away.

I walked over and unplugged it. Pulled up Lowell's number.

I was having a breakdown. He would fix me. I didn't have to deal with this alone.

The AC kicked on, and chilled air ruffled my sweaty hair. Traces of diesel smoke tickled my nose.

I dropped the phone as if snakebitten.

No. I'd been there. I'd seen it. This wasn't a hallucination, or dream, or whatever other BS story Lowell wanted me to believe.

Min's face popped into my head. She'd wanted to tell me something.

I felt a jolt of adrenaline.

Did she know about Black Suit?

Something zipped by the window. Heart in my throat, I crept over and peered outside.

My next-door neighbor was running up the street in a bathrobe.

I blinked. A Labradoodle puppy wandered onto my driveway, marking the ground every couple of feet. The woman overtook her dog, snatching, scolding, and hugging the animal all at the same time. As she turned for home, I could tell she'd been crying.

I turned on the TV, was instantly bombarded with heartbreaking images. People had talked about the Big One for years, but it was always California. The news was making clear that the Northwest had taken the knockout punch instead.

Flipping around, other news was just as bad. A twin tsunami caused by the quake had pummeled eastern Japan, leaving half of Hokkaido underwater. In Manitoba, stampeding cattle had trampled a mining town, charging north at full speed until the herd collapsed from exhaustion. Even the experts were stumped.

Eventually, I couldn't take it. The walls began closing in, a familiar claustrophobia tightening its grip around my neck. I had to get out of there. Needed to be somewhere I felt safe.

I switched the alarm to "away" and snuck out the back door.

Ever since I was little, I would hide there.

As the moon rose in a cloudless sky, I was high in the branches of a cedar. Only five minutes from my home, but it felt like a thousand miles.

My fort originated as a hunting platform. The ladder had rotted away, but the tree limbs were close enough to climb up by, if you knew the route. The hide was thirty feet off the ground, with room for three. Moss-covered sides made it virtually invisible.

Somewhere no one could find me. The only place I ever truly relaxed.

Gazing out over the valley, I chuckled softly.

Sixteen years old, and hiding in a tree house.

I thought back on what I'd witnessed in the alley, and a shudder ran through me. I didn't fight the sensation. It felt appropriate, so I let it have its moment.

Why would Fire Lake residents meet with a serial killer?

Was he a killer? I shifted, uncomfortable with the thought.

I was alive, obviously. Whatever was happening to me, I kept recovering from it. I refused to travel down the road of thinking I was *actually* dead. I'd believed myself crazy for too long to go there.

I straightened, remembering the guy in the uniform. A general? Why was *he* there? At first he'd seemed in charge, but only until Black Suit showed up. So was this a military thing, or something else?

Engine sounds. Down on Shore Point Road, headlights appeared in a line.

I peeked over the sill as heavy trucks rumbled around the lake. Soldiers hung from the bumpers, weapons glinting in the moonlight.

"What in the . . ." A group of vans passed with black starburst symbols on their sides. Then eight mammoth big rigs. I couldn't imagine how they'd gotten over the Plank.

There'd been talk of trucks cutting through town on Announcement night, but I hadn't seen them. Rumors said they drove onto the government land at the eastern end of the valley. As I watched, these vehicles disappeared into those same woods.

I sat back, perplexed. Troops and trucks were piling up, hiding in the one spot nobody ever went. Something was going on.

Suddenly, I felt very alone. I was up a damn tree, a thousand yards from anyone, all by myself. No one knew I was there. No one was waiting for me to return.

I slipped from the fort and climbed to the ground. Crouched, listening, one hand straying toward my pocket. A twig snapped, and my nerve broke. I ran as fast as I could, certain I'd feel a hand on my shoulder at any moment.

I unlocked my front door and leapt inside. Then nearly wet myself when the security system demanded a code. With trembling fingers I input the numbers, then slammed and locked the door, reactivating the alarm.

I was alone in the house. Dad was still in Europe—I'd gotten a text that afternoon griping about foreign food and canceled flights.

Black Suit could be hunting me at that very moment.

I stumbled to the living room and slumped down on the couch. Pulled the Beretta from my jeans. Holding it with both hands, I watched the door, preparing for a sleepless night.

22

PROJECT NEMESIS

File: INTERVIEW TRANSCRIPT: NOAH C. LIVINGSTON ("NL")

Date: JUNE 8, 2017

Specialist: DR. GERALD LOWELL ("GL")

Subject: TEST PATIENT B, BETA RUN, SESSION 15-F2

GL: Today I'd like to talk about your fourteenth birthday, if that's okay with you.

NL: [SUBJECT SHRUGS]

GL: It's been almost two years since that day. You told me what happened when I found you in the woods, but please remember what we're trying to accomplish when we discuss your dreams. Details are important. Consider it a mental housecleaning.

NL: I'm not feeling any better.

GL: Excuse me?

NL: About the dreams. We've gone over nearly all of them, and they bother me just as much. I'm still nervous all the time. I still don't feel safe. If you thought I'd be cured by rehashing them, you were wrong.

GL: These things take time, Noah. If you lance a boil, the wound itself still must heal. I think you'll find that this process achieves great results over time. Now, may we get started?

NL: [SUBJECT SHRUGS]

GL: This one was different from the others, was it not?

NL: No. That's the problem.

GL: But, more so than on your other birthdays, that day you actively tried to resist.

NL: [SUBJECT SIGHS] I woke up at dawn and took my father's fishing skiff out onto the lake. It's just a rowboat, really, nothing special. I thought, if I can get out in the middle of the water, and stay there all day, I'd be alone. Nothing could distract me. I'd stay awake. I hate boats, so how would I fall asleep on one?

GL: And you took further measures, correct?

NL: Yes. I traded Toby for some of his ADHD medication, the kind that's supposed to keep you awake. I also had a four-pack of Red Bull, and enough food for a week.

GL: Taking medication that isn't prescribed to you is dangerous, Noah. I understand why you did it, but I feel obligated to bring that up. Further, mixing a controlled substance with even something as common as caffeine can have unexpected side effects.

NL: I didn't care. I wasn't going to sleep for twenty-four hours, period. I'd stay out in the boat all day, then go to this bowling-alley birthday thing my friends we throwing that night. If I didn't nod off, I couldn't dream. And you can't sleepwalk across a frigging lake. Then I'd surround myself with people at the party. I'd beat my condition for once. Then . . . maybe . . . maybe it'd be over.

GL: [PAUSE] But it didn't work.

NL: [SUBJECT SHAKES HEAD]

GL: I know this is hard to hear, Noah, but your condition can't be cured by external measures like drugging yourself to stay awake. There's a switch inside your brain that is tuned to your even-year birthdays. You will sleep no matter how hard you fight it. Our job is to disable that switch by finding out what created it in the first place.

NL: You give me drugs. Why are they supposed to work?

GL: Your prescription is highly targeted to the complex chemistry of brain function. It aims to ease a path to an internal fix, not overpower the disorder, as you attempted to do with stimulants. But we're getting off track. Tell me what happened.

NL: There was no clear break. I was out there for hours. I put on sunscreen twice. Fished some. It was incredibly boring. Still, right up to the moment I heard the engine, I felt totally alert. [PAUSE] But it must've happened. Because suddenly there's another boat headed right for me.

GL: Did you recognize the vessel?

NL: [SUBJECT SNORTS] It was my dad's speedboat. I'm not allowed to touch it. Suddenly, I'm stuck in a rowboat in the center of the lake, and I realize how idiotic I've been. I can't escape a speedboat with two paddles, and—

GL: It's a dream, Noah. Don't beat yourself up. You can't outrun your brain in any sort of contraption.

NL: [SUBJECT NODS] You're . . . you're right. It's just, it was such a bad idea. You can barely see land from the middle of Fire Lake, much less hear anything. I'd made it so easy for him.

GL: Please continue.

NL: It was laughable. Black Suit cruised up right next to the skiff. He only looked at me once—like, just to verify he was killing the right person—then he tossed something into my boat.

GL: And?

NL: Boom. I barely had time to think before a wave of heat tossed me from the boat. I hit the water. Tried to swim, but my legs weren't working. I looked down, and the left one . . . my left leg wasn't—

GL: Move on from that, Noah.

NL: It wasn't there! I . . . sank. The light fell farther and farther away . . . only I knew the light wasn't moving . . . I was the one . . . dropping into the cold . . . I stopped fighting . . .

GL: Let's stop for a moment.

NL: [SUBJECT SHAKES HEAD] No! Why?

GL: I don't want to upset—

NL: [SUBJECT LAUGHS] Don't want to upset me, Doctor? We're talking about the day I was blown up and drowned. This was never going to be fun.

GL: You're distressed. We can pick this up another time.

NL: No. [PAUSE] Please. I'm sorry. I just want to finish. This is the last one.

GL: Very well. Tell me what you remember about waking up.

NL: It was just after sunset. I rolled over and cried. For a full hour. In a way, the cave has become a comforting place for me. Strange, isn't it? But I've never been hurt in there. And it's always over. I don't have to worry. [PAUSE] How could I have slept? I was in a boat, out on the water. How could I have rowed all the way back to shore while unconscious? It doesn't make *any*—

GL: Let's finish the details, please.

NL: You know them. You were there. Next thing I knew, you were kneeling beside me on the cavern floor. Telling me I was okay.

GL: I was worried about you. It was your birthday, but I couldn't get in touch. I went to your house first, but your father wasn't home.

NL: Of course not.

GL: I found your iPad. I know I shouldn't have, but I decided to use it to track your iPhone, just to be sure you weren't thinking of harming yourself. The program led me to the pond, and the cave where I found you.

NL: [SUBJECT NODS] Do I need to go over the rest? You took me home. I never said a thing. I even went to the stupid party, chilling with my friends while this silly girl drama played out, like some normal-Noah robot. That night was the first time I ever got drunk. Carol put me to bed and promised not to tell my father. I don't think she ever did.

GL: Was there anything else?

NL: I . . . Yes. I never told you the last part.

GL: Please do, Noah. We can't know what might be crucially important until we discuss it.

NL: [PAUSE] I woke up later that night and got sick. Then I snuck out, down to our boathouse. The skiff was there, just like always. I . . . I cried again. For a while.

GL: That must've been difficult. I know how certain you were that you hadn't slept. You stated it repeatedly on our drive to your house. Proof of the opposite couldn't have felt good.

NL: [SUBJECT NODS] I went back to my room and took my pill. Emptied my pockets. Found everything just like I'd carried it onto the boat, even Toby's pills. Then . . . then I . . .

GL: [PAUSE] Then you what?

NL: [SUBJECT FAILS TO RESPOND]

GL: Noah? Is something wrong?

NL: [SUBJECT FAILS TO RESPOND]

GL: Noah, what is it?

NL: [PAUSE] It's . . . nothing, I guess. I just remembered something.

GL: Yes?

NL: Right before I went to bed, I . . . I tried to check my phone. You said you'd called and left messages. But . . . it was completely dead. I remember now that the battery died sometime around noon, out on the boat.

GL: The messages were there. You told me you listened to them the next morning.

NL: Yeah. [PAUSE] Yeah, I did. But . . .

GL: Please, Noah. Tell me.

NL: How did you know where to find me again? In the cave, I mean. You can't track a dead cell phone that way.

GL: You must be mistaken about the phone. Probably because you fell asleep.

NL: [SUBJECT SHAKES HEAD] But . . . No . . . I . . . I remember being mad about forgetting to charge it. It was the only mistake I made in preparing, and it was a pain in the ass not having a working phone at the party. I'm almost sure—

GL: I'm so sorry, Noah, but we're going to have to stop now. I just remembered I have another appointment. We'll pick this back up another time.

23

I awoke in a cold sweat.

Sprang up from the couch. Despite everything, I'd zonked out. First time in days.

Nightmares. Real ones this time.

Black Suit, creeping up the stairs, and me with nowhere to run. Black Suit, stalking me through the halls of Fire Lake High, whistling tunelessly as I scrambled for a hiding place. He was everywhere. Inescapable. Implacable.

I hurried to my father's office. Checked the security feeds. Nothing. All clear. I collapsed into an oversized reading chair. Blowing out a ragged breath, I tried to think rationally. Black Suit was alive, but that didn't mean our pattern was suddenly meaningless. There was no reason to think he'd show up for a special "bonus" slaying tonight.

Then another thought struck me, and I sat up straight.

Black Suit *was* a real person. Which meant he had to eat, and sleep. Which meant, logically, he had to be staying somewhere.

In the valley, almost certainly—it was thirty miles to the closest town with guest rooms.

I can probably find him.

My father owned the largest resort in Fire Lake, and could access the integrated booking system used by every bed-and-breakfast and hotel in town. Normally that wouldn't help much—most places stayed at least half full, even in fall—but *this* year the Anvil had kept nearly everyone at home. Active reservations were scarce.

I logged in as my father. His password was a joke: EQUITY. The name of his first boat. Though forced to use them, Hunter Livingston disdained computers and the silly "online webs," mainly because he was hopeless with technology. Despising things he didn't understand was one of his favorite pastimes.

Inside the system, I found what I'd expected: blank ledgers across the grid. There were less than a dozen reservations, and half had been canceled. The rest were easily dismissible to someone familiar with our town. I didn't know much about Black Suit, but you couldn't keep a low profile at Waterfront Court, especially when no one else was staying there.

Disappointed, I tapped a few more keys. Nearly gasped.

There was a single booking at Powder Ridge Ski Lodge.

My father's resort.

"What is this . . ." I pulled the listing. A one-bedroom suite was blocked out by special code. *Indefinitely.* Even more strangely, the reservation was in the boutique chalet at the top of the slopes rather than the main lodge at the base of the mountain.

My fingers drummed the desktop. Rooms up there weren't

usually available out of season. Known as Chimney Rock, the facility was summerized from June until the first good snow, usually sometime in mid-October.

I sat back. Why would anyone be up there now? It was well out of the way, and there were cheaper places by the lake. Plus, the mountaintop village was closed. Literally everything you'd need was ten minutes downslope.

My shoulders tensed. The more I considered logistics, the less sense it made. There was no good reason for anyone to stay there this time of year. *Unless you're trying to go unnoticed.*

My hands began to tremble. This was it. I'd found him.

New questions dog-piled. Who made this reservation? It didn't follow the proper format. Which meant my dad had probably keyed it in personally, something he rarely did.

I went cold.

Had my father booked a room for my killer?

My breathing quickened. It all felt too big for me. Like I was juggling thirty knives at once. What did I know about conspiracies? I was the dope who'd listened to Dr. Lowell for years!

Min didn't. She figured that bastard out.

I had a sudden impulse to find her. Min said she had information that something big was going down. Maybe we could figure it out together.

You mean she could figure it out for you.

The self-reproach was like a slap. I didn't know anything yet. Had nothing but a hotel reservation. What would I actually tell Min? That I maybe sorta kinda thought a bad guy was staying on the mountaintop? That I needed her to check on it for me?

I'm going there.

I stood abruptly, terrified by my snap decision. But the idea firmed in my mind.

Black Suit always came for me. Found me. Killed me.

He was always the hunter.

But this time the story would be different. Screw the consequences.

I was coming for him.

I took the Tahoe. It's black with tinted windows, and runs quiet. The drive is longer heading counterclockwise around the lake, but I didn't want to be seen. Even that early—the dashboard said 6:58 a.m.—people might be up and about in town.

Plus, there was a loaded Beretta M9 resting on the passenger seat.

I'd waited two hours before leaving, anxiously pacing the house, timing my drive up the mountain so that the sun would crest as I reached its apex. I wanted to catch Black Suit unaware. See him in the flesh a second time. But perhaps even more than that, I wanted to catch him doing something basic. Something human. Watching my nightmare assassin engage in as simple an activity as combing his hair, or eating a breakfast burrito, might help chase away the terror still lurking in my brain.

I reached the eastern end of the lake and turned north. My eyes strayed to the woods on my right. I thought of the trucks I'd spotted from my tree house, one more unfathomable development in a week full of them. But I put that mystery from my mind. I was heading to my father's ski resort to intercept a serial killer, and I still didn't have a plan.

The gates were closed, but I knew the code. I pulled into a parking lot facing the main pavilion. All quiet. No lights or other vehicles. The place could not have looked more shut down.

I turned onto a narrow strip of blacktop winding up the mountain and killed the headlights, familiar enough with the road that I could drive it blind. The sky was morphing from charcoal to ash as I reached the summit. I pulled around behind the shopping village and parked out of sight. Turned off the engine. Then my movements grew stilted as I ran out of things to do inside the car. *This is where my genius ends.*

A glance at the gun. My stomach did a cartwheel.

Why'd I bring it? Sitting there in the parking lot, I became uneasy with my intentions. Back at home I'd had some troubling thoughts. Whispers of a dark idea. But up here in the rapidly growing light, it all seemed crazy.

I shouldn't be here.

I almost left. Turned the key, punched the gas, and fired downhill with my tail between my legs. Instead I shoved the gun into the glove box, opened the door, and stepped out. A footpath led to a small plaza in the center of the complex. I scurried forward in a crouch, feeling both foolish and exposed at the same time. The stores were all empty, with jaunty door signs saying things like, "Closed until . . . SNOW!"

Something caught my eye—a shiny object between two wooden benches. I crept over, discovered a small satellite dish on a mobile pedestal. As I watched, it swiveled sharply, making me jump.

I whirled to see if anyone was around. I knew for a fact this wasn't resort equipment—cable and Internet uplinks ran through a cell tower on the back side of the mountain. Whoever was up here had impressive hardware for company.

Light struck my eyes and I flinched, but it was just the sun topping the mountains. The world brightened. I shrank back, then hurried toward the slopes. As I emerged from the shops, the valley spread out below me. The view was breathtaking, even with the slopes naked and dry. A part of my mind whispered what a great surveillance point it made. Another voice gloomily noted how well you could see the front gate. Had I turned off my headlights before pulling in?

Stop wasting time. If you're going to spy, do it. Then get out of here.

The chalet was to the right of the village, set slightly back in a stand of the pine trees. I crept toward it as ski-lift chairs rattled in the breeze, haunting and lonely.

At the far end of the complex, I peered across a stretch of grass separating the buildings. The suite in question was on the slope-facing side. No cover if someone happened to be looking.

My hands began to sweat. I wiped them on my pants. Ran a palm across my face.

I can't do this. What a stupid idea.

An engine coughed to life. I pressed close to the wall, ready to bolt as soon as I figured out which direction to run. Squeaking tires, slowly fading. Someone had just left the Chimney Rock parking lot.

Go look. Find out if it's him. Then get the hell gone.

I sprinted across the grass. Ducked into a thicket, gulping air, exhilarated and terrified at once. This was so unlike me. I never risked anything. But today I was risking *everything*.

The suite was directly before me. A ski-out accommodation, it had a ground-floor patio accessed by a sliding glass door. For five solid minutes I watched it as the sun rose behind me. No sound. No movement. But I couldn't see inside.

Finally, I rose and bolted onto the patio, flattening myself against the wall and praying like hell no one was inside. When nothing happened, I reached out and pushed the door's handle. It slid open soundlessly.

Blood pounding in my ears, I took a peek. Let out a breath. Empty.

The room was tidy, but lived in. The bed had been hastily made. A towel hung on the bathroom door. Someone was staying there, but nothing indicated who it was.

I walked to the closet and opened it.

Three black suits hung in a row.

Swaying slightly, I looked down. Shiny boots lined the floor.

I was right. It's him. It's him, and I'm standing in his freaking hotel room.

I don't know what I'd been thinking, coming here. I couldn't do a damn thing about anything, but I could definitely get myself killed. As I spun for the door, I spotted a black iPad sitting on the nightstand.

Almost against my will, I crossed the room and picked it up. Pressed the home key. It sprang to life instantly, a program already running, tight lines of text scrolling down one side of the screen. I scanned the feed, eyes narrowing. The information consisted of real-time updates from around the globe.

As I watched, a seismic reading from Manila appeared, followed immediately by a series of tweets about volcanic activity in New Zealand. Next came a classified NSA report detailing fatalities from a CO_2 outgassing in Petaluma, California. On and on it went, a detailed summary of recent disasters and ominous reports.

In the center was a world map with arrows and links, cross-referencing events in the timeline. A digital clock occupied the bottom of the screen, counting down: "6 days, 15 hours, 54 minutes, and 12 seconds." A new report popped up: details of a whirlpool in the South China Sea. The clock changed in a blink, reducing the remaining time by eight hours.

"What the hell?"

I tapped the timer, but nothing happened. So I pressed the home button, closing the program. The screen beneath was blank except for an icon named "Project Nemesis." I tapped it, and a familiar landscape appeared. It took me a moment to grasp what I was seeing.

"The valley," I whispered.

An option at the bottom of the map was labeled "Beta Subjects." I pressed. Four glowing dots appeared onscreen. Two red. Two blue.

One of the blue dots was high in the northern slopes.

Directly over Chimney Rock Lodge.

It's me. I'm the blue dot.

He can track me.

The other blue dot was to the west, behind Miner's Peak.

"Min," I whispered.

Growing frantic, I checked the two red dots. They were right next to each other, somewhere in town. I was trying to figure out exactly where when I heard a door open inside the building.

The iPad dropped from my fingers.

I bolted onto the patio and across the grass. Was halfway to my car before realizing I hadn't shut the door behind me. I reached the Tahoe, slammed the starter button, and peeled out, roaring down the access road at breakneck speed.

"Let this be a dream," I mumbled. "Let this be a dream. Please, please, I don't want this. Let this be a dream."

I didn't stop driving for anything.

And I didn't wake up.

PART THREE

PROJECT NEMESIS

24

MIN

I woke to the smell of frying bacon.

Mom had put away the photo albums and washed her scotch glass. The shades were up, and warm sunlight filled the trailer.

Last night, she'd basically kept me prisoner. We'd sat and watched the news. Beyond the earthquake horror to the west, there'd been a story about a mass beaching in Thailand—hundreds of whales, swimming into the shallows and getting caught on sandbars.

I'd risen to wander outside, but Mom had forbidden it, perched in her rocking chair with red eyes. She rarely drank, and never more than one. But she'd refilled her glass several times as the TV looped footage of the devastation by the Pacific, paging through old pictures and mumbling about God's judgment.

The whole time I'd watched her from the corner of my eye, thinking three words.

Field_Observation_Report.

Breakfast was tense. Mom wouldn't meet my eye, seemed ashamed of her behavior. She barely responded to my feeble attempts at conversation.

Which made me mad. Because I had *many* questions, and desperately needed answers.

Numbers ran through my head. 091817. Monday's date.

If I was right, Virginia Grace Wilder had reported on me three days ago.

The day of the Announcement.

She still hadn't asked about my birthday. Where I'd been overnight.

For two days I'd carried the riddle of Project Nemesis inside me. I'd nearly demanded a reckoning a half-dozen times, but the signature in that Nemesis file always stopped me cold.

But I will *get answers. And soon.*

When I looked up, she was watching me, absently stirring her eggs, pushing things around on her plate rather than eating. I felt like she wanted to say something but couldn't bring herself to do it. I put down my glass.

"Mom."

Her hand froze.

"If something was going on . . . you'd tell me, right?"

For an instant she remained absolutely still, eyes unreadable. Then she looked away, busying her fingers once more. "I don't know what you're talking about." Mom rose and reached for her coat. "I have to go now. I'm late for work."

She wasn't. But before I could speak, there was a knock at the door. Our heads swiveled in unison.

"Yes?" Mom called out in a strained voice. The door opened and Tack stepped inside. We both relaxed, though Tack's usual smirk was absent. His jaw was as tight as when we'd fled Dr. Lowell's office two nights before.

I flashed back to that night—sitting on Lowell's floor, Nemesis folders piled all around me. The slamming doors had been our only warning. Tack had leapt to the window, then lurched away. Two gray jeeps, stamped with the black starburst symbol.

Military vehicles. In Lowell's parking lot. There was no mistaking why.

Luckily, I knew the place better than the men outside. We'd raced into the lobby and down a short corridor to a service door in the rear, firing into the bushes before our pursuers thought to circle. There we'd hidden like terrified rabbits as four soldiers charged inside, then hurried back out, shining flashlights into the trees as a pock-faced officer barked orders. It'd been ten minutes before we could sneak away.

Soldiers protecting Lowell's office. Soldiers!

Then yesterday had been a disaster. I'd rushed to school looking for Noah, but he'd been useless, meekly standing aside when Ethan and those jerks showed up.

I don't know why I thought he'd be useful.

Tack and I had met again after school, but with no idea what to do next. Then I'd made the mistake of checking in, and Mom had locked me down for the night.

"Morning, Tack." Mom seemed to welcome the distraction. "You want some breakfast before school?"

"No, thanks. I was just wondering if you'd heard."

"Heard what?" No chance it was good.

Tack scooped up the remote. The answer was playing on every channel.

"Sweet Lord in heaven," Mom whispered, covering her mouth.

I gaped at the screen, too stunned for words. An asteroid had struck India, and the devastation was . . . catastrophic. CNN was showing images from the International Space Station.

"Happened thirty minutes ago," Tack said quietly, squeezing his forehead. "Hundreds of thousands might be dead."

"Where is that?" I demanded, trying to grasp the magnitude of the disaster.

"Calcutta." Tack cleared his throat. "A bad spot. Lots of people there. They're saying this one was way smaller than the Anvil—the size of a motorcycle—but traveling faster. No one saw it coming. It hit like a nuclear bomb."

"Turn it off," my mother said.

I turned to face her, still numb. "What?"

"I *said*, turn it off." Her head was in her hands. "I don't want to see any more."

I was about to argue—how could she turn a blind eye? First Portland, now *this*—but Tack switched the TV off. I gave him a look and he shrugged.

The door slammed. I jumped. My mother had gone outside. I guess she didn't want me to see her upset. With her gone, Tack switched the news back on, which was now showing close-ups of the damage. Most of Calcutta was burning. Tears filled my eyes as I watched the horror taking place half a world away. Then Tack seized my shoulder, his face draining of color. "Min, look!"

He rewound, then paused, freezing an image of destruction

onscreen. I noticed two vans that were parked near the edge of the impact crater. Men in gray uniforms appeared to be taking samples of some kind. Black starbursts were stamped on both vehicles.

I gawked like the witness of a traffic accident. "That symbol! Just like the convoy!"

Tack nodded, anxiously licking his lips. "I spent two days trying to ID that. Didn't find a thing, which makes no sense. Unit designations are supposed to be recognizable. That's how they function."

I grabbed the sides of my head.

Troops in Fire Lake. Vans in Calcutta. Project Nemesis. Me. Noah.

Whatever this conspiracy was, it spanned the globe. Maybe it was even related to the disasters.

"Nemesis," I hissed.

Tack looked at me sharply. "We don't know for sure that these troops are tied to the project." He frowned. "Though why else would they show up at Lowell's office?"

I was barely listening. I *knew* it all connected. The scale of things was beginning to terrify me. "Myers said the project was almost complete."

"So did that memo we found in Lowell's spymaster boxes."

"Time is running out."

"So what do we do?" Tack asked in a small voice.

That question had been vexing me from the moment we'd fled Lowell's office.

Pieces on the board were moving. In a shadow war, you need intel to survive.

I thought of Mom, standing outside our trailer at that very moment. She knew something, I was sure of it. I could walk out and confront her. Fling everything we'd uncovered in her face, and demand the truth.

PN_FIELD_OBSERVATION_REPORT_SUBMITTED/FILED/091817.

With a suffocating feeling, I realized I didn't trust her. Didn't know which meant more to her, Project Nemesis or me.

She'd informed on me three days ago. Where did her loyalties lie?

If I asked questions, what would she do? File another report? Turn me over to them?

That I didn't know nearly broke me. I damn sure wasn't ready to find out.

It'll have to be another way.

"Min?"

I shook off the bleak thoughts. Locked them away for another time.

"We take the fight to them," I said finally. "Let's find out what our enemies know."

"Come on!" I hissed. We hurried around the corner to Principal Myers's office.

"This is insane," Tack whined. He was right, but I didn't care. Myers was part of Project Nemesis, same as Lowell. Maybe he had files, too.

Our diversion was simple, executed during Mrs. Ferguson's break. An anonymous call reported truants by the equipment shed. Worse, they were smoking. Myers *hated* that, had gotten so mad, he'd hobbled out there himself. Round-trip should take him at least ten minutes.

Get in, get a look, and get out. Hopefully no commandos would show up this time.

Tack frowned at the file cabinets behind Myers's desk. "That's a lot of paperwork."

"Then get moving."

The first two were a bust—personnel records and student discipline. On another day those might've been interesting, but we weren't there to play. I wanted Nemesis docs, and would have bet my life Myers had some close at hand.

Tack finished rifling the desk. "Nothing here. And I doubt he'd put anything sensitive on a school-issue computer."

I finished the second cabinet, with the same result. "Shoot."

I spun, scanning the room. There was nothing else to search.

"Maybe the conference room?" Tack suggested. "That's where he took the call, right?"

"No, wait!" I slunk outside. Across the hall was a locked file closet.

"Did you see any keys?"

Tack ducked back into the office, emerging moments later with a heavy set. "Sorry—there are like thirty of them."

I grabbed them and began trying until one finally turned. Inside, the room was long and narrow, with shelves along both sides. It'd take a week to search everything. "Look for something secure," Tack whispered. "He wouldn't store secret files where another administrator might see them."

"Yes, good!" Most of the boxes were old and dusty, but there was a cleaner section in back with a small safe. "Of course." I smacked the handle in frustration. Was surprised when the door swung open.

But my hopes were quickly dashed. The safe was empty.

"We're too late. Myers must've cleared out his files. He said things would be happening soon. Let's go before we get caught."

Tack held up one finger, then aimed it over my shoulder. "Those look familiar to you?"

Two plastic storage boxes were tucked into the corner.

"Tack, you're the smartest man alive!" I squeezed his arm, watched his pride swell. In seconds we had both down on the floor with their lids off.

Watch check. Myers could return at any second.

Inside were folders like the ones in Lowell's office, though in better condition. I flipped through them quickly, deflating once again. "It's the same stuff. Lowell must've made a copy set for Myers."

It was *something*—the boxes tied Myers to Lowell and Project Nemesis—but I already knew that much. I'd been hoping for another piece of the puzzle.

Then I found it.

At the back of the second box was a slim yellow folder. I flipped it open. Nearly wet my pants. "Tack, look!"

I handed him a routine cover letter from Lowell to Myers, but with one qualifier. Tack read that part aloud. "*The two beta patients under my jurisdiction—Melinda Wilder and Noah Livingston—are not included in this set. Their information has been sent directly to Control.*"

Tack shook himself. "Holy crap, Min."

I nodded. Noticed a blue folder in the other box.

Kneeling, I pulled it and looked inside. At first, it made no sense. "A bus schedule? Why would Project Nemesis be interested in . . ." I trailed off, considering the information. "Tack, what do you make of this?"

Tack had drifted toward the door and was listening. He hurried back. "Weird." He scratched his nose, eyes narrowing. "Seems to be what it says—a bus schedule. But why only sophomores?"

"Same as the background files. And it's not just that—there's too much info here. Names and addresses, sure. But why physical descriptions? And it's timed to the second."

"What are you thinking?"

"I'm not sure." I chewed my lip, trying to make sense of the document. Then it came to me. "Tack, this is a *collection* schedule. And look who authorized it!"

I pointed to a name scrawled at the bottom.

Sheriff Michael T. Watson.

Tack put a hand over his face. "Ah man, not the cops too! I can't take any more of this!"

I blinked. Almost couldn't believe it. Pieces were sliding together, but I still couldn't see the picture being formed.

Noah again. We have to talk, whether he wants to or not.

A bang carried from the lobby. Footsteps down the hall. Tack and I cringed like hunted animals as Myers's voice boomed through the door. "Buncha nonsense, Delia. Might be I got pranked. I'll be in my office."

I felt sick. If Myers noticed his keys were missing, we were dog meat. As quiet as humanly possible, Tack and I put the boxes back together and placed them on their shelf. Then we stared at each other, without the slightest idea what to do.

Loud beeping in the hallway. I looked at Tack, who mouthed, *fax machine*.

"Delia? Mrs. Ferguson?" Myers's chair squeaked, mutters flying as he trudged down the hall. I frantically waved Tack forward. Now was our chance.

Hearts in our throats, we crept out. Myers had his back to us, near the swinging door beside the counter. "How do you hook an incoming message?" he grumbled to himself, fighting with the machine.

I closed the door behind us, locked it, then tossed the keys under Myers's desk. Best I could do. Then I shoved Tack into the conference room.

"That way!" I pointed to the other door, accessing the outside corridor.

"Delia? You back there?"

We burst into the hallway, slammed the door, and fled in panic. Myers had to have heard, but I didn't care. I was out from under his grasp.

I intended to stay that way, whatever it took.

25

NOAH

"I'm telling you, it's a conspiracy!"

Toby tapped his temple. He and the others were gathered beside the Nolans' van. Last bell had rung fifteen minutes earlier, but the lot was still packed, everyone fully freaked out about the news from India.

I tried to ghost past them, still rattled from my spy work that morning. I regretted going to school at all, but Black Suit would surely know someone had searched his room. Keeping up appearances seemed like the safest play.

But Ethan spotted me and waved me over. With no polite way around it, I joined them, hovering at the periphery. *I'm better off with the group anyway.*

"The government knows *exactly* what's going on," Toby was ranting, getting all riled up. "But they aren't telling us jack! Meanwhile, I was in the liberty camp yesterday, and those guys have sources inside the military. Our troops are on high alert. They're being deployed across the globe."

"That doesn't mean anything," Jessica snapped, anxiously twirling her hair. "Soldiers are always moving around, right?"

"With all the crap happening, it'd be crazy if they weren't doing *something*," Chris Nolan said. Mike nodded, leaning back against their van. "Who knows? Maybe the Chinese are causing it all."

"What about troops in *our* valley?" Toby countered. "More trucks came over the bridge last night. They drove right by the camp."

"It's true," I said, before thinking better of it. "I saw them."

Heads turned. Sarah smiled at me. I nodded as neutrally as possible. Saw her expression curdle in the corner of my eye.

"So where'd they all go?" Charlie asked. "You can't hide a tricycle in Fire Lake, much less a whole strike force."

"That's the craziest part," Toby said, trying to wrestle back the center of attention. "They drove onto the government land. There must be a buttload of soldiers in there right now, doing God knows what!"

Significant glances. What was beyond that fence had been schoolyard gossip for years.

"There are a hundred reasons why the army could be here." Jessica rolled her eyes at Toby. "Maybe it's a . . . a science place. They could be setting up sensors or something. Because of the earthquakes."

"That's what they want you to believe." Toby elbowed Derrick, who shrugged. "Those dudes are probably *causing* the earthquakes."

"You think the United States military deliberately broke Oregon in half?" Chris Nolan laughed out loud. Even his brother smiled. "Yeah, *okay*, Toby. That makes sense. Did they suck in the asteroids from outer space, too?"

"The timing *is* weird," Charlie said, scratching a rash on the back of his neck. "Those troops must've already been on their way here during the Announcement. Seems like we're not being told enough."

Toby punched his thigh. "I'm telling you, they know about everything. *All* of it!"

Surprisingly, I found myself agreeing with Toby. Too much was happening at once. I'd seen the conspirators and troops myself.

"Whatever's going on, we need to be ready," Ethan said.

"Ready?" Derrick asked. "Like, how?" But Ethan only shook his head.

Glancing over his shoulder, I spotted Min standing on the curb a dozen yards away. Our eyes locked. She nodded left, toward the gym. Tack was slouching beside her, his gaze considerably less inviting.

I glanced at Ethan, found him watching me. "We boring you?"

Before I could respond, Spence Coleman ran over, his shaggy brown hair bouncing like a mop. "Guys, listen to the radio!"

Chris reached into the van. "What station?"

"All of them!"

Spence was right. The president's voice floated from the speakers. Chris cranked the volume so everyone could hear.

"*—the discovery was made just hours ago by NASA's Near Earth*

Object Program. A cluster of comets have diverted from their usual orbits and entered the inner solar system. Five of these bodies appear to be on possible collision courses with our planet."

Gasps. Shouts. Jessica began to cry. Sarah told her to shut up.

I listened, my jaw hanging open.

"*—are small, ranging in size from basketballs to cars, but they are traveling at high rates of speed. I want to reiterate—these objects are not potential planet-killers like the Anvil. The Earth is not in any kind of existential danger. However, at this time we don't know exactly where they will strike, except that the impacts will occur within the next forty-eight hours—*"

"What the hell?" Sweat dampened Derrick's temples. "Some outer space storm?"

"Shh!" Ethan's whole attention was on the radio. "There's more!"

"*—therefore, in accordance with the powers granted to my office by the Constitution, I am declaring a state of emergency for all fifty states. Martial law will take effect beginning this evening at nine p.m. eastern standard time. That's in two hours and thirty minutes. All citizens are ordered to remain inside their homes after dark. As of this moment, I am freezing prices. There will be no hoarding. There will be no lawlessness. Everyone needs to remain calm until the crisis has passed. This is a temporary—*"

"Screw that!" Toby lurched back from the van, eyebrows climbing his forehead. "I'm not getting caught with my pants down." He bumped into Derrick.

"What are you talking about?" Derrick snapped, pushing him aside. "You plan on leaving town now? Y'all need to remember what happened after the Announcement." He clicked his tongue. "City people are gonna lose it. Up here in the valley is the safest place to be."

"Supplies, you idiot!" Toby ripped his keys from his pocket. "I'm stocking up, *now*. Go ahead and follow orders like a bunch of sheep, but it's about to hit the fan!"

Toby ran to his car, triggering a flood. Students bolted for their vehicles. Doors slammed and cars raced away, some bouncing over the curb in an effort to escape more quickly.

Ethan and Sarah had their heads together, seemed to be arguing. They cut off abruptly when Jessica and the Nolan brothers approached. Derrick and Charlie lit out, and suddenly I was free. I ducked my head and slipped away. Where had Min gone?

I jumped into my Tahoe, started the engine, and shifted into reverse.

Nearly backed over Min and Tack.

Min marched to my window and rapped on the glass. "We need to talk."

"I know. Listen, sorry about yesterday. I didn't—"

She circled the SUV and opened the passenger door. Slid inside. Secured her seat belt. A back door opened and Tack jumped in. "Afternoon, slick."

I blinked, momentarily nonplussed.

Min waved a hand. "What are you waiting for? *Go*."

I reversed from my spot and joined the line of cars exiting the parking lot.

"Okay." More to myself than to them. I caught Tack smirking at me in the mirror.

“Where are we going?” I asked.

“Someplace we won’t be interrupted,” Min answered curtly.

I sighed.

“My place it is.”

26

MIN

I stepped from his Tahoe, trying not to look impressed.

Noah's house was a freaking castle.

We were up near the canyon rim, at the top of the valley's swankest neighborhood. Noah unlocked the front door and disarmed the security system, waving us inside. He hadn't looked at me once during the ride there.

"What a dump." Tack strolled in like he owned the place, dropping onto a leather couch. "Is this public housing?"

Noah ignored him. Reset the alarm. "Wait here a sec." He disappeared toward the back of the house, leaving Tack and me alone.

"Probably needs to check on his Sims." Tack bounced up, walked over to a bank of floor-to-ceiling windows overlooking the lake. "Pretty sweet digs. I wonder what the poor people are doing right now."

"Our neighborhood is right behind that peak."

Tack spun. "You could fit, what, seven trailers in this room alone? Seems a bit much for two people."

"Sometimes my dad's girlfriend stays over, too," Noah replied, returning from wherever he'd gone. "It can get downright cramped."

My eyebrows rose. Noah wasn't usually sarcastic. I think he'd had enough of Tack's wit for one day.

Good. A little spirit was a welcome change.

"Is your dad really out of town?" Tack said. "Helluva time for a vacation."

The barb landed. Noah's eyes tightened. "Flights were grounded after the asteroid hit India. I got a very thoughtful text explaining his predicament." He turned to me. "But you didn't come here just to insult my family, I assume?"

"Don't be so sure." Tack flopped back onto the couch.

I flapped a hand at Tack for quiet. But I didn't know where to start.

Noah seemed to sense this. "Sit. Please. Do you want something to drink?"

"Got any Dom Pérignon?" Tack's face was pure innocence. "Or a nice brandy?"

"Both." Noah didn't move.

"We're fine." I sat next to Tack and shot him a warning glare. He rolled his eyes. Shrugged. Then nodded. *I'll be a good boy.*

Noah sat in a recliner across from us. And waited.

Here goes.

"What do you know about Project Nemesis?"

Noah didn't flinch. "Nothing. Is that what it's called?"

"That's the name of an operation taking place here in Fire

Lake," I said slowly, choosing my words with care. "I first came across it ten years ago, when we got those shots at school."

Noah tensed. A hand rose to rub his shoulder.

Does it burn like mine?

"It's a large and well-funded conspiracy," I continued, "involving prominent people in town, the government, and the military. You probably think I've lost my mind but—"

"No," Noah said. "Actually, I think you're right."

I stiffened. "You do know about it? What *is* Nemesis?"

Noah looked at his shoes. "I have no idea. But I've seen things . . ." His head rose, but he didn't meet my eye. "It's the only answer that makes sense."

"What *things* have you seen?" Tack demanded.

Noah glanced at him, as if considering whether to answer. "Trucks, for one."

Tack shook his head dismissively. "We saw those too. The night of the Announcement."

"I saw them last night. A line of gray ones, vanishing onto the federal land."

"A second group?" I paused, digesting this. How many was that altogether? Suddenly, it felt awfully crowded in the valley.

"What else have you seen?" I asked.

Noah considered me a moment. "First, tell me what you wanted to talk about at school."

"I'm a patient of Dr. Lowell's. I know you are, too."

"You said that already." Irritation fought with embarrassment in his eyes. His therapy was clearly a touchy subject. I decided to not hold back. "I found your name on his laptop when I broke into his office on Tuesday night."

Noah's eyes widened. "Why'd you do that?"

"*We* did it," Tack interjected, but we both ignored him.

"I wanted a look at his notes. To see what he was writing about me." Noah listened without interrupting, but I could tell he was drinking in every word. "So Tack and I snuck in and had a look around. Found things."

I took a deep breath. Telling Noah was a gamble, but one I had to take.

"Lowell is using us like lab rats." I suppressed a shudder and forged ahead. "It's a classified experiment code-named Project Nemesis, and lots of people are involved. People we know and trusted. Lowell's computer has secret files under the Nemesis heading with our names on them."

Noah rubbed his palms on his jeans. "You said something about the shots?"

"I first saw the words *Project Nemesis* that day—on a form the doctor filled out. I remember Principal Myers talking with strange men in suits, too." I felt a slight quaver in my voice. "I don't think there really was a pesticide spill."

Noah squeezed the bridge of his nose. "Myers."

"He's been a part of it from the beginning." I didn't mention my mother, or their meeting that same day. Wasn't ready to share that yet.

"There's more."

Noah nodded, though based on his expression, I wasn't sure he wanted to hear it. "We found background files on *everyone* in our class." I told him about the boxes in Lowell's cabinet and the matching set in Myers's office closet.

"You broke into the file room at school?" Noah asked incredulously. "This morning?"

Tack nodded, flexing his biceps. "Never scared."

"I overheard Myers on the phone the morning after the Announcement. He was talking about Nemesis, and said everything was ready to go, whatever that means. He even mentioned Sheriff Watson."

Noah's face became unreadable. "Lowell, Myers, and Watson. In a military conspiracy code-named Project Nemesis. Happening here in Fire Lake."

"I know it sounds crazy, but—"

"It's not." He barked a laugh. "Not *at all.* In fact, I nearly crashed one of their meetings."

My turn to be stunned. "What? Where?"

Noah rubbed his eyes. "Yesterday. After the quake." He paused, as if deciding how much to tell. "I was down by the waterfront. Came up an alley, and stumbled onto them."

"Did they see you?" Tack asked sharply.

Noah shook his head. "It was Myers, Lowell, Watson, and some military guy. The other psychiatrist, Dr. Fanelli, was with them too." He opened his mouth again, then seemed to reconsider. "There's your conspiracy, right there."

My fingers dug into my hair. I couldn't believe it. Noah had actually *seen* the bastards together! *Fanelli? Him, too?* "Did you hear what they said?"

"No. I . . . I didn't stay." Noah rose and walked to the windows. He stared down at the lake without saying more.

I sensed he was holding back. Something potentially big.

Don't push. Not yet.

I chose a different tack. "The metadata on Lowell's computer," I began, hoping he'd come sit back down. "It described you and I as 'beta patients.' For what, I have no idea. But we don't have background files in the storage boxes either. Us and two others."

Noah's head turned at that. "Who else?"

"We don't know. The count was sixty files—four less than the entire class. I'm guessing there are two more betas."

"Terrific," Noah breathed.

"This isn't a joke." Tack leaned forward and tapped the coffee table. "We found a *collection* schedule in the file room. An exact route to seize every sophomore from their home, one by one. Sheriff Watson has a copy."

"Of course it's not a joke!" Noah pivoted, his voice shaking with emotion. "I'm a super-special test subject, remember? But for what?"

Now *I* looked away. We'd come down to it—the part of my story even Tack didn't know. The terrifying pattern I'd never shared with anyone. But I couldn't put it off any longer. Not after Noah had confirmed almost everything.

"I think I know," I said quietly, eyes on the carpet. "Some of it, at least."

Tack's head swung my way. I felt Noah's eyes dig into me.

Here I really go.

"Something's been happening to me." I hugged my knees to my chest, goose bumps rising all over my body. "For years. I've never told anyone about it. Not since I was little, anyway."

A soft thump. I looked up. Noah had dropped back into his recliner and was staring at me.

I continued before I lost my nerve. "I'm being stalked. No, worse than that. *Hunted.* Every two years, by the same person every time. No matter what I do, this man in a black suit finds me and attacks me. I'm never able to outrun him."

"What!?" Tack grabbed my shoulder, his face stricken. "Min, why haven't you told me this before?" Then a light dawned in his eyes. "Your birthdays," he whispered.

I nodded. Cleared my throat. I didn't look at Noah, wanting to get it all out before anyone started calling me crazy. "This man . . . He doesn't just hurt me. He *kills* me. I know it sounds insane, but he's murdered me five times already, and he'll do it again in two years."

And there it was. That look in Tack's eyes. The one I'd always dreaded.

Confusion, mixed with horror and . . . pity? Unease? Was it . . . embarrassment?

What do you think now, Tack? Am I still so great?

A high-pitched sound startled me. I whirled, eyes rounding.

Noah was bent over with his head in his hands, his mouth locked in a grimace. A keening escaped his throat, like an animal in pain.

Tack leapt up. "He's having a seizure!"

I grabbed my friend's arm as he lunged to help. "No! It's not that."

And I knew.

Seeing Noah's horrified expression.

Without a shadow of a doubt. Noah and I had the same problem.

I rose, walked slowly to his side. Tears were spilling down his cheeks. I reached out and grabbed Noah's hand. He flinched, but I didn't let go.

"Noah." As soothing as my voice could be. I lifted his chin until our eyes met. "It's okay. I think I understand."

His breathing slowed.

"Does your scar hurt sometimes?" I asked quietly.

He nodded.

"We share a birthday. Do you ever wake up in the woods?"

Noah sat upright in the recliner. Wiped his eyes, but wouldn't look at me.

He nodded again.

My legs almost gave out.

It's happening to Noah, too. I'm not alone.

Tack was standing behind me. "Will someone please tell me what's going on?" he asked quietly. So I turned and sat on the edge of the coffee table. Laid it out as succinctly as possible.

"Every two years, on my birthday, a man in a black suit finds me and kills me."

Tack blinked.

"I'm serious, Tack. It's been happening since I was eight. Remember when I disappeared from the park? I was actually thrown into the canyon."

"But you're not in the canyon," Tack said slowly.

I shook my head. Noah was coughing into his fist, seemed to be getting ahold of his emotions. "I don't seem to *die*, though," I said. "Every time, no matter how or where I'm killed, I wake up in the same clearing. I die in one place, and then I'm lying in another. I have no idea what happens in between."

"That's not possible."

"I'd agree, but it's been happening to me for years. Noah, too, I think."

"I call him Black Suit," Noah whispered, staring at his hands. "Dr. Lowell told me he's a bad dream, and that I'm a chronic sleepwalker. He said I have a—"

"Severe dissociative disorder?" My lips curled into a scowl. "Lying bastard."

"Wait." Tack held up a hand. "Just hold on a second. Let me get this straight: there's a deranged psychopath murdering both of you on your birthdays, but you don't actually die? How is that even remotely plausible?"

I shrugged, relieved to finally be talking about it. "It's *not*. But it's also true. And let's not forget, we just figured out that Noah and I are beta patients in a secret government shit-show called Project Nemesis."

"Holy crap," Tack whispered. "So Lowell's been playing you guys for . . . years?"

"And Myers." My jaw clenched. "Sheriff Watson, too. Whatever sick experiment is being conducted, it started at our elementary school ten years ago, under their supervision."

"But I got a shot that day too," Tack persisted. "Nobody's ever tried to kill *me*."

"Not *tried*. Understand, Tack—this man actually murders me. He *succeeds*. Every time."

I glanced at Noah, who nodded reluctantly.

"But who *is* he, then?" Tack pulled on his hair with both hands. "Where does this lunatic come from? And what's the point of this . . . insane . . . *blood sport*?"

"No idea. To me, he's always been a ghost."

"A nightmare," Noah mumbled. "Except he's *not* one. He was at the meeting, too."

I started. "What?"

"In the alley yesterday. Black Suit was there, with the others. He seemed to be in charge."

I was speechless.

There it was. The final connection.

The black-suited man, tied to Project Nemesis.

The killings are part of the program.

"I tracked him to his hotel." Noah slumped in his chair like he needed to change batteries. "He's monitoring us by computer. Tracking us somehow."

This was one blow too many. "You followed him to his *room*?"

Noah smiled faintly. "Wasn't too hard, actually."

I listened in amazement as he detailed his morning espionage. The chalet. The iPad. Glowing red and blue dots, and a countdown ticking toward zero. When he finished, I had no idea what to say.

"That was ballsy, man." Tack's voice carried grudging respect. "If that dude had seen you—"

"What?" Noah cackled harshly. "He might have killed me?"

I barked a laugh as well. Our eyes met, and I felt something pass between us. "Okay. So. We know the players, but almost nothing about the game. What are we beta patients *for*? What could these killings accomplish?"

"There were *four* dots," Noah reminded me.

I nodded. "We have to find out who the other betas are."

"The red dots were both in town, but I couldn't tell where before I bolted. The countdown was at six days, but the timer seemed to be accelerating." Noah waved at his television. "Right as things are spiraling out of control."

"Slow down." Tack held up both hands, shaking his head in astonishment. "I believe you guys. Honestly. It's freaking nuts, but I trust you. But what I *don't* get is how all of this"—he fluttered both hands—"*murder* business . . . ties in with what's been going on around the world. Project Nemesis might be up to some shady business here in Idaho, but they can't make asteroids strike Asia! Or start earthquakes in Seattle. That's impossible."

"*Everything* is connected," I said fiercely. "I can't explain it, but I'm positive."

"But how?" Tack whined.

"The vans on television, Tack! Don't forget."

Tack was silent a moment. "That's not enough. Those might be part of martial law or something. Could be a coincidence." But he didn't sound too confident.

"Vans?" Noah glanced from my face to Tack's.

I explained what we'd seen on TV. The starburst we couldn't decipher. Noah closed his eyes. "Too big," he muttered, pinching his nose. "Too much."

"That's the Noah I know!" Tack quipped.

Noah popped from his chair and stepped nose to nose with Tack. "I've spent the last *six years* of my life being told that my mind was broken, by the only person I ever really trusted. Who, it turns out, was using me as a guinea pig the whole time. My dad left the country over a week ago, and for all I know, might never come back. Meanwhile, a serial killer has been dropping by every twenty-four months and *murdering* me. Now I know he's real—I saw him yesterday, in town, chatting with the sheriff and my high school principal. The scheme they're running—the one *ruining my life*—is secretly backed by the US military, and may involve worldwide devastation. And we put all of this together roughly ninety seconds ago." He jabbed a finger in Tack's face. "So why don't you *cut me some freaking slack*, Thomas. Would that be so tough? Huh?"

Tack gaped. "Jeez. Noah. I'm sorry. I . . . I didn't . . ."

I pulled Noah into a hug. He resisted a beat, surprised, then clutched me back. After a long moment I stepped away, ignoring Tack's startled glance.

"We're in this together," I said to Noah. "From now on, no one has to be alone."

"Hey, I'm in too." Tack shuffled forward and self-consciously chucked Noah on the shoulder. "We'll figure things out. Together, like Min said. As friends."

Then he tried to lighten the mood. "Look at us. Team of heroes."

The three of us stood in an awkward circle.

On the mantel above the fireplace, a clock ticked.

27

NOAH

They left twenty minutes later.

Min's mother called, and, miracle, it got through. I checked my phone to see if Dad had reached out. Of course not.

We agreed to meet again later and form a plan. That's how far we'd gotten coming up with one, but what were we supposed to do?

I slumped on my couch, practically in a daze. The news was getting worse. Mobs had formed in several major cities, protesting the government's travel lockdown. Troops clashed with protesters, and reporters were being kept away. Churches were packed. In less developed corners of the globe, groups with old grudges were turning on each other, wild accusations being thrown left and right.

Right. Blame your different-colored neighbor for a comet storm. Great thinking, guys.

Stomach rumbling, I trudged to the kitchen, trying not to

let the madness infect me. As I put water on to boil—our cook hadn't shown up all week, and mac and cheese is the pinnacle of my culinary abilities—the president came back on the air, condemning the violence. *"Destroying each other gets us nowhere. This is a time for pulling together. We have to remain calm."*

But what came next blew that possibility out of the water.

"Minutes ago, I learned that three comets NASA is tracking will strike Earth in the next twenty-four hours. Let me be clear—these are small objects and do not *represent an existential threat. However, the local devastation will be severe."* A map appeared, with angry red circles over Germany, central Russia, and the Korean peninsula. *"NASA has calculated the likely impact zone for each comet. To those residing within these regions: if you have a safe means of exiting the area, please do so immediately. God bless you."*

A wave of relief swept over me—not Idaho, not America, and not Italy, where my father was—but it was quickly replaced by guilt. Fire Lake might be a hemisphere away, but thousands had just been given a death sentence. Even the president looked shaken.

A White House science adviser was projecting the impacts in terms of nuclear weapons, estimating the force of each would be "about 100 to 200 times Hiroshima." I gulped. Hordes were already clogging the roads in Germany, and casting off from the docks of Seoul in anything that would float. *Those poor bastards. At least Siberia is empty.*

The one thing no one could do was explain it. NASA understood that a group of comets in the Oort cloud had abruptly changed course and accelerated, but they were at a loss to explain why. Plenty of others had ideas, however. The Internet invited every crackpot with a theory into my kitchen, each certain they knew the "real" reason. Aliens. God. The Iranians. Thor. All were "attacking" our planet, along with too many others to count. It was the tinfoil-hat community's finest hour.

I stepped out onto my deck. Took a breath. The air was cool and damp, hinting at rain. I gazed down at the lake, which rippled in the fading afternoon light. The postcard view usually calmed me, but today it was almost a taunt.

Everything's fine, ha-ha, just kidding, it's really, really not.

I crossed the porch and stepped down to the driveway. Started walking. There's only one direction to go from my place—downhill—and soon I was by the waterfront.

The lake seemed less malicious up close. Relaxing a fraction, I began strolling west, toward the Plank, thoughts swirling as I walked. It felt like my private universe was in shambles, everything I'd considered firm suddenly unstable beneath my feet.

I'd been played for an idiot. Had naively accepted a buffet full of lies without questioning the narrative. My brain wasn't the scarred and scrambled mess I'd been led to believe.

So . . . who am I now? What am I?

Am I still the same person?

I found myself desperately hoping not. That I didn't like *me* came as no surprise. But I'd always operated under the assumption I was doing the best I could, given my condition. That was gone now. I could do more. *Be* more.

But my crutches were gone as well. Dr. Lowell and his pills. The handy explanations. A bottomless bag of excuses. Those things had been ripped from me, too.

I may not be crazy, but I'm still weak. And totally alone.

I was a mile down Shore Point Road before I realized where my feet were taking me.

I sped up.

Min wasn't weak. Her struggles had made her *fierce*. I didn't fool myself into thinking we were really friends—the only thing connecting us was Nemesis—but at least she understood. What an unexpected gift, even from someone who might not like me.

I nearly missed the cutoff. I'd never been to Rocky Ridge Trailer Park in my entire life. Dad might've grounded me just for suggesting it. *They have to live somewhere*, he'd grumble, on the rare times we'd drive through this part of the valley. *My villas don't clean themselves.*

I slipped through the gate, unsure where to find Min. A black-haired man in jean shorts gave me a suspicious look when I asked, but he nodded toward the back row. There, luck was with me—she was sitting in a lawn chair beside a cold fire pit, her legs curled up beneath her.

She started upon seeing me, running a hand through her hair. She wore a long-sleeved Vampire Weekend tee and jeans, a shade more casual than my khakis and blue sweater. I got the sinking feeling she wasn't happy to see me.

"What are you doing here?" she blurted, all but confirming it.

I froze in the act of sitting. "I, uh . . . went for a walk. Ended up here. I can leave if you want." My cheeks burned scarlet as I took a step back.

"No! Sorry." Was her face red as well? "It's just . . ." Min waved a hand, and I suddenly understood. *She's embarrassed.* "Not quite up to your standards," she finished, trying to make it a joke. I thought of how she must feel, having been in my dad's opulent house.

"I couldn't care less about that," I said, and meant it. So what if Min was poor? My dad's money didn't make me happy. It hadn't saved me from being a lab rat right alongside her, either. *Black Suit kills me just the same.*

After a moment, Min nodded slightly. "Honestly, you've never acted like a snob. I'll give you that much." Unspoken were the volumes she *wasn't* giving. Baby steps.

Min stood up as I sat. "If it's all the same to you, a walk sounds nice."

I rose eagerly. She was allowing my company. I'd take whatever terms were offered.

"Where to?"

"Wherever the wind blows us." Min smiled softly. I was struck again by how pretty she was. It felt like a secret only I knew about but should be obvious to everyone.

She led me behind her trailer to a fence bounding the park. Pointed to a break in the wire. "I keep this open, despite the coyotes." Her expression darkened. "I had to get out this way once."

I decided to test this new concept of sharing. "I once took a boat out onto the water." A snort escaped. "Can you believe it? A freaking dinghy, in the middle of the lake." Then my smile faded. "He still got me."

A floodgate opened. We began swapping stories, haltingly at first, then freely. Her experiences were so much like mine, yet different, too. We actually laughed when she described hiding behind the summer camp. I began to feel a little of what Dr. Lowell said would happen during our visits but never did. Some of the pain disappeared. But the mood dampened as I related my most recent murder.

Min was chewing on her thumbnail. "So he got *me* in the morning, then came for you after dark?"

I nodded. "You know how I said he never spoke? Well, he did on Sunday. He told me it was the last time."

Min stopped walking. Our path had taken us to the canyon rim.

"The last time, huh?" Min gazed out over the gorge. "Myers told someone Project Nemesis was a go. I saw a memo saying the same, and you found a freaking countdown clock in our killer's hotel room. Whatever they've planned, it's happening *now*."

"What can we do? We still don't know what the project is."

She gasped. Grabbed my arm. "On Lowell's computer the file names were gibberish after you and me, except for *one* other folder. It was named 'VHG Federal Land Reserve.'"

"Where the trucks went," I breathed.

"Where they took *us*, in kindergarten."

"In the alley, I saw a uniformed officer talking to Black Suit. We know for a *fact* the military is involved."

Min nodded. "Soldiers chased us from Lowell's office the night we broke in, and he and Myers are hiding military documents. The whole chemical spill story was clearly just a cover for Nemesis."

A pause. Min looked me in the eye. It was all I could do to not look away.

Why did she make me feel like such a fraud?

"Those troops are a part of this," she said quietly. "And we know where they're hiding."

I swallowed. Nodded weakly.

"Then that's where we go next."

"Not without me," a voice called. I spun, alarmed.

Tack emerged from the trees. "Thought I was invited to these meetings."

"It's not like that," Min said patiently. "Noah came by here without planning to. We talked about a few things, and just a second ago decided what to do."

"Then you must've been headed to find me," he said drily. "Saved you a trip."

His face was unreadable. I wondered how much he'd overheard. Had Tack been spying?

"We're going to see what's hiding in the eastern woods," Min said. "It could be dangerous."

"You go, I go. You know that."

Great. Should be fun.

I turned to Min. "When do you want to try?"

The sun was setting beyond the mountains, and soon it would be full dark. Min began striding back toward the trailer park.

"Right now."

28

MIN

"Right now" ended up being six hours later.

When I ducked into my trailer, Mom insisted we have dinner. I knew there was no getting out again without a string of questions I couldn't answer.

A late-night raid was a better idea anyway. Tack had grudgingly offered to have Noah over to his place, but Noah elected to walk home. He promised to pick us up, which made things easier. You can hike across the valley—Tack and I thought nothing of it—but a car was better for a quick getaway. Especially since we were breaking the curfew.

As Mom and I watched more puzzling reports—a massive bird die-off in New Zealand, an apparent shift in the orbit of Pluto's moon Charon—I stole glances at her. Did she know what happened to me? Had she ever met the black-suited man?

I wonder when her next report is due.

I shivered, covered it. Focused on my plans for that night.

Finally Mom rose and kissed my cheek. She disappeared into her room and closed the door. I changed into yoga pants and a hoodie, then sat on my bed and waited.

I thought back to that drive after the inoculations. Try as I might, I couldn't remember any details about the property past the fence. I knew I'd been taken to a building. Then a room. Beyond that, I had nothing.

Then let's go see what's there.

At 2:55, I snuck across the trailer, wincing with every squeak. Slipped outside. Tack was waiting down by the gate. "Cutting it close," he admonished, toying with a fence wire in faded jeans and a Seattle Sounders sweatshirt. "Although, who knows if that dork will actually show? He's probably hiding under his bed."

"I wanted to be sure Mom was asleep."

I ignored the jab. We both knew Noah would be there.

On cue, headlights knifed through the darkness. Noah's Tahoe rumbled to a stop, and we hurried over to meet it. Tack opened the front door, but I slipped inside ahead of him, shooting him a reproachful look. He grumbled something about me needing a car seat, but then climbed in back, and we pulled away.

"Any problems?" Noah wore a tracksuit and a plain black baseball cap pulled low over his eyes. He gripped the wheel tightly as he reversed in a circle.

Tack giggled. "Dude, what are you wearing? You're not the American Sniper."

Noah's jaw tightened. "Do you have a plan?" he asked, addressing only me.

"Not much of one, sorry. Let's drive as far down Old Fort as we can, then ditch the car and go in on foot. I'm not sure how deep the woods are, but it can't be more than a couple miles. Whatever's in there should be easy to find."

Noah nodded. "As good a strategy as any."

"Sounds great," Tack chirped, planting himself in the middle of the backseat.

We drove through the dark and silent town. Minor quake damage was visible here and there—a busted streetlight, boarded windows at the Laundromat, cracks in the sidewalk where a water main had ruptured. Stark reminders of the devastation to the west.

Connected to Project Nemesis. I know it.

Tonight I'm going to prove it. Just don't ask me how.

We exited to the east and Noah picked up Old Fort Run. No more businesses or homes. The only thing ahead was our target. Noah slowed, relying on moonlight to navigate the bumpy dirt road. A chain-link fence appeared.

No lights. No people. No signs of occupation.

The place looked like we'd always believed it to be: utterly abandoned.

Spotting a gravel lane, I tugged Noah's sleeve. He turned, rumbled fifty yards into the darkness, then stopped. Idled. Noah stared through the windshield, eyes far away. I could almost hear him gathering his nerve.

"While we're young, Livingston." Tack opened his door and stepped from the vehicle. Noah killed the engine. Took a deep breath. I understood—my heart was hammering too. Noah's evident reluctance felt more real to me than Tack's bravado.

"Ready?" I asked softly.

"As I'll ever be." Exiting the vehicle, he left his hat on the seat.

The fence was twenty yards ahead across a wet, grassy field. Fading yellow signs warned that this was restricted government property, and that everyone should stay the hell off it. The access road was quiet, neglected, and uninspiring. Listening hard, I detected nothing beyond the usual chirpings of an alpine forest at night.

"Look." Tack pointed to a section of rusty links to the left of the gate.

"Those vines?" Noah whispered.

Tack nodded. "Creepers like that grow in a mat first, then shoot upward. They must've gotten under the fence somehow, to cover that much of it. We can get in there."

"Lead the way," I said.

Tack arrowed forward. I went next, with Noah bringing up the rear. I resisted the urge to make sure he actually followed.

The grass soaked my shoes and legs, but we crossed without incident, regrouping beside the fence. One look made clear it hadn't been repaired in years. By all indications, it was exactly as it appeared—a decrepit barrier long past its prime, guarding an empty forest no one cared about.

"There's not even barbed wire." Tack pointed to the top. "How are these guys running a global conspiracy if they can't maintain a perimeter fence?"

I shrugged, though I'd been thinking the same. Lowell and Myers had been loose with their files, and it looked like anyone could stroll onto this base. Not exactly the stuff to inspire confidence. Or fear.

"This program's been running since we were six," Noah whispered, "but we didn't know it existed until this week. They can't be that bad at it."

"Whatever." Tack wiggled a hand under the fence and pulled. A three-foot section curled up off the ground, the lowest links sheared through their middles. "See? The plants pushed through. Nature finds a way, people."

"Everybody still good?" I looked to Noah, who gave a shaky nod. Moonlight sparkled his eyes. For an instant, I imagined leaning forward and kissing him. He was tall and strong, but so vulnerable, too. Sweet. Not at all the person I'd thought him to be.

I flinched. Turned away. Twenty-four hours ago, I'd basically hated him.

Was I attracted to Noah simply because he understood my experiences, having shared them? I'd never considered the possibility before. Maybe the need to make sense of my life was clouding my judgment.

"Noah could stay here and guard the car?" Tack suggested casually. "We need to be surgical in there, and Min and I have done this kind of thing before."

Noah gave a curt head shake. "I'm going. I won't let you guys take all the risks."

"We're *all* going." I gestured for Tack to proceed. "Let's not waste any more time."

Tack grunted something, but forced the opening wide. Noah and I crawled through. Tack slipped under last, spreading the leaves with his hands to mask our passage.

We crept into the woods. A branch snapped, and I froze. Noah bumped me from behind, then mumbled an apology. It wasn't his fault—it was nearly pitch-black. I reached out and grabbed his hand. At first he pulled away, but then he gripped back tightly. When I felt certain no one was lying in ambush, I stole forward, pulling Noah along with me.

Just like when we were kids. Life is so strange.

Something clawed my other arm and I nearly squealed. But it was just Tack, moving up on my opposite side. He wrapped his fingers around mine.

We slipped forward in a ragged line, listening intently. We went a quarter mile, then another, never spotting a soul. Not even a parked vehicle. "Could they have driven *through* somehow?" Tack said.

"Not possible," Noah whispered back. "You can't cut a road through these mountains. I know—my dad scouted the whole ring looking for new slopes, but everything on the backside is too sheer."

"*Your* backside's too sheer."

"*Shh!*" I punched Tack's arm for silence. "Listen."

The sound was barely audible. A low hum. Mechanical. Maybe electrical. I pulled Noah's ear close. "There's something beyond that hedge." He nodded, muscles rigid. I pivoted to Tack, but he was already creeping forward.

Reaching the bushes, Tack carefully pulled a branch aside. The access road was only ten yards from where we crouched. There was a gatehouse of some kind, dark and unmanned, with a crooked yellow sign. Tack powered up his flashlight. Xenon light reflected brightly, destroying my night vision. He turned the beam back off and sat on his heels. My pulse raced as I waited for an alarm that never sounded.

"What are you doing?" I scolded.

"This checkpoint isn't in service. Look."

I gave the building a closer inspection. Vines had grown around the barrier arm. A windowpane was broken and hadn't been repaired. Tack was right. This gatehouse was falling apart. I stood and stepped onto the road. Nothing happened. We were alone.

"Did you read the sign?" Noah asked. Tack's head bobbed in the moonlight.

I'd missed it. I walked over and examined the sign closely. "I don't understand. What's an ICBM?"

"Intercontinental ballistic missile," both boys said at once. At a sharp glance from Tack, Noah shrugged, began fiddling with the gatehouse door.

"Giant missiles," Tack explained. "An old launch facility must be up ahead, probably from the Cold War. ICBMs were designed to be fired from underground silos, delivering nuclear warheads thousands of miles. In theory, at least—obviously, a war like that never happened, or we'd all be dead. ICBMs could travel across continents, and level whole cities. They're basically doomsday weapons."

"And the government built one here? A missile silo, I mean."

Tack nodded to the sign. "Looks like it. The military built hundreds of them in secret, mostly in remote places without a lot of people around. The idea was that if the Russians ever tried to nuke us, we'd fire all these suckers at once from all over the country, and wipe them out no matter what. The Russians did the same thing."

"Mutually assured destruction," Noah added, giving up on the gatehouse door. "It actually kinda worked. Those insane missiles might be the only reason we never had a third world war. The consequences were too scary for either side to shoot first."

I rubbed my cheek, annoyed to still be confused. "So this is a nuclear bomb facility?"

Tack shook his head. "The military doesn't use giant ICBMs anymore. We put nukes on submarines now, which works better. The older missiles are dinosaurs. Decommissioned. The government even started selling off some of the silos to the public. You can live in one now, if you like remote Wyoming."

Noah looked around thoughtfully. "It makes sense that they put one up here. Fire Lake is the exact type of isolated location they were looking for. It also explains why they *stopped* coming."

My hands found my hips. "So why armed soldiers this week?"

"Maybe they still keep warheads on the property?" Noah suggested. "Martial law might trigger a defensive response."

Tack snorted derisively. "With security this weak? The military might be lazy, but it can't be *that* bad."

Noah frowned. "Okay, you tell me. Why'd those soldiers come in here?"

"And where are they now?" I whispered, staring down the road. Was there a glow in the canopy up ahead? I remembered the humming sound we'd been tracking. "Let's keep moving."

Noah hesitated. "Maybe we should—"

"Quit whining, Livingston." Tack strode past him down

the asphalt. "We didn't come all this way to punk out now." Tack disappeared into the gloom, forcing us to hurry after him. I didn't say anything. What was the point? We moved briskly along the broken pavement, trying not to jump at every sound.

We were rounding a bend when Tack's hand shot out. A second later he pulled me into the woods, motioning for Noah to follow.

"What?"

"Look!"

Twenty yards ahead, light was peeking through the trees. We snuck to a gap in the trunks. Peered down at a windowless one-story building surrounded by a gravel lot. Two gray jeeps were parked beside a steel door. A generator growled in the darkness. The place didn't jog any memories.

Hands tight to his chest, Tack pointed with both index fingers. "I'll bet my handsome good looks people are in *there*," he whispered.

He looked at me, but I was gazing past the building. Though a hillock blocked our view, a nimbus of illumination covered the forest beyond it. Engine noise carried over the rise.

Something is around that bend.

I was about to suggest a flanking maneuver when the steel door opened. Three figures emerged from the building.

Noah sucked in a breath.

I recognized Lowell and Myers immediately. The third man wore a military uniform. I glanced at Noah and he nodded, his face deathly pale—it was the officer he'd seen in the alley.

The men of Project Nemesis were here.

A fourth person exited. Small and compact, with short black

hair, he wore the same gray uniform we'd seen on the convoy personnel. He started a jeep, and Myers and Lowell both climbed in. The three men drove past where we hid as the officer went back inside. In moments, we were alone.

Noah fell back on his butt, breathing rapidly.

"We need to get in there," Tack whispered.

I reached out and touched Noah's shoulder. He nodded tersely. Flashed a thumbs-up.

I pulled back. "We should see what's down the road first. What that noise is about."

Tack was already pushing through the gap. "We can buzz the door on the way. I want to—"

Something clicked. Red lights sprang to life high above us.

"Oh, no." Tack jumped back as if burned. "I think—"

An alarm blared from the branches overhead. I watched in horror as soldiers surged from the building.

Tack spun, hands covering his ears.

Noah was staring at me, naked terror on his face.

A scream erupted from my lungs, shattering the still night air.

"*RUN!*"

29

NOAH

I knew this was a bad idea!

I fled in panic, racing full throttle through the woods. Flashlight beams sliced through the canopy overhead. I heard engines fire, then the screech of burning rubber.

I didn't know where I was going. Where Min and Tack were. The fence. The lake. The road. My Tahoe. I just wanted to get away as fast as possible, but had a sinking feeling we were screwed.

I spotted Min up ahead, then Tack to my left, cursing as he ran through a pricker bush. I couldn't see more than ten feet, kept narrowly avoiding branches and hidden ditches. *I'm going to charge straight into a tree, knock myself unconscious, and get arrested. The perfect end to a perfect day.*

I didn't even want to be there. Sneaking into a military facility at night? How was that a good idea? This was *exactly* how I'd pictured our "adventure" ending.

I'd almost said something, but Tack loved making me look bad in front of Min.

Now I'm running from armed soldiers through the woods. Thanks a lot, pride!

A tree materialized in front of me. I lurched sideways, dodging the trunk but slamming into Tack.

"Watch it!" He shoved me ahead of him, onto a narrow deer track that knifed through the understory. I was too scared to protest, busy imagining the punishment for trespassing onto a nuclear weapons facility. Then I skidded to a halt as someone stepped from the bushes.

"Guys!" Min waved anxiously, then pointed to a clearing just ahead. "I saw lights go by. I think they're in front of us now, following the road."

Tack peered across the open field. "The fence can't be much farther, right?"

Min looked at me. I flashed my palms. I hadn't been paying attention to anything beyond my next step.

"The road is over there." Min nodded to the right. "So we have to cross this field and stay left. As long as we keep heading west, we'll hit the fence eventually. Then we climb out and find the car."

I swallowed. My Tahoe was just sitting there, waiting to be discovered.

She and Tack began jogging across the meadow. I followed, shoulders hunched, every sense on high alert.

Didn't matter.

They were on us in seconds.

Bushes exploded as two ATVs launched into the clearing.

Min spun, grabbed my hand. We tried to follow Tack, who was bombing across the grass.

The four-wheelers were faster. In moments they skidded to a halt in front of Tack, cutting him off. Then, like a bad movie, they began circling, hemming us together in a tight bunch.

My heart was racing out of control. *We're in so much trouble.*

Someone shouted a command. The ATVs stopped on opposite sides of us. Four troops dismounted, wearing night-vision goggles and carrying automatic weapons. No one addressed us, but we put our hands up on instinct. One soldier said something into his shoulder radio.

"Hey, guys," Tack ventured. "What's going on?" A pause. "Is something wrong?"

No response. Stone-carved faces. Sweat erupted all over my body.

"Good talk," Tack deadpanned.

Tense minutes passed as we stood in silence, staring at the four men with guns trained on us. Then a third ATV entered the field. It pulled up closer, headlights blinding me.

Two men stepped off. The first was a gray-uniformed soldier with a pockmarked face and the bearing of an officer. The other troops tightened up noticeably under his scrutiny.

"It's him!" Min whispered to Tack, who nodded tightly. Then she spoke out of the side of her mouth to me. "That's who chased us from Lowell's office the night we brcke in."

Then I recognized the second man. Felt a wave of relief.

"Sheriff Watson?" I said.

The officer made a gesture. His men flipped up their night-vision goggles. They were younger than I'd expected—

hard-faced dudes in their early twenties. One shouldered his weapon and hustled between the ATVs. He activated halogens atop each, creating a harsh field of light like a crime scene.

Sheriff Watson examined us with tired eyes above his thick mustache. With a shake of his head, his gaze dropped to the grass. I felt a twinge of panic.

The officer turned to the nearest pair of soldiers. "Shoot them," he ordered. "Dump the bodies in Grid Four, then return to base."

Watson flinched. Min gasped. My knees buckled, the light blurring as all the blood in my body rushed to my head. *That's it. We're dead.*

"Wait!" Tack's voice cracked as he frantically waved his hands. "You can't do that! We're Americans. We're kids!"

Watson rounded on the officer. "Now hold on a minute, Captain Sigler."

The soldiers who'd received the command glanced at one another. Across the circle, the other pair shifted uncomfortably. "New orders this evening," Captain Sigler boomed, clearly annoyed at having to explain. "Trespassers are to be liquidated. This base is now a Class Alpha facility. We're moving to DEFCON One."

"There's no point in those orders!" Watson shouted. "For what, a couple days? Just take them prisoner or let them go. None of this matters anyway."

"Sheriff?" Min took a tentative step toward him. The soldiers trained their weapons in response, and she stiffened. "Sheriff, it's me! Min Wilder!"

Oh God, don't shoot her. Please, please, don't shoot her.

Watson's eyes widened, as if only now recognizing us. He spun to face the armed men. "Wait! Wait! Damn it all, *wait*!" The soldiers hesitated, unsure which man to obey. Frowning, Captain Sigler raised a hand. "Hold your fire."

"Open your eyes!" Sheriff Watson jabbed a finger at Min. "That's one of the damn betas right there! I've known her since she was a baby!"

"Thomas Russo, too!" Tack was shaking like a leaf as he moved to stand protectively next to Min. "And that's Noah Livingston, Sheriff. You know his dad, I'm sure. Look, we made a mistake, but we're all friends here, right?"

Watson stepped into Sigler's personal space, fuming. "*Two* betas! And the other one's part of the experimental group. Half the damn project is standing in front of you, and you almost mowed them down!"

"My orders were clear." But Sigler sounded less confident.

Watson ran a hand over his face, suddenly looking exhausted. "The project's in motion, Keith. We can't risk changes at this point, and killing these three would be a massive curveball. You have to release them for now."

Sigler considered for a long moment, then nodded slowly. "They can go."

I almost collapsed in relief. I glanced at Min, and we exchanged shaky nods.

But the captain wasn't finished talking. "The betas only. I can't let the other one leave. My orders gave no exceptions, and he's not a core variable. Losses from the wider subject group are considered acceptable breakage."

My eyes shot to Tack. His whole body was trembling. But he

stepped away from Min, swallowing a lump in his throat. "Go on," he told her in a strangled voice. "Take Noah and get out of here."

"No!" Min grabbed Tack by the arm and tried to shove him behind her. "You can't do that!" she yelled, choking back tears. "We'll do whatever you want, just don't shoot anyone!"

"This is pointless!" Watson raged, but Captain Sigler wasn't swayed this time.

"As you said, Sheriff, the project is under way." His voice was glacial. "We've reached *the* critical moment in our forty-year history. Discipline must be maintained."

Sigler nodded to his men. "The boy in jeans. Take him down. That's a *direct* order from your superior officer." A shadow fell across the captain's face. "It's happening, men. We knew this day would come. Now isn't the time for cold feet."

The soldiers raised their weapons. Took aim.

"No!" Min screamed, trying to shield Tack. But they had us surrounded.

Panic overwhelmed me. Paralyzed my limbs. I stood statue-still as the scene unfolded.

Helpless. Hopeless. Feet frozen in concrete.

Min struggled to protect her friend. I didn't move an inch.

Tack grabbed Min by the shoulders. Hugged her tight, kissing the top of her head. Then he shoved her away forcefully, toppling Min to the ground. Tack squeezed his eyes shut. "Love you," he whispered.

A shot rang out.

"No!" Min screamed, lurching up from the grass.

I dropped to my knees.

Tack's dead. I did nothing.

But when I looked up, Tack was still standing there, quivering, face soaked with sweat.

My eyes darted to Sigler. He was lying facedown on the ground, a dark puddle spreading beneath him.

"Nobody move!" Watson was behind the first pair of soldiers, his service pistol pressed to one man's temple. "Stand down! All of you, right now!"

The captured soldier swallowed. "He shot Captain Sigler."

The other three slowly lowered their weapons, bewilderment on their faces. "Toss the rifles!" Watson shouted. After a moment's hesitation, they did as ordered. Watson stepped back and prodded the pair in front of him. "Kneel, or it's your last damn breath." Moments later he had all four troops on the ground in a line.

Watson turned and shot out the tires of the closest ATV. "Go on now, kids. Take the other two and head that way." He pointed across the field. "The road swings back around, and you can follow it to the gate. Don't stop for anything."

"You'll die for this," a soldier growled.

Watson laughed harshly. "What a stupid thing to say."

Something grabbed my arm and I jumped. It was Tack. "Come on, Noah!"

Min was mounting an ATV. I slid onto the seat behind her, letting Tack have the other one. At that moment I could barely form sentences inside my head—off-roading through a pitch-black forest at night was out of the question.

Tack revved his engine, obviously familiar with the machine. "Let's go, Sheriff."

Watson shook his head. "No place for me to hide from this, boy. Not anymore."

Min turned and stared at Watson. Something passed between them. A tear leaked from the corner of her eye. "What is Project Nemesis, Sheriff? What were those shots about, really?"

"Oh, Min. It's so much bigger than that. You have no idea how deep this goes."

"Then tell me!" Min shouted, rising in her seat. "Tell us what's going to happen!"

"Keep your mouth shut, Sherriff." The surly soldier glared up at Watson. "Captain Sigler was right—we never should've let you locals into the program."

Watson cuffed the man's head. "Shut up, moron. *Let* us in? *Ha!* I've spent more years on this than you've been alive. I've given more than you can possibly imagine."

Tack pulled his ATV around next to ours. "We have to go," he whispered. "They could send more troops after us at any time. Maybe they already have."

Min stared at the old man holding a gun on four restless soldiers. "Whatever you've done, Sheriff, there's still time to make it right. Tell us what you know. Who's after us?" Her body tensed like a piano string. "*Who's been killing me?*"

Watson shook his head. "You have no idea what we tried to accomplish," he said softly, then looked away. "Or what's coming."

The soldiers shifted restlessly, exchanging glances. Watson stepped back, trying to cover all four at once. If they broke for him, he'd lose. "Better move now, Min. You'll learn it all soon enough. Take care of your friends. I believe in you most of all."

Min shrieked in frustration, slamming the handlebars with her fists. Then she gunned away without another word. Tack fell in behind us as we raced across the field. There was a path, then the road. Two minutes later we reached the gate.

We ditched the vehicles, slipped under the fence, and sprinted to my car. I was unlocking the doors when I heard the first shot, followed by several more.

A pause, then two more shots in rapid succession. I turned startled eyes on my companions. "Did Watson shoot those guys!? How's he gonna get away on foot?"

Min kicked the glove box, snarling. "Just drive!" Startled, I yanked the car into gear and peeled out. We hit pavement, and I raced toward town. No one followed.

Min was sobbing, head buried in her chest. Tack reached a hand toward her, then thought better of it, slouching back. Confused, I met his eye in the rearview.

Tack glared at me. "Watson wasn't getting away, you dope. He could never handle all those guys at once. The fat old bastard was buying us time." Tack looked away, trying to keep his composure as he stared out the window.

"Those last shots, Noah? That was Sheriff Watson's execution."

30

MIN

I slept until midmorning.

Only a few hours—after sneaking past Mom and curling up on my side of the trailer—but I'd needed them badly. The memory of last night would scar, I knew.

Two men had died, at least. Tack nearly, too. And for what? Just a glimpse of some men we already knew were conspiring against us.

School was canceled, so there was no point getting up early. Martial law at least got me away from Principal Myers. Eventually I trudged into the living room to find that my mother had left me breakfast on the coffee table.

I flipped on the news. Nothing about the violent death of our sheriff, not that I'd expected anything. His body was probably in a ditch somewhere in "Grid Four."

Sheriff Watson was part of Project Nemesis. Had served it for decades. He'd helped the government experiment on *school-*

children in his jurisdiction for at least a decade. Such evil was hard to fathom.

But he saved Tack's life. Gave his own.

Too little, too late. Watson had let the monsters through the door. I thought back to him questioning me as a child. Those memories now had a sinister quality. Had he known then what was happening to a scared little trailer-park girl?

My mood hardened.

I ate my cold eggs slowly, watching the comet panic. Riots had closed the port of Tokyo. Large sections of Frankfurt were burning. There was fighting on the floor of the UN General Assembly. The president made another address, trying to ease tensions, but crowds still filled the streets of major US cities, protesting military control.

Also freakier stuff. The Australian Seismological Society reported increased activity along fault lines in the Pacific Rim. Volcanoes were smoking across Indonesia, and portions of the wild bird population had fled.

Things were falling apart. Right as Nemesis was ramping up.

We're running out of time.

I jumped as the door opened and my mother stepped inside. "About time you were up," she said briskly, unwrapping her scarf and hanging it on the hook. "Just because school's out doesn't mean you should sleep the whole day away."

I watched her cruise the trailer, attending to tasks she'd neglected over the previous few days. She seemed . . . different. Not as scared. Or morose. Or just plain numb. There was purpose to her movements as she squared away our tiny domain.

Upon completing her tasks, Mom nodded to herself. I noticed she'd never removed her jacket. "There's nothing to eat in this place. I'm heading down to the store, rationing be damned. Is there anything you need, Min? Anything at all?"

We made eye contact for the first time. I saw a well of emotion, quickly shielded.

Hard questions fluttered to the tip of my lips.

Why'd you sign the form, Mom? Do you know what happens on my birthdays?

"No. Nothing."

She nodded, eyes lowering as she slipped back outside.

I rose and went to the window, watched her stride out of sight. There was more lurking in that woman than most people saw.

I don't trust her.

I punched the wall, tears burning in my eyes. I *hated* this. Hated what Project Nemesis had done to me. To my family and friends. My town. It was a hidden cancer destroying everything it touched.

I wondered again at the name.

Nemesis.

Does it refer to him? Is the black-suited man my nemesis?

But that made no sense. Why build a secret government project around a psychopath killing teenagers? What purpose could that serve? The idea gave me the shakes.

Or did it go deeper? Darker? I rubbed my eyes, tired of thoughts that ran in circles. Maybe "Nemesis" had come up in a random name generator and meant nothing at all. Wouldn't that be perfect?

I picked up my cell. No signal, so I tried the landline and

got a dial tone. Score one for old-school tech. I was about to call Tack, then hesitated. He'd been hard to deal with lately, wrapped up in his disdain for Noah. Though, admittedly, Noah hadn't covered himself in glory last night. He'd locked up when the soldiers cornered us, and never snapped out of it, still in a daze as he dropped us off at the trailer-park gate.

He's all alone in that big house.

Then I sucked in a breath.

I hadn't told Noah something. Something important.

But would he really want to know?

I would. And I'd be furious if he kept it from me.

With a heavy heart, I punched in his number.

We met in town. Almost nothing was open, but rocking chairs lined the waterfront by the marina and we sat. The temperature was cool but not cold, fall holding on gamely in the face of winter's approach. The sky was gloomy and overcast, with a steady breeze lapping waves against the pier.

For a while, neither of us spoke. Then Noah nodded toward the burned-out mechanic's shop at the end of the wharf. "The Portland quake caused that fire. I came down here to avoid Ethan and the others, and saw it blazing like a matchstick." He pointed to a side street. "That's where they met. The Nemesis men. I saw Black Suit with them, and ran."

He bowed his head. "I'm pretty good at running from things."

"Hey." I touched his arm. "Stop it. You're officially allowed to run away from a serial killer. It's in the rule book and everything."

Noah smiled. He had such a strong face when he wasn't

moping, or totally checked out. "What was it you wanted to tell me?" he asked.

"I . . . I was thinking about something Tack and I found in Lowell's office."

Noah nodded for me to continue. I hesitated. He was already down about so many things. Why add to it?

Noah must've sensed my reluctance. "It's okay, Min. I can tell it's bad, and involves me. Might as well just tell me and get it over with."

Deep breath.

"My consent form—the one for Nemesis, that my mother signed? It wasn't the only one in Lowell's files. There was one for you, too."

"Figured as much." Noah rocked back in his chair and sighed. "I'm not surprised. Honestly, I'm shocked my father even cared enough to sell me. But my *God*, what an unbelievable prick. All my life he's mocked my problems. Therapy. The way that I am. Yet he knew the whole time."

I stared at the floorboards. "Your father didn't sign the form, Noah."

He straightened. I felt his eyes. "Then who did?"

"Your mother signed it."

Noah popped up from his rocker. He took a few steps backward, staring at me, then turned and strode away down the wharf.

I hurried after him. "Noah? You okay?"

He didn't answer, continuing along the waterfront at a brisk pace. As we neared the center of the town, he slowed, then stopped, thrusting his hands into his pockets.

"Noah, I'm so sorry. Maybe I shouldn't have—"

A hand rose. He stared out at the lake. "Thank you for telling me."

I drew closer, but didn't speak. Hoped my presence might provide some comfort.

"You know, it's weird," he said slowly. "In a way, I'm kind of relieved. At least my dad didn't betray me for my whole life. He's a jerk, and we hate each other, but it's honest. I bet he has no idea about Nemesis. He'd never allow a *Livingston man* to be used like that."

"Hey, I got you beat," I quipped, trying to keep my voice light. "My dad abandoned me when I was a baby. He didn't even stick around to ignore me. But my *mom* hugged me every day before school, for years, despite signing that form."

His sparkling green eyes locked onto mine. I had to look away.

I kicked myself. Why'd I bring up my parents?

"You're right." Noah's voice was full of self-recrimination. "I didn't even consider . . . Typical me. Spoiled little rich boy, wrapped up in his own problems. Never thinking about anyone but himself."

"No!" I turned him to face me. "I didn't mean it like that. The last thing we should do is make each other feel bad." I forced a crooked grin. "It occurs to me we have a lot in common."

"We do?"

I nodded. "Our fathers are total disasters. And our mothers—"

"Have secrets. Sold us like lab rats, and we don't know why."

I ran a hand through my hair. Spotting a bench, I motioned for him to join me. We sat together this time, his leg pressing against mine. I didn't pull away.

"This one's tough," Noah said candidly, scuffing his shoe on a plank. "I don't remember much about my mother, but what I do is . . . nice. Warm hands. Silly songs. I like to think my life would've been different had she lived. Finding out she signed me over to Lowell . . . That's hard to take."

I put my hand over his. "I see my mother every single day. It *kills* me. The thought that she's been a part of my misery for all these years, and kept it from me . . . I sometimes can't even breathe. But I still can't talk to her about it."

He flipped his hand over, twining his fingers with mine. "I'm sorry, Min. For both of us. It seems impossible that they would do this. There must be a reason why."

"I'm going to find out. I *will*."

Noah sighed. "Sometimes I wonder if we should even bother. No one cares about our problems. Not right now."

"It's all connected!" I squeezed his hand without meaning to. "Our murders. These disasters. That's impossible, I know, but somehow it's true. I don't care if the planet implodes *tomorrow*, I'm going to find out what's been happening to me. Why these men did this."

He wrapped an arm around my shoulders. "I think you will, too. No matter what. That's what makes you, you."

I didn't pull away. "I keep going over everything we've learned. There has to be a pattern. And what did that countdown clock you saw mean?"

"Let's just sit for a minute. Relax. Think."

He pulled me in. I let him, resting my head on his shoulder. Noah shifted, brought his other arm around me, hugging my back to his chest. I nuzzled closer.

We sat like that for a long time, gazing at the lake.

It felt good.

31

NOAH

Min was in my arms.

I steadied my breathing, willed my heartbeat to slow. Tried to act natural, but my entire manner was fake—pretending to be relaxed when my body was on fire. Not that I wanted it to stop. Far from it. The moment was surreal. Magical. Wonderful. I wanted to keep my arms around Min for as long as she'd let me. It felt so . . . safe.

So of course it didn't last.

Voices on the wind. Min glanced down the waterfront, then pulled free of me in a rush.

Toby and Chris were strolling along the dock, trading shoves and raucous laughter. They spotted us at the same time. Toby's eyebrows quirked. He turned and whistled. Derrick and Mike spilled from an alley behind them, followed by Ethan and some of the girls.

Ugh.

Min stood up quickly as the group approached.

"Don't get into it with them," I whispered, hoping to avoid a showdown. Tack wasn't around, but I didn't know where Ethan stood with Min. I prayed he'd moved on to other things.

"Yo!" Derrick waved, smiling slyly. "Didn't know it was date night, bro. My bad!"

Toby scooped up a rock and chucked it out over the water. It skipped twice before hitting a fishing skiff, causing him to cackle.

Min's temper flashed. "That's somebody's boat, genius."

My eyes snapped to her, begging for restraint, but she ignored the warning.

Toby smirked at Chris, who grinned back at him. "She doesn't get it, does she?"

"Perhaps we could show the lady?"

"Indeed!"

Toby and Chris walked over to the bench we'd been sitting on. They nodded to each other, then kicked it in unison. The wood shivered but held, so they kicked again. This time the backrest broke off and went sliding, leaving just the seat intact.

"Huh." Toby rubbed his chin. "How about that! Bolted to the ground."

Derrick ran up and spiked a trash can on the bench's remains, generating howls from all three. Min glanced at me, but I could only shrug. I knew where this was going, and it made me tired all over.

Ethan shook his head as he approached. "Really, Noah? It's the end of the world, and you're dumpster diving?"

I felt Sarah's eyes. Knew it burned her, finding us together. I resisted an urge to shy from Min's side.

"So you're just breaking things now?" Min snapped, tightening the noose around my neck. "Real smart. The country's under martial law, you know. Police will arrest you for stuff like this."

Ethan scooped up a bottle at his feet, then casually fired it at the store behind us. Glass exploded like fireworks. "Look around you, Min. There's no one here. The cops are all off planning evacuation routes or whatever. Oregon and Washington are *demolished*, and comets are about to pummel Asia. Nobody cares what we do."

"My dad says more crackdowns are coming," Toby said. "The guys in the liberty camp, they've got killer sources. People in the know. Everything's gonna get worse."

"Two comets hit today." Jessica stood next to Sarah, dry-washing her hands. "The Russian one is still coming, and those wackos might nuke it. What if they miss, and their missiles end up here?"

Mike shook his head, actually spoke. "Won't miss. Question is, where do the fragments land?"

Min shot me a troubled glance. We'd been unplugged and missed the news. How many people had died while we were cuddling on the bench?

"You guys still don't get it!" Toby went on, working himself up. "The government is lying! On ham radio, people are reporting weird stuff all over. Plus there was some kind of mass suicide in Oklahoma. Like, hundreds in a cornfield, or something. Soldiers arrested a film crew on the scene and took their cameras. They don't want people to see."

"Up to speed, Melinda?" Ethan kicked trash into the water, a cardinal sin in this tourist town. "With all that going on, I'm not too worried about our local cops rounding up vandals."

"You have *no idea* what's going on," Min spat. "Everyone in this town needs to be careful or . . . or . . ."

"Or what?" Ethan asked, suddenly intent. "What are you saying?"

"Nothing. Just . . . it could get dangerous around here."

Chris snorted, pulling his fiery hair into a ponytail. "In Fire Lake? Whatever. We live in a mountain fortress. All we have to worry about is boredom."

"And supplies." Ethan ticked off fingers. "Food. Water. Ammo. We should gather as much as we can now. There's no telling what might happen. Some of the smarter West Coast dips might realize what we've got up here and try to take it from us."

Toby leaned forward, eyes dancing. "The camp has a plan for that. I'm not supposed to talk about it—or even *know* about it, but Uncle Danny can't shut up when he's drinking. There's something *serious* in the works."

"What trash are you talking?" Chris scoffed. "Man, you don't know jack."

"The hell I don't! You watch. I'm not saying any more about it."

Derrick pointed toward Main Street with a mischievous smile. "You guys really want to act like doomsday preppers? Nobody's watching the hardware store right now."

Ethan straightened. "Anyone around up there?"

"Get serious," Min growled. "You're not going to rob Buford's. You wouldn't get ten feet. Not after I called the owners, anyway."

All heads swung her way. "You heard us," she said, glancing at me for support.

Something in my face must've betrayed me.

"Noah?"

I wanted to back Min up. Take her side, and stand up for what was right.

Ethan smirked, enjoying the hard place in which I'd landed. "You gonna rat on your friends, Noah?"

I nearly told Ethan what I thought of him. What I thought about *all* of them, really.

Instead, I shrugged. "I don't care. Seems stupid, but whatever."

I heard Min's intake of breath. Her entire body radiated disappointment.

She turned on Ethan. "Well, I *do* care. Touch that store, or any other, and I'll tell Sher—" Min stumbled in her words, then finished quietly. "I'll tell the police who did it."

Then Min glared at me. "Good-bye. I'm going to find Tack. I need to decompress with a friend for a while."

The guys whistled and laughed as she left, shouting overwrought apologies and begging for her to come back. The girls hid wicked smiles. I said nothing as Min disappeared around a corner. I'd never felt more ashamed.

Why am I so worthless? God, I hate myself.

Anger detonated inside me. My head rose, lips forming a snarl.

"Why are you such a prick all the time?" I said to Ethan. "You need to leave Min alone."

He stopped dead. Silence fell like a scythe.

“Excuse me?” Ethan said, casually moving closer. “Did you just say something?”

“You heard me.”

I took a step toward him, about to do something very, very stupid.

BOOM.

BOOM. BOOM. BOOM.

Blasts echoed across the canyon.

Everyone flinched. “Oh my God!” Jessica cried. “Earthquake!”

“No, no!” Toby ran down the wharf, waving for us to follow. “This is it! This is what I was talking about! C’mon!”

The others set off after him. I followed in spite of myself, as curious as the rest.

“Where are we going?” Ethan demanded.

“The Plank!” Toby reached the Nolans’ van and started pounding on its side, eyes wild. “Head for the bridge!”

Everyone piled inside. Sarah ended up on my lap. I shifted uncomfortably, wondering why I was even in the car as Mike sped west. Then he slammed the brakes. “What the hell?”

Thirty yards from the canyon, half a dozen cars were parked bumper to bumper across the highway. A Fire Lake police cruiser idled next to the makeshift barricade, with two deputies standing beside it and furiously whispering to each other. Beyond them, a dozen armed men were blocking access to the bridge.

They were scruffy types in jeans and dirty overalls, bearded, wearing sunglasses and bandanas to cover their faces. Smoke was rising from the span behind them and drifting across the gorge.

A small crowd had gathered, some yelling angrily, others

cheering the men on. The deputies pointed and shouted, but to no avail. One jumped inside the cruiser and started hollering into her radio.

"Holy crap!" Derrick's eyes darted nervously as we joined the onlookers. "What are they doing out there? Were those explosions we heard?"

I shook my head, baffled. Then the answer clicked home.

"They're trying to blow the bridge."

Heads turned to me in surprise. Toby nodded, elated.

"Sealing off the valley," he said proudly. "We'll be safe from everything to the west. Liberty men planned this whole op last night. *Told* you I knew something, Chris! Nobody's coming up here and taking *our* stuff."

"But that's the only way in or out." I glanced around for support. Sarah and Jessica looked too stunned to speak. Chris was smiling like a zealot, while Mike was stone-faced. Ethan rubbed his cheek, his expression guarded. Only Derrick seemed to share my horror.

"What if *I* want to leave, Toby?" Derrick threw his hands into the air. "My sister's down at Boise State. She won't be able to get home!"

"What if we run out of food?" I asked. "We have one supermarket."

"You've seen the news," Toby said firmly, eyes glued to the bandits. "The country is about to catch fire—this way, we don't burn with it. We can start planting crops like the Indians used to. Run our *own* government."

Ethan looked sharply at Toby.

Chris Nolan pointed. "Heads up!"

A man in a ski mask came running off the bridge, waving his hands. The other gunmen scattered, taking cover. There was another series of ear-shattering booms. I watched in horror as smoke billowed skyward.

Seconds ticked. The smoke cleared. Gunmen emerged from their hiding places, looking confused. Several threw anxious glances into town as sirens began to wail.

A long metallic groan. Then a loud crack.

We watched in silence as the bridge split in the center, cables snapping as the two sides swung apart and smashed into the canyon walls. A cloud of dust erupted, choking and blinding everyone. When the air cleared, the Plank was gone.

"Oh my God." I ran both hands over my scalp. Those lunatics had done it. Our only link to the outside world was now at the bottom of the gorge.

Derrick was stomping back and forth with his fists clenched. "Why didn't the cops stop them? Where's Sheriff Watson?"

I stiffened. Watson couldn't help us, or anyone else, ever again. Maybe it was his absence that had allowed this nightmare to happen. I glanced at the cruiser. The deputy still outside it was discreetly pumping a fist. Was there another conspiracy in Fire Lake, involving the liberty camp? Maybe the police had reacted slowly on purpose.

Engine noises behind me. I turned. Nearly leapt from my skin.

"Get out of here!" I yelled at the others, already booking it for the woods. But I tripped and fell, rolling into a roadside ditch.

Ethan frowned down at me. "God, Noah, you're such a wuss. It's embarrassing." Then he saw the gray vehicles that had sent me scrambling.

I staggered to my feet. "Guys! Get out of here, seriously! Those dudes are dangerous!"

No one listened, watching in silence as a wedge of jeeps and Humvees rolled to a halt behind the car barricade. Caught in no-man's-land, I ducked back into the ditch.

Soldiers leapt down and pushed through the crowd, covered by others manning machine guns atop each Humvee. Fire Lake residents began shouting questions, spooked. To them, these grim-faced troops must've dropped straight out of the sky.

The soldiers were silent and efficient, taking up positions in seconds. The liberty campers had gathered at the edge of the ruined bridge, caught off guard by the military response. But they remained defiant. Four-letter words floated on the breeze.

An officer with short black hair stepped up beside one of the machine guns. I recognized him immediately—he'd driven Lowell and Myers away last night, before everything went bad. A chest patch named him Captain Harkes.

Harkes surveyed the gunmen through a pair of binoculars. I saw one give him the finger, to the roaring approval of his comrades. A sandy-haired man in a yellow bandana cupped his hands to his mouth. "What are you going to do, make us rebuild it? This is *our* valley! You're not wanted here!"

Captain Harkes pressed a finger to his ear. Nodded. Then he raised a gloved fist.

All down the line, the soldiers took aim.

Yellow Bandana froze. Then his hands shot up. "Hold on! Okay, you win. We surr—"

"Fire," Harkes ordered calmly.

A line of bullets tore through the liberty men, cutting them in half. They fell in a bloody mass, each body pierced a dozen times.

Residents screamed, fled in terror. A pair of injured gunmen broke for the woods. I watched, horrified, as three soldiers stepped out onto the road, knelt smoothly, and shot them in the back.

It was over in seconds. The liberty men were dead. The crowd had scattered, their shouts echoing off the canyon walls. But I was still crouching in a ditch like an idiot, ten feet away from an active death squad.

Get out of here, you moron!

Ethan and the others were scrambling into the van. I saw Jessica throw herself inside, blubbering uncontrollably to Sarah, followed by Derrick, Chris, and Toby, who was screaming something about his uncle.

Ethan was last. He spotted me as Mike fired the engine and waved for me to hurry.

I spun, ran into the woods. Had only one thought in my head.

Min. I've got to tell Min.

32

MIN

"Told you he's a jackass." Tack wore a satisfied smile as he poked the fire with a stick. "Noah Livingston is a silver-spoon waste like the rest of them. We don't need him."

I didn't reply. After Noah's cop-out by the lake, part of me agreed.

He was just so . . . frustrating.

Right after we had that moment, too. For a minute I thought . . .

Tack tossed another log into the pit. The temperature had dropped off a cliff that afternoon, winter gusts swirling in off the mountains. We'd get snow soon, a thick carpet of white to cover the trailer park's dirty lanes. I'd always liked that time of year.

Then suddenly, he was there.

Tack and I sat up as Noah came tearing down the path toward my trailer. Tack rolled his eyes. "God, does he *ever* learn?"

Noah skidded to a stop, gripping his knees as he gasped for breath. He'd obviously run a long way. "*Min! Did . . . you . . . hear?*"

Tack slouched back in his chair, clearly annoyed by the intrusion. I debated ignoring Noah, still furious with him. And hurt as well, to be honest. But curiosity got the best of me. "Hear what?" I huffed.

"The Plank." Noah sucked in a lungful, finally getting his wind back. Then his eyes lost focus, as if he couldn't believe what he was saying. "It's gone. *Destroyed*. The liberty campers blew it up and it fell into the canyon!"

"What!?" I shot to my feet. "Are you serious?"

Noah nodded grimly, and I spun on Tack. "You said that was fireworks!"

Tack's face turned red. "I just assumed, because of the cheering. I didn't know some yahoos would blow up the damn bridge!"

"Why would anyone *do* that?" I pressed my temples. Had the world gone crazy?

Tack was shaking his head. "They're all crazy separatists. They must think we're better off severed from the rest of the country. Who knows, maybe they're right."

"That's *nuts*, Tack." The magnitude of Noah's news was sinking in. "Fire Lake isn't self-sufficient. We don't even have a hospital! Without the Plank we're trapped, and help might be a *long* time coming."

The Pacific Northwest had been devastated. Oregon and Washington were federal disaster areas, with millions trapped in desperate conditions and trillions of dollars of damage to infrastructure. Where would fixing the bridge to Fire Lake rank on the list of emergency repairs? Low. *Extremely* low.

Noah swallowed. "I haven't told you the worst part."

The door to my trailer swung open and Mom emerged. She was in her nightgown, a patchwork blanket thrown around her shoulders against the chill. "What happened, Noah? After those fools blew up the bridge." She'd clearly heard us talking.

Noah hesitated, his face paling. "It . . . it was bad. The soldiers showed up."

I stopped breathing. "The ones from the silo base?"

Noah nodded, rubbing his forehead. "They surrounded the campers. Those liberty guys are stubborn. They didn't know . . . The officer barely even paused . . ."

My mother strode over and put an arm around him. He leaned into her embrace like a starving man. It occurred to me that Noah had been living alone for a week, without anyone else.

"Tell us," my mother said.

"They opened fire." His eyes glistened.

"Any survivors?"

Noah closed his eyes. Shook his head.

Tack was pulling his hair with both hands. "Holy sh—"

A crash of metal echoed up the hill.

"You kids stay here!" Mom ordered. The blanket fell to the mud as she rushed down the lane.

I looked at Tack, who rubbed his palms on his jeans. "No idea. What should we do?"

"Come on!" I grabbed Noah's arm. We stumbled to the common, found my mother standing in her nightgown with a hand to her mouth, staring at the gate. Gray combat vehicles were rolling up the main drag, black sunbursts gleaming on their doors.

Tack pulled me a step toward the back fence. "Let's bail!"

"Stand right there, Thomas!" my mother shouted, startling us both.

Tack let go, uncertain. Two jeeps and a Humvee drove to within a dozen yards. Soldiers popped out, including a thin officer with a blond mustache. His men surrounded us, weapons at the ready. Any chance to escape had vanished.

Principal Myers levered himself out of the Humvee, wheezing as he leaned on his cane. He limped over to the blond officer and said something sharp, handing him a metal clipboard. The man gave him a hard look, but turned and shouted, "Lower your weapons!"

The soldiers complied, but didn't relax. Tack shifted nervously, trying to watch everyone at once. Myers was sweating despite the cool temperature. "No need for alarm, kids. No one's gonna hurt you." He shot a nasty glare at the blond officer. "Commander Sutton! Tell your men to stand down."

"Stay in your lane, Myers. You're here as local liaison only."

Sutton glanced at the clipboard. Suddenly, I could guess what was on it.

"Melinda J. Wilder. Thomas Russo. Under Section 2.43A of FEMA Special Emergency Preparedness Act 580, you are hereby ordered to attend an emergency assembly, to be held in the town square of Fire Lake. These men will escort you. Attendance is mandatory."

"What's happening?" Tack whispered.

"He's got the collection schedule," I said. "The roster with names and addresses."

The color drained from Tack's face. Noah's throat worked. Then my mother marched forward, ignoring the guns as she stormed to stand in front of Myers.

Their eyes met. He broke first, dropping his head.

Mom regarded him for a moment. Then slapped him across the face.

Soldiers moved to restrain her, but Myers waved them back. He faced my mother alone. "It's time, Virginia. I'm sorry it's happening like this. Our calculations were off, and things got sped up."

"Keep your word, Andrew! Make this *mean* something, after everything we've done!"

"I promise, Virginia."

The world stopped spinning.

My heart ceased beating.

The sun halted in its path across the sky.

Tack was tugging my arm, whispering urgently, but I didn't notice. I couldn't see or hear a thing. I'd retreated to a deep recess in my mind where only one fact existed.

Mom knows everything.

She turned and hurried to my side. "Min, you need to listen to me," she whispered. "You have to go with these men. Don't run away or resist."

I gaped, unable to breathe. Was about to be sick. Then I shoved her with both hands, suddenly and explosively furious. "*How could you!?*"

For the first time in days, Mom met my eyes squarely. "I did what I had to. I'm sorry for what it's cost you."

I stared in disbelief. Wanted it to be a dream. But I'd known this was coming since the moment I saw my mother's signature.

"What is this, Mom? What's going on?"

She seemed about to answer, but Commander Sutton spoke over her. "That's enough. Get them into the Humvee. We're running behind as it is."

"Livingston is here, too," Myers said.

"Bring him. I'll notify Control. But we have to leave *now*. The trouble in town might spread, and the assets aren't all in place."

The soldiers closed in, began herding us toward the vehicles. Tack shrugged off the first man to prod him, but two more shoved him while a third trained his rifle. Noah shuffled forward with his shoulders hunched. He looked close to losing it.

I stumbled along in a daze. Then whirled. "*Why*, Mom? What'd they promise you?" Our eyes met, and my voice broke. "Was I really such a bad daughter?"

Myers flinched. He glanced at Sutton, who shook his head.

Mom flew forward and wrapped her arms around me, then held me by the cheeks, our faces inches apart. "No! *No*. You're the best daughter a mother could have. Don't ever doubt my love for you, Melinda J. *Ever*. I love you with all my heart. This isn't your—"

A soldier pulled me away. Dragged me to the waiting vehicles.

I saw my mother trailing us in her bedclothes, glaring at Myers and shaking her tiny fist. "Make this *count*, Andrew! You and that other one. You asked for too much, and we'll never get clean. But cross me now and I'll make you pay!"

"I'll see it through, Virginia. You have my word. His, too."

Mom turned, began slowly walking back toward our trailer. She seemed smaller. Older.

Something told me I'd never see her again.

Tack twisted suddenly and kicked the closest soldier in the crotch. The man dropped, writhing in pain. Tack attempted to leap over him, but three other guards converged and wrestled him to the ground, Tack bucking and snarling like a wild animal until one of them struck him on the head with a rifle butt. He went limp, and they loaded him into the Humvee.

"Easy!" Myers bellied up to the soldier who'd struck my friend. "These are core subjects. Don't damage them!" The man looked back impassively for a moment, then pushed past him.

Noah climbed in beside Tack. I followed without a struggle, too shattered to think. Myers wedged in beside me and closed the door. In seconds we were barreling for the gate.

Myers spoke into a radio. "Lowell, Myers here. We have Livingston with our task group. Proceeding to staging area. Myers out."

I looked up at him. "Staging for what, Principal Myers?"

He winced, perhaps at my use of his title. A reference to his position of trust. He seemed about to speak, but a rumbling in the hills cut him off. The jeep slid on the narrow gravel driveway up to Quarry Road, but managed to find traction. We reached pavement and turned for town.

Myers sat back, wiping sweat from his face.

"Principal Myers?" I repeated, but he shook his head, his mouth a grim line.

"Almost time," was all he said.

33

NOAH

I could barely breathe.

Min was shouting at Myers, who refused to respond. Tack's head was on my shoulder, still stunned from having it cracked. I sat still, unspeaking, locked up to the point I was almost unable to function.

It's happening.

We were prisoners of Project Nemesis, which was operating in the open now.

The Humvee raced down Main Street to town square, which was surrounded by a confusion of people and vehicles. Gray-uniformed soldiers had formed an armed cordon around the entire plaza. Townsfolk were pressing the barriers, shouting and pointing angrily toward a group of nervous-looking teens huddled by the fountain at the square's center.

The Humvee stopped just short of the protesters.

"Everyone out," Myers ordered gruffly. "Join your classmates on the lawn."

"Why?" Min demanded. "So you can shoot everyone at once? What's going to happen to us? How could you *do* this?"

He paused. "I'm sorry, Min. Especially for you betas. I had to make a hard choice."

"*Sorry doesn't make this okay!*" Min shouted, her face purpling. She started punching him again and again in the shoulder. Myers made no attempt to defend himself.

I watched, immobilized, unable to react.

This has to be a dream.

A soldier opened the door and removed Tack, then ordered me out. A squad stood a few paces off, watching the crowd intently. Shouts and threats carried from the barriers—Fire Lake citizens, demanding access to their children. The troops held their weapons ready.

A soldier thrust Tack at me. I caught his weight and swung an arm under his shoulder, holding him up as best I could. Tack swayed, mumbling incoherently as more soldiers hauled Min from the Humvee. Myers remained inside, staring at his hands as blood trickled from a cut on his forehead, unnoticed. For some reason this scared me more than anything else.

"Form up!" Sutton commanded. Troops raced to obey, surrounding us in a tight phalanx. We marched past the Nolans' van, pulled up on a curb outside the cordon. I could see Ethan and a few others inside the assembly area, milling anxiously, watching the guards with a mixture of resentment and fear.

Tack stirred. Pushed me away, his head lolling on his shoulders. "Wha—?"

"Take it easy." I kept an arm out just in case. "We're being moved."

"We have to do something," Min whispered, but Sutton was already issuing new orders.

"Deliver them to the holding zone," he told our escort, then addressed us directly. "You three: proceed to the center of the square and remain there. Don't get cute. Noncompliance will be dealt with harshly." Then he turned and strode away.

Min's hands were fists. I could see blood on her knuckles, and nearly got sick.

"We should do what they say," I said quickly.

Her eyes whipped to me. She thought I was being spineless again, but I'd witnessed the massacre at the Plank. *We can't test these men.*

A hand gripped my shoulder. I spun, nearly shouted.

Dr. Lowell had wormed his way to my side. He looked ridiculous in a military uniform, his fiery red hair at odds with the drab fatigues. His gaze bore into me, his fingers tightening like a claw. "Listen to me, Noah. You can do this! I believe in you. Just trust yourself. Trust your *instincts*, the real ones we buried so deeply. Do you understand?"

I shook my head, stunned. Of course I didn't understand. But then Min lunged across me, trying to get a piece of Lowell. "I know what you did, you monster!"

Lowell stepped back through the guards, who didn't impede his movements. "I'm not worried about you, Min. You've always had spirit. Godspeed to you both. I'm sorry I didn't do more." Then he disappeared into the mob.

Our escort carved a path through the protesters, using force when necessary. A sawhorse was pulled aside, the lines parted, and we were shoved into the open space beyond. The soldiers were arranged in a double formation—an inner square facing the kids by the fountain, surrounded by an outer square holding back the townspeople. They were stone-faced and heavily armed. All wore gray uniforms with the black starburst emblem.

Without another option, we hurried over to join our classmates. Ethan intercepted us halfway, his expression unreadable. Min tensed, and I worried her anger would erupt again. *The last thing we need right now.*

But Ethan merely nodded. "You too, huh? Thought maybe they skipped the trailer park." He jabbed a thumb back at the fountain. "Almost everyone. The whole sophomore class, rounded up like criminals. They jammed the cell tower, too."

His gaze flicked behind me. A disturbance was working through the crowd to the edge of the cordon. "I'll bet anything that's Hector, Benny, and Darren Phelps," Ethan said. "They're the only ones still missing."

The troops parted and Hector Quino stumbled onto the grass, followed by the two other boys Ethan had named. Benny Erikson hustled over to the group, but Darren whirled and ran at the guards, trying to break the line. Three soldiers tackled him. Darren continued to struggle until a soldier punched him in the stomach, shoved him down, and drew a pistol. Wide-eyed, Darren crawled away, gasping, until Hector helped him to his feet. The soldier watched them retreat, then coolly holstered his sidearm and rejoined the line.

The crowd seethed, shouting and cursing at the troops. I recognized parents and business owners, people I'd known my whole life. They were scared, *outraged*, but the assault rifles were keeping them at bay.

Myers hobbled over and screamed in the face of the soldier who'd drawn on Darren. The man ignored him. Red-faced, Myers limped toward a knot of officers at the corner of the square.

"Everyone's here?" Min asked sharply. She'd gotten ahold of her temper.

"Yes," Ethan replied, for once choosing not to be difficult. "You six make sixty-four on the nose." He smiled without humor. "Think they're planning a Hunger Games?"

Tack pointed to the command post Myers had joined. "We're about to find out."

Vehicles formed the northern edge of the security cordon. As we watched, Myers heaved himself onto the back of a flatbed truck and began fumbling with a bullhorn. But before he could speak, there was a disturbance on the street.

Tack gasped. "*Oh no.* Dad!"

Wendell Russo was trying to fight his way into the square. He caught a soldier with an uppercut, knocking him to the turf. A second man charged him, but Wendell captured his arm and launched him sideways. Three more troops converged, and they all went down in a pile of bodies.

Tack lurched forward, but Min caught his arm. "Tack, stay here. You can't do anything."

The fight ended quickly. Two soldiers lifted Wendell and held him between them. Blood ran from a broken nose. "Let go of me, you bastards. I'm a veteran! Where's my son?"

Captain Harkes strode over and said something. Wendell spat in his face. "Piss on you and your threats. I know my rights, sunshine soldier. Who are you guys, anyway? You can't just grab people off the streets."

"*No no no*," Tack whispered.

Min locked her arm around his.

Harkes wiped the spittle from his cheek. He nodded to the soldiers holding Wendell, who dropped his arms and stepped aside.

Harkes drew his gun and fired twice.

"*DAD!*"

Tack lunged, but Min held on until I could grab him, too.

Wendell dropped to his knees, then toppled forward and lay still. The crowd erupted, scrambling away from Harkes, who strode back to the command post. "Safeties off!" he ordered. A pair of soldiers began dragging Wendell's body away and the defensive line re-formed, only now with fingers on triggers.

"You son of a bitch!" Tack fought to free himself, choking on tears. "He was unarmed! He wasn't going to do anything!" We wrestled him to the ground and held him there, even Ethan lending a hand. Min was crying, but I was too rattled to feel anything but shock.

"Let me go!" Tack growled, but no one did. He struggled futilely, then gave up. Slowly, his breathing calmed. When he spoke again, his voice was almost normal. "Seriously, let me go. I won't do anything stupid, I swear. But get the hell off me, I mean it!"

I released him, watching like a hawk. We weren't friends or anything, but I didn't want Tack getting himself killed. He rose slowly, then stood there, clenching and unclenching his fists as he stared at the captain. "I'm gonna kill that man. I will."

Ethan gaped at the bloodstained curb. "They just . . . shot him. No warning. No anything."

Behind us, I could hear classmates panicking. Toby jogged over, his face a mixture of wonder and fear. "Ethan, we gotta do something! Mike and Derrick have an idea, but we need your help. Come on!"

Ethan nodded, waved for me to follow. "Let's go, Noah."

I flinched. Min was suddenly watching me. It felt like the docks all over again.

All my life, I've taken the easy way.

"Come on, Noah." Ethan's voice carried a note of warning. "You belong with us."

I shook my head, avoiding his eye. "I'm gonna stay here. Help with Tack."

"Really? So that's how it is?"

"Yes."

Ethan clicked his tongue. "I'll remember this." Then he and Toby jogged away.

I snuck a peek over at the fountain. Ethan and Toby were huddling with Chris, Mike, and Derrick. Jessica was crying beside Sarah, who was staring at me. My head jerked away.

Min was holding Tack as he sobbed. She mouthed her thanks.

I nodded.

I might never see my father again, but I didn't care. And screw what the others thought. I was done with all that.

Min can be my family.

The instant I thought it, the ground began to shake.

34

MIN

The earth heaved beneath my feet.

I fell to the grass as the rumbling intensified. Windows shattered up and down the block. The crowd, already spooked by the execution of Tack's father, scattered for cover. Alarms began blaring all over town.

Then, just as abruptly, the shaking ceased. Rattled faces rose, looked around. When nothing happened, my classmates and I climbed nervously to our feet. Ethan and Derrick made a break for a gap in the line, but the soldiers closed it quickly, marching them back at gunpoint. No one doubted they'd shoot.

Myers finally got the bullhorn to work. "May I have your attention!" his voice boomed.

We all fell silent, years of training heeling us to his voice like dogs. "There's no need for anyone to panic. We have everything under control."

My rage burned white-hot. Myers had been my principal

since I was six. Though never warm and fuzzy, he'd always been reliable. Solid. A comforting, unyielding presence in my life. The weight of his betrayal pressed down on me as he played spokesman for soldiers who'd just killed Wendell Russo in cold blood.

What'd they promise you, Myers? What's in your deal with the devil?

His shoulders slumped as he addressed us. "I love each and every one of you. I . . . I did my best. Whatever happens next, this is all on me. Put it on me." His head sank to his chest.

Two more people climbed onto the flatbed. The taller man was Dr. Fanelli, incongruously dressed in a natty three-piece suit. The shorter man gently took the bullhorn from Myers, who surrendered it without resistance.

"*Lowell*," I spat like a curse.

Before he could speak, the earth bucked again, then vibrated ominously as the mountains groaned. Screams caused me to whirl—the fountain was shaking to pieces, bone-crushing chunks of stone collapsing to the cobbles below. We all scrambled away.

A thunderous crack echoed across the valley. Startled, I glanced around, trying to locate the source. Then I watched in horror as a peak to the south split near its apex, sending a landslide of rock and earth tumbling downslope, wiping a section of mountainside clean before rumbling to a halt by the lakefront.

The quake ceased.

The proceedings acquired a new urgency.

Officers barked orders. Two squads peeled off from the inner square and surrounded an eighteen-wheel truck parked beside the flatbed.

Lowell regained his feet, seemingly unperturbed. "To the

sophomore class of Fire Lake," he intoned, his amplified voice floating over the plaza. "I wish you all the best of luck. Our part is now done."

Lowell handed the bullhorn to Fanelli. The two men shook hands. Then, putting an arm around Myers, he helped the old man down from the truck. Left alone on the flatbed, Dr. Fanelli ignored the bullhorn. Instead, he pointed into the crowd of frightened teens, then tapped an index finger against his temple. Finally, Fanelli raised a fist and shook it madly, his placid expression morphing to fierce encouragement.

I spun. Was Fanelli signaling someone? With dazed students stumbling everywhere, it was impossible to tell.

The ground hummed once again.

"Something's happening." Noah pointed to a fragment of stone that was dancing between his sneakers. "The earth is still moving, even though we can't feel it. I don't like this."

"I'm gonna kill that captain." Tack was staring at Harkes as he conferred with Lowell and Commander Sutton. "I just need a chance. Only one. That's all."

Behind them, a van door slid open, revealing a mass of computer equipment inside. "That must be their nerve center," I said, then braced as another tremor shook the block. *What is going on?*

Suddenly, Noah howled.

I grabbed his shoulder. "You okay? What is it?"

He didn't respond. I pivoted, following his line of sight.

The black-suited man was standing fifty feet away.

After consulting an iPad, he said something to Commander Sutton, who saluted and hurried away. Alone, Black Suit regarded the penned-in students through his sunglasses. Then he stiffened. He was looking right at me. And knew I saw *him*, too.

A switch flipped. I stormed forward, making no effort to disguise my approach.

"Min?" Tack called. "Hey, what are you doing?"

Noah started, as if coming out of a trance.

I strode directly toward the murderer of my nightmares.

Soldiers ordered me to halt. Raised weapons. Took aim.

Black Suit barked something. The muzzles lowered. A pair of guards grabbed my arms, stopping me at the line.

I heard Tack and Noah run up behind me. The troops took aim again. Black Suit said nothing this time, watching impassively.

I threw my hands out by my sides. "Stop! Guys, stay back."

Black Suit nodded, then signaled his men. They released me.

There were a thousand things I wanted to scream in his face, but the words piled up in my head like a freeway crash. "You're a monster," was all I could manage.

"I know."

"You *ruined* my life, you psychopath. I hope you burn for it."

"I will. Good luck, Min."

The ground convulsed, harder than before. Black Suit's head snapped up, then he strode to the control van and disappeared inside.

That wasn't enough. I needed more. A fight. Closure. Something. Muscles tensing, I prepared to force my way past the soldiers, whatever the cost.

Instead, everything went crazy.

The grass began rolling like a ship at sea. Buildings around the block collapsed. A water main burst, shooting mud into the air.

In the confusion, a knot of parents attacked the barricades, trying to break through. The soldiers opened fire. Townspeople broke and ran, fleeing down side streets that cracked and split beneath their feet. Then the shaking stopped.

The troops tightened their formation, kicking bodies aside. New orders traveled up and down the line. The ones facing us advanced, forcing everyone onto the cobbles surrounding the broken fountain.

"Holy crap!" Derrick screamed. "They're gonna kill us!"

Ethan and Toby scooped up pieces of the stone, while behind them, Hector and some others had begun to pray. At the northern edge of the square, soldiers dragged sawhorses aside, opening a lane to the eighteen-wheeler. Black Suit emerged from his van as the big rig's rear doors swung open.

A group of men in hazmat suits climbed down.

"What the hell?" I glanced at Tack, who started chewing on his fist.

The men walked through the gap into the square. Each wore a strange backpack of some kind, with a long hose looping around to the front, topped by what looked like a fire extinguisher nozzle. They spread out around the fountain, encircling us.

"Screw this!" Ethan took a step toward the closest balloon man, but a spray of bullets at his feet stopped him short. The soldiers advanced again, packing us in even tighter. Then Commander Sutton shouted something. The soldiers withdrew smoothly, leaving the entire class backed against the fountain, surrounded by men in outbreak gear.

The earth groaned. A rent opened in Main Street. Tack and Noah pressed in on either side of me. I saw Black Suit yell something at Sutton, then hop into the van and slide its door shut.

"We're done for," Noah croaked.

Something exploded across town. The tremors increased in intensity.

Commander Sutton lifted a fist above his head.

I reached out and took Noah's hand. Grabbed Tack's on my other side.

Sutton paused. Saluted us with his other hand. Then brought his fist crashing down.

"Engage!"

The hazmat brigade flipped switches on the tops of their backpacks. A thin green mist spewed from the nozzles, filling the air with a viscous film. In seconds the oily spray reached the cobblestones.

Ethan was closest. He dropped to his knees, face purpling as he clawed at his throat.

Then Toby fell, eyes bulging, his mouth working like a fish out of water.

Poison! They're gassing us!

I tried to run, but my legs gave out on the first step. Crumpling like a pillowcase, I lost hold of Tack and Noah. The mist seeped in everywhere—through my pores, my eyes, and finally my lungs, sealing them shut and blocking out oxygen.

I crawled on hands and knees, trying to get clear.

Tack collapsed beside me, twitching in a ghastly way. Noah was scrabbling toward the fountain, vomit staining his shirt. He dragged his upper body over the rim, then flopped face-first into the water and went still.

Classmates writhed on the ground, tears and mucus coating

their faces. The agony was unbearable—a burning, stinging horror that tore at the skin. The moans were piteous and inhuman. Through blurry eyes, I saw Commander Sutton put a pistol to his temple and pull the trigger.

I rolled onto my back. My tongue felt too large for my mouth. I was blacking out, knew I'd be dead in moments. None of this made sense, but I was past caring.

I stared up at the sun, suddenly hypnotized by its blazing presence.

I lose. So I die. For realsies this time.

Lightning filled the sky in a spiderweb grid.

A bright pulse, then a boom like breaking the sound barrier.

My head scrambled. I felt a ripping sensation.

Everything went fuzzy, then snapped into laser-sharp focus, then went supernova.

Light, sound, and sensation disappeared.

A soft breeze ruffled my hair, sending shivers through my body.

I opened my eyes. Blinked. Sat up.

Daylight.

I was lying beside the fountain in town square. Except the fountain was whole and unmarked, its statue unbroken.

The ground was still. The sky clear. Our valley peaceful. Quiet.

Around me, Fire Lake sophomores were sprawled about like driftwood.

Sixty-three souls, unconscious on the grass.

Everyone else was gone.

PART FOUR

FIRE LAKE

35

NOAH

Hands gripped my calves, and I was dragged backward.

I flopped down onto something hard.

I couldn't breathe, felt an odd heaviness in my chest.

Someone was pounding on my abdomen. It was awful. I rolled to my side and puked a gallon of water.

"He's breathing," a voice said. Ethan? Dad?

"Noah? You okay?" A girl. *Min.*

I tried to respond. "Gah."

Not my best effort. I hocked more liquid from my mouth. Rubbed my head.

"He'll live." Heavy feet stomped away. *Definitely Ethan.*

My eyes fluttered open. Then snapped shut, bright sunlight searing my retinas. When the pain faded, I sat up gingerly, cracking my lids more cautiously a second time.

I'm still in the square.

"Go slow," Min warned, rising from my side. "Your head

should clear in a minute. I'd offer you some water, but I'm guessing you'll pass."

"Ha!" I scratched my face. Blew a snot rocket.

When Min next spoke, her voice trembled. "You have to see this, Noah. It's like . . . like nothing . . ." She trailed off as something else caught her attention. Min grunted and strode away, leaving me alone for the moment.

I ran both hands over my scalp, waiting for my head to stop spinning. I tried to think back, but my mind kept shying away. Last thing I remembered was a bunch of plastic-covered men with fire hoses . . .

I jerked upright.

Men in hazmat suits. Gassing us. *Killing* us.

The valley had been shaken to pieces, but that hadn't stopped those psychos from spraying us with poison. Unable to breathe, I'd crawled toward the fountain to wash my burning face. But I'd fallen in instead.

I shivered in my wet clothes, reliving the sensation of water entering my mouth, my nose, my throat. My arms had stopped working, every muscle seizing painfully before going limp. My head had struck bottom as my lungs filled with fluid.

Drowning. Dying. I had a terrible flash of dejà vu.

Oh, God.

I ran my hands over my body. No cuts, bruises, or broken bones. I was quite clearly alive.

Like all the times before.

I shot to my feet.

It was then that I noticed my surroundings. I was standing in the town square with all the other kids in our class, everyone picking themselves up off the dirt. Several blinked stupidly, as I had, struggling to get their bearings.

The hazmat squad was gone. So were the soldiers, the townspeople, even the bodies. The entire block was empty—no trucks, sawhorses, or equipment of any kind.

But that wasn't all.

The grass was smooth and manicured, the fountain unbroken. Every building on Main Street was standing with its windows intact. Sidewalks and alleyways were seamless, without cracks or rents. Everything looked normal, as if the earthquake had never occurred.

I spun on wobbly legs, trying to make sense of what I was seeing. The valley looked the same as it always had. Better, actually—last week's damage had disappeared, too. Crystal waters lapped gently against the waterfront. Even the *rockslide* was gone, the formerly shattered peak now standing tall and firm to the south.

Everyone was chattering nervously, pointing out different aspects of the repaired landscape. I looked skyward. Clear mountain air and a yellow sun. A picture-perfect, postcard day in Fire Lake.

Tack was sitting on the grass a few feet away, massaging his temples. Red-rimmed eyes regarded me with incomprehension. "What the hell?" he rasped. "Are we dead?"

I shrugged. "I don't know. I don't feel dead. Do you?"

"Not sure. Don't have a handle on that one." Tack staggered to his feet. "Where's Min?"

I looked around, spotted her alone on the opposite side of the square. "There."

Wiping his hands on his jeans, Tack headed over to join her. After a moment's hesitation, I followed. Min turned at our approach, her forehead creasing as she waved a hand. "Are you seeing this?"

Tack nodded. "It's insane. How could they fix *everything* while we were unconscious?"

"Impossible!" Min pointed across the lake. "I don't care who those guys are, no one can put a mountain back together. No . . . This is something else."

I shifted, trying to get my brain to function properly. "What do you think went wrong?"

"Wrong?" Min gave me a surprised look. "Why do you say that? Whatever's happening now might be exactly what Project Nemesis intended."

Tack crossed his arms. "The government spent a decade secretly inventing a way to make themselves disappear?"

Min shrugged, her irritation plain. "I don't know. Maybe they're not really gone. It seemed to me like they completed their plan, whatever it was. We have to figure out what they're doing."

"That mist," I began, shuddering at the memory. "It was *definitely* killing me. I couldn't move or breathe. And at the very end, I swear it did something to my head."

She nodded. "I felt it, too. Like my mind was being balled up like Play-Doh, then forced through a press. I've never felt anything like it before."

I hesitated, but we couldn't avoid the topic. "Not even—"

Min shook her head. "It's not like that for me. When I'm killed, I just sorta . . . stop. My mind blinks out. This was different. Like . . . like I was being torn to pieces. Inside my head."

Tack spat on the ground. "Same. It felt like my soul was on fire. Not pleasant."

The more I thought about it, the more I agreed. This was different from the murders. I'd woken up dazed and sick to my stomach—which never happened in the cave—and *I wasn't in the cave.* "To me, it was like my brain was shredded, then sewn back together."

"This is something new, I'm sure of it." Min wheeled slowly, examining the surrounding area. "Still. Where *is* everybody?"

Back by the fountain, sixty-one classmates were starting to freak out. Spence Coleman shouted that his cell phone wasn't working. Piper Lockwood began screaming for her parents. Neb Farmer and his two best friends began jogging away, heading for their neighborhood higher up the slope.

A dam broke. The group scattered in a dozen directions, most running to check on their families. *Not me. Dad wasn't here before. Why would he be now?*

Min didn't feel the same. "I'm going home. I want to see if . . . I have to talk . . ."

Her eyes tightened. My heart went out. I hadn't trusted my father in years, but it'd been less than an hour since Min's mother stabbed her in the back. *Hell—in the front.*

"I'll go with you," I heard myself say. Min nodded. Tack didn't speak, but fell in.

We started down Main Street at a brisk walk. There were no other people anywhere. Passing the home entertainment store, I spotted Charlie Bell prowling inside, messing with a TV. I stopped and waved, and he stepped outside.

"Thought I'd try to get the news," Charlie said, scratching

his pimply cheek. "But my mom's not here and I can't get the cable to work. Can't get an IP address either, which is weird. There's power, but no signal. Everything's offline."

"Crazy, man. Keep trying." I hurried after Min and Tack.

When I caught up to them, Tack was scanning a side street and shaking his head.

"What are you looking for?" I asked.

He threw up his hands. "Cops! Trucks! Troops! The bastard who killed my father! *Any-damn-one*, Noah!" Tack closed his eyes, sighed. "But they're all gone. Either they rolled the whole show back into the woods, or two companies of soldiers and an entire vacation town just evaporated into thin air. But why go to the trouble? Why round us up only to vanish and leave us alone?"

I had no answers, but plenty of my own questions. Where was Black Suit? Myers and Lowell? With a shudder, I remembered Commander Sutton taking his own life, right before I passed out. My skin crawled. I began to sweat.

How does a statue repair itself? Who could piece a mountain back together?

I stopped walking. Put my hands on my knees.

Too much. Too fast.

"Noah?" Min had stopped ten paces ahead. Tack waited at her elbow, rolling his eyes with barely concealed impatience.

I opened my mouth. Closed it. Couldn't frame a response.

My mind was blank. My limbs like jelly. I wanted to curl into a ball.

Voices carried up the block. Suddenly, Min and Tack were beside me, pushing me into a recessed doorway. Seconds later,

Ethan and Toby stormed past, so intent on their conversation that neither spotted us. When their footsteps receded, I blew out a relieved breath.

"Come on." Min eased me back onto the sidewalk. "Let's get to my trailer. We can relax there for a minute while we figure out what to do next."

I nodded, not trusting my voice. It was so silly, her guiding me up the street like an old lady. I was twice her size, at least. But I was thankful. As I put one foot in front of the other, my tension began to ease.

At the edge of town, Tack halted abruptly. "Should we check the Plank?"

Min hesitated. "After. I want to go home first." Tack shrugged, and we turned up Quarry Road. Five minutes later we reached the trailer park.

Ghost town. Not a soul around.

Tack's eyes were troubled. "Okay, this is officially too bizarre. Where is everyone?"

Min broke into a trot. Reaching her trailer, she found it unlocked. Tack and I waited outside while she looked for her mother, but it took less than a second.

"She's not here." Min cleared her throat.

"I'll be back." Tack turned and sprinted down the lane.

"Where's he going?" I asked.

"To check on his dad."

"But . . . we saw—"

"I know that, Noah," Min said sharply. "Doesn't mean he can't look."

She took a deep breath. Softened her tone. "Maybe Tack

needs a minute alone, okay? He hasn't had any time since . . . since the incident. Do you want to check your house next? I'll go with you if you want."

I was touched, but had no interest. My father wasn't there.

"There's no point." A helpless feeling was creeping over me. "Where'd they go, Min? How could a whole town just disappear?"

"I don't know. But I'm going to find out."

"*We're* going to find out," I corrected, speaking before I knew it.

I stole a look at her, suddenly embarrassed. But Min smiled and nodded.

36

MIN

My trailer park was empty.

The unnerving part was, nothing seemed out of place. Cheap lawn furniture still surrounded the fire pits, undisturbed. Cars were parked here and there like always. Everything seemed normal. Except for the fact that every single person was gone.

"We should go back downtown," I said finally, after investigating a fourth empty row. "We don't know how long we were unconscious. It's possible the soldiers rounded everyone up and evacuated the valley."

Noah nodded. "We should still check and see if the bridge is down."

"You said it fell into the canyon."

"It did. But I also saw downtown collapse into rubble, so . . ."

I repressed a shudder. "Okay. We'll grab Tack, then swing by there. After we'll head into town and . . . and"—I fluttered a hand ineffectually—"find *somebody*."

We walked back to the main thoroughfare, where hours before armed soldiers had taken us prisoner. But had it only been hours? A glance at the sun confirmed it wasn't much later in the day. *But is it the same day? Who knows how long we were out.*

Noah sat down beside the water pump to wait. I joined him, thoughts racing.

I was sure this was somehow a part of Project Nemesis. Myers and Watson had said things were in motion, and a forced-at-gunpoint assembly definitely fit the bill. Those soldiers had been ready for protesters. Gassing us must've been the objective.

They *shot* people. Lots of them. But what purpose did any of it serve?

I kicked the dirt, drawing Noah's gaze. "You okay?"

I shook my head, worries spilling out. "What *happened* back there? Knocking us out and abandoning us was their grand plan?"

"Maybe they wanted us out of the way. To take everyone else somewhere."

"Then why all the tests? Why involve the schools, for years? Why was a psychopath stalking and killing us, over and over? So they could kidnap the population of an isolated town and leave sixty-four kids zonked out in a courtyard?"

"Maybe it's all a mind game," Noah said quietly, eyes far away. "The asteroid, the earthquakes, everything about this past week. How do we know any of it actually happened? They might be messing with us right now. I . . . I don't trust anything. Not even the things I see. Sometimes . . . I . . . I don't even know if I'm awake."

His voice cracked. I took his hand. Had forgotten how fragile he could be.

"I'm awake, Noah. Lean on me."

He smiled wanly. "You're tiny. I'll squash you."

I felt a flutter in my stomach. Tamped it down. But I didn't release his hand.

Gravel crunched, and I turned. "Am I interrupting?" Tack asked.

I looked down, realized Noah and I were still holding hands. I released his quickly, face reddening. When had we become so comfortable with each other? Hours ago, we'd been strolling along the waterfront, sharing our deepest feelings. Minutes later, however, he'd caved in front of Ethan and left me high and dry.

He chose differently in the square. Noah stuck with Tack and me.

"We have a plan." I rose quickly.

"Well, by all means, tell me what to do."

My temper slipped a notch, but I held it. Tack had just watched his father die. I knew it was eating at him, though he'd never let anyone see. "We should check the Plank, like you suggested, then head back into town and see what we can find. *Who* we can find."

Tack nodded, began striding down toward the gate.

I glanced at Noah. He shrugged. *What can you do?*

A bell was clanging somewhere deep in town.

"That's a church," Tack said, shielding his eyes to peer down Main Street. "Sacred Heart, I think. I wonder who's there."

We were headed that direction, having checked on the bridge. Its twisted remains were barely visible at the bottom of Gullet Chasm.

There was still no way across the gorge. No route into or out of Fire Lake.

I stumbled on a curb and Noah caught my arm, steadying me. I smiled ruefully, but it died when I noticed Tack watching us. He didn't like Noah touching me, even to prevent a face-plant.

"What should we do?" Noah asked.

"Answer the bell. What else?" I wanted to know who it was.

Sacred Heart is a boxy white building bordering town square. Other classmates were hurrying toward its large wooden doors. Gazing up, I spied two silhouettes in the steeple. Chris and Mike Nolan. They'd climbed up beside the bell and were whacking it with hammers.

"Idiots," Tack muttered, then cupped his hands. "You know there's a rope for that, right?"

Chris Nolan gave him the finger. "This is more fun! Now get inside."

"Guess those dopes are forming a club." Tack rolled his shoulders, working out the kinks. "What's the opposite of Mensa?"

I snorted, but had an uneasy feeling. I could tell Noah shared it. The twins didn't make decisions like this on their own. We both knew who did.

But there really wasn't much choice. As I stood there, hesitating, a dozen classmates filed past me into the church. Like it or not, a meeting *was* taking place. Better to stay in the know than wonder what was going on without us.

Derrick was manning a stool in the foyer. "And you three

make sixty-four," he said with satisfaction. He nodded at Noah, who returned the gesture. "Amazing. When was the last time we had perfect attendance for anything?"

Derrick popped up, and we followed him inside. The pews were nearly filled. Ethan was up by the lectern, hands clasped behind his back.

We slunk to a back row and sat. Noah's foot began tapping as Derrick conferred briefly with Ethan, then leaned back against the Communion rail. I spotted Sarah in a chair beside the pulpit. Then Toby and the Nolans entered through a side door and flopped down on the steps in front of Ethan.

"Okay," Ethan began, pitching his voice to carry. "Good. Everyone came. That's a great first step. We need to stick together from now on, and maintain order."

In the front row, Jessica shot up from a tight huddle of sophomore cheerleaders. Raven-haired Susan Daughtridge. Melissa Hemby, a quiet girl with luminous hazel eyes. Six-foot Kristen Fornelli and her best friend, Tiffani Bright, petite and athletic, the top of the pyramid.

"What happened?!" Jessica shouted. "Where is everyone?"

"I have no idea," Ethan replied. "Does anyone?" He waited patiently, and the silence stretched. People glanced around, as if the answers might be hiding somewhere inside the room, but fear and confusion were reflected on all faces.

"I went through the same thing you did," Ethan said finally. "The ground was shaking to pieces, then those jumpsuit bastards sprayed us with something toxic. I passed out, and now I'm here. That's all I know."

"The soldiers *killed* people!" Jessica yelled, visibly shaking, her perfect features stretched in an ugly grimace. "They fired on the crowd! And that spray was choking me! I . . . For a minute I thought . . ." She dissolved into tears, sitting quickly, instantly smothered by her teammates.

Leighton Huddle stood, curly blond hair framing pale skin and ice-blue eyes. His father headed the valley's medical practice and Leighton was class president. "When the spray hit me, I started to hallucinate. It felt like my mind *bent* somehow. I can't describe it."

Lars Jergen rose beside him. As stocky as his friend was tall, he had reddish-brown hair and the only full beard in our class. Lars shook his head. "I swear I had a seizure or something. My head exploded. Colors. Light. It hurt like hell. Next thing, *boom*, I'm lying on the ground."

Voices cried out in agreement. The crowd was restless, people jabbering to their neighbors about their own experiences. Ethan let it go on for a few moments, then clapped his hands for silence. "*Whatever* happened after the gas hit," he said loudly, "it knocked us out. Now our families are missing. So is everyone else, including the soldiers. We have to find out why."

Spence Coleman lurched up, anxiously fidgeting with his jacket zipper. "Why'd they only kidnap *our* class? Where are the other kids? We all saw Principal Myers working with the soldiers, along with those two head doctors. They were helping them!"

Charlie Bell waved his phone overhead. "All networks are down. Cable and satellite providers, too, including Wi-Fi. My mom's store couldn't pick up anything all afternoon. Even the landlines are dead. It's a total blackout."

"What happened to the earthquakes?" Jessica screeched from her cheer-friend cocoon. "How'd the buildings get put back together?" She buried her head in her hands.

"I went to my house," Vonda Clark announced in a shaky voice. She was tall and heavy, with dark brown skin and cinnamon eyes. Her father was deputy mayor, the first African American elected in our lily-white town. "My little brother is *gone*. My parents are *gone*. My grandmother's *gone*. But everything we own is still there. It's insane! Where'd they go?"

"Those Nazis shot my dad." Carl Apria's dark brown eyes simmered with hatred. A descendant of the Nez Perce, he had the copper skin and thick black eyebrows common to his ancestral tribe. Carl sat next to his cousin Samuel Oatman. Their athletic builds and matching fauxhawk haircuts made them look more alike than the Nolan twins, though Carl was taller and had a snub nose. "I saw him cut down in the street, but we can't find his body."

Tack tensed beside me. The same had happened to his father.

A dozen conversations broke out at once. The crowd was becoming frenzied, each story adding to the fire. The enormity of our situation had begun to sink in. We were all alone, with no idea why, or what to do next.

A heavy thud silenced the room. Eyes whipped to the front.

Ethan drummed his fingers on the thick Bible he'd slammed on the pulpit. "As you've noticed, we have a lot to figure out. But it won't happen overnight. Right now, we need a plan to survive on our own for however long that may be. We also need to protect ourselves."

Ethan signaled Chris and Toby, who snagged stacks of papers

from the Communion table and began passing them out. Sarah rose and stepped behind a lectern.

"Everyone's been given an assignment." Sarah wore athletic pants and two brightly colored tanks, one over the other, her strawberry-blond locks pulled back in a ponytail. "People will work in teams of five, with each group handling a separate task."

Murmurs from the gallery. Classmates frowned at the page being distributed.

Aiken Talbot stood. A professional slacker with greasy brown hair, he was holding hands with his girlfriend, Anna Loring, a sour-faced pixie with black doll's eyes. "No offense, but who put you guys in charge? None of you have spoken to me in years. Now I have an *assignment*?"

"We have to pull together, Aiken," Ethan said. "That means everyone doing their part."

The sheets finally reached us. Eleven groups were listed, each with five names. I elbowed Noah. "Nine people aren't on here," I whispered. "Wanna guess who?"

"We're split up, too. No chance that's by accident."

I didn't notice Tack rising from his seat. "Your Majesty?" he called, and all heads turned. "Are we still using the bathrooms on our own, or is there a special toilet commission? Because I'd be a natural for that one."

Ethan's jaw tightened. "Watch it, smart-ass."

Tack ignored the warning. "I'm curious to know who chose you as leader." He extended his arms to encompass the whole church. "Was it Jesus? Do you guys talk, or was it, like, a Snapchat anointment?"

Laughter, mixed with mutters of agreement. Several cliques

were giving Ethan's group the side-eye. Before anyone could respond, Darren Phelps stood. Short and solid, with broad shoulders and a cocky attitude, he wasn't impressed by the "in" crowd. His dad was a welder at the marina and known for explosive bouts of temper. Darren was a chip off the old block.

"I don't see *your* name, Ethan," Darren said. "Or Sarah's. Or Toby's. Or anyone else up there. I'm not taking orders if you guys are just sitting around doing nothing."

Ethan was eyeing Tack, so Sarah answered. "No one is exempt from work. The people not listed have other tasks. Ethan, Derrick, and I are the executive committee. We're in charge of planning, and stuff like that. Mike, Chris, and Toby are in charge of security."

Tack sighed loudly. "Why are the dumbest always cops?"

"Shut up!" I whispered, but he was a boulder rolling downhill.

Tack raised one hand as if testifying, placing the other over his heart. "I hereby propose that I'm not doing anything you jokers tell me to do. And I *further* propose that everyone else do the same. This whole meeting is ridiculous."

Toby popped up from the steps and strode to where Tack was standing beside me. Leaning an elbow on our pew, he placed his other hand on his hip and grinned. "You're gonna be a good boy and do what Ethan says, Tack. It's for the common good."

Tack laughed in Toby's face, but a warning light had begun blinking in my head. This meeting. Ethan and his friends. The typed lists. It was all so . . . prepared. Like they'd spent a lot time considering things, even though that wasn't possible.

Ethan seems totally ready to run things. How did that happen so fast?

It occurred to me how precarious our position was. Ethan had a grudge against Tack and me, and there was no one around to police him. He could do anything right now.

Toby leaned closer to Tack. I didn't like the look in his eyes, but his relaxed demeanor never wavered. "Ethan and Sarah have a plan," Toby said in a chipper voice. "A good one. So we're going to listen to them. *All* of us. Understood?"

Tack's mouth opened, but I punched him in the side. "Just do what he says," I warned. Then in a lower voice. "*For now.*"

"Fine," Tack grumbled, slumping down in his seat. "I'll do my part. Just get this monkey off my back."

"*Monkey on your back.*" Toby straightened with a giggle. "I like that. You've always been funny, Tack." He sauntered back to the front, all eyes following him as he flopped down on the steps next to Chris.

Ethan continued with "we're all in this together" briskness. "The first order of business is scouting the valley. We need to find out if anyone else is around. While you're all doing that, the committee will work on securing supplies."

Noah clicked his tongue. "I'll bet my trust fund he's rounding up guns."

I nodded grimly. This was getting more disquieting by the second, but I couldn't see anything to protest. Though it burned to admit it, Ethan's plan made sense. Then I remembered having news to share. I stood. Ethan frowned, but didn't try to stop me.

"The Plank is down," I informed the room. "I'm not sure if everyone knows this already, but before the soldiers rounded us up, a group of liberty campers blew it up. We checked and it's still gone. There's no way across Gullet Chasm."

Round eyes. Furious whispers. Half the kids hadn't known we were trapped.

Ethan smiled oddly. "Then I guess we're stuck here. Does anyone else have something they want to share?"

He waited.

No one spoke.

"Perfect. Let's get to work."

37

NOAH

Last box of mac and cheese in the house.

I ate straight from the pan, unable to enjoy it. The cook hadn't come around since my dad left. There was no food anywhere. I might have an industrial-sized fridge, but it'd be empty soon. What was I supposed to do then?

Thinking of groceries, I experienced a shock. Ethan's family owned the only supermarket in town. With no adults around, he'd pocket the keys for himself.

Ethan controls the food supply. We'll have *to follow his orders.*

I was sitting on my back porch, watching the sun sink behind the mountains. The valley was as quiet as I could ever remember. Not many cars on the road—just a few classmates racing here and there, doing whatever Ethan and his friends had assigned. I was mind-boggled by how swiftly they'd taken over, but wasn't going to make a big stink about it. Who wanted that job?

I finished scraping the pan and carried it inside. Noticed my father's Beretta was still sitting on the kitchen counter. Before the disaster in town square, I'd been too afraid of Black Suit not to have it close. Now, an uneasy feeling told me to keep the weapon handy. *What if the soldiers aren't really gone? What if Black Suit shows up out of nowhere, like he's done so many times before?*

I walked back outside and dropped into a chair. Tired. My group had been sent door-to-door through my neighborhood and two others close by. Ferris Pohlman had been in charge, a beanpole kid with short blond hair atop a narrow head. He'd treated Zach Grey as his second, since their mothers were the two dentists in town and they lived on the same street. Neither had the guts to order me around, however. I was still a Livingston. Old habits die hard.

Rounding out our party were Rachel Stein and Liesel Patterson, as dissimilar as two girls can be. Where Rachel was dark-haired and beautiful, Liesel was tall, plump, and as plain-faced as possible. Rachel spent the whole time bitching about having to walk up and down the steep streets. Liesel never opened her mouth once. Her parents owned a bed-and-breakfast in town, and she worked there during summers, actually getting her hands dirty. Of the pair, I much preferred her.

Street after street, the houses we'd checked had been empty. All morning there'd been a mounting tension I couldn't place. A *wrongness*, hiding just out of reach. After the fifth or sixth property, the cause dawned on me.

Dogs.

I hadn't heard a single bark.

Despite passing numerous fenced yards, there hadn't been a single animal in sight. We'd stopped at Rachel's house for twenty minutes while she searched for her cat. No luck. Whatever drove all the people out had taken their pets along with them.

Afterward, the girls and I pleaded out of the walk back into town, since our homes were on this side of the valley. Zach and Ferris agreed to report without us. Waving a welcome good-bye to them all, I'd climbed back up to my inconveniently placed home and collapsed onto the couch. Only the need for sustenance caused me to stir.

For the hundredth time, I wondered what Min was doing. Tack, too, though I didn't miss his constant potshots. I knew I'd been given a cushy assignment—scouting my own freaking neighborhood—but I doubted they'd been as lucky. I hoped whoever was heading their squads weren't being jerks.

Staring down at the lake, I shook my head. The whole thing was surreal. Only this morning, Fire Lake had been a normal town living through troubled times. Now the troubles had disappeared, but they'd taken all the people with them. My mind couldn't wrap itself around the absurdity of it all.

Like creeping phantoms, doubts began to consume me. I had no idea what to do next. I didn't really want to take orders from Ethan, but honestly, what choice did I have? I grudgingly acknowledged that at least *he* had a plan.

I don't want to deal with a world-changing calamity. I'd even take my sad old life back.

I straightened, disturbed by the thought. But it was true. A week ago, the murders were just dreams, I had little blue pills for comfort, and Lowell would hold my hand through the truly dreadful moments.

Now? Chaos. Disorganization.

Everything I'm not built for, happening at once.

As the light died, I spotted movement to the east. Another group was descending from the canyon rim, snaking down from where Summit Pass cut through the encircling mountains. That trail wasn't for the faint of heart—and was open only in summer—but an experienced hiker could exit the valley that way, traversing a series of treacherous switchbacks to the canyon floor.

With the Plank down, Summit Pass was the only other established way out of the valley. I was eager to hear what they'd discovered.

Cupping my hands, I shouted to the group. "Hey there! Yo!"

Corbin O'Brien glanced up, waved. He was a sturdy redhead with farm-boy arms and pale, sunburned skin. I wasn't surprised to see Isaiah Cantrell and Neb Farmer as well, since the three were inseparable.

With them were blond-haired Casey Beam, the best smile in school, and Lauren Decker, solidly built with short brown hair and a pug nose. Both played on the soccer team and were exceptional athletes, which probably explained the assignment.

"How's the pass?" I called.

Corbin gave me a thumbs-down. "A rockslide spilled across the trail, blocking the whole thing up. No getting down that way."

My spirits sank. We truly were trapped.

I waved good-bye, then retreated inside, wondering if there was a way to find Min. With the phones down my options were limited, since I had no intention of asking Ethan where she'd been sent. I was considering a drive over to the trailer park when my doorbell rang.

I stared at the door, debating whether to answer it. Then it opened anyway—how had I left it unlocked?—and Min stuck her head inside. Spotting me, she sighed in relief. "Thank God. For a minute I thought I'd trekked all the way up here for nothing." She waltzed in and dropped onto the couch, closing her eyes.

I hadn't moved. Was locked in place by the surprise of her arrival.

Min was here in my house, alone. I didn't know how to process this turn of events.

Her eyes snapped open. "Your doorbell works. There's power in the valley."

"That's good," I said, chagrined not to have noticed. "It'll turn cold any day now."

"Yes, but that's not my point. Everyone disappears, our communications don't work, but the electricity keeps running?"

I shrugged. "Don't look a gift h—"

"Don't say it," Min interrupted with a laugh. "Tack might hear and present a dissertation on the phrase." I gave her an odd look, but she waved the comment away.

I let it go. "Did you notice the pets are all gone, too?"

Min nodded, stretching out on the cool leather. "*All* animals, as far as we could tell. I was in a group with Akio Nakamura and Finn Whittaker. Both of Akio's parents are gardeners, and Finn's father does landscaping. They were seriously spooked, because the birds are missing. And it *is* freaky, if you think about it. One more thing on top of everything else."

I shook my head. What could scare birds away?

"What was your job?" I asked.

Her face soured. "I got stuck in Charlie Bell's group, with Kristen Fornelli, the blond stork. We had the delightful task of inspecting those warehouses over by the Plank. Nobody was ever going to be there, and the buildings are nasty. I'm *sure* it was just the luck of the draw."

"God only knows what they sent Tack to do."

"We're all *required* back at the church tomorrow morning." Min scowled at the ceiling fan. "For new orders, I assume. I swear, sometimes I want to punch Ethan in the balls."

Someone pounded on the door.

I locked eyes with Min, but she shook her head. It could be anyone.

For the second time, it opened without being answered. "Incoming!" Tack warned. Seeing Min on the couch, he muttered something I didn't catch, then walked to my kitchen and cracked the fridge.

"Make yourself at home," I said sarcastically.

"Way ahead of you." Tack grabbed a bunch of grapes, then strolled back to the living room and flopped into an easy chair, leaving me the only one standing. "Thought you guys might be here. Still no one at the trailer park. It's eerie."

I sat down on the love seat, frowning as Tack ate my last grapes.

Min perked up, impatient to hear about his day. "What'd they have you doing?"

Tack snorted. "I was part of a select group of champions sent to investigate the woods. The ones north of town, where there's absolutely no one on a regular day. It was riveting. No deer, though—did you guys notice all the animals are gone?"

I nodded along with Min, who asked, "Who was in your group?"

Tack noisily popped grapes as he listed companions. "Leighton and Lars—I can't *stand* those guys. Dakota Sergeant. Emma Vogel. The boys were trying to boss everything, of course. Barking orders like we were slaves. I lasted thirty minutes and bailed. Don't need that crap."

"Ethan will hear about it," I warned. "He's not tight with those two, but they talk."

"I couldn't care less. I'm not bowing and scraping for him. Things might be crazy around here, but that doesn't make Ethan some kind of warlord. That dude flunked geometry."

His cavalier attitude irritated me. "You're just giving him what he wants, you know. If you make waves, he has the excuse to crack down on everyone. Don't think he won't."

Tack flapped a hand, popping the last grape. "Those guys aren't going to do anything."

I'd thought the same earlier, but hearing it from Tack made me reconsider.

Who knows what people might do in this situation.

A familiar crawling sensation squeezed my heart. I bowed my head, trying to hide my nervousness. When I stole a glance at Min, I thought she looked disappointed in me. I sank even lower. *She doesn't understand. No one does.*

My panic disorder hadn't disappeared with the townspeople of Fire Lake. And now I was alone, with no help. No drugs. No smiling doctor to put me back together. I had to white-knuckle the occurrences, something I'd never done well.

The room wobbled. My breathing quickened.

Neither Min nor Tack seemed to notice, arguing about the morning. After some arm-twisting, Tack reluctantly agreed to attend the meeting, if only to see what Ethan had planned. By the time they remembered me, I'd semi-recovered.

"Good. Sounds fine." Trying to sound as normal as possible. Outside, full dark had descended. "Are you guys sleeping here tonight? You're both welcome—I have plenty of room."

Suddenly, more than anything, I didn't want to be alone.

"Yes, yes, you have a castle." Tack rolled his eyes. "How very nice for you."

"*You* don't have to stay if—"

"Tack, quit being a jerk." Min glanced outside, let out a deep breath. "I suppose there's no point hiking all the way back to an empty trailer. And I wouldn't mind having friends around tonight. Thanks, Noah."

I nodded, relieved. "I'll make up the guest rooms."

"I like pillow mints," Tack called after me.

With no TV or Internet there wasn't much to do, and everyone was tired. Tack and Min both grabbed a quick Hot Pocket, and then we all headed upstairs. I showed them to their rooms.

"'Night, Noah. Thanks again." Min squeezed my hand before closing her door. I smiled dumbly as her light winked out, then noticed Tack watching me from his doorway. He gave me a dark look, but for once I didn't let it get to me.

Back in my room, I lay awake for hours, trying to come to grips with what had happened. Found I couldn't make sense of anything. The only thing cheering me was the thought of Min, just down the hall.

On a mad impulse, I slipped from bed and snuck down the corridor. Stood outside her door, listening. Then I slowly turned the knob, cracking the door an inch until I could see her lying in bed. A feeling of peace swept over me, even as part of my mind screamed that I was acting like a pervert.

Min rolled over in her sleep, suddenly facing me. She yawned.

I shut the door and fled.

Back in my bedroom, the bad feelings returned.

Who am I kidding? I can't keep up. Min's stronger than me. Better than me.

I vowed to get my act together. To become a person Min might respect, instead of the Spineless Noah Livingston I always was.

Then I shut my eyes and drifted off at last.

38

MIN

I awoke with a start.

The dream was fading fast. Something about running, jumping into water. The details slipped away before I could gather more. I looked around, experienced a second jolt. It took me a moment to remember where I was.

Noah's house. Tack and I slept over.

I rose quickly and pulled on yesterday's clothes. Cracked the door. I could hear someone puttering around downstairs. I closed the door, used the bathroom, then made myself as presentable as possible. Seconds later I bounded into the kitchen, tracking the distinct smell of bacon.

Noah was manfully attempting to cook breakfast. I could tell immediately he had no idea what he was doing. Patting his shoulder, I lowered the heat on the eggs and scrambled them, then checked the microwave. The bacon was still soggy. I gave it another two minutes.

Noah nodded gratefully. He was standing over some sort of juicing contraption with a bag of oranges. *That* machine, at least, he seemed to know how to operate. Together we finished preparing the meal and filled three plates. Tack stumbled downstairs just in time to be served without having to help.

"I swear you planned that," I scolded. "Slacker."

Tack yawned theatrically. "I was born with good timing."

There were four seats in the breakfast nook. Tack and I took chairs next to each other, and Noah sat on the opposite side of the table. I dug in, thanking Noah profusely for his efforts. Even Tack grunted appreciatively. The day was off to a good start.

But as I watched Noah, I could tell something was bothering him. He picked at his food, stealing glances at me as I ate. But when I looked up, he avoided my eyes. I got a weird vibe that *I* was bothering him somehow. I had no idea why, but the feeling persisted.

"You still good with going to the church?" I asked, hoping to draw him out. But Tack answered before Noah had a chance.

"Master Fletcher's plantation?" Tack scoffed, gnawing on the last of his bacon. "I most certainly am not."

Noah's eyes flashed, but when he spoke, his voice was neutral. "We *have* to go. It's the only way to keep on top of things." Then he twitched, as if just remembering something, and told us what the Summit Pass explorers had discovered.

I blew out my lips. "No Internet, radio, or TV. The Plank is gone, and the pass is blocked. Like it or not, Ethan's jerk network is the only 'organization' in the valley. We have to keep an eye on it until we come up with a better plan."

"I've already got one." Tack burped loudly, then pushed back from the table. "The three of us should form our *own* group, based in this luxurious home of Noah's. Get the normal kids to join us. Then we can stop bowing and scraping to those dorks."

Noah was shaking his head before Tack finished. "Who needs some big showdown right now? It's not like their ideas have been bad so far."

"Who cares?" Tack sat forward, speaking excitedly. "I've been thinking about it all night. Sixty-four sophomores, right? Most don't run with Ethan's crowd—they've been lording it over the rest of us for years. The *not*-cool kids have the numbers! We could run things instead of Ethan. And do a better job, too."

"But that's not how it should work either." I set down my fork. Spoke patiently. "We should all be working together. Voting on things, or whatever. No one should be railroading anyone."

Tack rolled his eyes. "Good luck with that."

"Ethan would still have the edge," Noah said irritably, ruffling his hair in a way that stirred me further awake. I looked away. Didn't want to be distracted. Even just out of bed, Noah looked good. "He has the jocks on his side," Noah continued, "and those rich girls scare the crap out of the others. It's not just head count, Tack. It's personalities."

"And *you* can jump back to their side any time," Tack said, rising and walking to the stairs.

Blood rushed to Noah's face, but I held up a hand. "It's not worth it," I whispered. "I'm going to talk with him today. The friendly fire has to stop."

Noah nodded, seemed suddenly uncomfortable. He gathered

all three plates and carried them to the kitchen. I sighed, downed the last of my orange juice, hoping the rest of the morning would go more smoothly.

Everyone came. I wasn't surprised. We were trapped in a mountain valley with no adults and no way to escape. Where else would you be?

Ethan was whispering with Derrick and Sarah by the pulpit. I was starting to get a feel for how things worked. Those three seemed to be the brain trust. Derrick relayed their orders to Toby, Mike, and Chris. Charlie Bell had joined the staircase group, along with Tucker Brincefield and Josh Atkins, two of the biggest guys in our class.

Tack bristled when he noticed the last two. Tucker and Josh were linemen on the football team, but had never been friendly with Ethan in the hallways. Tack had probably counted them on his side of the ledger.

"Smart," Noah murmured. "They added extra muscle while weakening any possible resistance. Someone really thought this through."

I cursed silently. It was true. In less than a day, Ethan had somehow consolidated a rough dictatorship. Still, the grumbling was louder this morning. Shock had cowed everyone yesterday, but that was before people had been sent marching all over the place. I suspected things wouldn't be so easy this time around.

"Look at those idiots," Tack griped. We were sitting closer today, and he was making no attempt to keep his voice down. "Like a preschool model UN."

Toby glanced up. Spotting Tack, he smiled and waved, then

leaned back and put his hands behind his head. An uneasy feeling stole over me. Toby looked like someone expecting a show, and I couldn't fathom how that'd be good for us.

Shuffling up front. Ethan stepped behind the pulpit.

"Here we go," Noah breathed.

"Everyone is present and accounted for," Ethan boomed. "So let's get started. Sarah will summarize what we learned yesterday."

Sarah walked confidently to the lectern, moving like a cat in yoga pants and a Lululemon top. "Eleven teams searched eleven different quadrants. There isn't anyone else around. As far as we can tell, Fire Lake is deserted."

Whispers in the crowd. Sarah held up a hand. "What's even stranger is that the animals are gone, too. Cats, dogs, deer, even birds. Whatever scared our people away also removed all wildlife from the valley."

Rachel Stein stood, dark eyes furious. "My cat stays indoors. By choice! Misty did *not* run away—someone had to have gone inside to get her. Which means all our houses were probably invaded. What kind of sick joke is this?"

"Nobody can explain it, Rachel." Sarah was a picture of icy calm. "Personally, I'm more interested to know how buildings can stand back up again. But today is about *security*. We don't know where those troops are."

"The power's still working," Richie Lopez called from a pew. Deeply tanned, with soft, almost yellow eyes, he had the whipcord build of a distance runner. "My group checked the transformers yesterday, and they're humming like always."

Sarah nodded. "But still no communications. Right now we have no way of contacting anyone for help, and no way of learning what's going on everywhere else. I'm working on this personally. We have to find out what's happening down the mountain, and where everyone is."

A clamor rose as several classmates tried to speak at once. Ethan walked over and handed Sarah a stack of papers. "We have new assignments for everyone today. Some are related to supplies, while others involve checking what still works, like water and gas. A few are just jobs that need doing."

Derrick began passing the sheets out. Leighton stood, his blond eyebrows dropping into a V. "No offense, Ethan, but I'm not up for another day of wandering through the hills. I'll pass."

Ethan watched Leighton silently for several seconds, which made the skinny class president shift uncomfortably. Finally, "Everyone will complete their assignment, or they won't get their food allotment."

Voices erupted in unison. "Food allotment?" Leighton said, confused.

Oh no. I glanced at Noah, who was shaking his head.

Ethan folded his arms over his chest. "My father owns the supermarket. He's gone, and I don't know where. But in his place it belongs to me. And no one will get so much as a fish stick unless they do their part. Understood?"

Leighton's expression soured, but he sat back down. "Fine. Whatever."

"And I expect *everyone* to see their jobs through to the end." Ethan looked pointedly at Tack, who glowered back. *Oh yes, he knows Tack skipped out yesterday. Wonderful.*

"When you check back in tonight, I'll explain how the rationing will work."

Noah whispered without moving his lips. "I can already explain—he'll keep all the good stuff and we'll get canned beets."

I nodded slightly. This could get bad, quick.

Derrick paused before handing a sheet to Noah. "Interesting seat choice, Livingston. You fall on hard times?"

Noah's eyes dropped. Derrick grunted and moved on.

I scanned the handout. It was immediately apparent that Tack and I were being punished.

"Firewood collection?" Tack growled. "Goddamn it."

"I have sanitation plant inspection, Tack. Sound more fun to you?"

Tack's nose crinkled. "Look at the favoritism. It's so *blatant*. I'm telling you, we should just bail. Right now. This whole thing is a farce, and there's nothing stopping us."

I wavered, on the point of agreeing. It was the brazenness that stung the most. Then I noticed Noah's assignment. "Sporting goods? That doesn't sound bad. At least you'll be inside."

He shot me a guilty look. "Ethan is keeping me close. Under his thumb."

"Right where you like to be," Tack muttered.

"Tack, stop it!" But before I could say more, there was a disturbance in the front row. Aiken was trying to force his way past Chris. "I said *no*." Aiken's face was a mask of irritation. "I'm not about to spend the day counting generators in a warehouse. I've got my own food, bro. I don't need this." His girlfriend, Anna, stood beside him, black eyes tight with anger.

Toby and Mike came off the steps. "What made you think this was voluntary?" Toby asked. Then he removed a 9 mm pistol from his waistband and pulled back the slide. Toby held it loosely in one hand, scratching his head with the muzzle.

I recoiled as if slapped. The air in the room stood still.

Toby had always been a little crazy, and now he was holding a gun.

He raised an eyebrow at Aiken. "You were saying?"

"Whoa!" Noah barked, half standing up. "Take it easy! What are you doing?"

Behind Toby, Mike pulled a gun from his baggy pants, followed by Chris, Charlie, and the two linemen on the steps. Derrick frowned, but kept his position at the rail below Ethan, who was watching intently. Standing behind the lectern, Sarah never flinched.

Aiken rolled his eyes. "Dude, enough. I'm not impressed. My dad's got three Glocks locked in our garage. Quit being a jerk, Toby. You're still the kid who crapped his pants on the sixth-grade trip to Walla Walla."

Surprisingly, Toby laughed. Then he stepped forward and rabbit-punched Aiken in the stomach. Aiken collapsed, coughing, unable to draw a breath. Anna screamed, but Mike held her back by the shoulders.

Toby pivoted slightly, then kicked Aiken in the side. Once. Twice. Three times.

I shot to my feet. "Stop it!"

Mike glanced my way. "He will. When Aiken agrees."

Aiken was sniveling on the floor. He lifted his head, trying to say something, but was unable to catch his breath.

"That's enough! You're hurting him!" I wriggled past Noah—who was staring, slack-jawed—and took two steps down the aisle. Then froze. Mike was pointing his gun at me. "I'd stay there, Min. Seriously, I would."

Toby knelt close to Aiken's face. "What's that, buddy? You say you'll be a productive member of the team?" Aiken nodded weakly.

"Super!" Toby helped him up and patted him on the back. Then he guided Aiken into Anna's arms. The pair collapsed onto the first pew, staring fearfully at their armed classmates.

Silence filled the chamber like a living, breathing thing. Finally, Ethan spoke. "I hope that doesn't happen again. Really, I do. But we can't keep the town safe without order. *Structure.* Now, everyone please go. We *expect* to see you here tonight at six sharp. No exceptions."

Classmates began filing out. Noah turned and spoke across me. "Still want to fight the power, Tack?" My friend looked away.

I ground a fist into my thigh. "We'll play along, then strategize tonight. Deal?"

Noah nodded. A vein was throbbing in Tack's neck, but he bobbed his head as well.

Glancing up, I found Ethan watching me. Then he turned and said something to Derrick. I rose and sped for the exit, seething like a thunderstorm.

39

NOAH

I stacked sleeping bags in a row.

Twenty-seven total, in various shapes and sizes. Then I walked up front and gave Ferris the count. Nodding his pointy head, he recorded the number on his clipboard. "Canteens next."

I shrugged, headed back down the aisle. Camping gear was kept in only two places inside the sporting goods store—the outdoors section and along the rear wall of the storage room. The job was easy. I'd already tallied coolers, camp stoves, axes, and waterproof matches.

I could hear Rachel and Liesel in the next row. Or rather, I could hear Rachel whining while Liesel silently did all the work. "Who cares how many flashlights are in this stupid store?" Rachel grumbled. "The electricity works. Everyone has one at home anyway. He's just making us do stuff to feel like a big shot."

I somewhat agreed, but kept it to myself. Although I could

see the logic in counting how many batteries we had—and having Zach inventory the guns locked behind the counter—some of this stuff was available all over town. Plus, how long did he think we'd be stranded up here? Eventually *someone* would notice that the entire town of Fire Lake had stopped venturing out of the mountains. A scout would be sent, the bridge discovered, and help would arrive. We were talking days, at most.

Unless there's nobody out there, either.

The thought sent a shiver down my spine. With communications out, we had no way of knowing what was going on beyond the canyon. What happened with the comets? They must've played a part in the blackout. The quakes had clearly stopped, but we didn't know the severity of the damage.

A corner of my mind rebelled against these rationalizations. *Stop ignoring the real issues. Soldiers disappeared like ghosts. Buildings spontaneously reconstructed. Half a damn mountain put itself back together!*

My body tensed. I stopped moving, fingers balling into fists.

I didn't want another panic attack, but it was never up to me.

Anxiety. Fear. Helplessness. That old cocktail, infecting my psyche like a virus. I closed my eyes, unable to dispel the tension. Or the self-loathing that came with it. I wanted a blue pill in the worst way. To lie down, and sleep, and have all this be over.

Normalcy. Anonymity. Numbness. I wanted them all back, if only for a moment.

Want your executioner back too, you putz? You're pathetic.

Anger erupted inside me. *God, I'm such a waste.* Locking up like a hunted animal in the middle of a sporting goods store? Because life was suddenly more complicated?

What a joke.

Like picking a scab, I wondered where Black Suit was at that moment. He hadn't lost his cool in the square when things started falling apart. Who was he, really? It seemed like he'd been operating outside the hierarchy.

So where did that place him? I tried to imagine someone applying for his role and actually laughed out loud. *Job available: serial killer. Must be willing to slay the same teenagers multiple times.*

"Something funny?"

I winced. The last person I wanted to see.

Ethan strolled down the aisle with a smile of contentment, like a man appreciating the fruits of his labor. It took me a second to notice that Sarah was with him. She fluttered her fingers in a coy wave. She was wearing a skirt now, which for some reason I found weirdly out of place.

"What's the joke?" Ethan asked casually.

"Nothing." I straightened, unsure how to act. I'd hung out with them almost every day for years, but things had changed recently, and we all knew it. "It's just . . . all this. What's been going on, you know? I can't seem to wrap my head around it."

Ethan nodded, even looked sympathetic. "It's been a crazy week. I remember sitting at home just last weekend, totally convinced that we were all gonna be Anvil pancakes. Then they called a miss, but somehow things got even crazier."

"You said it." Still wondering what they were doing there. Random spot check? I didn't think so.

"We've missed you, Noah." Sarah flashed perfect white teeth. "I'm not sure what's been going on, but you don't have to hang out with the trailer-park kids. Your friends want you back."

"No. I know. Things have been . . . complicated."

"But it's *not* complicated." Ethan's voice carried an edge. Sarah put a hand on his arm. He took a breath, then spoke in a milder tone. "Listen, we've been butting heads lately, but that's what friends do every now and then. No hard feelings, right? We gave you this sweet gig, didn't we?" He playfully punched my shoulder. "Screwing around in here with no adults or rules, like we dreamed about in middle school? I'm jealous!"

I remembered Ethan knocking things off shelves and yelling, "*Run*," leaving me in the lurch, but I didn't argue the point. He was trying to be nice, so I let him.

"We want you to rejoin our team," Sarah said. "It's where you belong."

Ethan winked. "We have a spot for you in our inner circle. No more assignments, just running things. Sound good?"

I hesitated. I didn't want to spend a single minute trapped inside a room with these two, but how could I turn them down without making things worse? Ethan didn't take rejection well under the best of circumstances, and these weren't those.

Sarah must've sensed my reluctance. "Or you could work with Derrick. I guess he's kind of like our team captain. Delivers orders, and things like that."

Ethan's eyes narrowed. "Unless you *like* pawing through back rooms."

"No," I blurted, fumbling for a way out. "It's not that. I appreciate the offer, honestly."

"Then what, Livingston? Are we not good enough for you anymore?"

"*Ethan*." Sarah shot him a warning glance, then aimed her

megawatt smile at me. "You can have whatever role you want, Noah. Seriously. Come back to the church with us and we'll figure it out. Just like always."

She reached out and squeezed my arm. I cringed. Accidentally pulled back.

Her smile evaporated, replaced by a hurt look, which slowly morphed to anger.

"You guys are great, I mean it," I said quickly. Then I noticed Rachel and Liesel spying on our conversation from the next row over. "I just don't want to ditch my team right now, is all. It wouldn't be right for me to bail and leave them stuck with all the work. I'll catch up with you guys at the meeting."

Neither Ethan nor Sarah said anything. I forced a smile, pulse racing.

Ethan shook his head. "You're gonna have to make a choice, Noah. *Soon.* You're either with us or against us. I'm done screwing around." He walked off, not waiting for Sarah.

"See you tonight, Noah." Her voice was chillier than before. "He's right, you know. You need to step up, or you might get run over. There aren't many places to hide these days." With that, she turned and left.

Releasing a pent-up breath, I replayed the confrontation in my head. Had the sinking feeling I'd come out farther behind than when I started.

"Thanks for not ditching us, Noah." Liesel smiled at me through the shelves. I think it was the first thing she'd said all day.

"Don't *thank* him," Rachel huffed. "He's an idiot. They just offered him a free ride, and he choked. I hope I'm next in line. *Ow!*"

Liesel lifted a toolbox off of Rachel's foot. "Oops. Sorry."

I ignored Rachel's aggrieved tirade, still reeling from the ambush. And, being honest, I was surprised at myself. Why hadn't I gone with them? It would've been so much easier to just join their stupid dictator club. I could fade out and do nothing, like always.

You know why. She'd never forgive you.

Min.

Was it really that simple?

Ferris's voice echoed down the corridor. "Hey guys, get up here! Something's happening outside!" *Oh God, what now?* I hustled to the front with the girls. Out in the parking lot, a handful of people were pointing and laughing. When I saw why, I couldn't help but chuckle, too.

Someone had spray-painted the bank window next door. A crude figure with blond hair was giving a Nazi salute. It had a Hitler-style mustache and was shouting, "*DO YOUR PART!*" in a word bubble. A red circle with a slash through it surrounded the whole thing, with a message in block letters below. DEATH TO FASCISTS.

Though fairly slapdash, it was obviously a caricature of Ethan. I looked for him in the crowd, but he wasn't there—he must've missed it heading the other way. "It captures his likeness pretty well," Benny Erikson joked, sweeping shoulder-length black hair from his eyes. "I give it eight out of ten."

"Ethan's gonna flip," Alice Cho murmured, her smooth features forming an apple-shaped face. "I hope whoever drew this doesn't get caught." Beside her, Emily Strang rubbed her chubby arms. "I don't like it. Why mess up the bank? The buildings around here are nice, and there's no one to clean stuff up anymore."

"I watched this whole block *collapse* yesterday," Jamie Cruz muttered, her chestnut curls bouncing as she shuddered. "But now look at it. I don't like the future at all."

I spun, brow furrowed. "The future?"

Jamie nodded. "Where else could we be? That mist they sprayed us with must've shot us forward in time, to some point after these buildings were repaired. That's why everyone's gone."

"That's not it," Benny argued, scratching his dirty flannel shirt. "There'd be people here in the future too, dummy."

"Okay, hotshot, *you* tell *me* what happened," Jamie fired back.

"Wormhole," Benny said confidently. "Those men pushed us into another dimension. One where everything is exactly the same, only no people. We're in a new *universe*, dudes. It's wild out." The two began hotly debating their theories, but I stepped away. I had enough on my mind without trying to guess the impossible.

Alice Cho trailed me, worry lines creasing her forehead. "What do you think, Noah?"

Her question caught me off guard. I couldn't remember talking to her much before—Alice had only moved to Fire Lake in high school, and she took the arty classes I avoided like the plague. I shrugged, uneasy with the topic. "Couldn't it be as simple as us being knocked out? Maybe we imagined everything falling down. An early effect of the gas."

Alice nodded, but I could tell she wasn't persuaded. Against my better judgment, I asked if she had a theory. For a long moment she didn't answer, staring at the wall art. Then she looked me in the eye. I nearly flinched at what I found there.

"I think we're dead," Alice whispered. "I think the gas killed us all."

She turned and walked away.

My mind recoiled from her pronouncement, but I didn't have time to process. Another crowd was forming down the block. Toby and Mike appeared at its heart, dragging a struggling captive between them.

All other thoughts fled.

I turned and ran.

40

MIN

The place reeked.

Not surprising for a sanitation plant, but that didn't make our job any less awful. I wasn't even sure what we were supposed to be doing. "Inspect" the waste treatment facility? Okay, sure. None of us had a clue how these systems worked.

I caught dark looks as we forced the door, everyone's noses crinkling at the stench. The others blamed me for this terrible assignment, and I was sure they were right. Ethan had sent me to the sewers on purpose.

Akio and Finn, at least, kept their opinions to themselves, tying bandanas around their noses as we wandered the rusty complex. The boys were good friends even though they looked like polar opposites—Akio short and slender, with spiky black hair and traditional Japanese features, Finn towering like Thor walking among us, tall and strong, with piercing blue eyes and golden hair. Finn had a rudimentary knowledge of plumbing from helping his father install sprinkler systems, and was doing his best to confirm that Fire Lake toilets would keep flushing.

Charlie was much less circumspect. "This is the worst," he grumbled for the hundredth time. "I've never done anything to Ethan! I'm even part of the security team now. How come I got sent down to Piss River?"

"Why do you think?" Kristen jerked her head at me, six feet of quivering indignation as she stood with her arms crossed. "She might as well be an anchor."

I smiled tightly. "He put you in my group, Kristen. You must not be a favorite either."

She blinked, as if the idea had never occurred to her. I moved deeper into the building, unwilling to trade barbs. This was a terrible job that we didn't know how to do. A lap around the complex should suffice. If not, Ethan could come back and inspect the works himself.

Suddenly, the door behind us rocketed open. We all jumped as Noah burst inside.

I sprinted over to him. He could only be looking for me, and it wasn't going to be good.

"Min!" Noah ran a hand over his sweaty forehead. "You have to come. They got Tack!"

Shit. Shit shit shit.

"What'd he do?" I raced past him to his Tahoe in the parking lot. Noah jumped into the driver's seat and threw the SUV in gear. We tore out, heading for Main Street. "Toby and Mike were dragging him toward the church. It looked . . . It looked bad."

"*What did he do?*"

"I don't know! I just saw him being manhandled." Noah's eyes darted to me, then back to the road. "I . . . I have a guess, though." He told me about the bank's new wall art.

"Damn it!" I squeezed my eyes. Tack had been uncooperative from the start, trash-talking Ethan to anyone who'd listen. Most of our classmates just laughed—Tack being Tack—but now he'd pushed things too far.

I should've seen this coming.

A crowd had already gathered. As I fired up the church steps, classmates whispered and pointed. *Not a good sign.* Inside, Tack had been forced into a chair beside the lectern. Toby and Mike stood behind him, making sure he didn't escape. Ethan was leaning against the pulpit with his arms crossed.

"What the hell is this?" I stormed to the foot of the steps. Noah trailed me, stopping at the front row of pews. "Ethan, let him go."

The crowd slipped in behind me. Maybe forty in all.

"We were waiting for Tack's counsel to arrive," Ethan said, straight-faced. "He's accused of slacking, but we're not monsters here. He gets an attorney."

I wanted to strangle Ethan. "I'm *not* an attorney. This *isn't* a court. And *you're* certainly not a judge. So stop being an idiot and let him go. *Now.*"

"An advocate, then." Ethan cleared his throat. "Thomas Russo is accused of abandoning his team and failing to do his job. He also probably drew that picture of me, which is vandalism."

Hate seeped from Tack's eyes. "Of course I drew it, you jackass!"

"Oh, neat! A confession. You guys think he captured my good side?"

Scattered snickers. I glared at Ethan. Laughing at himself. Playing to a crowd. He seemed completely in control of the room. Strong. Persuasive. Self-possessed.

Formidable.

And he's putting my best friend on trial.

Tack jabbed a finger at Ethan, his temper slipping past the point of common sense. "You don't tell me what to do! I don't work for you, and I'm not collecting firewood like some kind of indentured servant. Get your own sticks."

Ethan's cheek twitched, and he absently brushed it. Tack tried to rise, but was forced back down by Mike and Toby. The silence stretched, became suffocating. I needed to intervene, and fast.

"Ethan—" I began, but he spoke over me, turning to address the crowd.

"If we don't work together, nothing will get done. Therefore, failure to do your assignment is a punishable offense."

Tack sneered, then laughed maniacally. "I don't have to do your bidding, asshole. I can do whatever I want. We *all* can. This whole damn thing is a sham, and I'm done playing. If the others want to be your errand boys and girls, whatever. I'm out."

Ethan shook his head, explained as if to a child. "There is no 'out.' Not until we know what happened in the square, where everyone went, and what's happening beyond the valley. We could be trapped up here a long time, and we can't have people running around, taking whatever they want and not sharing the rest."

"You're the one taking everything," I countered loudly. "First the grocery store, and now you're gathering up all the essentials. If anyone isn't sharing, it's *you*."

"Rationing isn't stealing—everyone will share. But I won't leave our largest food source unguarded for people to ransack."

Tack snorted. "Pretending *you* own your dad's supermarket. What a chump."

I spoke fast. "Tack's upset because those guys grabbed him on the street. Anyone would be." I swallowed bile, forcing myself to continue. "We'll follow your lead, because it *is* better if we all work together. Tack agrees with that, even if he's too worked up right now to admit it."

Tack shot me a hurt look, but I only had eyes for Ethan.

He seemed to consider my words. "Okay, here's the deal. I'll forget the graffiti, but Tack has to clean it up. Afterward, he does two days in Watson's lockup for ditching his group. Bread and water only—let him think about whether he wants to be a team player."

Tack tried to stand again. "No way! You can't do that!"

My mind raced. Ethan was serious. I knew he'd secured the sheriff's office and the two holding cells inside. He really could hold Tack prisoner if he wanted to.

Noah shifted uncomfortably on the pew. Whispers spread as people realized Ethan's sentence was real, and that he could do it to anyone.

"Ethan, come on." I adopted a pleading tone, forcing myself to play along with this sick charade. "That's way too harsh for a first offense. Nobody knew that would be the penalty."

"It's called deterrence, Melinda." Ethan stole a glance at Derrick and Sarah. "We have to set an example. Tack will be fine if he just shuts up and accepts his punishment." He gave Tack a condescending look. "Can you do that, Thomas? Can you be a good boy?"

"Go to hell," Tack fumed. "Everyone here thinks you're dumber than crap, I'm just the only one willing to say it. None of these people like you, Ethan. You're a loser and a fraud. Just a redneck piece of trash like me. Kill yourself."

Silence like the total vacuum of space.

Hands covered mouths. No one moved an inch.

Ethan's face went slack. He shook his head sharply, as if trying to dispel something. Then he strode forward and punched Tack between the eyes.

"Ethan, stop!" I sprang up the steps, diving between them. Ethan shoved me aside as though I were a kitten, thrusting me into Toby's arms. Noah shot to his feet, but was intercepted by Tucker and Josh. The linemen shook their heads slowly.

"Easy now, Min," Toby whispered into my ear, his tone almost apologetic as he pinned my arms to my sides. "You can't help that boy." I tried to pull away but couldn't. Ethan was leaning over Tack, who was sprawled on his back with blood dripping from his nose. "Anything else to say, Thomas?"

Tack jerked upright, spat a red gobbet full into Ethan's face.

Ethan's head jerked back. He straightened, wiping his cheek with his sleeve. "Just like your old man." Then he laughed strangely—a short, high-pitched giggle. No one laughed with him.

Tack rose unsteadily, eyeing the larger boy. He'd gone too far, and knew it.

"I've changed my mind," Ethan announced. "Tack won't go to jail. That's a punishment for slacking, not treason."

A well opened in my stomach. "What are you talking about?"

He nodded to himself. "Treason has only one possible sentence."

Ethan pulled something from his pocket. His hand shot forward.

His henchmen reared back in surprise, gaping at the knife buried in Tack's chest.

The world caved in around me. I dropped to my knees.

Screams echoed in the rafters.

"*Ooh . . .*" Tack backpedaled a drunken step, turning to look at me. "Min?" he pleaded weakly, a hand reaching out. Then he collapsed onto his side. His chest rose once, twice, then went still. Glazed eyes stared unblinking at the ceiling.

"*NOOOOO!*"

Pandemonium.

Classmates tried to flee, but Toby recovered quickest and ordered the doors secured. His team reacted instinctively, cutting off the exits and herding everyone back, pushing and shoving those who resisted.

I didn't see any of it. On my hands and knees, I crawled over and took Tack's hand. Tears streamed down my cheeks. Then I whirled, staring up at Ethan, who hadn't moved since killing my best friend.

"How could you?" It was all I could muster.

"I was born for this, Min," he said quietly. "It's my time. I suggest you fall in line."

Hands found me. Noah. Pulling me back, away. I resisted at first, then collapsed against him, crying in earnest.

Ethan shouted for silence. When everyone quieted, he spoke

succinctly. "I'm declaring martial law in the valley. No more 'please' and 'thank you.' You'll do what you're told or pay the price. Does everyone understand?"

Fearful nods. Not a word of dissent.

A spreading pool of red ran down the chancel steps. Sarah draped a tablecloth over Tack's lifeless body, but the knife's hideous outline stuck up under the linen. I turned and threw up on the floor.

Tack was dead.

And our nightmare was only beginning.

41

NOAH

The branch nearly struck me in the face.

I ducked just in time, shooting a glare at Mike Nolan, who smirked over his shoulder. He walked along the trail ahead of me, a handgun bulging from his jeans. We'd arrived south of the lake only minutes before, and things were already tense. I rounded the next tree carefully, unable to shake the feeling that I was a traitor.

What was I supposed to do? Take on the whole church?

Tack is dead. He's freaking dead.

Ethan had *stabbed him in the heart.* In front of dozens of witnesses!

A kid he'd known for most of his life. It was *impossible.* I'd thought Ethan's crew would abandon him right there, given their expressions, but Toby kept them in line. In the end, no one but Min had said a word. I still couldn't believe it.

Min had gone after Ethan like a banshee, clawing at his face.

He'd had trouble defending himself, blinking and moving robotically. I think he'd been as shocked as everyone else. Then Toby and Mike had wrestled Min away and marched her off to jail.

We all watched a murder. And did nothing. Not even me, not even when they manhandled Min from the building. Spineless Noah Livingston strikes again.

Things happened quickly after Tack fell. Ignoring the execution that had just occurred, Sarah ordered everyone to gather supplies from lists she'd drawn up. We were supposed to meet back in an hour. I'd stumbled to the sporting goods store in a daze, filling buckets with batteries, unable to make my brain work.

I couldn't believe how many people actually returned. Only a dozen had gone missing, which was *crazy* to me, even though I was there, too. I'd told myself I had to cooperate so I could help Min, though how following Ethan's orders was going to improve her situation, I still couldn't say. Ethan had blown a gasket at the absences anyway. Which was why I found myself on the opposite side of the valley, inspecting a shuttered summer camp.

Ethan had assembled a "tracking party" to find our "delinquent" classmates. Mike led, assisted by the hulking linemen Tucker and Josh, along with Charlie, Lars, Leighton, and Ferris.

I'd been sent along too, likely to keep me busy. And under watch.

Hector and Darren were also in the group because they lived south of the lake and knew the area. Neither looked comfortable. We were searching for the Nez Perce cousins, Carl and Sam—rumor had it they'd bolted as soon as the doors opened, whispering they were headed for the summer camp and that others should join them.

Several girls apparently followed. Piper Lockwood. Maggie Knudson. Kayla Babbitt and Cenisa Davis. Jacob Allred was also missing, along with his best friends Hamza Zakaria and Floyd Hornberry. Ethan wanted them all rounded up and returned, even against their wills.

Personally, I hoped we didn't find a soul. Carl and Sam weren't fools—they'd have armed themselves the minute they disappeared. No one was going to order those two anywhere, and I wasn't about to try, regardless of the company I was keeping.

One person was already dead. This was doubling down on insanity.

We reached the field surrounding Starlight's Edge. Mike and Charlie ordered everyone to sit tight in the woods while they scouted. The camp looked abandoned—no lights, fires, or visible signs of occupation. I smiled. The cousins had probably laid a false trail—they could be anywhere in the valley by now. I wished them luck.

I bumped into the person next to me and whispered an apology. It was Hector. He barely noticed, his light brown eyes fixed on the ground. He wore black jeans and a bright orange T-shirt that was less than ideal for sneaking through the woods.

"You okay, Hector?"

Hector looked up, and I was startled by the pain in his eyes. "How can I be okay? Despite everything I did, I'm here. Did you know today is Sunday?"

I didn't understand, but Hector was obviously struggling. I

know what that's like. "We'll figure out what happened, man. Everyone's working on it. You just have to have faith. That things will work out."

My words had the opposite of their intended effect.

"*Faith*." He covered his face, his voice cracking. "You don't get it. None of you do. I already *know* what happened."

My eyebrows rose. "You do?"

Hector nodded. "This is purgatory, Noah. We were murdered by those men, and now we're chained to this place. A private hell. I . . . I thought I'd lived a good life, but I was wrong. This is our punishment."

I relaxed. He was talking crazy. Hector was leader of the youth group, so I wasn't surprised he was acting all religious. That was his thing. "You'd know better than me, but I don't remember the Bible mentioning an eternity kicking around your hometown with classmates."

Hector shook his head. "It's a holding place. Somewhere you're judged. And tested. I think . . . I think it's going to get very bad, Noah. Tack was just the beginning. His blood stains all our hands."

I didn't like that talk. "If we're in purgatory, how could Tack die?"

"I don't pretend to understand, but I know the truth." His head dropped. "I miss my family. I . . . I don't think I can survive this place."

"Hey, Hector, listen—"

But whatever I was going to say was cut off by a shout up ahead.

"Let's go!" Lars called, and we emerged into the bright sunshine. Mike and Charlie were waiting in a dell behind the camp. "Nobody's here," Charlie said as we joined them.

I almost sighed in relief. Maybe I could go straight home.

Mike dashed those hopes. "Ethan said to check the woods behind the camp, too. In case they're hiding in there to wait us out."

Groans, even from the security guys. No one wanted to bushwhack through the forest all afternoon, chasing shadows. "This is pointless," Lars grumbled, scratching his beard. Leighton and Charlie nodded in agreement.

"We should go back," Ferris whined. "I forgot to put on sunblock."

"You guys hear about Town Hall?" Darren said, his coal black hair swirling in the breeze.

"What about it?" Lars asked.

"It won't open. My group was supposed to check inside, but we couldn't get the doors to budge. We tried for an hour and got nowhere."

Leighton's blue eyes rolled. "You couldn't open a door. Great story."

"I wasn't finished," Darren said matter-of-factly. "After a while, we said screw it, and went to bash in one of the windows. But *those* wouldn't break, either. Any of them. We couldn't even scratch the glass."

I rubbed my chin, intrigued in spite of myself. "Bulletproof, maybe? Like, for terrorism or something like that?"

Darren shrugged. "I guess it's possible. The point is, there's no way to get inside. We tried everything we could think of. Kinda creepy, actually."

"Did you climb the walls?" Lars asked. Darren shook his head.

"There's gear at the sporting goods store," Ferris said. "We could get up on the roof and see if there's a way in from there. That'd be way more interesting than rooting through the bushes for Sam and Carl and a bunch of chicks. Honestly, who cares if they took off? I never liked those guys anyway."

Mike's eyes narrowed. "You want to tell Ethan we quit?"

That silenced the group. "I didn't think so," he said, rubbing his gelled red hair. "Let's get this done and report back. We can try to crack the hall later. Three other parties like ours are out looking. We can't quit early, or everyone will know."

With a last few mutters, we divided into pairs and spread out behind the buildings. I ended up with Ferris, who sighed loudly and started into the forest, not looking to see if I kept up. I followed his beanpole frame a dozen yards, then stopped.

Three other parties?

I hadn't known there were other teams besides ours. Three other groups meant at least forty people were out combing the valley. And they'd need nearly every reliable guy to fill them out, if they wanted enough muscle to intimidate the cousins into coming back.

So who's watching Min?

I felt a jolt in my system.

What was I doing? Searching the forest for people I didn't want to find?

Min is being held hostage.

Ferris glanced back at me from the shadow of a giant cedar. He was twenty yards ahead, barely visible among the trunks. "You coming, Noah?"

I plastered on an apologetic smile. "Give me a minute. I have to take a leak."

"Whatever." Ferris resumed his desultory march into the woods.

The minute he disappeared I turned and ran, across the field, around the camp, and over to where I'd parked my car by the side of the road. Thank God I'd agreed to drive. I slammed my seat belt on and peeled out, carving a rut in the gravel as I raced back toward town.

I was abandoning my team.

Ditching out on my job.

Maybe even committing "treason."

But I wasn't going to leave Min alone in a jail cell. This time, I was going to fight for what I believed in, no matter the consequences. I was going to *do* something.

I just didn't have any idea what.

42

MIN

I couldn't stop crying.

I was slumped on the floor of Sheriff Watson's holding cell, sobbing into my hands.

Tack was dead. Gone. Killed right in front of me.

And I hadn't been able to stop it.

Guilt pummeled me in waves. Tore me up inside.

Toby was perched on a stool down the hall, reading an old *Entertainment Weekly*. Ethan's right hand. Yesterday, I'd worried *he* might be the bigger threat, but that was foolish.

Ethan. Always Ethan. Before. Now. Always.

I'm going to kill him.

The violent thought swept away my complacency. Provided a counterpoint to grief and self-recrimination. Brought heat to my face. I stood up and gripped the bars.

If Ethan wants a war, I'll give him one.

But I had to get out of this stupid cell.

The sheriff's office was a dull affair. The front was a large square with a door leading out to Main Street. Two desks, some chairs, and a wooden counter dividing the room. Behind it ran a narrow hallway with locked rooms and two wide cells. A staircase at the far end descended to a basement level below.

Toby was sitting behind the counter, where he could watch the door and the hall at the same time, though he wasn't doing much of either. The keys were in his pocket—he'd made a production of showing them after shoving me inside the cell.

"Cool off, Melinda," he'd said lightly. "You'll be in here until you get with the program."

I'd tried to grab him through the bars, but only managed to smash my face against the cold steel. Toby had walked off, chuckling, twirling the key ring on his finger. He was enjoying his power trip. I'd collapsed in a corner and lost track of time.

Based on the light slanting across Toby's face, it appeared to be early evening. I needed to get out of there. But how? This was an actual, real jail cell. I couldn't escape without a key. I considered a dozen plans to lure Toby inside, but none were practical. For all his pigheadedness, Toby had a base, savage cunning. He'd be on guard for tricks.

"Hey, Toby!"

He looked up.

"I haven't eaten all day."

"Bummer." Toby resumed reading.

Okay, that didn't work.

"I also have to go to the bathroom."

"There's one in there," he answered in a bored voice.

"Yes. And you can see it. Which isn't comfortable for me."

Toby flashed a wry smile. "I'm not letting you out, Min. Someone will bring us food, and I'll look away if you need to drop a deuce. But I'm not opening that door so you can shiv me with a jagged piece of tile." His grin soured. "*Although*, at least that'd be interesting. Who knew being a prison guard was so boring?"

Hinges squeaked, and a tiny bell jingled. Someone had come through the front door.

"Finally," Toby said, dropping his magazine on the counter. "I thought you guys forgot about me. Find those cousins?"

Muffled reply. Someone placed a tray on the counter. Toby picked up half a sandwich and shoved it into his mouth. Then a fist flashed out, cracking him across the bridge of his nose. Toby toppled backward with a garbled howl.

Noah vaulted the counter. Toby attempted to rise, a hand reaching for his waistband. Noah kicked him in the face, snapping his head back. Toby crumpled against the wall and lay still.

Noah put his hands on his knees, panting wildly. Then he glanced down the hall and spotted me. "It worked."

It took me a second to recover. Noah had destroyed Toby in a few heartbeats. I'd never seen that side of him. But we didn't have time to waste. "Keys. They're in his pocket."

Noah dug through Toby's pants, tossing aside the gun he found there. He removed the ring and raced down to my cell, only to stare at the gaggle of keys in confusion.

"It's the biggest one. Old looking. Here, just give them to me."

He handed them over gratefully, eyes darting back to where Toby lay sprawled out on the floor. "I hope he's okay. Concussions are no joke, and I . . . I kicked him pretty hard."

"Screw him," I said fiercely, slotting the right key home. "I hope he has brain damage."

Then I stopped, tears welling. "They killed him, Noah. Ethan slaughtered Tack like a pig."

"I'm so sorry, Min. I had no idea th—"

I grabbed his wrist through the bars, startling him. "I'm going to make them pay, Noah. *All* of them. For Tack." In a voice so cold, it scared me. I looked deep into his eyes. "You with me?"

He swallowed. Nodded. Then flashed a nervous grin. "I just ninja-kicked the director of security. Pretty sure I'm on the outs now."

Impossibly, I laughed. Hadn't realized how badly I needed his support. I pushed the gate open and we crept to the front. "Where'd you get food?"

Noah went to the door and peered outside. "I've been lurking across the street for twenty minutes, trying to think of some excuse to come in here. Then I saw Jessica walking up the block with that tray. Convincing her to give it over was easy."

"Smart. Where is everyone?"

"After what happened, some kids freaked out and bailed, so Ethan organized search parties to track them down. That left less than a dozen people in town. I figured it was the perfect time to break you out."

"Then we should get going." Taking a deep breath, I slipped outside, eyes canvassing the neighborhood. No one in sight. "Where to?" Noah asked.

I hesitated. "Not my trailer, that's too obvious. Or your house."

Noah's eyes lit up. "The ski lodge! I know where there's a spare key. It's secluded, too."

I nodded excitedly. "Perfect. Let's go."

"My car's over there." He pointed across the street.

The sheriff's office is beside Town Hall, across from the square. Bad memories came flooding back, but I pushed them aside. Glancing left and right like cartoon villains, we scurried across Main Street to the lot beyond the green. I shivered. Noah's Tahoe was parked right where the Nemesis trucks had been.

How could they all have disappeared?

Noah clicked open the doors. I let out a relieved breath.

Too soon.

"Hey! Look!"

My head whipped. Back across the square, Derrick was pointing in our direction. Ethan appeared, followed immediately by several others.

"*Come on.*" Noah fumbled with his seat belt as they ran toward us.

"Hurry!" I shouted, then winced. The last thing I wanted to do was ramp up the pressure on Noah. But seconds later he backed us out, hopped a curb, and sped away down High Street. But we were going in the wrong direction. "The ski lodge is the other way!"

"I know where it is!" Noah snapped. "What do you want me to do, drive across campus? I'll swing around at the next block."

"Don't! They're piling into the van. We can't lead them to where we're gonna hide."

Noah's knuckles whitened on the steering wheel. "Where, then?"

"Head for the lake. Make them think we're going to your house, then double back."

A rattle, then a cough, then a thump. Noah's face went white.

"Uh . . . we're going to need a different plan." He glanced at me like a child caught doing something naughty. "I'm out of gas."

"*Out of gas?*"

"When was I supposed to fill up? There's nobody at the station!"

Noah turned left at Quarry Road, coasting downhill on fumes. We reached the junction where the highway becomes Main Street. "Turn right!" I shouted, forming a plan on the fly. Noah punched the gas for a last kick and we rolled into the industrial area at the foot of Miner's Peak. "Park in the sanitation lot."

Noah made the turn and stopped. I snapped off my seat belt. "Let them think we ran into one of these buildings, since I was inspecting them today. Instead we'll sprint for the bridge and take a hiking trail around the rim to the trailer park. They might come looking, but there are dozens of mobile homes in there. We can try to hide until nightfall." Dicey, but without a working car, we were boxed in. Had to chance it.

Noah shot from behind the wheel. "Works for me!"

We ducked into the woods. A minute later I heard squealing brakes. They'd seen Noah's SUV and had hopefully drawn the wrong conclusion. Working steadily through the trees, we angled toward the ruined bridge. The footpath I was aiming for wasn't popular—there was a chance only trailer folks knew about it. With luck we'd ditch them, go to ground in a random unit, and then trek across the valley after dark.

We emerged on a rocky hillside near the canyon. The Plank was dead ahead—what was left of it, at least. I was searching for the trailhead when I noticed Noah had stopped. Shading his eyes, he peered down at the bridge.

I followed his sight line. Spotted a flash of bright orange. Someone was standing by the precipice. "It's Hector," Noah whispered in surprise.

"Noah, we have to go. They could be here any second."

"Yeah, but . . ."

Hector was at the edge of the broken span, staring down into Gullet Chasm.

Noah turned to me. "I need to check on him for a second."

I gave him an impatient look, but Noah was already jogging toward the bridge. I followed reluctantly, keeping an eye on the road. Noah approached Hector cautiously and called out, "Hector? You okay?"

Hector was staring into the gorge. "I can't do it, Noah."

Noah seemed to understand. "I think you're being too hard on yourself, man. We're all in this together, right?"

Hector shook his head. His legs began to shake. "This is *my* punishment. How do I know you're even real? I . . . I think I'm alone here. Tack proved it. This isn't everyone's purgatory, it's just for me. And I . . . I'm not strong enough."

One of Noah's hands reached out. "Hey. Hector, come on. Don't talk like that."

"Good luck, Noah. For what it's worth, I never thought you were so bad." Before either of us could react, Hector stepped into space and vanished.

"*Hector!*" Noah shot forward, skidding dangerously close to the edge. He looked down into the canyon, then jerked his head away. I ran over and threw my arms around him.

I didn't look myself. I'd taken that drop on my eighth birthday. Knew what happened at the bottom.

"*He didn't have to do that!*" Noah said miserably, tears on his cheeks.

"I know," I soothed, hugging him close. My mind was in shock, but I could tell Noah was close to the breaking point. I had to be strong.

"He thought he was already dead." Noah pulled away from me, wiping his eyes. "Who knows? Maybe he's right." I didn't know what to say, but it didn't matter.

"Holy crap, he jumped!"

Our eyes shot to the road. Ethan and his gang were standing a hundred yards away at the top of a rise. Based on their astonished faces, they'd seen Hector's fall as well.

"*Ethan,*" Noah spat, with a bitter heat I'd never seen before.

I took his hand and began dragging him toward the forest. "We have to go. Now!"

He fought me for a moment, then relented, sprinting by my side.

Behind us, pounding feet echoed across the canyon.

They were coming.

43

NOAH

Full dark out.

No voices on the wind. No sounds of pursuit. I finally began to relax.

Min was by the window, peering through a gap in the shades. All the lights were off, and would stay that way. We'd picked a run-down unit on the western side of the trailer park. Close to where Tack had lived, or so Min said.

Ethan and those guys hadn't known about the trail and we'd lost them, locking ourselves in before they'd figured it out. We'd heard footsteps and hushed conversations carrying from the main drag, but they hadn't come close to finding us. That was at least an hour ago.

Min sighed. Stepped back. Sat down next to me on the couch. This trailer had only two compartments—an open living area and a cramped, sour-smelling bedroom at the far end. If I stretched, I could probably touch the front and rear walls at the same time.

"Any idea who lived here?" I asked, breaking the silence. For some reason I used the past tense.

Min nodded. "One of the Jenkins brothers. I forget which. He spends most nights outside by his fire pit, drunk off his ass."

The dead air returned. I couldn't think of anything to say. It was gloomy in the trailer, with only moonlight for illumination. I could just make out Min's face in the shadows next to me. I knew she was thinking about her friend.

"There was nothing you could do," I said quietly.

"Yeah."

"I'm serious." I reached for her hand. "Once Tack went off like that—the stuff about being a fraud—Ethan was never going to let it go." I shifted, disturbed by the memory. "I mean, I never thought he'd actually *kill* anyone . . . Even the other guys were, like . . . No one saw *that* coming."

Min's shoulders were shaking. Her other hand rose to cover her mouth.

I stopped talking. I was only making things worse. On instinct, I pulled her close and wrapped my arms around her. A dam burst, and she began sobbing in my arms.

"He was so angry!" Min blubbered, bottled-up emotions pouring out. "Maybe if . . . if . . . I'd paid more attention, or . . . or if . . . I should've *listened*!"

"Hey. Hey!" I eased her back, looked directly into her eyes. "Tack's death isn't your fault. *Ethan* murdered him. *Ethan* is responsible, and no one else. I know you feel guilty because of how he died—so do I—but we're not to blame. I'm serious, Min."

She held my gaze, hungry to believe. The moon had risen

above the mountains, twinkling her eyes and painting her face in a soft blue glow. I had a sudden desire to kiss her. She looked so beautiful. So vulnerable. I wanted to bring her into me somehow. Connect with her. Make her a part of me, and never let go.

She's crying over the murder of her best friend, you scumbag. A friend who had a crush on her, which she probably knew about. Show some freaking respect.

I released her awkwardly, shame burning my ears. What was I thinking?

Min tensed beside me, pushing jet-black hair behind her ears. Was I crazy, or did she miss the contact, too?

She looked at me then, stormy gray eyes boring into my soul. I glanced away. Began fiddling with my hands. I didn't know what was happening. Between us. Inside me. With the world in general.

My foot started tapping on its own. Reality was crackling around me.

Death. So much death.

Tack. Hector. Sheriff Watson. Those poor people mowed down in town square.

And me, too. I shouldn't forget my own private murders. Or Min's.

I stole a glance at her. She was watching me.

My muscles tightening like snare drums. I felt the panic start to build. It was happening again, right here, inches from the only person I trusted. The last person I wanted to witness this.

A girl I wanted to have faith in me. Rely on me. Believe I was strong.

A hand on my shoulder. Then my face.

Min turned my head to face hers. Looked me in the eyes.

"It's okay. I'm here."

She leaned forward and kissed me.

For an instant, I actually tried to pull away, like a spooked horse. But Min didn't let go, sliding forward into my lap. My body responded. The fear melted. I folded my arms around her slender body, buried my face in hers, and let it all wash away.

I woke up beside her on the couch.

Min's eyes were open, studying me. I should've felt self-conscious, but didn't. "How long have you been awake?"

"Long enough." She raised her arms and stretched. I caught her around the waist and pulled her close. Buried my face in her neck. Our lips met again, and for a while all other thoughts fled.

Finally, I came up for air. "We didn't go to the ski lodge."

"No, we didn't." She kissed me again, then rose and stepped into the kitchen. "We might have to hide here all day now. Go tomorrow night."

I sat up and yawned, working a crick in my neck. "I'm good with that."

I realized I was deliriously happy. And I'm *never* happy.

Min opened the fridge and frowned. "We'll have to scout around for food. Unless you want to eat Bud Light tall boys for breakfast."

"I've heard worse ideas." A goofy smile wouldn't leave my face.

Min flopped back down beside me. She took my hand in hers, her eyes growing serious.

"I want to thank you."

"Thank me? For what?"

"For what you said yesterday. About Tack."

My mood deflated. "I meant it. Tack's death isn't anyone's fault but the asshole who killed him."

She looked away. "I know. It's just . . . I think it's going to haunt me."

I nodded. Didn't say something stupid like, "It'll get better with time," or "Think of the good stuff." All the well-intentioned crap I'd heard after my mother died. A grieving person needs to grieve. It's better to just be there.

Min's expression darkened. "Ethan's a monster and a murderer. When you found me, I was upset, and said some things I regret. But I *am* going to make him answer for what he's done. Will you help me?"

The plea in her voice caught me off guard, but I didn't hesitate. "I will. What's the plan?"

"Part of our class splintered yesterday." She pulled her knees up to her chest, flashing what I'd come to think of as her thinking face. "We need to exploit that. Let's find the kids who took off and see if they'll help us."

I was about to point out that forty people had already failed in that task, but stopped. I'd heard something outside the trailer. Min's feet hit the floor. She'd caught it, too. Bringing a finger to my lips, I slowly began to rise. The door crashed open. Toby's shaved head popped inside.

He had a Band-Aid across his scalp, one eye purpling on its way to black. "In here!" he called over his shoulder, then smiled as we scrambled to our feet. "Hey, Min. Hey, Noah." He winked at me, like he'd just won a friendly game of hide-and-seek. "Helluva takedown back at the jail, bro. Hat tip."

I blinked, unable to respond. There was no other way out of the trailer.

"What do you want?" Min spat through clenched teeth. "Haven't you done enough? Just leave us alone!"

Toby shook his round head. "Not how it works, Melinda. You guys come on out. It'll be pretty embarrassing for everyone if we have to drag you."

I glanced at Min. We had no choice. Bristling like a cat, Min stormed past Toby, shouldering him aside as she exited. He giggled, then swept his hand grandly, allowing me to pass as well. I stepped outside, the hairs on my neck standing at attention.

There were six of them. Ethan. The Nolan twins. Toby and Charlie Bell. Tucker Brincefield. More than enough to handle the job. Ethan was staring at me with cold eyes, arms across his chest. He pointed at Min without looking.

"Her I get. She's always been trash. It's no surprise she can't follow directions. But you, Noah?" Ethan shook his head in disbelief. "We were friends. You could've stuck with your own and run things, but instead you ran and hid behind a skank's skirt."

My eyes flashed. "Watch your mouth, Ethan."

"Or what?"

Min took a step toward Ethan, but Tucker grabbed her arm from behind. She stopped, but didn't turn, eyes blazing. "You *murdered* Tack. I won't let you get away with it. Ever."

"Tack had a choice. He got what he deserved."

"Says who? You?"

Ethan's face reddened. "That's right, *me. I'm* in charge, whether you like it or not. That's how it's supposed to be!"

Min glared at the other boys. "Are you listening to him? He's insane!"

Charlie's head dropped, but no one else moved. Ethan waved a dismissive hand, spinning to face me. "You were warned, Noah. Now you're all out of strikes." He turned and barked orders. "Throw them in the van and let's get out of here. We'll settle this back at the church."

Chris took Min's other arm, and they marched her down the lane.

I hadn't moved. My legs wouldn't respond. Four sets of unfriendly eyes watched me.

"Let's go, Noah." Toby shoved me in the back. "Or I can repay you now for this shiner."

I went quietly.

Chris parked near the square. Most of our classmates were hanging around outside—apparently no work had been assigned while the search for us was active. Ethan and Mike led us toward the church, with Tucker, Toby, and Charlie boxing us in from behind. Kids I'd known for years cast sidelong glances, but no one made a move to help, or spoke out in our defense. Not that I expected anyone to.

Ethan halted on the steps to address the group. But before he could begin, a shout caused everyone to turn. Chris Nolan was streaking down the sidewalk, his long red hair flapping behind him as he pointed back down the block. "Ethan! Guys! Look!"

Squinting, I could just make out someone walking down the center of Main Street. The person was moving slowly, head down, hands by his sides. He had dark hair and wore a bright orange shirt.

My eyes popped. "Oh my God."

Min's gaze shot to me, no less shocked. "How?"

I shook my head, mind-blown.

Hector Quino stumbled along the pavement in a daze. As silence filled the square, he turned the corner and began walking toward the church.

"Impossible," Charlie breathed. "I watched him jump."

Ethan began nervously scratching his neck. "Toby. Charlie. Bring him over here."

Toby glanced at Ethan, eyes fearful. "Dude, he's *dead*. I looked into the gorge. Hector hit the bottom. I *saw* his body!"

"Go get him and we'll find out what's going on," Ethan growled. The church door opened. Sarah and Jessica rushed outside. One glance at Hector slogging up the block and they both turned white.

Min grabbed my arm. "*Noah!*" she whispered urgently. "Hector is *alive*!"

My hands started to shake. "He fell the whole way, Min. I looked, too."

She gripped harder, a wild light in her eyes. "Hector fell. But *now* he's alive."

Understanding hit me like a hammer. "You think—"

"Shh!" Min slipped past our guards, who were too distracted to notice. Ethan and Sarah were hurrying down to where Charlie and Toby had confronted Hector.

"Hector?" Charlie said tentatively. "You okay, man? What happened?"

"I was a fool," Hector mumbled, staring vacantly at the sidewalk. His eyes were blurry and red, as if he'd cried out all the tears he possessed. "My punishment isn't over."

"What are you talking about?" Ethan crossed his arms, eyeing Hector warily. "I saw you jump, Hector. What happened when you . . . when you hit the rocks?"

Hector shrugged miserably. "Everything went black."

Ethan shifted, rubbing his jaw. Jessica moaned. Sarah was staring at the pavement.

"How'd you get back up here?" Toby asked quietly. "I don't know anyone who can climb the canyon wall. It's practically vertical."

"I didn't wake up in the canyon. I was somewhere else."

"Where?" Ethan blurted. "Tell me."

The group tightened around Hector, mesmerized. No one was paying the slightest attention to Min or me. I tried to catch her eye, but she was watching as intently as the others.

"Somewhere south." Hector absently waved toward the other side of the lake. "A hollow above the tree line." Then he held up his arms and stared at them in wonder. "Like this. I don't have a scratch on me."

Ethan grabbed Hector by the shoulders. Looked directly into his eyes. "You jumped from the bridge into the canyon, but woke up in the woods. Is that what you're saying, Hector?"

Hector nodded, his face a mask of grief. "God isn't done with me. It was stupid for me to think I was in control. I won't defy him again."

Nervous chattering broke out. No one knew how to take the news. One more impossible thing in a week full of them.

But I was ice-cold.

I knew.

Hector had reset, just like I'd done so many times before.

Ethan was forcing him to repeat every detail of his story. I looked over at Min, who nodded. We slipped away from the circle, unnoticed. Then she grabbed me by the shirt. "Did you hear that?" she hissed.

"Yes. It's the exact same. Hector must've—"

Min shushed me. She'd gone rigid, eavesdropping on a conversation behind us.

"I don't know, man, but it's gone! What do we tell Ethan?"

Pivoting slowly, I caught sight of Derrick and Lars huddled on the church steps. "You really think somebody *stole* a dead body?" Derrick shivered. "Man, I can't handle any more of this crap."

"No idea." Lars began pulling on his beard. "But it's *not* there. And now Hector comes walking down Main Street like he didn't just swan dive into the gorge. That dude rose from the frickin' *dead*, bro. I'm bugging out!"

Min tugged my arm. Pointed behind the church. I nodded. We scurried out of sight, then took off running for three blocks. At the post office we ducked behind a mail truck. I was puffing and blowing, but Min looked energized as she gnawed her bottom lip.

"What is it?" I wheezed.

"You heard them! Tack's body is missing!"

A wave of revulsion swept through me. "Oh, God. *That's*

who they were talking about? Who'd steal a corpse?" I immediately regretted the words, but Min was on another trail entirely.

"No! Don't you see!?"

I shook my head, lost. I'm not great under pressure.

"Hector didn't die, Noah!" A frenzied smile appeared on Min's face. "No one can survive that drop—but he woke up in the woods, like we've been doing for years! *And Tack's body isn't where they left it.*"

Comprehension finally dawned. "Oh, damn."

Min nodded fiercely.

"Tack's not dead, either!"

44

MIN

Lightning coursed through my veins.

Tack could be alive!

Impossible, but wasn't all of this, from the very start? I'd never pretended to understand my birthdays, but Hector's revival didn't require my comprehension. It was a real thing. I'd seen it. Tack could've done the same.

So where is he?

Noah watched me pace, his expression dazed. I knew the strain was getting intense, but I needed him with me on this. He was the only one who might get it.

I stopped and took his hand. "Listen! I know it sounds crazy—"

He barked a laugh. "We're *way* past crazy. I can barely think."

"True. But Hector woke up in the woods alone, without any injuries. That's exactly what happened to me when I was pushed into the canyon. Somehow he reset!"

Noah's eyes widened. "You think Hector is one of the blue dots? A beta?"

I shook my head vigorously. "Did he look like someone who'd been through that before? Plus, today isn't his birthday. And he wasn't killed by Black Suit, he jumped."

"Okay." Noah was thinking it through. "So . . . then how did it happen?" His jaw tightened. "Are we dead after all, like Hector said?"

A twinge of fear, but I shoved it aside. *Trust your instincts!*

"For some reason, Hector just had one of our experiences. Now Tack's body is missing! It's not a stretch to think it happened to him as well."

"Okay . . . so where is he?"

"No idea!" The words tumbled out of me. "He could be hiding in the woods, totally freaked out. He wouldn't walk back into town like Hector did. Not after Ethan stabbed him. He's probably up a tree somewhere, alone and scared out of his mind."

"Then how do we find him?"

I'd been wondering the same. "I don't think he and Hector came back in the same place. They probably would've seen each other. But maybe Tack reset in one of our spots? My clearing isn't far from here. Let's check it. If he's not there, we can circle around to your cave. If both are empty, we'll try to find the place Hector described."

"Right. Sure."

"He's out there, Noah. I can feel it. Trust me, please."

Noah smiled. "I do trust you, Min."

I smashed his mouth with a kiss. Then pushed away.

"Let's go find our boy."

• • •

We reached the meadow where I'd awakened so many times. No sign of Tack. The forest was eerily quiet without birds, a chilling reminder that more was wrong in the valley than just missing townspeople. I took the risk of calling out, but got no response.

So we started hiking over to Noah's cave, skirting the northern edge of town. There we had a stroke of luck. An unlocked car had its keys inside—not unusual in our town—and the tank was full. Opting for speed over stealth, we drove down Quarry Road, then shot south along the water.

We didn't see anyone else. Whatever Ethan and the rest were up to, they didn't seem to be looking for us. Noah drove as close as we could get, then led me the rest of the way on foot, to a hidden fissure in the rocks beside a small pond. The cozy little vale would make an amazing campsite, but it was plain that no one was there.

Noah pointed to a sheet of mud stretching across the entrance to the cave. "No footprints. I don't think he was here."

I ground my teeth. *He's alive. Somewhere. We just have to find him.*

Noah knelt, drew a circle in the dirt. "Look. This is the lake." Then he made three dots around the circle. "Here's your reset point, in the north. Mine is to the west. And the area Hector described is over here, to the south. What do you notice?"

The answer was obvious. "They look like compass points." My mind made the leap. "The Nemesis docs described four beta subjects, but we know of only *three* reset points so far."

Noah made a fourth mark in the dirt. "Here. To the east."

I clamped a hand on his shoulder and squeezed. "Brilliant!"

"Ow!" He scuttled sideways with a laugh, then rose to tower over me again. I could tell he was pleased by my praise. We hurried back down to the car.

The trip took thirty minutes. We drove south around the lake, hoping to avoid notice, though anyone watching from the hills would've spotted us. I wondered what Ethan was doing. His reaction to Hector set my teeth on edge. Did he know more than he was letting on? Was he still after Noah and me, or had Hector's return somehow changed the game?

Worries swirled inside my head, forming a ball of tension I couldn't dispel. I wanted to scream at the car to go faster. For a hot second, I missed my mother desperately. Yearned for her soft hands and levelheaded advice. But I pushed those feelings away.

Mom had betrayed me. She'd made me the centerpiece of a conspiracy involving my repeated execution. Anyone who could do that to her own flesh and blood wasn't worthy of trust. I could only count on myself.

And Noah. He's proven that much, now.

We reached the eastern woods. Without a better plan, Noah parked in the same place we'd used the night Sheriff Watson was killed. Everything felt like it was coming full circle, though we were no closer to figuring things out.

Project Nemesis remained a total mystery. Its architects were ghosts.

Noah led me to the edge of the woods. "Where should we look? There's a lot of acreage back here."

I'd been thinking about it on the ride over. "Reset points seem to be empty spaces. Let's find the field where those soldiers trapped us." *Where Sheriff Watson was executed*, I left unsaid, but I could tell it was on his mind as well. We hopped the fence. The hike took ten minutes. We reached the clearing, but not a soul was present.

My spirits sank into my shoes. I'd been wrong.

Tack wasn't there. Which meant Tack was dead.

I didn't even have the heart to call out.

Bushes rustled. I spun.

A skinny kid emerged with greasy black hair stuck to his forehead. His clothes were filthy, but there was a devilish gleam to his blue eyes.

"What took you guys so long? I was running out of berries."

PART FIVE

THE GUARDIAN

45

NOAH

Tack strolled into the clearing.

He faked a yawn, trying to play it cool. But his relieved eyes betrayed him. I could tell he was *extremely* glad to see us. Then Min tackled him in a flying bear hug.

"Tack!" Tears streamed from her eyes. He laughed, begging for mercy as they toppled to the ground.

I stood rooted to the spot. *He's alive. She was right.*

Logically, I knew that finding Tack alive was the object of our trip—what we'd been desperately hoping for—but seeing him in the flesh nearly overwhelmed me.

I watched him die. Saw the light leave his eyes.

Yet here he is, like it never happened.

Min was straddling Tack and punching him in the chest as he lay pinned to the ground. "Tell me everything!" she demanded. "How are you here?"

"Get off me first!" Tack croaked, though I suspected he was perfectly content. Min relented and they both stood up. Tack glanced over at me. Gave a head nod, which I returned. Then he turned back to Min, eyebrows climbing his forehead. "I have no idea how I got here. The last thing I remember is collapsing in the church."

He flinched involuntarily. I understood. I knew what it was like to be murdered.

Min pulled him into another quick hug. "Just tell us what you remember."

Tack seemed to focus inward. "I felt the knife go in. Felt it . . . pierce my heart." His breathing picked up, a sheen of sweat dampening his brow. "I went numb. My brain stopped working, and I hit the floor. Then . . ." His hands rose, accentuating an impossible description. "Nothing. I woke up here. Not even a rip in my clothes."

Tack looked at Min, then me. "Just like you guys described. How is that possible?"

"We don't know, but you're not the only one." Min told him about Hector.

"So, what, *no one* can die now? We all reset like you guys?"

"No idea," Min admitted, brushing hair from her face. "But it's a possibility."

"Has it always been like this?" Tack wondered aloud. "I've never freaking croaked before, but maybe I would've reset every time, too."

"Kids in Fire Lake *have* died," I pointed out unhappily. "Remember Mary and Pete? They didn't come back." My thoughts were racing down tunnels, a dark idea taking shape. "I keep circling back to town square. They obviously gassed us for a reason. This might be it."

"But you and I have been resetting for years," Min said, tapping her thigh with an index finger. "We died and came back *five times* before they rounded anyone else up."

"We're the betas, remember?" The idea gathered steam in my head. "Project Nemesis used four test subjects as guinea pigs in the early trials. Then they gathered our whole class together to activate their final plan. That mist was probably some kind of experimental chemical. Maybe they were . . . *infecting* everyone, giving our classmates the same thing *we've* had since we were kids."

Min was slowly nodding. "The shots in kindergarten. They took Noah and me into the woods. We could've been injected with something, then had our responses tested for years. Until the bastards were ready to infect the whole sophomore class."

"But where did they go?" Tack countered. "Noah's theory doesn't explain why everyone vanished while we were unconscious, or . . . or"—he shuddered, then forged ahead—"or *dead* in the square. And how did the valley repair itself? That part blows my mind, no matter what angle I come at it from. Buildings don't fix themselves."

Min groaned. "You're right. I think Noah's close, but we're still missing something."

I ground my teeth. The answers felt tantalizingly close. I didn't want the moment to slip away. "The damage could've been a mass delusion. Maybe the earthquakes, too." My eyes popped. "Oh man, I suppose it's possible that even the Anvil was invented. All of it—the reports, the natural disasters, everything—faked from the beginning. Our whole last week could've been one giant head game! Part of the Nemesis experiment. We're isolated up here in the valley. They could've manipulated *everything*."

Min was rubbing her forehead. "At this point, I don't trust anything. Certainly not the government. But faking natural disasters? Hacking CNN, Fox News, and all the others, while also putting together clips as believable as disaster movies? It's too much. In fact, I think the opposite is true—everything did happen, and it's all tied to the project. I think Nemesis *caused* the chaos."

"Now who's reaching?" Tack muttered, but didn't say more.

"Don't forget," Min said quietly, "Sheriff Watson was shot to death right here. That wasn't a hoax."

Tack's jaw tightened. His father had been gunned down, too.

Min sighed in resignation. "So we're nowhere. Right where we started."

"No!" I said, drawing their eyes. A strange feeling was welling inside me. I felt a sudden release of the tension I'd been carrying for days. Hell, *years*.

I realized my anxiety was gone. Something had shifted. Loosened. I almost laughed with relief, but was too exhilarated. Puzzle pieces were snapping together in my mind. There were blank spaces, sure—holes that would have to be filled—but the big picture suddenly seemed so much clearer.

Project Nemesis had changed the rules we lived by.

I was a centerpiece of that. A crucial element. A keystone.

"No, *what*?" Tack demanded finally, when I hadn't spoken for several seconds. "You have some miracle plan to deal with Ethan and the rest?"

"We fight them," Min answered automatically, her expression darkening. "We can't let Ethan run things. Not after what he did to you."

"Fight them how?" Tack shuffled his feet in a desultory manner. "Ethan's got the whole class on his side—or afraid of him, which works just as well. I say we pick a good place to hide, then find some way out of the valley. Let that prick have his Kingdom of Morons."

"You really think we can leave?" Min looked as if she'd never considered the idea. "I'm not so sure. Plus, you missed a few things while dead. There's trouble in paradise."

Min began catching Tack up on current events, but I couldn't bring myself to contribute.

All my life, I'd been plagued by fear. Self-doubt. A crushing insecurity. I'd been told these problems were caused by a flaw in my psyche. The deranged conjurings of a broken mind.

But that simply wasn't true.

The murders *were* real. The resurrections, too.

I wasn't flawed. Or broken. I was being tested.

I cannot die.

Heavy curtains opened inside me, allowing sunlight to pour in.

What was I so afraid of all the time? I wasn't *crazy*. I'd endured a crucible *no one* could suffer through unscathed. Frankly, it was a miracle I ever stepped outside my bedroom door. Who could've done better than me?

The murders were obstacles to overcome. I'd survived them all.

My spirit soared as the realizations dog-piled on top of one another.

I can be strong now. No, more than that.

I can be powerful.

"That's another thing," Min was saying. "Who are the other two betas?"

"We need to find out," I said. Though suddenly, I thought I could guess.

"Does it matter?" Tack made a face. "No offense, but if everyone resets now, you betas aren't different from the rest."

My head swiveled. I flashed an almost condescending smile. "We're the *most* prepared, Tack. Whatever this cycle is, we've been living it for a decade. We need to find the other betas and figure out what they know."

Min shivered. "That shouldn't be a problem, I guess. We can just ask around."

"And give away our advantage?" My tone was incredulous. "No way. We have to keep this secret from everyone until we know how to exploit it."

And it *was* an advantage, I just knew it. I was special. Chosen. Picked first.

I noticed they were both looking at me funny.

"What do you think is happening, Noah?" Min asked slowly. Tack had crossed his arms, was watching me with interest.

"I don't think the project failed." It was hard to explain, this feeling of purpose that had stolen over me. The answers suddenly felt so obvious, I found them difficult to express. "I think this is what we were prepped for. What our birthdays were leading up to."

"*Prepped?* That's what you're calling it?" Min's eyes narrowed. She spoke in a quiet but forceful voice. "When I was eight years old, I was pushed off a cliff. At ten, I drowned in a creek. On my twelfth birthday, I was run over. When I turned fourteen, the black-suited man *bashed my head in with a rock*. He shot me to death on Sunday. I wasn't *prepped* for anything, Noah. I was terrorized throughout my childhood, and you were, too. Don't forget that."

Her rebuke was like a slap. "No, no! You're right. That's not what I meant." I wasn't explaining this well. "I'm not minimizing what was done. I'm just saying our experiences give us an edge."

"For what?" Min snapped. "Over whom? What are we trying to do, take over the town ourselves?" She took a breath, but the heat didn't dissipate. "I'll be honest, Noah—I don't like what I'm hearing right now. You're starting to sound like Ethan."

I flinched. Bit my tongue. *How could she say that?*

"We need to work together," Min continued, a bit more calmly. "We should attack this mystery by involving everyone as equals. We need to share information, not build private sand castles."

Irritation sparked—why didn't she understand?—but was swiftly doused by shame.

God, Min was right. What was I talking about? I *did* sound like Ethan.

Another failure of character. While she aces every test.

"You're right. I'm sorry. I don't know what came over me." When that seemed deficient, I added, "It's been a long day."

Her posture softened immediately. "It's okay. We're all under a ton of pressure." She reached out and squeezed my hand.

I thought back to the night before. Remembered her body cradled in mine, our lips inches apart as we slept, sharing the same breaths. Then my face reddened. Tack was watching us closely, his expression guarded.

He doesn't know. And I doubt he can adjust.

I turned away, pretending to stretch. Couldn't help but slightly resent the situation. Min always came to the right conclusion, while I always blew it. We were both betas, but not equals. Faced with the same obstacles, she'd become twice the person I was.

Tack broke the silence. "So what's our next move? I haven't eaten anything today, and I smell like Smokey Bear. I need a shower and a turkey sandwich. After that, we can declare war on Ethantonia."

"I'd think hard before doing that," a voice said.

I spun to face the forest.

Two figures were watching from the shadows.

Both held guns.

46

MIN

Ethan and Sarah walked into the clearing.

"Oh crap." Noah took an involuntary step back.

Tack squinted at the tree line beyond the pair. "They alone?"

"Yes," Ethan answered. Sarah kept pace, watching Noah with a tight frown.

I considered our options, but there weren't any. They had weapons, we didn't.

"We just want to talk," Ethan said, though the gun he was holding signaled the opposite. "That's why we left the others in town."

With a jolt, I realized they didn't seem surprised to see Tack alive.

"*You*," I breathed. "You're the other betas."

"I felt the same about you." Sarah eyed the two boys beside me. "Which one?"

"Me." Noah's expression was almost prideful. He'd been so weird since we'd found Tack. I didn't understand, but now wasn't the time.

Ethan made a show of stuffing the gun into his belt. "Sarah figured out Min. Took long enough, but we didn't know much about Dr. Lowell until this morning. We had no clue who the last beta was." He winked at Noah. "You didn't strike me as the type."

Despite the clear menace of their appearance, I couldn't contain my excitement. They knew about Project Nemesis! What information did they have that we didn't?

"So you weren't Lowell's patients?" I thought back to the square. "Did you see Fanelli about the murders?"

Ethan and Sarah exchanged a look. "I told you it was different for them," she said.

Ethan nodded, scratching his chin. "Tell us what you know about the experiment."

"You first," Tack shot back.

Ethan snorted. "Great to see you again, Thumbtack."

"Screw you."

A flush began creeping up Ethan's neck. Sarah put a hand on his arm. When she spoke next, she only had eyes for Noah. "Did you know we all share a birthday?"

Noah's brow knitted. "Huh? Your birthday is in June. Ethan's was three weeks ago."

Sarah shook her head, golden tendrils shimmering in the midday sun. "I saw Fanelli's records. Ethan and I were both born on September seventeenth, just like you two. Our parents gave us fake birthdays our whole lives. Isn't that twisted?"

My heart began to pound. "Why would they do that?"

Sarah glanced at me briefly, then returned her attention to Noah. "For the project. You and Noah are local, but Ethan and I were imported. They needed *four* betas, but I guess they thought the class parties would be too big. *Suspicious looking.* So they lied. It's kind of funny when you think about it."

Noah's face scrunched in confusion. "What does our birth date have to do with anything?"

Sarah gave a full-bodied shrug. "But facts are facts. I wonder who's oldest?"

My mind was racing. So many questions filled my head, I couldn't think straight. We were doing this out of order. "Were you guys murdered on Sunday? Does he come for you on your real birthdays or the fake ones?"

They both wore blank looks. "Who?" said Sarah.

Now Noah and I shared a glance. *She said it was different for them.*

Ethan's eyes narrowed. I could tell he was as hungry for information as I was. "This person—you said he *murdered* you?"

I decided to play ball. At least a little. "On our even-year birthdays, a psychopath in a black suit tracks down Noah and me and kills us. We were told these executions were delusions."

Ethan looked legitimately shocked. "*Jesus.* That's harsh. Who is the bastard?"

"We don't know. But I think he's the power behind Project Nemesis. He was running the operation in town square."

"Min shared what she knows," Tack interrupted. "Now you."

Sarah slipped her gun into the pocket of her Windbreaker. "Since I turned nine, I've had to visit Dr. Fanelli every other year on September seventeenth. He'd perform hypnosis on me. I always woke up right here."

Noah had been right. This *was* a reset point. But why had Tack appeared here?

Ethan snorted. "*Hypnosis.* That's what Fanelli called it, even though I'd never remember a thing, and regain consciousness south of the lake. We just finished grilling Hector—he's barely holding it together, but described my spot exactly. Sarah guessed you'd check both places, looking for Tack. Do you guys wake up here, too?"

I shook my head, trying to process it all. "Above town, in the northern woods."

They looked at Noah. "West," he said. "A cave."

"Like a compass." Ethan nodded thoughtfully. "Sure. Why not?"

Dr. Fanelli. I'd assumed all four betas were under Lowell's control, but now the picture was clearer. "They split us up. Different doctors, different tactics. Different years."

"Just like a government plan," Ethan quipped. "Redundancies everywhere. We didn't even know Fanelli was killing us during our visits until Sarah cracked his files. If I ever see that bastard again . . ."

"Where'd he go?" Noah asked. "Where'd they *all* go?"

"We don't know. Fanelli said our treatment was some radical new therapy. Our parents signed us up when we were little. Leaving us in the woods was supposed to test our survival skills, or something. Make us stronger. Which is freaking stupid, since I always woke up in the exact same place."

"Wait." Noah extended a hand toward them. "Did you guys know about each other?"

Sarah nodded. "I saw Ethan leaving Fanelli's office a few years back. We talked, and found out he was doing the same thing to both of us. Eventually we confronted him, and Fanelli began treating us in joint sessions."

I couldn't believe what I was hearing. "Treating you for *what*?"

"We don't know." I could tell the admission burned. "The other files on his computer are encrypted. All he left us was a freaking note."

I lurched forward a step. "What did it say?"

Sarah and Ethan shared a look. "Might as well," she said quietly. "It's why we came."

It was a moment before Ethan spoke. "He left an instruction. Fanelli liked to talk about what we should do if something strange ever happened. Something huge and inexplicable." He barked a bitter laugh. "I'm guessing the entire class being gassed qualifies."

"And?" Tack urged impatiently. "What was the message?"

Ethan looked directly into his eyes. "He told us to dominate. Sarah and I are supposed to take over if things go bad. I never understood Fanelli. Honestly, I thought he was crazy. But he was ahead of the game all along. He *knew* those troops were coming."

"Please tell me exactly what the note said," I persisted, mouth dry.

Ethan rolled his eyes, but Sarah spoke, reciting from memory. "*Dominate the situation, by whatever means necessary, for as long as you can.* It was addressed to both of us."

I nearly growled in frustration. "That doesn't *explain* anything!"

"Of course it does!" Ethan fired back. "The adults ditched us, and now we're locked in this valley with no way out. Fanelli absolutely knew it was going to happen. His instructions are clear as day: the betas are supposed to run things now."

In the corner of my eye, I saw Noah nod slightly. It set my teeth on edge.

"What *things* are we supposed to run?" I countered, trying to regain control of the conversation. "We don't even know what happened. We don't know where everyone went, and we've got no contact with the outside world."

"There *is* no outside world. Don't you see?" Ethan's finger shot toward Tack. "I stabbed him in the freaking heart, and he's perfectly fine. That's not possible, but it's true. None of this is possible! But it's *exactly* what Fanelli warned us about."

Tack took a step toward Ethan. "When you stabbed me, did you know I wouldn't die?"

Ethan's eyes slid away.

"Bastard," Tack hissed.

Ethan's scowl hardened. "I was told to dominate, *by whatever means necessary*. You got in my way."

"And I'm gonna *stay* in your way, you stupid—"

"Stop it!" I yelled, grabbing Tack's arm. "This got us nowhere before, and it's even more pointless now." He jerked away. I knew he was furious, but we needed to learn everything we could.

"Min's one hundred percent right," Sarah said calmly, shooting Ethan a pointed look. "We didn't come here to fight."

"Nice guns," Noah said softly.

"They might as well be props, since we all know they're pointless." To prove it, Sarah slipped hers out and tossed it into the field. Ethan made no move to follow her example. "We could've shot all three of you, but honestly, what's the point? You'd just reset, and we'd be right back where we started."

Her words hit me like a bucket of ice water.

My God, she's right. We can't die.

"What do you want then?" I asked in a shaky voice.

"A truce."

Sarah nudged Ethan, who spoke grudgingly. "We're offering you a place," Ethan said. "You're betas, like us." He was deliberately not looking at Tack. "The beta patients were clearly meant to be in charge."

Noah was nodding again, but I was repulsed. "You don't seem to get it: I don't *want* to boss everyone around. Why is it so important to be a dictator?"

"It's what I was *specifically* told to do," Ethan growled. "We don't know what's coming next, but I'm going to be ready."

He was glaring at me, eyes tight with anger. In that instant, I knew I could never work with him. Not on those terms. "You don't get to be warlord just because the adults disappeared," I said. "I don't care about your doctor's note. You *stabbed* Tack in front of everyone, just because he disagreed with you. And you *didn't* know he'd come back. You're a murderer, not a leader."

Ethan's head snapped to Sarah. "I told you this was pointless."

She sighed, turned to Noah. "Come back with us, Noah. You don't belong with these two. You understand what needs to be done. I can see it in your eyes."

Noah didn't respond. For a terrifying moment, I thought

he'd actually abandon us. Walk right off this field with them, and never look back.

But Noah shook his head. "Sorry. I'm staying."

A spasm of anger rippled her features, then disappeared as quickly. "Mistake."

"I should kill you all." Ethan removed the gun from his waistband.

"We'll just come back," Tack taunted, clapping his hands together. Then he raced over and scooped up Sarah's gun. Rejoining the group, he pulled the slide, chambering a round.

"This is *my* time, not yours." Ethan's eyes glittered. "You want a war? You've got one."

The gun rose. I could practically taste his hunger for violence.

Tack fired a round into the dirt, startling everyone. "Three against two," he warned, his face a stony mask. I knew he'd shoot if it came down to it. Any excuse to pay Ethan back for what had happened in the church.

Sarah put a hand on Ethan's arm. "Let's go. We can visit again with more friends."

"Trailer trash," Ethan scoffed. "And a spoiled little rich boy. I'll tear you three apart." He spun and strode into the trees.

"I wouldn't have done that," Sarah said, almost casually. "He's taking this whole 'messiah' thing pretty seriously." In some ways, her calm demeanor was scarier than Ethan's bluster. She alone hadn't flinched when the gun went off.

"Why are you helping him?" I asked.

"Means to an end. Whatever this is, I intend to survive."

Sarah waggled a finger at Noah. "You're so weak, Noah. You think like a child. Why am I always surprised?" His face went scarlet as she turned and strolled away. "Enjoy my meadow," Sarah called over her shoulder. "I've always found this place . . . comforting. Like an old friend." With a soft giggle, she disappeared into the woods.

"What a bitch," Tack breathed.

Noah was staring at his shoes. Sarah's parting shot had hit the mark. I reached out to him, but he pulled away. "So what do we do now?" he asked quietly.

For the first time in days, I had an answer.

"If this is all some sort of game, we need to know the rules. We have to solve the riddle of Project Nemesis."

"Okay, sure," Tack said. "But how?"

"By going to the source." I spun, pointed into the forest behind us. "We finally find out what's back there."

Tack scratched his cheek. "That didn't go so well last time. Guards. Guns. All that."

"You forget, Tack. Fire Lake recently suffered a massive population reduction. For all we know, that base is just as empty as the rest of the valley."

"Or maybe that's where everyone is," he countered. "It was the soldiers' show, after all."

I shrugged. "Either way, at least we'll know."

Noah abruptly sprang into motion. "Then what are we waiting for?"

Without a backward glance, he started across the meadow.

Tack and I exchanged a surprised look before hurrying after him.

47

NOAH

I didn't check to see if Min and Tack followed.

I knew they would, and needed space to breathe. My emotions were a mess as I plunged into the woods, grappling with a simple truth: Ethan and Sarah had made a lot of sense.

What else was the beta testing for, if not to prepare us? Maybe we really *were* supposed to lead. Dr. Fanelli had directly said so in his note! He had no reason to lie that I could think of. Sarah and Ethan had been working with better information from the beginning.

But Min didn't see it that way. And I understood *her* point, too. Ethan had been willing to murder Tack with his bare hands to take control. The memory repulsed me. How could we work with him after that, even if we were supposed to?

My elation had vanished the moment Ethan and Sarah appeared, replaced by doubt and uncertainty. I'd been prepared for something special, but was I up to the challenge? Min seemed more clear-headed about everything. Shouldn't I just follow her lead?

Always a follower, huh, Noah? Sarah was right.

Her casual insult was a hot coal searing through my chest. Mainly because it was true.

I *was* weak. I *did* act like a child. I tried and tried and tried, but always came up short.

Who could respect that?

I kept ahead of them until we reached the abandoned guard-house. Min and Tack broke off a whispered conversation. Discussing me? Probably. I could barely meet her eye.

"Ready?" I asked.

Min nodded without saying more. We followed the road to the low building we'd spotted on our first trip. I wondered again at the poor security. I guess the first line of defense had always been secrecy.

The forest's silence was unearthly. No scampering creatures. No birds. It felt like every crunch of leaves was a blown whistle, but nobody appeared. The woods felt as abandoned as the rest of the valley. Maybe the sixty-four of us truly were all that was left.

"Should we try the door?" Tack whispered.

Min was peering beyond the building, to where the road curved out of sight. "I want to know what those lights were the other night."

Tack nodded. "Let's circle. We can peek around the bend, then sneak inside."

"Perfect. Lead the way."

Blood pounded through my eardrums as we scurried across the access road. When no alarm was raised, we swung wide, behind the building, to where we could see deeper into the valley. What we encountered took my breath away.

An area the size of a football field had been cleared, with lights erected along its perimeter. Dozens of Humvees, jeeps, and trucks were parked at one end—the same gray vehicles with black sunbursts that had been popping up all week. Tack whistled. "I guess we found the convoys."

"But where are the soldiers?" Min said.

Temporary structures filled the rest of the field. Rows of tents. A field kitchen. Supply dumps. Even a hastily rigged ropes course. The arrangement was efficient and tidy—every inch laid out with discipline and a sense of order. But there wasn't anyone there.

I sighed. "Well, that answers one question."

Min looked at me curiously. "What's that?"

"Whether our neighbors were forcibly evacuated here. Doesn't look like it. Seems like even the military blew town."

Tack shot Noah a skeptical look. "How'd they leave the valley without a bridge?"

"No idea. How'd they fix a mountain that broke in half?"

Min swiveled to face the building. "Maybe they're all inside."

I nodded. Couldn't decide whether I wanted it to be true or not. We approached from the rear, eyes on the single door. I worried it was locked.

Tack stopped suddenly, glancing at Min. "How come Sarah and Ethan haven't been back here yet? You realize Sarah's reset point was *inside* the security fence, right?"

Min paused. "You're right. Plus, they had groups canvass the whole valley that first day, but no one came in here. Why didn't they check on the troops?"

“No one’s accusing Ethan of being a genius,” Tack snarked.

“But Sarah isn’t stupid.” Min’s face was troubled. “I’m not sure who’s really in charge between them.”

“Ethan said they ransacked the psychiatrists’ offices,” I offered. “Between that and running their little empire, maybe they just haven’t had time.”

Min’s frown deepened. “Or maybe they came here days ago. We could be behind.”

Tack shrugged. “It’s pointless worrying about it now. Let’s go and see.”

We abandoned stealth and walked straight for the door. After the barest of pauses, Min reached out and tried the knob. It turned easily, the door opening with an outrush of hermetically sealed air.

Inside was short white-walled corridor. There was a door to our left, but it was locked. I peered through its window at a large assembly room with an exit on the opposite side. With a shock, I recognized the space. I’d been taken through it when I was six.

I stepped aside so Min could see. One glance, and her eyes darted to meet mine. She nodded grimly. She remembered, too. I yanked on the handle in frustration, but the door wouldn’t budge.

“There’s something up ahead,” Tack said, pointing down the corridor. It led to a burnished slab of metal connected to a keypad. This portal looked like it could withstand a tank blast, but when Min tried the handle, it swung open without resistance, revealing a staircase that descended a dozen switchbacks.

“I don’t like this,” I muttered. “It’s almost like they’re inviting us in this way.”

"Why wouldn't they?" Tack hopped down a few steps, the clang of his shoes echoing into the depths. "You guys are their star pupils, right? Here come the betas!"

I looked at Min, who shrugged. "What choice do we have?" she said.

We began to descend, listening for any sign the building was occupied. At the bottom we reached a pair of sliding metal doors. Beside them appeared to be a retinal scanner and handprint touch pad, but the doors swished open at our approach.

Min looked almost offended. "Why install this stuff if you're not going to use it?"

I shook my head, baffled. We stepped into an elevator with only one button. "I think . . . *this* one," Tack said, pressing the glowing circle. Surprisingly, the car jerked sideways. I had the unpleasant sensation of passing through thick walls—like rolling into the belly of a hollowed-out mountain—and then the lateral movement stopped. Seconds later we plunged at breakneck speed before gliding to a stop.

The doors opened. We stepped out, and my breath caught.

"Wow," Min gasped.

Tack leaned over a guardrail, gaping straight down. "Holy crap."

We were standing on a steel catwalk bolted to a wall of solid rock. Before us, an enormous hole stretched thirty yards across and dropped hundreds of feet. The catwalk circled to a miner's cage on the opposite side of the chamber. I could see a track descending into the depths. Yellow lights blazed every ten yards, both along the catwalk and down the track. Otherwise, we'd have been in total darkness.

I looked up. A roof of solid concrete enclosed the massive space.

Tack spun to face Min, eyes bright with excitement. "Do you know what this is?"

"The world's most secure parking garage?"

Tack laughed, clearly excited by our find. "This is an old missile silo! For one of those ICBMs we talked about. They've converted it into . . . into . . . *something*. Sealed it from above, too."

I peered into the inky depths, swallowed. "Why would they do that?"

"No idea. But whatever they're hiding, you can bet it's at the bottom."

Min pointed to the cage on the other side of the shaft. "Then that's where we go."

As we circled the empty silo, I tried not to look down again. I couldn't imagine this place existing just a few miles from my house. It must've taken years to repurpose. How had they done it under everyone's noses?

They must have a secret way into the valley.

I filed that away to think about later.

Min stepped into the cage. Tack and I followed with wildly divergent levels of enthusiasm. I wasn't sure I wanted to see the bottom. I was *very* sure I didn't want to ride a flimsy metal box down the cavern wall.

"Most of this facility is underground," Tack was saying, closing the gate behind us. We immediately began to descend, thankfully at a slow pace. "Why would they do that?"

"Maybe they really, *really* wanted to keep people out," Min suggested.

"Or in," I muttered.

As we rattled downward, another catwalk came into view. It circled the silo like the one above it, but this level had chambers cut into the rock wall at regular intervals. Boxes of various shapes and sizes were stacked within each alcove.

A light began blinking on the cage's control panel. But when Min hesitated, we continued past the catwalk, plummeting deeper into the pit. Tack stood on his tiptoes, squinting into the closest alcove. "The boxes are labeled. I think one said 'sewing machine,' if you can believe it."

Another catwalk appeared. This time when the button flashed, Min pressed it. We slowed, then stopped. Min opened the gate and we stepped out, walking to the nearest chamber. The cases within were small and dusty, stacked in straight lines. "Seeds," she said, surprised. "Wheat. Corn. Potato. Soybean."

I wandered deeper into the room. "These big ones are labeled 'Farm Equipment.'"

Min's head swung left and right. "What *is* this place?"

Tack hustled to the next alcove, where larger crates were stored. "Tractors! Two of them, boxed up like Christmas presents! And a buttload of diesel fuel."

As we did a slow circuit, I became more and more bewildered. Each alcove contained a mountain of supplies. Camping equipment. Hard drives. A set of generators. Water filtration systems. Iodine pills. Copper wire. By the time we reached the cage again, Min was chewing on her bottom lip, eyes worried.

"This is a doomsday prepper's dream," Tack said. "Survival goods for an entire village. Hell, a city! Everything you could possibly need seems to be in here, boxed up and ready to go. But why would the *government* build a hidey-hole like this?"

"For the Anvil?" I suggested. "In case it was actually going to hit Earth?"

Min looked thoughtful. "That makes sense. But then, why abandon it? Plenty else has gone wrong since the asteroid miss was announced. More, honestly. You'd think places like this would be locked down right now. Hell, even *filled*."

She was right. The place was a gold mine. "I'll bet everything I own that Ethan and Sarah haven't seen this yet. No way they'd leave it unguarded."

"The bottom," Tack insisted, pointing into the abyss. "We have to hit rock bottom."

Poor choice of words, but he was right. We couldn't stop now.

We descended a dozen more levels without stopping, content to read whatever labels we could glimpse as the cage rolled past. Instruction manuals. Firewood. Matches. Pots and pans. One large alcove was filled with shiny ATVs. Another housed a fleet of motorcycles. A whole world of supplies, crated and stored, slowly gathering dust.

The temperature dropped as we moved farther underground. Something struck me as odd.

"All this stuff is boxed," I said. "Nothing seems prepared."

"What do you mean?" Min asked.

"There aren't any sleeping quarters. Or kitchens. No meeting rooms, or places for people to congregate. I haven't seen any perishable goods, either. No livestock, or living plants. Nothing is fresh or assembled. How would anyone survive in here?"

"You're right." Min began scanning the silo with new eyes. "It doesn't seem built for habitation. Just storage."

"The bottom," Tack repeated. "And here it comes."

The silo floor was an unbroken sheet of solid concrete. The cage descended past it, however, into a narrow chute that burrowed another twenty yards before screeching to a halt in some kind of basement. The gate clattered open. A narrow corridor led to a glass door. Beyond was a room filled with blinking red lights.

We stood silently for several heartbeats before Min pushed.

Unlocked. Indeed, the door didn't even appear to *have* a lock.

Inside was a control room to make NASA jealous. Workstations on descending levels faced three giant panels that filled the front wall. The outer two appeared to be computer screens. The middle section was actually a window into a much larger chamber beyond this one, where a breathtaking machine sat alone on a pedestal. It looked like an elaborate computer.

Both spaces were empty of people.

"Oh, man! Check it out!" Tack was gawking at the back wall. I spun. Bookshelves full of plastic binders lined the rear of the control room. Each spine displayed a black sunburst followed by a two-word label.

PROJECT NEMESIS.

48

MIN

This is it.

I walked to a shelf. Pulled a binder at random. Noah and Tack crowded behind me, reading over my shoulder. No one spoke, as if the moment were too big for words. We were finally going to get answers.

The riddle of my entire life, explained within these pages. Somewhere.

But the first binder was no help—the pages contained a series of technical specs and complex math equations. I couldn't make any sense of it, not even the captions. I shoved it back with a grunt.

"Maybe start at the beginning?" Noah suggested, pointing to the top left-hand row.

Nodding, I grabbed the first volume and carried it over to a workstation. Despite a burning impatience, I had to acknowledge this might take a while.

The opening pages contained nothing but dire warnings about the confidential nature of the information to follow. Tack shook his head. "This is as top secret as it gets. Look at the stamps at the bottom. DoD. DARPA. Homeland Security. Everything about this project is the *blackest* of black ops."

I almost laughed. "We're in a secret military bunker hundreds of feet below ground, built less than five miles from town without anyone knowing about it. I'm not surprised it isn't public knowledge."

"More than that. Look!" Tack jabbed a paragraph with his index finger. "That's the security clearance list. It's fewer than twenty people."

"It says these are just the civilians." Noah read out familiar names. "Andrew E. Myers. Dr. Gerald Lowell. Dr. Piro D. Fanelli. Dr. Perry B. Harris. Sheriff Michael T. Watson." Then he closed his eyes. "Barbara K. Livingston."

"Virginia G. Wilder," I whispered.

I'd already known, but that didn't make seeing it on paper any easier.

There were a half dozen more people on the civilian list. Doctors, mainly. The next section authorized the creation of a special military unit for Project Nemesis. I recognized a few names in the command structure: Commander Sutton. Captain Harkes. Captain Sigler. The rest I didn't know. "The top line is redacted," Tack complained. "They blocked out the head of the pyramid."

"Black Suit." I was sure. Even now, his identity eluded me.

I'll find you one day. I promise.

Twenty-five people in total. The entire conspiracy, laid bare.

"There are page numbers next to each name." Tack flipped ahead. "Let's see what these bastards got for betraying us."

Sheriff Watson was page 213. "Bingo. Here we go. This is dated twenty years ago!"

The section began with a detailed memorandum examining Watson, including a physical description and psychological profile. Next came a list of duties and assignments. My anger sparked as I read what his role had been. "*Prepare the town of Fire Lake for physical isolation. Block the creation of new access points to Fire Lake valley. Protect military property G14-88645 for use as a primary hosting location.*"

"Jesus," Noah breathed. "He's been working for Nemesis since before we were born."

"I want another." Tack located the section on Principal Myers. "'*Administer initial DNA testing protocols under public health misdirection.*'" Bitterness crept into Tack's voice. "'*Monitor beta patients and broader subject pool, providing access for regular medical updates and rapid collection.*' What a prick."

I scanned ahead, growing more horrified by the line. "He was tracking our specific class. Myers kept getting himself promoted to stay in charge of us, but never took a job that would pull him away. He turned down three promotions to stick with our year through the system."

Tack found the pages for Dr. Lowell. "'*Monitor beta patients A and B. Manage reactivity and establish controlling narratives. Administer test phase medication.*'" He turned the next tab. "More of the same for Dr. Fanelli."

"Did you see this part?" Noah went back to Lowell's first page. "'*Four beta patients will be selected, each possessing the specific electromagnetic neural alignment essential to withstand the phase shift process.*' I don't understand a single word of that," he admitted sourly.

"'*Beta testing must be completed no fewer than ten days before the E.L.E. becomes unmanageable.*'" Tack sat back and scratched his neck. "That part is underlined. What the hell does it mean?"

"It confirms Lowell was manipulating me from the first session," Noah muttered.

"Before," I corrected bitterly. "Don't forget the consent forms. But we still don't know what this project *is*. What's their ultimate objective? What's an E.L.E.? Why did these people dedicate their whole pathetic lives to ruining ours?"

Tears abruptly threatened, but I refused to let them fall.

Not now. Not when we're so close to the truth.

Tack was reading ahead when he flinched. His gaze slid to Noah, then he tried to close the binder.

Noah's hand slapped down on the page. "What?"

"Huh? Nothing." Tack shot me a loaded glance, but I didn't understand.

"You're hiding something," Noah said softly, forcing Tack to meet his eye. "What don't you want me to see?"

"Noah, man, trust me. You don't want to know. It's got nothing—"

Noah pushed Tack's hand aside. "Ah. My mother's page." He began reading silently. All color drained from his face.

"Noah?" I was suddenly afraid. "What is it?"

He didn't answer. Head bowed, Noah turned and stumbled a few feet away. I quickly scanned the text.

"They killed her!" I gasped. "Oh my God, Noah. I'm so—"

"So *what*?" he spat, not looking at me. "Sorry? Why? My mother *sold* me to these people, Min. Same as yours. Why should I care what they did to her in return?" But I could tell it was ripping a hole inside of him.

"You didn't finish!" I shouted, holding the binder up before me. "Noah, they killed her because she tried to *remove* you from the project. She wanted to take you out, but they wouldn't let that happen. It's all right here!"

Noah strode back to the workstation and read silently. When finished, tears glistened on his cheeks. "Well," he stammered, "at least she didn't abandon me. That's something, I guess."

I felt a flash of hatred for whoever had given the order.

Tack gently took the binder from Noah and flipped to the next page. "Get this: after Barbara Livingston rebelled, the project decided it was too risky to involve any more outsiders. They stopped asking for consent forms, and adopted Dr. Fanelli's 'hypnosis treatment' for 'Beta Patients C and D.' Ethan's and Sarah's parents came *here* and verbally agreed. Can you believe it? They just handed their kids over to a government experiment! Amazing."

Then his head snapped up. He eyed me with a grimace, no doubt wishing he could take back his last comment.

"But what *is* the experiment?" I said, pushing the painful reminder aside. "What's the damn point?" I glared at the rows of gleaming binders, vowing to examine each and every one if that's what it took.

Tack's slip had cut me deep. Being this close to answers only made it worse.

"Maybe this could help?" Noah lifted a silver DVD case from

the next workstation over. "It's labeled 'Dark Star—E.L.E.' That mean anything to you guys?"

E.L.E. Those letters again.

"Is there a place to play it?" I asked.

Noah's station had a computer. He located a keyboard and tapped the space bar. At the front of the room, the left-hand screen sprang to life. "There's a drive, too." Noah inserted the disk. Surprisingly, an old TV documentary began to play, a buttery voice surrounding us as an image of our planet appeared onscreen.

"*For twenty-six million years, Nemesis, the dark star of legend, has hidden from the Earth, distant and invisible in the vast depths of space. But its implacable orbit will once again return to wreak havoc, as it has done in the past and will again in the future.*"

I shot a startled glance at the boys, but they were staring at the screen. The image changed to animation of our solar system in motion. "*Most people think our sun is alone in the solar system, with only its eight planets to keep it company. But recent scientific findings point to an altogether different possibility.*"

The scale expanded, ballooning well past Neptune to include an enormous ring of asteroids and even larger comet cloud. Beyond even those, in the farthest reach, a dark red ball appeared, glowing with fiery menace.

"*What if our sun* isn't *alone in its spiral around the galaxy, but is instead part of a binary system with a distant, nearly invisible companion?*"

The word *NEMESIS* appeared in bright red letters.

Tack frowned up at the screen. "What is this, an astronomy lesson?"

The voice continued as a new simulation played. "*For years, scientists have been alarmed by anomalies in the Oort cloud, a sphere of icy bodies that bounds our solar system. It's from this frozen realm that comets originate, sometimes falling inward toward the sun.*"

The video cut to a scientist sitting on a boulder in the desert. "The geological record is clear—every twenty-six million years, our planet undergoes a massive die-off during which nearly all life on Earth is eradicated. The most commonly known example is the demise of the dinosaurs, but these extinction-level events are as regular as clockwork. What we didn't understand was *why*." He gave the camera a shaky smile. "Until now."

My whole body went rigid.

Extinction-level events.

E. L. E.

Noah glanced at me. He'd caught it, too.

"Archaeological evidence points to regular periods of environmental disruption in our planet's long history," the man continued. "What we've been searching for are the *trigger events*—the root causes of these cataclysms. Most assume that comet or asteroid impacts were to blame, and to an extent that's true. But those theories are missing the *much* bigger picture. They fail to account for Nemesis."

Nemesis.

I felt a rush of blood to my head.

The original narrator returned. "*Often dubbed the 'Death Star,' Nemesis is believed to be a red dwarf star one-tenth the size of our sun, barely glowing and therefore invisible from Earth by telescope. But what we can't see* can *hurt us.*"

A dark-skinned professor appeared, speaking with a smooth,

Africanized British accent. "Nemesis is much smaller than our sun, and on an elliptical orbit, meaning that for long periods it remains far away from the solar system. But when the dark star returns, its massive gravity—over a hundred times that of Jupiter—creates instability in the Oort cloud, sending thousands of comets streaming into the habitable zone. Nemesis also rattles the asteroids of the Kuiper Belt. The result is a galactic turkey shoot during which the Earth cannot help but be pummeled."

"*The results have been devastating.*" A chart flashed onscreen, listing a series of planetary extinctions with corresponding dates. "*Every twenty-six million years, life on Earth is pushed to the brink. The only solution that fits this pattern is Nemesis.*"

The first scientist was back, smiling inanely. "As Nemesis moves closer, its gravity will even disrupt our planet's plate tectonics, causing eruptions, earthquakes, and other disasters. Earth will become a living hell. Humanity has never seen Nemesis before, but we can't survive it. And there's nothing we can do."

"Why is that lunatic *smiling*?" Tack demanded, shaking his head. "He's talking about the apocalypse like it's a freaking One Direction concert. Weirdo."

The program shifted to a pair of guys throwing tennis balls into a trash can, apparently to demonstrate some gravitational law. Minutes later it ended. My thoughts turned inward, vividly recalling the events of the last week.

Everything described in the video had been happening. Then it all stopped.

Everyone also disappeared.

Nothing makes sense. None of it. Not one damn thing.

"So those scientists think a rogue star is going to ravage the planet," I said, thinking aloud. This was different from what I'd been expecting, and I didn't know how to react. The "nemesis" here wasn't my personal serial killer, it was a ball of burning gas somewhere in deep space. "In response, our government secretly built this emergency bunker and stocked it with supplies. That part makes sense."

"Preparing for global catastrophe." Noah nodded slowly. "Okay. Sure."

Tack started. "The Anvil. This death star must've tossed it at us. Those comets too, I guess. Jeez, Toby was right for once. The government really did know all about it."

I slapped my palms on the desktop. "So what happened? It all just . . . stopped? The earthquakes. The eruptions. Ash-filled skies. All that stuff is simply *gone* now, along with—oh, right—*everyone we've ever known*. How can that be?"

"No one's even using this place," Tack said. "We walked right in. All that effort, for nothing?"

"Why send a man to kill me, over and over?" I was nearly shouting. "Why experiment on students? Why isolate our town? They *shot* people. Gassed sixty-four kids in a park! What does *any* of that have to do with an invisible star orbiting a billion miles away?"

"And one other thing," Noah said softly.

"What?" I asked, almost afraid to hear it.

"Where's the death star now?"

49

NOAH

Min and Tack were slogging through the binders.

"For a week we know nothing," Tack grumbled, dropping another into a growing discard pile. "Now there's *too* much information available. Great joke, universe."

He turned to Min. "Whatcha got?"

She blew a stray hair from her mouth. "Telemetry studies. Projected movements of celestial bodies. Comet decay and orbit aerodynamics. In other words, nothing that explains what Project Nemesis actually intended. You?"

Tack pointed to the closest shelves. "Those up top are about satellite tracking systems. I think. I'm honestly not sure—this is the most boring stuff I've ever laid eyes on. The middle ones seem to be the 'What the Hell Should We Do?' section. There's a whole binder about building a giant space station, but the front page is stamped 'DISCONTINUED.' Guess that idea never got into orbit. Same with the one about a cave complex in West Virginia."

He lifted the binder in his hands. "This guy here discusses a missile defense strategy. Spoiler alert—it's a no-go. Seems like they spent a long time debating what to do about the death star, then decided nothing would actually work."

But they did something, I wanted to shout. *We're alive, and Nemesis is gone.*

I was sitting at a workstation, making no effort to help. I'd promised to investigate the computers, but had immediately run into a firewall. Everything was password protected. Engrossed as they were in the endless wall of binders, Min and Tack seemed to have forgotten I was there.

I didn't mind. Events were moving too fast. An opportunity to gather my thoughts was more than welcome.

Because I felt *great* again. Like a weight had been lifted.

My mother hadn't abandoned me.

She'd made a mistake turning me over to these lunatics, but she'd also tried to reverse it. And the ruthless SOBs had killed her for it. *My mother died fighting for me. She cared about me to her last breath.* I nearly choked up just thinking about it.

Had she ever really had cancer? Was she poisoned, or infected somehow? Or was she removed more directly, under some cover story? I'd probably never know. I briefly wondered if my father was in on it, but dismissed the possibility. Hunter Livingston would never let the government take something he considered his.

As terrible as the knowledge was, it didn't stem my exhilaration. In the past few days I'd learned that my mother hadn't abandoned me, and that I wasn't actually crazy. Quite the opposite—I was special. *Chosen.* The centerpiece of something important.

Min moved to attack the last row of binders. I almost shook my head. Obsessed with the mechanics of the conspiracy, she wasn't seeing the big picture.

The two of us were a part of something that would shape world history.

No, not just a *part*—we were the fulcrum of the whole thing. The files said as much! I didn't know what to do, or how to act, but my worthless feeling had evaporated, maybe for good this time. Whatever came next, I wouldn't be afraid.

I was born for this. *Built* for this. I could handle anything Project Nemesis threw at me.

Tack shoved another binder aside and stood, stretching his arms and legs. He spied me doing nothing and rolled his eyes. "Care to lend a hand, Noah? Or is this your smoke break?"

Irritation flared, but I covered it. "The system is encrypted. I can't access any files. I'm surprised the DVD played, to be honest."

Tack nodded unhappily, glancing at the window into the sealed chamber beyond. "I'm guessing that's the computer in there. Looks a little more intense than a ThinkPad."

Across the room, Min grunted. "Come look at this," she called.

She was examining the bottom row of the last bookcase. "See the dust pattern? There were more files here at one point, but they're gone. I'll bet you anything they explain what the troops did to us in town square."

"What does the last one say?" Tack asked.

"Most of this section catalogs natural disasters around the planet. Seismic readings. Volcanic activity. Tsunamis. All the bad stuff, even some of those weird animal reports. I think they were recording possible symptoms of the approaching death star. What's spooky is that these records go back almost forty years. How long have they known about Nemesis? How'd they keep it secret?"

"The no-joke possible end of the world?" Tack scoffed. "By whatever means necessary."

His gaze flicked to me, then away. They'd killed my mother to protect their secret, and that was nearly a decade ago. *Who knows what else they've done?*

Min was scanning the room. "We need an index for these files, or we'll be here forever."

"Doubt we have that long," Tack said seriously. "Ethan and Sarah will come looking for us eventually, and the doors are all unlocked."

"Can you work on that? Sealing this building up, I mean. Not to lock us in necessarily, but definitely for when we leave. I don't want Ethan having access to these records until we have a plan for how to deal with him."

"We *could* stay in here for a while," I said, thinking aloud. "There must be some supplies that are ready to use, and this is a perfect place to hole up."

"Hiding underground." Tack's lips quirked. "That a specialty of yours?"

"Do you have a better—"

"*Enough*," Min said wearily. "Noah might be right, Tack. Just see if the silo can be secured. If not, there's no point in staying. This could be a giant prison as easily as a safe house."

Tack turned, spoke grudgingly to me. "The doors above are

computerized. We probably need network access to activate them. Did you check every terminal in here?"

I shook my head, suddenly feeling defensive. "These computers must all be on the same network. I doubt there's an unsecured access point in the same room."

Tack rolled his eyes, stomping down to the second tier of workstations. "We won't know until we check, now will we?"

Min was squinting at the shelves, trying to decide where to look next. She pulled a binder at random and opened it. Moments later she slammed it back with an angry grunt. "That one had Lowell's student files in it. Looks like everyone got a copy of my dental records."

She half turned. "Want to help?"

I nodded quickly, hoping she wasn't disappointed in my systems search.

"Pick a spot and dig in. Maybe we'll get lucky."

But before I could move, Tack shouted across the room. "Guys? Think I have something!"

I spun, red-faced. Tack was hunched over a terminal on the lowest tier. One I hadn't bothered checking, too caught up in how special and important I clearly was. Cursing myself, I followed Min as she hurried to join her friend.

"Whatcha got?" Min asked eagerly.

Tack shot me a smug glance, then turned back to the monitor in front of him. "This one didn't ask for a log-in. When I jiggled the mouse, it came up right away."

The screen was empty except for a red circle. Inside it were two words in black letters.

ENGAGE PROGRAM

We stared, no one moving or speaking. There was zero ambiguity.

"Seems pretty straightforward," Tack said finally.

"But engage *what*?" Min rubbed her forehead, as if hoping an answer could be physically wrung from her brain. "For all we know, that button might lock us in."

"Let's check the rest of the stations first," I said quietly.

"Like you didn't do the first time?" But Tack was already moving. We tried the last few. All required a password, so we returned to the monitor with its single perverse option.

Tack glanced at Min. "We might as well just do it. You know we're going to eventually, so it's pointless to drag this out. What if this command allows access to the computer in there?" He pointed to the machine beyond the window.

"What if it launches a nuclear missile?" Min countered, but she spoke again before Tack could respond. "You're right. We're going to do it anyway. Go ahead." Her gray eyes shot to me. "You okay with that, Noah?"

I nodded, shoulders tense. "There's not really a choice to make."

"*Always* take the mystery box!" Tack crowed, cracking his knuckles. "Here we go!"

Mouse. Click.

The circle blinked once, then disappeared.

A Klaxon began blaring. Red lights flashed.

Every muscle in my body tensed. Then slowly, ponderously, the control room began to spin.

No. It's an optical illusion. Only the front wall is moving.

A curtain of solid metal was sliding into place behind the

central window. That, or the chamber beyond was somehow rotating out of sight. Either way, the result was the same—view of the machine vanished, replaced by a steel barrier several feet thick.

"I think we just sealed the computer away," Min whispered.

I swallowed. "Let's hope it was just that room, and not this one."

Tack ran to the door and disappeared. Seconds later he was back. "The cage is still here. I don't think we're locked in."

I exhaled in relief.

An image appeared on the two big screens. I recognized it instantly. "That's a map of Fire Lake. The whole valley, actually."

Min was staring at the display. "What's that glowing dot?"

"Town square?" Tack guessed. "Did these jerks watch the gassing from here?"

My pulsed quickened. "No, it's a building. That's Town Hall."

Min's eyes glittered with reflected light. "Where no one can get inside."

"Oh crap, look!" Tack was pointing down at the workstation. A drawer had slid open, revealing a single unmarked keycard inside.

I held it up. "Seems pretty clear, right? *Go there.*"

Min bit her lip. Nodded.

Tack snatched the card from my fingers. "Let's do it."

An earsplitting siren echoed from the center of town. I could guess where.

We parked a block away and snuck in on foot. Tack had managed to lock the outer door to the silo before we left and was confident he could get back inside. The drive had been tense and silent. It'd been forty minutes since we'd "engaged the program" in the control room. I worried that whatever we'd set in motion, Ethan and Sarah would find it first.

Most of our class had gathered on the sidewalk before Town Hall. Ethan and Derrick were trying to force the door while the Nolan twins paced the roof, searching for a way inside. Everyone else watched with their hands over their ears.

Peering around the corner of a nearby building, I didn't see any of the group who'd fled after Tack's murder. Carl and Sam must've eluded the search parties. Good for them.

"What do we do?" Min whispered.

I rubbed a hand over my mouth. We had the keycard, but there was no way past the mob. "Maybe wait for them to leave, then come back?"

"Screw that." Tack straightened. "Just follow my lead."

He strode into the street, heading directly for Town Hall.

"Tack!" Min whisper-shouted, but he didn't break stride. She covered her eyes for a beat, then fired after him. Without a better option, I followed.

Tack reached the group before anyone noticed him. Then heads whipped his way. Shouts erupted—another classmate, back from the dead. Everyone gave him a wide berth as he strolled up the steps like he was about to mail a letter.

Ethan turned, shock registering at finding my friend right behind him. Tack grinned.

Ethan was gripping a crowbar in one hand. "Thumbtack! You're an idiot for coming here. Thanks for making things easier."

"Close to opening that?" Tack shouted over the siren. "Doesn't seem like you've made any progress."

Ethan took a step, but Derrick held up a hand, eyeing Tack nervously. "So you're back, too, huh? What's going on, Tack? You're not dumb enough to show up here without a reason."

"I missed you guys. I thought we could get a group marriage license."

Ethan's jaw worked, but he made no move.

I was standing with Min at the bottom of the steps. She looked ready to pounce if necessary. One of my hands unconsciously adjusted my belt. *I'll help if it comes to it. I will.*

Derrick wiped sweat from his brow. "Last chance, man. Don't give Ethan another reason to pound your ass. Unless you *like* getting smacked around."

Tack spat on the flagstones. "Better than getting stabbed in the heart."

Derrick winced. "Let's not do this right now, okay? Both you guys. I'm tired. I don't understand how you're standing there. I just want that damn alarm to stop wailing before I go nuts!"

"Maybe this will help." Tack held up the keycard.

"Where'd you get that?" Ethan demanded sharply.

"I bought it on eBay."

"You think I won't—"

"Y'all chill!" Derrick shouted, stepping between them. "Tack, if you think that'll work, be my guest. Just turn off that freaking horn!"

Tack stepped around the larger boys, approached the port, and applied the card. For a moment, nothing, and my spirits sank. Then the sensor blinked green twice. The alarm ceased.

"Oh thank God." Derrick placed both palms over his eye sockets. "I was about to lose it." Ethan said nothing, but a pink wave was creeping up his neck.

The door to Town Hall swung open. A second, louder siren sounded. Everyone recoiled, holding their ears as they retreated down the steps. After ten seconds, it stopped. I found myself shoulder to shoulder with Ethan, who was staring back up at the door.

A figure emerged.

Gliding from the shadows, it halted at the top of the steps.

The blood drained from my face.

Black Suit.

He paused, observing us from behind his sliver sunglasses.

"Bastard!" Min charged the steps, but Tack snaked forward and grabbed her around the waist. "You son of a bitch!" She fought to break free, but he held on doggedly. "Don't, Min! He's a killer. Use your head!"

Min was beyond caring, rage twisting her delicate features. "You did this! *All* of this. I'll kill you, I swear it."

Black Suit regarded her dispassionately. "You'll kill me?"

Min stopped struggling. Stared daggers at our lifelong tormentor.

"I *will*. Or die trying."

"How, Melinda?" the black-suited man said softly. "You're already dead."

50

MIN

I stopped fighting.

My muscles froze as my brain spiraled.

Instinctively, I did a systems check. Pulse. Breath. Sweat. I was hungry. My left heel was blistered. Not the traits of a spirit in the afterlife.

Liar. Remember, that's what he does.

Tack released me, his face sickly pale as he stared up at the black-suited man. Noah was a few feet away, beside Ethan. His whole body was trembling. The rest of our class was gathered behind us in shocked silence. I felt like an actor in a Greek tragedy.

Finally, I found my voice. "I'm not *dead*. I don't believe you."

Black Suit pivoted slowly, surveying the assembled teens. Then he addressed the whole group. "A quorum is present, and the preconditions have been met. Phase One is complete."

"Phase One?" Tack's voice shook. "What are you talking about? Who are you?"

"I am the Guardian. I will clarify your circumstances, if you have the patience to listen."

I bit my tongue, swallowing a thousand insults I wanted to hurl. When no one interrupted, Black Suit continued. "Project Nemesis is now complete. Beta testing concluded on Day Minus-Nine. System components were installed on Day Minus-Four. The master program commenced full operation precisely one hour ago, marking this as Day Zero."

A lifetime of frustration exploded. "What is Nemesis?! What have you done to us?"

"The planet has been destroyed. You are all dead."

Gasps, but no one spoke. I swayed on my feet. I wanted to scream—curse him as a liar—but suddenly, I wasn't sure.

"Earth has suffered a cataclysm," he explained, inflectionless, a robot describing the weather. "Gravitational pressure from space has generated a storm of comet impacts while also triggering a sequence of deadly seismic events. Earthquakes. Eruptions. Tsunamis. The result has been an extinction-level event."

Town Hall's second-level bay window shimmered, became a giant screen. A picture of hell appeared. Smoke-choked skies roiled over a dead landscape. Lava flowed through valleys of steaming rock. Explosions detonated without warning, shooting flaming gas into the atmosphere. There was nothing alive in sight, not a single green leaf, for endless miles.

"The planet's surface has been virtually sterilized. Every human being is dead. *You* are dead. At least, your bodies are."

Soft moans behind me. Quiet sobs. "Why?" someone shouted in a shaky voice.

The image winked out. "Our sun is paired to another star known as Nemesis. Every twenty-six million years, when its orbit swings closest, the dark star's gravity ravages the solar system." Black Suit's face was impassive. "There is no defense. No place to hide. Humanity has always been doomed—we simply didn't know it. Which brings us to you."

The screen sprang to life again, displaying an underground chamber with a red zone illuminated at the bottom. My eyes shot to Tack, who swallowed and nodded.

We'd been there less than an hour ago. Clicked a red button.

"Project Nemesis was designed to preserve a sliver of humanity in defiance of extinction. Since you were young, this class of Fire Lake students has been studied and tested with a single goal in mind: to perfect the process of recording, digitizing, and uploading a human being into a supercomputer buried below Earth's surface."

My mind reeled. Pieces slotted into place.

"The project completed its mission. Though your bodies died, the program successfully preserved sixty-four electrochemical blueprints. These were uploaded into the mainframe on Day Minus-Four after final measurements were taken. You now exist as autonomous lines of code within the MegaCom master program."

I blinked, anesthetized.

I wanted to deny it all, but suddenly everything made sense.

The repairs to the town and valley. The lack of communications. The isolation.

The disappearance of everyone we knew.

What we'd considered impossible wasn't, because the world

we now inhabited was a fiction. A computer-generated reality, designed to house our ghosts.

I'm dead. Mom's dead. Everything is dead.

There was nothing left at all.

Black Suit droned on, every word a hammer blow. "Your digital sequences have been inserted into a virtual re-creation of your hometown, to make you as comfortable as possible."

Tack cleared his throat. "The gas killed us, didn't it?"

"Your brains were required to complete formatting. We brought you online as close to the moment of death as possible, to reduce disorientation."

"This is nuts!" Derrick staggered backward, shaking his head. Then he punched a marble pillar and held up his bloody first. "I'm not dead! This building isn't fake! Stop messing with my head!"

Black Suit lifted a hand. Around us, the block shimmered, then faded to a network of glowing yellow lines on a pure black field. Stunned, I looked down. My body had disappeared, replaced by a running sequence of numbers and letters.

I tried to scream, but had no mouth. No face. No tangible core. I didn't exist.

Then everything snapped back to how it was.

Derrick had fallen to his knees, was staring at his hand. The cuts were gone, all traces of blood removed. Behind me, classmates shouted in fear. A few collapsed. Most stared fearfully at the black-suited man as he lowered his arm.

No one doubted anymore.

"That was a demonstration," he said. "Your true plane of existence has been deemed unsuitable to accomplishing the program's goals. Therefore, you will permanently reside in a simulation of Fire Lake valley." His voice became rigid. "You still must eat and drink. You must shelter from weather, and avoid hazards. You can be injured. You can be killed."

"No, we can't." Ethan pointed at Tack. "Or *he* wouldn't be here." Ethan spun to face his classmates. "I was a test subject for Project Nemesis. They killed me over and over, but I always came back. Always!"

Black Suit regarded Ethan coldly. "Four subjects were chosen to test aspects of the program in the beta phase. Wilder. Fletcher. Harden. Livingston. That phase is now complete."

I lurched forward, seeing red. "*Five times* you slaughtered me like an animal, but I came back. *Alive.* In the *real* world, before all this. That wasn't virtual reality. What was the point?"

He ignored me, addressing the group. "System rules have been upgraded. Codes will now reset *only* within the updated parameters of the program. Reset points have been randomized, and are out of bounds. Only those undergoing a reboot process will have access." The window screen blinked off once again. "I will not appear again until the current phase is complete."

He turned for the open door into Town Hall.

"Wait!" I shouted.

The black-suited man paused.

"That's it? You murder us, stick us inside your insane videogame world, and now you're abandoning us? *What are we supposed to do?*"

His face was stone. "I am the Guardian. Though I bear his likeness, I am merely an avatar of the MegaCom creator. My programmer did not preserve his own life. He gave all in service to Project Nemesis, so that some spark of humanity might survive, but the scars were too much. He rests now. I exist solely to fulfill his ambitions."

My mind reeled, reassessing everything I thought I knew.

The conspiracy. Those evil men. Their lies, and tests, and casual brutality.

They'd been working to . . . *save* us. Had dedicated their lives to giving us a chance.

I thought of the pain in Principal Myers's eyes. How broken he'd seemed as I cursed his name. Sheriff Watson had made the ultimate sacrifice. Lowell and Fanelli had tried to encourage us before the gassing, at the bitter end.

Mom.

She knew.

She signed me up for a lifetime of fear and pain, to give me a shot at a future.

And it broke her heart. Every single day.

Suddenly, I understood. And my heart broke, too.

Project Nemesis had been a desperate attempt to keep us alive. They were all dead now. Each had known they'd die. Even the approximate date.

All that sacrifice, so that we could continue to exist.

They're heroes.

The revelation stunned me. Dropped me to my knees. Brought tears to my eyes.

Then a new thought struck, frightening me to the core.

I looked up at the Guardian. Project Nemesis was complete. The conspiracy done. Brave men and women had sacrificed everything for sixty-four teens in the Idaho mountains.

But no one in Fire Lake had been involved in the MegaCom design.

My assassin had built it. What was *his* plan? What was the ultimate purpose of the program?

The Guardian's eyes hid behind sunglasses as he addressed us a final time. "Phase One is now complete. Phase Two has begun."

"What does that mean?" I whispered, but he heard.

A ghostly smile appeared.

"Would you like me to tell you?"

51

NOAH

Euphoria.

As the Guardian spoke, all my doubts faded to nothing.

I'm part of something. I'm special.

It was almost religious, finding my place after years of loneliness and doubt. Until now, my life had been a disappointment. To my father. My friends. Myself. But that was all washed away. The Guardian had revealed my true purpose—the hidden meaning to a decade of pain and insecurity.

Adrenaline surged through me as I listened. The picture being painted was remarkable. I was one of the last surviving members of the human race. A keystone in the government's grand design, selected and preserved against impossible odds. A last stand.

The feeling was indescribable. Intoxicating.

Everything has been leading to this moment. I was chosen. I matter.

I glanced at Min, who was glowering at the Guardian. I understood the rawness of her feelings—I'd been his victim just as many times—but she didn't get it. That wasn't Black Suit up there. It was an illusion. It was like getting mad at a picture.

Things were completely different now. Didn't she understand?

Project Nemesis hadn't been torturing us—they'd been *preparing* us, for an epic struggle they wouldn't live to see. We should be *thanking* the Guardian, not shouting at him.

He molded us for greatness. We just have to seize it.

The Guardian's last question was practically a taunt. Min clamped her jaws, refusing the bait. I listened, enraptured, as my former nightmare explained. "Phase Two has begun. Uploaded sequences must be sorted. You must discover your place within the system."

His pronouncement was met with silence.

"What the hell does *that* mean?" Tack said.

"How are we supposed to do that?" Ethan shouted at the same time.

"You must create the proper population size and alignment. No more information will be given. Those who remain will move on."

Those who remain.

I thought furiously. We had to be *sorted*? What was a proper alignment?

A dark corner of my mind whispered an answer.

Resets must happen for a reason. That's how the betas were tested.

Min stormed up the steps to stand before the Guardian. "What you're saying is inhuman. You want us to do what, *battle* each other? That's sick! We're not pawns on a chessboard. How can conflict be a purpose?"

"The purpose is to save the human species," the Guardian replied icily.

My heart swelled. Energy infused my limbs.

His words rang like a clarion call in my soul.

Save humanity.

The ultimate purpose. I wanted to cry tears of joy.

Yet Min was still arguing. Insulting the Guardian. Trying to undermine his instructions.

I couldn't understand it. Felt a flash of anger. *Why can't she see?*

"What is Phase Two really?" she demanded. "Why are you doing this?"

"Aggregation," the Guardian replied, his tone indicating the matter was closed. "The program will enforce its rules beginning now. I will not appear again until the cycle is complete."

He turned and walked back into Town Hall. The door sealed.

But in my heart, I felt reborn.

52

MIN

My hands were shaking.

The Guardian was gone, but I sensed anarchy in his wake.

"That's it?" Tack's hands flew up. He raced to the door and swiped the keycard. When it didn't open, he grabbed a brick and slammed it against the closest window. The glass didn't even wobble. Tack grunted in pain, shaking out his fingers.

We're on our own.

Alarm was rippling through the crowd. People clustered together, whispering frantically. It's not every day a hologram tells you you're dead.

My eyes kept darting around the square. Everything *looked* real. I pressed my hand against a pillar, felt cool, coarse stone beneath my fingertips. Nothing about it felt "virtual," yet I'd seen for myself that it wasn't really there.

Whispers became shouts. The group began to froth like a pot of boiling water. No one had any idea what to do. "How can we be dead?" Jessica screeched, clutching Sarah's arm. "I'm *not*! I'm right here!" Sarah shrugged her off, hurrying to where Ethan was huddling with Toby and the Nolan twins.

We've got to get out of here.

Several students had collapsed, shell-shocked. Hector was crying softly, while Lars and Leighton were slumped side by side on the steps. "This is all just . . . some computer thing?" Lars asked his friend, fluttering a hand at the sky. Glassy-eyed, Leighton didn't answer.

Tack hustled down to me. "What should we do?"

Heads turned, a circle of desperate faces. I heard "beta" whispered as classmates edged closer to hear my response.

Noah hadn't moved since the Guardian's exit. His head rose when I called out, but he didn't join us. I worried the revelations had been too much for him.

"You *know* that Guardian dude?" Cash Eaton asked in a shaky voice. "Tell us what he meant! Are we really dead, Min?" The others—perhaps a dozen in total—were listening intently.

"I . . . I think we are. We all saw the programming."

"Oh my God, they *killed* us!" Anna was clutching her boyfriend's arm. "It's not fair. I don't wanna be dead!" Aiken patted her shoulder, his other hand running a shaky path through his oily hair. People covered their faces. They were about to panic.

Say something.

"Everything he said *might* be true," I began, "but we're not totally dead. We can't be. We're *here*, right? Still thinking. Still ourselves. Whatever this existence is, maybe it's a . . . a way to go on."

Traces of hope lifted a few heads. The tension lessened by a hair.

Gather as many as you can.

I spoke so everyone could hear. "We can cooperate and survive, whatever that monster said. We can't let a stupid program dictate our lives. If we stick together, maybe—"

"You heard the rules!" Ethan climbed the steps to the position vacated by the Guardian. "Order must be established, and the hierarchy is clear. I'm a beta. I've been a part of this project for years. Sarah, too. We're in charge."

His gaze shifted to me. "Min's proven she can't handle the situation, so she's out." He nodded to the Nolans, who'd snuck to the back of the crowd, behind me. They made no move, but I was hemmed in. *Damn it.*

Ethan swung to Noah. For a second his eyes were poisonous, but he took a deep breath. "Noah, I can't believe this, but I'm offering you one last chance. You're a beta, like me. You can join us and run this town. Are you in?"

Noah blinked, as if only slowly becoming aware of what was happening. Then he surprised everyone by laughing in Ethan's face.

"You don't get it, do you?" Noah scoffed.

Yes! If we acted fast enough, we could rally a resistance. *We* were betas, too. Noah and I could give the others an alternative. "You're falling into a trap!" I shouted. "The Guardian wants us to rip each other apart, but I don't care. This program doesn't define *me*, even if I am dead. I reject it! We have to *preserve* our humanity, not abandon it."

Ethan signaled the Nolans. "Grab her." Then he motioned

to Toby, who'd positioned his crew around the group. "Playtime is over. We're in charge, and that's all there is to it. Everyone is ordered to the church. *Now.*"

Mike and Chris each put a hand on my shoulder.

"Don't make a scene," Chris warned. "You're going to the cell either way." Tack tried to shove them off me, but Derrick swooped behind him and wrapped an arm around his neck. "You too, Thumbtack. Captain's orders."

Noah still hadn't moved. None of Ethan's guys were close to him.

"Noah, run!" I shouted. If he escaped, there was hope.

But he didn't react. I wasn't even sure he heard me. Noah's brow was furrowed, like he was working through a complex math problem.

Commotion to the rear. Tucker and Josh were bouncing Benny Erikson between them like a ping-pong ball. Then Benny spun and kicked Josh where it counts. Josh groaned and fell. Benny tried to lurch past him, but Tucker snagged him by his long black ponytail.

Benny howled, dropping to his knees. "Leave me alone, you prick! Nobody put you in charge. You heard the computer guy—*it's every man for himself.*"

Toby strode to where Benny knelt. Shaking his head, he put a gun to Benny's temple and pulled the trigger.

The shot boomed across the park.

Screams.

Benny slumped to the ground, a red mess where his head had been.

Tucker stared at the fistful of hair still clutched in his fingers, then dropped it as if burned. He shook his hand frantically and rubbed it against his pants, trying to dislodge the loopy strands.

Everyone stopped moving. For a moment, no one breathed.

Then Benny's body disappeared.

All hell broke loose.

Kids scrambled away from the bloodstained pavement. Ethan was shouting, but I couldn't hear what he said. I spotted Sarah slipping away with some of the other girls. Toby was pointing at me, but a mass of panicked students blocked his path.

More shots.

Shrieks.

Hysteria.

Tack whirled and elbowed Derrick in the gut, dropping the larger boy. I smashed a fist into Mike's face and felt his nose crack. Chris grabbed me, but Tack dove at his knees, knocking him over. I kicked Chris in the head twice, and he lay still.

"Let's go!" Tack yelled.

I pointed to Noah, still frozen like a statue. "We have to help him!"

Tack bugged his eyes, but didn't waste time arguing, darting forward and seizing Noah's arm. Toby and the linemen had managed to corral most of the class, but were barely maintaining control. We had precious seconds to escape.

Tack yanked Noah roughly. "Let's go, you moron!"

Noah stayed rooted to the spot. I ran over, tried to get him to look at me. "Come on, Noah! It's okay. We'll figure it out later, but we have to get out of here!"

"Oh, crap," Tack muttered. My head whipped. Ethan was arrowing straight for us.

"Noah, we have to go right now!"

Ethan tried to shove someone out of his way, but Cole Pritchard was as big as he was. Cole's farm-boy arm flailed, catching Ethan in the ear. Ethan stumbled and fell. He sat dazed on the pavement for a moment, trying to shake the cobwebs.

I tried to pull Noah in the opposite direction. We could slip behind the building and escape toward the lake. But he shook me off, pointing at Ethan. "We have to get him now, while he's down!"

I reared back. "What?"

Noah's eyes burned with intensity. "We can kill him now! That'll buy us some time!"

"I'm not killing anyone! What's wrong with you?"

Noah gave me a strange look. "We have to obey the program, Min. It's all that's left."

I couldn't believe it. I grabbed him by the shoulders. Tried to reach the boy I'd fallen for in that trailer. "That's insane, Noah. We don't have to do what the Guardian says!"

Something moved behind his eyes. I prayed I'd gotten through.

He shrugged from my grip. "You're making a mistake," he said in a callous voice.

Words like daggers.

"What's wrong with you?" I whispered.

"Nothing." His face was granite. I didn't even recognize him. "For the first time in my life, everything is right."

Tack tugged my arm, shooting a hateful glance at Noah. "Come on, Min. We have to go." Unable to speak, I let Tack pull me a step, hoping Noah's face would soften. It didn't. So

I turned to run, to leave Noah behind, my heart breaking with every footfall.

A loud bang.

Searing pain in my back.

I looked down. There was a smoking hole in my chest.

Tack was screaming, his clothes spattered red.

I fell.

Tack backpedaled, staring over my shoulder in horror. Then he turned and ran, vaulting a low wall and disappearing from sight.

I rolled to my back as a detached voice in my head explained the situation.

I've been shot. A bullet ripped through me. I'm going to die.

My head lolled. I saw Noah stalk over to Ethan, who scrambled to his knees. Ethan threw out a shaky hand, babbling something as Noah aimed.

Two shots. Ethan crumpled and lay still. Seconds later he vanished completely.

Whoever hadn't fled by then, did, even Toby and his crew. In seconds the steps were clear. Noah nodded thoughtfully at the place where Ethan's body had been. Then, noticing me, he walked back to where I lay in a pool of my own blood.

The gun was held tightly in his hand. I recognized it from his father's collection.

How long has he been carrying it? Hours? Days? All week?

I could feel warmth leaving my body. Blood filled my lungs in an all-too-familiar way.

Our eyes met. I wanted to cry, but refused. So I asked the same question I always did.

"*Why?*"

Noah shook his head, seemed upset I didn't understand. "You can't go against the program, Min. That's wrong. The stronger sequences must eliminate the weaker ones. It's a mandate." He blew out a frustrated sigh. "I intend to be strong, and you clearly don't."

I tried to speak, but no longer had the strength.

Noah glanced at the sky, then closed his eyes and took a breath. When they reopened, I saw no trace of the boy I knew.

Part of me died, but another piece exploded.

"*Bastard,*" I hissed.

The sun was radiant, illuminating his silhouette as though he were a Greek god. Or maybe that was the blood loss talking. "Everything is clear now." Sadness tinged Noah's voice. "I can't be weak anymore, like you make me feel."

My lips parted, but no words came. I was dying, and soon.

"Don't you see?" Noah whispered, his voice almost plaintive. He pointed the gun straight at my heart. "It was *you*, Min. All along. *You* are my Nemesis."

The muzzle flashed, and I saw nothing more.

EPILOGUE

My eyes slid open.

Blink.

Blink blink blink.

The clearing was soundless, no woodland noises to disturb my rest.

I ran a hand across my chest. Unhurt.

I sat up. Felt rage sweep through me like I'd never experienced before, not even with the black-suited man.

Noah.

He'd betrayed me. Killed me.

Worse, he'd let me down. Thrown me away like garbage.

I rose, surprised to be in my usual spot. The Guardian had said we couldn't take that for granted anymore, though he hadn't explained. Like so much else.

Get back to the trailer park.

Tack might be there. We needed a plan from now on, in case we were separated.

In case we're killed, you mean.

A hundred yards from the clearing, I felt a tingle run down my spine, as if I'd stepped into a freezer. I turned. Reached a hand behind me. My fingers struck an invisible barrier, one I'd obviously just passed through. I pushed with both palms, but there was no give.

So. The reset points really are off-limits.

"I already tried that," a voice called.

Tack was sitting on a boulder, chewing a stalk of grass. He spit it out as I cursed him for giving me a heart attack. Then we charged forward into a hug.

"Why'd you come here?" I asked. "Resets are supposed to be randomized now."

"Seemed as good a place as any. I was *really* hoping you'd walk out and not Ethan."

I released him and stepped back. "What happened in town?"

Tack's grin faded. "Bloodbath. Toby's dopes gunned down a few more people trying to keep control, but they weren't ready for a full-scale riot. Then all the bodies disappeared. After Noah killed Ethan, they broke and ran, and the whole class scattered. I doubt *anyone* knows where anyone else is, though some of the bigger jerks bolted for the church. Ethan's gang will probably hole up in there, waiting for him to . . . to come back."

I didn't want to ask, but had to. "Noah?"

Loathing twisted Tack's features. "Ghosted. No idea where. Good riddance."

I thought for a second. "Which way did he go?"

"North."

Ski lodge. Rage flared inside me. Another day.

"What now, Min. What are *we* going to do?"

I rubbed the spot on my chest where Noah's bullet had exited. The wound was gone from my flesh, but not my soul. The fury returned, and this time I let it simmer.

I'm your Nemesis, Noah? Fine. I accept.

"I'll tell you what we're going to do." I met Tack's eye, saw my anger reflected there. "We're going to gather everyone who still has some decency left. Then we're going to find Noah. And Ethan. Sarah and Toby, and all the rest. Anyone who wants to rule by stepping on people's throats."

I gazed down at the glittering lake in the heart of the valley.

"We're going to fight them."

A bitter taste filled my mouth, but I choked it back.

Let the mountain breeze chill me.

"And we're going to win."

ACKNOWLEDGMENTS

Nemesis is a dark, quirky, crazy book that took me years to finish. I have more people to thank than I could possibly remember, so if I leave you out, know that it's because I'm an idiot and not because I'm not eternally grateful for your help.

This book would not have been possible without the tireless efforts of my wonder-editor, Ari Lewin. Thank you for all the time you've put into this project, and for enduring all of my manic phone calls along the way. Thanks as always to the wonderful teams at Putnam and Penguin Young Readers. This book stands on your capable shoulders. And special thanks to Elyse Marshall for steering *Nemesis* to market with grace, wit, and hustle. Sorry for making you run through large convention centers.

More thanks to Jennifer Rudolph Walsh, Margaret Riley King, Anna DeRoy, Janine Kamouh, Simon Trewin, Eric Reid, and the whole team at William Morris Endeavor. You believed in *Nemesis* from the start and found my insane book wonderful homes. WME launched my career and helped me become the writer I am today. I will always be grateful.

Oh, and thanks, Mom. For all of it.

To my earliest readers, I owe you big-time. Limitless thanks to Carrie Ryan, Kami Garcia, and Margaret Stohl—you turned my somewhat-of-a-mountain-holiday-travelogue called *Death Gates* (awful) into a usable writing sample, and gave the whole concept much-needed focus. More thanks to Renée Ahdieh for helpful notes on the first draft (which you read while sitting in front of me on a flight to Dallas, in first class, while I languished back in coach—stupid upgrades).

My career has been incubated by the constant encouragement and support of my YALL-family. Love to Margie, Mel, Kami, Veronica, Sandy, Rafi, and Jonathan, as well as West Coasters Marie, Tahereh, Ransom, Leigh, Holly, and Richelle. And *of course*, Emily, Tori, and Shane. YALLFEST and YALLWEST are the best two weekends of my year. You guys make me feel like a real writer who can do this for a living. Priceless.

More thanks to my later readers, many of whose names grace this book with their gracious praise. I won't list you all here, but you know who you are, and I'm forever in your debt. Thanks to Jodi for fighting for me based on nothing but belief. Special thanks to Todd Humphreys and Paul and Jennifer Hudson, who helped me out with some tricky mathematical calculations I still don't understand. Sadly, I decide not to go with Paul's character suggestion of Dr. Spacey McHudson. And I could never forget the wonderful support of my VCFA family, who allowed me to read and workshop portions of *Nemesis* in a safe environment and were kind enough not to throw rocks at me. Special shouts to my classmates for their nonstop encouragement. I name you all my dear friends.

I need to specifically and individually thank my good friend, classmate, and colleague Ally Condie, whose name could've appeared in almost all of the above paragraphs. Your support and relentless enthusiasm for *Nemesis* kept my spirits up when they were down and helped calm my publishing neuroses. Thanks for always being in my corner. Go, Lake Monsters. Always be NeCaPPing.

Most important, thank you to my beautiful wife, Emily, to whom this book is dedicated. It never would've happened without your unconditional support and occasional brutal insults. Because of you, our kids are alive and well adjusted to this day, despite my frequent absences from home. I love you and the little ones very much and can't wait until they are old enough to read this book.

Finally, to my readers, know that you are the point of all of this. Your support has given me a career that I love and a happy, exciting, fulfilling life. I hope I have served you well in turn. Thanks upon thanks until the end of time.

TURN THE PAGE FOR A FIRST LOOK AT

BOOK TWO IN THE PROJECT NEMESIS SERIES

1

NOAH

We went there to kill them all.

Fire and blood.

Blood and fire.

I stalked through the midnight-dark woods, making as little noise as possible.

Kyle was beside me. Akio a step behind. We stole through the bare trunks like smoke, stepping lightly in our snowshoes, a pack of hungry wolves scenting prey. The target was still a football field away and a hundred feet downslope, but experience had taught me to be wary.

I'd been killed twice that week already, ambushed both times. Had no interest in another death. Resetting in new places had been disorienting. Unnerving. The rules had changed, and I didn't know all the new ones yet. But I'd learn.

Reaching the tree line, I dropped to a knee and freed my boots from the snowshoes. An icy wind smacked me in the face, tingling my cheeks and scraping my nose like sandpaper. I peered down the plunging mountainside before me, a barren stretch of slope barely dusted with white despite deep drifts piled up on both sides.

A full moon hung low and huge in the sky, glowing like a candle. Squinting, I could see our objective: a log cabin at the bottom of the run—simple, rough-hewn, topped by a cedar-chip roof and a stone chimney. Soft yellow lamplight spilled from two blocky windows. Inhaling, I caught faint traces of burning pine.

I shook my head, nearly snorted in disbelief.

These classmates were cocky. They'd planted a double line of tiki torches that stabbed up the center of the slope. Angry orange flames danced in the heavy gusts, reflecting off the frozen landscape, creating pools of shadow and light among the encroaching trees.

The kids inside probably thought the torches made them safer. They didn't.

Echoes of their laughter had risen all the way to our base at the mountaintop chalet. I was living in the same suite the black-suited man had once occupied, back in the real world, before it died. Stepping out onto the ice-covered patio, I'd heard voices. Tasted wood smoke. Spotted the flickering pinpricks a mile away.

I clicked my tongue at the memory. This cabin was firmly outside of downtown limits. An expansion into my territory. They were testing me. Mistake.

I glanced right, across twenty yards of open ground to a thicket on the opposite side of the slope, searching for the second prong of my strike force. This empty stretch would've made an excellent moguls trail. My father had earmarked it for development—a project that would never happen, in a future that would never be.

Did time mean anything now? Did it exist inside the Program?

It'd been three weeks since the Guardian revealed the true nature of our existence. How the planet had been destroyed by a series of cataclysms, our physical bodies burned to crisps. That the sixty-four members of Fire Lake's sophomore class were all that remained of humanity, existing as digital lines of code inside a supercomputer buried deep underground.

Some couldn't accept it. Couldn't wrap their heads around the idea of being nothing more than ones and zeros. They walked around like zombies, or hid. A few even defied the Program, questioning its purpose. Refusing the Guardian's instructions, as if things were somehow up for debate.

Idiots. The Program *was* purpose. The last hope of our species. It was the greatest gift anyone had ever received. To rebel against it was madness. *Heresy.* The smartest minds on Earth had crafted a single way forward for a few lucky souls. Who were we to question its dictates?

I'd been murdered over and over back in the real world, never knowing why, wracked by the pain and humiliation of thinking I was crazy. But I'd had it all wrong.

I was being trained. Prepared. I'd been chosen to lead the human race. I was *special*, to a nearly paralyzing degree. The *hell* I'd give the middle finger to the defining achievement of all human existence. The stakes were way too high.

During the chaos at Town Hall, I'd been momentarily conflicted. The Guardian had disappeared back inside without further instructions. But I'd rallied quickly, focusing on what we'd been told. We had to sort ourselves. There'd be winners and losers. I needed to dominate the situation. And the first step was to carve out my own space.

So I did. Shooting Ethan had changed everything, for everyone.

Shooting Ethan? You mean shooting Min.

I flinched. Felt a heaviness in the pit of my stomach, even as I gritted my teeth.

She'd made her choice. Had given me *no* choice.

Min had rejected the Guardian, ignoring what we'd been prepared for. Everything we'd suffered through, *our whole lives*, as beta patients for Project Nemesis. She'd refused to see the truth—that the Program was our salvation. We *had* to follow its plan.

I'd been so angry. So frustrated and disappointed. I'd shot Min to make a point. To her and everyone else. *This* was our world now. Min would reset and be perfectly fine. The old rules didn't apply. The Guardian's rules were all that mattered.

It's not like I'd enjoyed it.

After the massacre, everyone had scattered. I'd retreated to my father's ski resort atop the northeastern slopes, the most defensible spot in the valley. To my surprise, several classmates had followed. People who understood the truth as I did.

The Program was everything. It required conflict. We would provide it.

But you don't even know why. You're flying blind.

I shook my head sharply to clear it. Try as I might, I hadn't been able to stamp out a nagging voice that was determined to weaken me. My failures in life—the sad puddles of self-recrimination and doubt that had hounded me for years—were trying to sabotage me here, but I rejected them. I was strong now. I'd stay strong. Spineless Noah Livingston was dead.

Movement across the gap. I spotted Zach, skinny and moon-faced, standing upright and exposed, and waving like a human archery target. Behind him Morgan and Leah were motioning for him to get down, but he ignored them, even shaking off Morgan's outstretched hand.

Smart girls. I should've put one of them in charge instead of Zach. Too late now.

Not all of my followers were brilliant. Zach had even killed himself once, just to see what it was like. Moron. Suicide *had* to be against the Program, and was therefore unthinkable. I was fully committed to winning this phase, whatever that meant. And right then, it meant giving the people down in that cabin a really bad night.

I lifted a single fist overhead, then made a chopping motion and pointed at our target. Zach straightened, scratching his cheek, but Leah flashed the okay sign. Her father was a National Guardsman, and her family owned the quarry at the western edge of the valley, which was why I'd chosen her for this mission. She had experience with flammables. Lifting two plastic canisters, Leah shoved one into Zach's stomach and began picking her way downslope. Zach stomped after her, with Morgan bringing up the rear.

"Let's go," I said to Akio and Kyle, keeping my voice firm.

I didn't relish what was coming, but I wasn't agonizing over it. And I could never show weakness in front of the others. They had to believe *I* was the scariest thing on the mountain. Or else why would they follow me? Who'd follow the Noah Livingston from life, a guy who never stood up for anything?

Min would.

Heat rose to my cheeks. Min shamed me, brought out all of my failings. All of the things I couldn't afford to be in this world. Would my flaws always haunt me, even here?

This was a mission.

Feelings didn't matter.

Not here, not in this virtual proving ground we inhabited.

I was doing what I was supposed to do.

Akio's soft features tightened as he handed a fuel canister to Kyle. He didn't want to do this, but could be counted on to follow orders. Fine by me. His conscience was irrelevant so long as he did his part. Akio had been the first to join me. If I trusted anyone, it was him.

Kyle smiled darkly. He was looking forward to the carnage, and I didn't care about that, either.

Snowshoes hidden, we crept down the mountain, sticking to the trees as we mirrored our teammates on the opposite side. Zach quickly became a disaster—stumbling through the frozen underbrush, snapping branches and grunting in annoyance. Morgan hissed at him, but he ignored her warning, stepping out onto the slope to avoid a patch of pricker bushes.

I shook my head. I shouldn't have included him, but I'd asked for volunteers and he'd spoken up first.

The wind sighed down to nothing. The night was as still as

death, and nearly as cold. No birds. No chirping insects. Every sloppy footfall echoed down the icy hillside between the bordering woods, setting my teeth on edge. Zach drew level with the first pair of torches, casting a long black shadow that arrowed sharply back up the mountain.

A clicking sound.

Leah and Morgan froze.

Zach stomped a few more steps, then stopped abruptly, glancing back over his shoulder.

Shots rang out. One. Two. A half dozen.

Zach dropped like a puppet with its strings cut, a dark stain spreading on the icy ground beneath him.

Leah dove behind a round-bellied oak and rolled, her thick braid whipping like a bicycle spoke. Morgan's body jerked as more cracks boomed up the mountainside. Then she slumped onto her butt, blubbering, glossy liquid spilling from her mouth.

Out on the slope, Zach's body shimmered and disappeared.

Leah was up and running, ignoring her fuel canister and Morgan's grasping hand as she bolted deeper into the forest. Three figures in dark ski jackets lurched from the shadows. After a cursory glance at Morgan, they tore after Leah, fanning out in an attempt to encircle her. Behind them, Morgan toppled over and stopped moving. Seconds later she vanished.

Two dead, another outnumbered and on the run. I didn't care.

These people weren't friends. The idea was nonsensical. As far as I was concerned, every kid in Fire Lake was my rival. I'd work with those I needed to, but I'd never lose sight of the goal. I had to win. I had to follow the rules and complete the phase.

Killing without knowing why? How is that strength?

"Enough," I hissed, startling my companions. Cheeks burning, I schooled my face to stillness. Doubt was poison, and I was letting it infect me at the worst time possible.

Dr. Lowell. Principal Myers. Sheriff Watson and all the others. Even Black Suit. They'd dedicated their lives to Project Nemesis, planning every detail. All so we had a chance to go on. I had to fulfill their vision. I had to live up to the faith they'd placed in me. I had to make the Program proud. Plus, Morgan and Zach would be back in the valley in a matter of minutes.

Kyle and Akio were backing away from the slope, preparing to bolt. I snapped my fingers, freezing them in their tracks. "Our scouts counted ten people," I whispered. "Three just went after Leah. Our job got easier."

Akio shifted, a hand shooting up to rub the back of his neck. Kyle swallowed, gave me a shaky thumbs-up. I turned and set off downhill, not watching to see if they followed. I knew they would.

We ghosted the remaining distance, sticking to the woods on our side, avoiding the flickering torchlight. I stopped in a copse of pine trees directly across from the cabin. The single window facing us was dark, perhaps a bedroom. It made for a clean approach.

A freezing gust swept down from the snowcapped heights, rattling branches and leaching the heat from my skin. I rubbed my flaking nose. Scanned for any sign we'd been seen. God, it was cold. But not for long.

I turned. Met the eyes of my companions in turn.

"Ready?"

Two nods.

I led them across open ground, past the line of torches to an ancient, billowing cedar standing beside the cabin like a sentinel. Just then the front door opened. We dove to the ground, crawling under the cedar's low-slung branches. Flattening onto my stomach, I held my breath, one hand creeping toward the pistol in the back of my waistband.

Derrick Morris stood blinking in the doorway, his silhouette unmistakable, skyscraper-tall and haloed in yellow light. He was woefully underdressed in jeans and a short-sleeve T-shirt. I don't think he was even wearing shoes.

"Lars? Charlie?" he called. "What the hell are y'all shooting at?" Derrick listened for a moment, rubbing his dark skin to ward off the chill. Then he shook his head, muttering to himself. "Trigger-happy derps, always popping off." The door closed. Voices rose within, but no one else came outside.

I eased up into a crouch. One of Ethan's top lieutenants was here, and he wasn't paying close enough attention. No guards. No lookouts. I guessed those people were all chasing Leah up the mountain. The rest weren't taking any extra precautions, even after hearing shots fired. We'd teach them quite a lesson.

I swiveled on one knee, tapped the canisters in my companions' hands, then pointed at the cabin. Spun an index finger. They nodded—one excited, the other scared to death. But they both moved forward, slinking toward the dark side of the house.

No shouts of alarm rang out. The door stayed firmly shut.

Akio and Kyle split apart, hugging the outside walls as they circled the building, dousing its wooden foundation with liquid. Then they scurried back to my position under the cedar, tossing the now-empty canisters aside.

On his knees, Kyle dug into his pocket and withdrew a book of matches. Leering darkly, he started to rise, but I stopped him with a hand to his chest. Kyle frowned, then nodded and sank back down.

I was in charge. I'd light the fire.

Crawling from beneath the branches, I gave the cabin a final inspection, every sense on high alert. It was time to finish the job.

I strode directly for the front door, making no effort to disguise my approach. Passing a woodpile, I snagged a long, thick branch, twirling it in my hands as I mounted the porch.

The door had a wide, refrigerator-style handle. I ran the branch through the opening until it extended all the way across the door frame. I paused, then stepped down and grabbed another tree limb, doubling the barricade.

No one came to the door. I almost laughed. A dark part of me was tempted to call out and give them a far-too-late warning, but I resisted the urge. The Program wanted results, not grandstanding.

I walked down to the yard. Grabbed a torch and carried it back to the house.

The wind dropped like an accomplice. The forest held its breath. Time stood still.

Because it *was* still. Time was as dead as me.

I tossed the torch at the base of the doorway. Felt the bone-deep concussion of fire being born as it raced along the fuel-drenched logs. Orange tendrils sprang up around the foundation, encircling the cabin, eating hungrily into wood.

Shouts. Screams.

The door began jerking inward as flames engulfed it, but the branches held. Then fists began to pound, rising in intensity as shrieks erupted to match. I stepped back into the yard, removed my father's Beretta 9 mm, and racked the slide. The wind returned, and a furnace blast of dry heat struck my face, forcing me to retreat a few more paces.

Smoke billowed. Enveloped the house in a whirly black fist.

The screaming reached a crescendo. The branches finally splintered and the door flew open. I fired into the inferno, emptying the Beretta's magazine. I quickly reloaded, but no one emerged. No one even got close. I put the gun away and watched the fire rage. Heard Akio throwing up behind me.

Six at least. Maybe seven.

Then I felt something . . . twist in my head. An electric charge that snapped and sizzled, matching the conflagration reflected in my eyes before vanishing as quickly as it came.

Kyle was yelling something, but couldn't get close. The cabin burned like a Roman candle, entrancing me. Then Akio raced forward and grabbed my arm, covering his face with a sleeve as he pointed toward the trees. I nodded as if coming awake. We should leave. Everyone inside was surely gone, transported to one of the four reset zones, waiting to rejoin the Program's version of reality.

This was a minor victory. A slap on the wrist. A warning.

My head felt thick and gummy. The front of my parka was a melted ruin. But the screech of breaking glass snapped me back into focus. Shrugging free of my companions, I trotted around to the rear of the cabin, dazed and confused but determined to finish anything left undone.

A girl had launched herself through the back window in a desperate attempt to avoid the flames, but it was clearly too late. The fire had left her unrecognizable. Breathing raggedly, she lay on the ground, her hands making red lines as she pawed at the snow.

The girl's eyes opened. She stared up at the sky with a silent plea. Then her head lolled, and a lock of gleaming black hair spilled onto her ruined cheek.

My heart stopped. The air left my lungs. I lurched forward, one hand shooting out as bile climbed my windpipe. Then I noticed the girl's melted leather boot with a smiley-face sticker on its heel. I gagged, coughed hard.

Not Min. But I knew who it was.

Something shifted inside me. A hairline crack. Water seeping into stone.

I swallowed, fingers trembling as I dropped my hand and squeezed it into a fist. I stood there, frozen, breathless, waiting for the body to disappear. Guilt—sharp and stinging—exploded within me. Burning like that must've been excruciating.

Inhuman.

I tried to brush the thought aside. This girl would wake up unharmed in minutes, alone in the woods without a scratch on her. She'd have done the same to me.

Piper. Her name is Piper Lockwood.

Piper's eyes found mine. We'd never been close, but she'd sat two rows in front of me in English Comp. She'd tap her toes under her chair when bored, stickered boot heels smiling back at me.

The rift inside me deepened. Cracks spread like spiderwebs.

No. I wouldn't go back. I'd worked too hard to bury my demons.

But her body was still there, still quivering, still slumped atop a pile of dirty leaves. Her hand spasmed. A silver ring had melted around her pinky finger. The smell of roasted meat filled my nostrils, and I nearly emptied my stomach.

My teeth dug into my bottom lip. A cloud slipped in front of the moon, swamping the yard in darkness, leaving only the flames to whisper what we'd done.

My hand rose. Two shots rang out.

Akio gasped beside me, staring at Piper's now-still body as tears cut tracks down his ash-covered cheeks. "She didn't . . . This wasn't . . ." he stammered, his chin dropping to his chest.

I put a hand on his shoulder, somehow freed by his show of weakness. It clarified things like a magnifying glass. This was a different world, with different rules. Only the strong would survive, and that meant doing hard things. I had to be vigilant against my own inadequacy. "It's okay, man. It's best to send people along quickly."

So why'd it take you so long?

Akio nodded, staring at his boots. He wasn't cut out for this. Then a new wave of energy struck me, dwarfing the one from before.

My scalp tingled. Electricity ran up and down my limbs. It filled me. Remade me.

Suddenly I was back in the park beside town square, playing

basketball with my friends. Ethan and I were on the same team for once, and we were passing circles around the Nolan twins. The air was crisp, the sky so blue it felt unfair. A slight breeze swept up off the lake, ruffling my hair and tingling my sweat-slicked skin. I knew I was on fire, couldn't be guarded. That no one could stop me that day. Ethan knew it, too. He threw me the ball, backing up to give me room. I dribbled through my legs, wobbling Mike, then stepped back and shot over his outstretched hand, the ball sliding through the net like prophecy. Ethan lifted me up and we whooped like idiots. I glanced over and saw Min sitting on the grass with Sarah and the other girls, her eyes rolling as she shook her head at us. My smile grew ten times wider.

The scene—memory?—winked out, but the elation remained.

I drank in the sensation. Felt galvanized, head to toe. I stared at my hands, flexing and unflexing my fingers. I was so close to the Program I could weep.

Fire and blood.

Blood and fire.

Program wants? Program gets.

This was my world. Or it would be soon.

"Guys?"

I glanced over at Kyle, who was chewing on his thumb, his face lit up by the bonfire raging behind us. He pointed. "Why's she still here?"

I turned. Stiffened. Piper had stopped moving, but hadn't vanished.

My blood ran cold, a dark corner of my mind jabbering for

attention. Piper was still lying on the frozen ground. She wasn't miles away, restored and repaired, waking up with only a bad memory for her trouble.

She wasn't moving. Or breathing. She refused to fade away.

Inside me, something snapped. Surety dissolved like a sand castle at high tide.

Piper's scorched body defied me like an accusation. The truth was inescapable.

Someone inside the Program hadn't reset.

You're a murderer.

READ THE VIRALS SERIES BY BRENDAN REICHS
AND BESTSELLING AUTHOR KATHY REICHS

"If you like the TV show *Bones* (I do) or *Maximum Ride*, you'll love *Virals*." —James Patterson